Jersey, and grew up in Brooklyn, New York. After graduating from Harvard, he served in the South Pacific during World War II. He published his first book, *The Naked and the Dead*, in 1948. Mailer won the National Book Award and the Pulitzer Prize in 1968 for *The Armies of the Night* and was awarded the Pulitzer Prize again in 1980 for *The Executioner's Song*. He has directed four feature-length films, was a co-founder of *The Village Voice* in 1955, and was president of the American PEN from 1984 to 1986.

NORMAN MAILER

The Deer Park

With a preface and notes by the author

An Abacus Book

First published in Great Britain by Allan Wingate Ltd, 1957
This edition published by Abacus 1997
Reprinted 1998, 2002

A CIP catalogue record for this book is
available from the British Library.

ISBN 0 349 10997 4

Printed and bound in Great Britain by
Clays Ltd, St Ives plc

Abacus
An imprint of
Time Warner Books UK
Brettenham House
Lancaster Place
London WC2E 7EN

www.TimeWarnerBooks.co.uk

To
ADELE MY WIFE
and to
DANIEL WOLF MY FRIEND

Preface to *The Deer Park*

There are books which are born like endangered children, and they battle for their lives and change the nature of the parent – in the case of this analogy, the author. *The Deer Park* is a book like this, and it had a lurid history, which is to say it came out loud in the press and livid in the heart of the writer. A few years after publication the author was still brooding sufficiently over what had happened to desire to write about its reception, and that sustained passage called The Last Draft of *The Deer Park*, printed in *Esquire* and then in *Advertisements for Myself*, is reprinted here at the back of this book after the novel.

It is purposely placed at the back of the book. The story of *The Deer Park* stands after all – or at least one hopes it does – in fair shape by itself. I would not wish to distort a new reader's impression by having him read about its history first, particularly since it is I think of all my novels the one which shows the fewest signs of the work which went into it, and I like it that way. So the reader is requested to enjoy the novel first, if he chooses to, and then take his opportunity to learn of *The Deer Park*'s inner history, a private account of the relation between the novel and the author. It is on occasion a relation as interesting as many a marriage.

... the Deer Park, that gorge of innocence and virtue in which were engulfed so many victims who when they returned to society brought with them depravity, debauchery and all the vices they naturally acquired from the infamous officials of such a place.

Apart from the evil which the dreadful place did to the morals of the people, it is horrible to calculate the immense sums of money it cost the state. Indeed who can reckon the expense of that band of pimps and madames who were constantly searching all the corners of the kingdom to discover the objects of their investigation; the costs of conveying the girls to their destination; of polishing them, dressing them, perfuming them, and furnishing them with all the means of seduction that art could provide. To this must be added the gratuities presented to those who were not successful in arousing the jaded passions of the sultan but had nonetheless to be paid for their submission, for their discretion, and still more for their being eventually despised.

MOUFFLE D'ANGERVILLE
VIE PRIVEE DE LOUIS XV:

ou principaux événements, particularités et anecdotes de son règne

Please do not understand me too quickly

ANDRE GIDE

Part One

1

In the cactus wild of Southern California, a distance of two hundred miles from the capital of cinema as I choose to call it, is the town of Desert D'Or. There I went from the Air Force to look for a good time. Some time ago.

Almost everybody I knew in Desert D'Or had had an unusual career, and it was the same for me. I grew up in a home for orphans. Still intact at the age of twenty-three, wearing my flying wings and a First Lieutenant's uniform, I arrived at the resort with fourteen thousand dollars, a sum I picked up via a poker game in a Tokyo hotel room while waiting with other fliers for our plane home. The curiosity is that I was never a gambler, I did not even like the game, but I had nothing to lose that night, and maybe for such a reason I accepted the luck of my cards. Let me leave it at that. I came out of the Air Force with no place to go, no family to visit, and I wandered down to Desert D'Or.

Built since the Second World War, it is the only place I know which is all new. A long time ago, Desert D'Or was called Desert Door by the prospectors who put up their shanties at the edge of its oasis and went into the mountains above the desert to look for gold. But there is nothing left of those men; when the site of Desert D'Or was chosen, none of the old shacks remained.

No, everything is in the present tense, and during the months I stayed at the resort, I came to know it in a way we can know few places. It was a town built out of no other obvious motive than commercial profit and so no sign of commerce was allowed to appear. Desert D'Or was without a main street, and its stores looked like anything but stores. In those places which sold clothing, no clothing was laid out, and you waited in a modern living room while salesmen opened panels in the wall to exhibit summer suits, or held between their hands the blooms and

11

sprays of a tropical scarf. There was a jewellery store built like a cabin cruiser; from the street one peeped through a porthole to see a thirty-thousand-dollar necklace hung on the silver antlers of a piece of driftwood. None of the hotels – not the Yacht Club, nor the Debonair, not the Yucca Plaza, the Sandpiper, the Creedmor, nor the Desert D'Or Arms – could even be seen from outside. Put behind cement-brick fences or wooden palings, one hardly came across a building which was not green, yellow, rose, orange, or pink, and the approach was hidden by a shrubbery of bright flowers. You passed through the gate to the Yacht Club, the biggest and therefore the most exclusive hotel in the resort, and followed its private road which twisted through the grounds for several hundred yards, expecting a mansion at the end, but came instead to no more than a car-port, a swimming pool in the shape of a free-form coffee table with curved-wall cabañas and canasta tables, and a set of lawn-tennis courts, the only lawn in all that part of Southern California. At night, along yellow sidewalks which crossed a winding artificial creek, lit up with Japanese lanterns strung to the tropical trees, you could wander by the guest bungalows scattered along the route, their flush pastel-coloured doors another part of the maze of the arrangement.

I blew a piece of my fourteen-thousand-dollar fortune and stayed at the Yacht Club until I picked the house I was to rent for the rest of my stay in Desert D'Or. I could describe that house in detail but what would be the use? It was like most of the houses in the resort; it was modern, ranch-style, of course, with light furniture and rugs which felt like poodle wool, and it had a garden and a wall which went around the garden, the standard fault of Desert D'Or architecture; along the desert table, the walls were made of glass to have a view of mesa-coloured sand and violet mountains, but the houses were so close to each other that the builders had to fence them in, and the result was like living in a room whose walls are mirrors. In fact, my house had a twenty-foot mirror which faced the wall of plate-glass window. No matter where I stood in the living room, I could never miss the sight of my rented garden with its desert flowers and the lone yucca tree.

During the dry season which lasted for nine months of the

year, the resort was parched by the sun. Every twilight the spray from a thousand sprinklers washed dust and sand from the grey foliage; morning and afternoon the sun scorched the sap from the plants and the desert circled the resort, its cacti standing on the horizon while croppings of dusty rock gathered like scavengers in the distance. The blue sky burned on the pale desert. It would come on me at times that Desert D'Or was a place where no trees bear leaves. The palms and the yuccas lifted a foliage of tufts and fans and fronds and shoots, but never leaves, and on some of the roads where tall palms lined the way, their dead fronds hung from the trunk like an ostrich's muff.

During the off-season, most of the activity took place in the bars. The bars were a village in the town, or at least a kind of main street in the absence of any other, yet they were as different from the warm front of Desert D'Or as the inside of one's body is separate from the surface of one's skin. Like so many other places in Southern California, the bars, cocktail lounges, and night clubs were made to look like a jungle, an underwater grotto, or the lounge of a modern movie theatre. The Cerulean Room, to take an example, had an irregular space of rose-orange walls and booths of yellow leatherette under the influence of a dark blue ceiling. Above the serving bar with its bank of bottles, its pyramids of citrus fruit, a smoky-yellow false ceiling reflected into the mirror behind the bar and coloured the etching of a half-nude girl which had been cut into the glass. Drinking in that atmosphere, I never knew whether it was night or day, and I think that kind of uncertainty got into everybody's conversation. Men lacquered with liquor talked to other men who were sober, stories were started and never finished. On a typical afternoon in the air-cooled midnight of the bar, you could see a fat old man in a Palm Beach suit talking to a young girl with orange lipstick and the deep sun tan of Desert D'Or, the girl more interested in the old gent than the gentleman in her. Promoters and tourists, middle-aged women with new-coloured hair, and high-school kids who had competed in running hot-rods across the desert, were jammed together. The talk was made up of horses, stories of parties the night before, and systems for roulette. Running along the heavy beat of a third-rate promoter trying to raise money, there would come the solo shriek of one hysterical blonde or another, who seemed to be laughing in that tune which goes, 'I'm dumb, I'm dumb, but you're a scream.'

In such a way, afternoon was always passing into night, and drunken nights into the dawn of a desert morning. One seemed to leave the theatrical darkness of afternoon for the illumination of night, and the sun of Desert D'Or became like the stranger who the drunk imagines to be following him. So I spent my first few weeks doing little more than pick up the bar checks of all those small sharp prospectors for pleasure from the capital, and in the capsule biography by which most of the people knew one another, I was understood to be an Air Force pilot whose family was wealthy and lived in the East, and I even added the detail that I had a broken marriage and drank to get over it. As a story it was reasonable enough to pass, and I sometimes believed what I said and tried to take the cure in the very real sun of Desert D'Or with its cactus, its mountain, and the bright green foliage of its love and its money.

2

To most of the bar-flies in Desert D'Or I must have been passing impressive. I had my First Lieutenant's bars and my wings, I had combat decorations from that Asiatic war which has gone its intermittent way, I even looked the part. I had blond hair and blue eyes and I was six feet one. I was good-looking and I knew it; I had studied the mirror long enough. Yet I never believed I was convincing. When I would put on my uniform, I would feel like an unemployed actor who tries to interest a casting director by dressing for the role.

Of course, everybody sees himself through his own eyes, and I can hardly know with any confidence how I looked to other people. In those days I was a young man who felt temporarily like an old man, and although I believed I knew a great many things, I was able to do very little I wanted to do. Given the poker money, however, and the Air Force uniform and me with our arms around each other, most people assumed I was able to take care of myself, and I was careful not to correct their impression. There is that much to be said for having the build of a light-heavyweight.

I saw only a few people regularly. It would have taken too much effort to find new friends. In the off-season, any celebrity who lived in Desert D'Or was surrounded by a court. It did not matter where you went to visit; dependably there would be the same people pouring the host's drinks, laughing at his remarks, working I suppose as servants of his pleasure, so that his favourite games were played, his favourite stories were told, and the court was split into cliques which jockeyed for his favour. Nothing was so unusual as to find two celebrities who liked to see each other often.

At Dorothea O'Faye's home which she called The Hangover

– it was the place I went to most often, Dorothea having picked me up one night in a bar and taken me home with her friends – the court was made up of a garage owner and his wife, a real-estate operator and his wife, a publicity man for Supreme Pictures, an old show girl who had been a friend of Dorothea's years ago, and a drunk named O'Faye who had been married to Dorothea, had been divorced, and now was kept by her to run odd errands. Dorothea was a former personality who had been an actress of sorts, a night-club singer of some reputation, and had temporarily retired at the age of forty-three. Years ago, a friend advised her to invest in Desert D'Or property, and it was said now that Dorothea was rich. How rich she was no one could guess, however, for she had the secrecy about money which gives itself away in being generous and stingy by turns.

Dorothea was handsome with a full body and exciting black hair, and she had been notorious as a show girl years ago, and famous again in her night-club days as a singer. Her boast was that she had been everywhere, had done everything, and knew everything there was to know. She had been a call girl, a gossip columnist (at separate times, be it said), a celebrity, a failure; she had been born in Chicago and discovered in New York, her father had been a drunk and died that way, her mother had disappeared with another man. Dorothea had done her father's work when she was twelve; he was a sort of a janitor, and she collected rent from tenants and put the garbage out. At sixteen she was kept by the heir to a steel fortune, and a couple of years later she had an affair with a European prince and gave birth to his illegitimate son; she had made money and lost money, she had been married three times, the last to a man of whom she said, 'I can't remember him as well as guys I've had for a one-night stand.' She had even had her great romance. He was an Air Force pilot who was killed flying the mail, and she would tell me that was why she took to me. 'I never knew a guy like him,' she would sigh. When she was on the sentimental side of her drinking she would decide that her whole life would have been different if he had lived; sober, or very drunk, she thought the opposite. 'If he hadn't died,' she would say, 'we'd have killed it. The great thing is when something good hasn't time to be spoiled.'

Known for her rough wit and the force of her style, Dorothea was considered a catch by that revolving troupe of oilmen, men who made their money in the garment industries, and men ... let me not pursue the series. What characterized most of them was that their business allowed them to travel and they worked for the reputation of having women who opened the eyes of other men. I admired the convenience of their itinerary which was triangulated by California, Florida, and the East. Generally, these men were seen with young women – models kept by millionaires, or child divorcees so fortunate as to be mixed in scandal – but Dorothea offered, in contrast to these girls, a quick mind and a tough tongue which was respected greatly. My theory is that her men took her out like a business partner, and in all the sweat of a night club, they found Dorothea easy, they could talk to her. By the parade of her admirers I was always told, 'She's a great kid. She's one of the best.' To which Dorothea might answer when asked her opinion, 'He'll pass. He's a bastard, but no phony.' She had categories. There were good guys, bastards, and phonies, and the worst was a phony. A good guy, I learned by example, was a guy who made no excuses about looking out only for himself. A bastard was a man who had the same philosophy but took extra pleasure in hurting people. A phony was somebody who claimed to be concerned with anything but himself. For a while, she had trouble with me, she hardly knew where to set me in the cosmos of good guys, bastards, and phonies. I was out for a good time as I always told her, and she approved of that, but I also made the mistake of telling her I wanted to write, and writers were phonies in her book.

All the same, she had her points. Her loyalty was strong. To be her friend was to be her friend, and if she was rough in business, as I often heard, it was her code never to leave you in needless trouble. She was a generous woman. There were always people for dinner, there was always whisky and though she had two living rooms in her house puffed with heavy velvet furniture, the court stayed in the panelled den with its big home bar, its television set, and its night-club posters of old engagements Dorothea had played. Now, at Dorothea's, all that was played were the games she liked, the gossip was told which interested

her, and we spent evening after evening in doing almost exactly
what we had done the night before. Her favourite was the game
of Ghost, and I had to admire the heat with which she worked
to win. Dorothea had had no education, and to be able to spell
down everybody in the house left her in a fine mood.

'What are you thinking, cupcake?' she would say afterward,
chucking the old chorus girl under the chin.

'You're tremendous,' the friend would say adoringly.

'Oh, Dorothea's great,' the garage owner would rumble.

'Angel, make me a small Martin,' Dorothea would say, and
hand her glass to someone.

Dorothea had lasted. If her night-club days were finished, if
her big affairs were part of the past, she was still in fine shape.
She had her house, she had her court, she had money in the
bank; men still sent airplanes for her. Yet when Dorothea was
very drunk, she was violent too. She always had liquor inside
her, she was always restless, she used up people and time – you
could go to her place for breakfast and eat scrambled eggs at
four in the afternoon after hours of drinking – but unless she was
very drunk, Dorothea was agreeable. Very drunk, she was
unmanageable; she abused people, she threw things. Once she
was even slapped around by a man and woman in a roadside
brawl. A really drunken evening had to end with Dorothea
screaming, 'Get out, get out you son of a bitch before I kill you.'
She could say it to anybody in the court, it did not matter who;
she was most fond of saying it to one of her rich men friends.
She hated to be alone, however, and such tantrums were rare.
One could spend whole days with her and all of the night, and
at six in the morning when Dorothea was ready for bed, she was
still coaxing us in her rough deep voice to stay a little longer. So
automatic became the habit that on those week ends and odd
nights when Dorothea was away on one of her dates, the court
still gathered at The Hangover, still drank in her pine-panelled
den. Nobody knew how to stay away. Hours before going there,
I could sense the worry that there was no other way to spend the
evening.

About a month after I met her, Dorothea settled on one rich
man. His name was Martin Pelley, and he had a pear-shaped
head, a dark jowl, and sad eyes. He had made a lot of money in

oil wells, but there was something apologetic about him, as if he were explaining, 'I learned how to make money, but I never learned nothing else.' Recently, his second marriage had been finished off in Desert D'Or. I remember his wife who was a platinum blonde with a neck corded by tension. They had had fights. You could not go by Pelley's suite at the Yacht Club without hearing the terrific abuse she yelled at him. They were now getting a quick Mexican divorce, and Martin Pelley had found his way to The Hangover. He adored Dorothea. His big body would sit heavily in an armchair through the evening, he would chuckle at the quips of the court, he would have an anxious scowl on his forehead as though looking for some new way to win our approval. When Ghost was played, he was the first to go out. 'I'm a bonehead for this sort of stuff,' he would say easily. 'I'm not quick like Dorothea.'

All the same, he was a spender. His preference was to invite everybody out from The Hangover for steak and drinks at a desert roadhouse, and when he was drunk he was very genial. Any young woman he called 'Daughter,' and he would tell us over and over again, 'I had a little girl, you see, by my first marriage. The cunningest little bugger. She died, age of six.'

'You got to get rid of it,' Dorothea would say.

'Ah, I just think about her once in a while.'

For two weeks he was at Dorothea's every night. The first time he found her out for the evening, he paced the floor and did not hear a word we said. The court learned from Dorothea about the fight which followed.

'You son of a bitch,' Dorothea said, 'nobody owns me.'

'What are you, a tramp?' he asked her. 'I thought you had character.' He gripped her shoulder. 'You always said you wanted to get married again and have kids.' This was one of Dorothea's favourite themes.

She twisted herself loose. 'Get your hooks off me. What do you think, you're throwing some pipes around?'

'I want to marry you.'

'Go blow.'

The quarrel ended with Pelley taking Dorothea to bed. Nothing happened.

He could not get it out of his mind. He apologized to Dorothea

19

again and again. The apology was painted on his face. I overheard them one night in a corner, and I think he wanted me to overhear for he did not speak softly. 'I used to be great, you see,' he told her. 'When I was a kid, I'd do it so much I got a strain. I had to see a doctor, that's the truth. I know there's no way you can believe me, but I was great.'

Dorothea cuddled to him, her bold eyes full of sympathy. 'For Christ's sakes, Marty, I don't hold it against you.'

'I got a strain. You don't believe me?'

'Sure, I believe you.'

'Dorothea, you're a champ.' He held her wrists in his large paws. 'I tell you, I was great. I'll be great again.'

'There's no rush. Listen, there was a guy I knew. He was the greatest in the hay, and in the beginning he was the same as you.'

Dorothea grew tender toward him. Their romance began on the sure ground of his incapacity. Pelley would have been absorbed into the court at The Hangover if it weren't for the many times he insisted on standing treat. Dorothea's evenings with other men came to an end. Now her rich friends were asked to visit the house, and hours were spent at Ghost with Pelley working sullenly against the new visitor. Finally, everybody accepted him as Dorothea's boy friend. There even came the night when the fat ex-chorus girl telephoned me and announced excitedly, 'Marty made it. He and Dorothea finally made it. They want to celebrate.' When I didn't answer immediately, she added, 'Don't you even want to know how it was?'

'What do I care?' I said.

'Dorothea didn't tell me, but she kind of hinted it was just a beginning.'

We celebrated that night. Pelley acted like a new father passing out cigars. He not only bought champagne for everybody, but he nursed Dorothea through the meal as if she had just left the hospital. 'You're a bunch of champs,' he said to the people at the table, 'you're all champs, I never knew such champs,' including by this the fat show girl, the garage owner, the realtor, the wives, the press agent, myself, all the friends of Dorothea, even the drunk O'Faye who had once been her husband.

3

That was a story. When I thought of it, I would be sorry for O'Faye. A natty little sport with a smile and a hair-line moustache, I could never believe that years ago there were nights when Dorothea wept because she had lost him.

She was seventeen when they met, and he was a vaudeville hoofer on the crest of a vogue. Dorothea lived with him, she was crazy about him as she swore, worked out song-and-dance routines to support the act they did together, and suffered his cheating, for he liked a different girl every night. They got nowhere together: she was always hinting that she wanted to settle down, to have children, and he would smile and say she was too young and ask her to look at the silk shirt he had bought that day. She thought how to save money and he thought how to spend it. When she found herself pregnant, he gave her two hundred dollars in cash, left the address of a doctor friend, and moved his belongings out.

Dorothea sang in night clubs, she had a pattering little song for trade-mark: 'I'm Sighin' For my Scion Who's a Yale Man,' and her audiences loved it. Her name was well known, she was nineteen and beautiful, and she was secretly pregnant again. That was the passing affair with the passing European prince and it delighted a pure vein in her. She was the janitor's daughter and she now carried royal blood. She could not bring herself to extinguish such a creation. Three months went by, four months went by, it was much too late. O'Faye saved her. His vogue running down, his drinking begun, he dropped in to see her one day and sympathized with her predicament. O'Faye was a rolling stone, he would never marry a girl who carried his own child, but he considered it right to help a friend out of her trouble. They were quickly married, and as quickly divorced, and her child had a name. Marion O'Faye she called him, and starred in a musical comedy that year. Later, years later, after Dorothea had made money and lost it and made it again, when she was retired in Desert D'Or, her gossip column sold and her court formed, O'Faye showed up again. He was a wreck, no doubt of that. His hands shook, his voice had lost its size, his working days were over. Dorothea was pleased to take him in; she hated to owe a debt. He had lived at The Hangover ever since, and she gave him a modest allowance. Between Marion Faye the son (as a boy he had dropped the 'O') and the nominal father, there was nothing at all. They looked at each other as curiosities. For that matter, Marion looked at his mother in the same way.

When she was drunk, Dorothea could never resist bragging that her son was the gift of a prince. Marion had known this since he was a boy and maybe it can explain a few things about him. At twenty-four, he was very special. Slim, tight-knit, with light wavy hair and clear grey eyes, he could have looked like a choir boy, I suppose, if it had not been for his expression. He had an arrogance which was made up of staring at you, measuring your value, and deciding you weren't there. At the present time he was living in Desert D'Or, but not at his mother's house. They got along too badly for that, and besides, his occupation would have interfered. He was a pimp.

I often heard that when he was a child one would have predicted another career. He had been a high-strung boy, and he cried easily. When Dorothea had been able to afford it, there had been nurses and servants, she had always been pleased to spoil her son, to forget him, to love him and match his tantrums with her own. There was a story she would tell about Marion when she was feeling sentimental and mourned the distance between them. Once, so long ago, she had been crying in her bedroom – over what, she no longer knew – and he had come in, he was three and a half at the time, and he had stroked her cheek. 'Don't cry, Mommie,' he had said, beginning to cry himself, and consoled her the only way he knew. 'Don't cry, Mommie, 'cause you're so pretty.'

He was a dreamy boy at school. She would tell me how he had been fascinated by railroad trains, by Erector sets, by collecting stamps and butterfly wings. He was shy, he was spoiled, he would be desperate at times with a desperate temper. In the first fight he ever had (it was with the tubby son of a motion-picture producer), he had been pulled screaming off the other boy's neck. Somewhere in those years between ten and thirteen, changes occurred in him, he no longer seemed so sensitive; he turned surly and communicated with himself. To her amazement he told her once that he wanted to be a priest. His intelligence was startling at times, at least to Dorothea, but he had become difficult. He was always causing trouble, he was ahead of his teachers, smoking, drinking, doing whatever was not allowed. Before he graduated from high school, Dorothea had been forced to put Marion in one private academy after another, but no matter where she put him, he had a talent for making friends outside the school. At seventeen, he was arrested for driving eighty miles an hour on one of the boulevards of the capital. Dorothea had fixed that, she had to fix many things he did. On his eighteenth birthday, he asked her for three hundred dollars.

'For what?' said Dorothea.

'There's this girl I know and she needs an operation.'

'Did you ever hear of precautions?'

He had stood before her, patient, bored, his clear grey eyes looking at her. 'Yes, I've heard of them,' he said, 'but you see, I was with two girls at the time, and I guess we got . . . distracted.'

Dorothea managed to write a sentimental column about her son the day he went into service, but that was the last she could write about him. When he came out of the Army, he refused to work, he refused to do anything he did not care to do. She got him put on as an assistant to a well-known executive at a movie studio; three months later, Marion quit. 'They're preachers,' was all he would say, and moved in with her at The Hangover.

In Desert D'Or he knew gangsters, he knew actors, he knew show girls and call girls and bar girls – he was even a pet of those few residents of the resort who might be considered international set, and with it all, since he was capable of spending days in one bar after another or hours at the Yacht Club patio, since he knew the headwaiters of the best clubs in the resort and was respected by them because he valued them so low, he had access to the pool of businessmen, entertainers, producers, tennis players, divorcees, golfers, gamblers, beauties and near beauties fed to the resort by the overflow from the capital. When Dorothea kicked him out after a quarrel over money, assuming she could force him to work – for her son she wanted respectability if for nobody else – he found his trade ready to hand. When Dorothea learned, she pleaded with him to come back, and Marion laughed at her. 'I'm just an amateur,' he said, 'like you.' She hadn't even dared to slap him; somehow it was years since anyone had tried that.

His operations were modest. He stayed away from the professionals; he did not care to take on the organization that would have meant, and many of his arrangements were unusual. He knew girls who would take a date once, and then never again, at least not for several months; he even knew a woman who did not need the money and merely was drawn to the idea of selling herself. As he had explained, he was an amateur, he dabbled. To work at a business was to be the slave of a business, and he detested slavery; it warped the mind. Therefore, he kept his freedom and used it to drink, to push dope on himself, and to race his foreign car through the desert, a gun in the glove compartment instead of a driving licence, for the licence had been suspended long ago. I drove with him once and tried to avoid it thereafter. I was pretty good with a car myself, but he drove like nobody I ever knew.

From time to time he still would drop in at The Hangover, but he was contemptuous of the court, and they were uneasy with him. Of all the people there, he could tolerate only two. I was one of them, and he made no pretence about his reasons. I had killed people, I had almost been killed myself, and these were emotions he considered interesting. Out of the cat's grace with which he held himself, he asked me once, 'How many planes did you shoot down?'

'Just three,' I said.

'Just three. They lost money on you.' His mouth showed nothing. 'You'd have shot down more if you could?'

'I suppose I would have tried.'

'You dig killing Asiatics?' Marion asked.

'I didn't mean it that way.'

'They know how to train you characters.' He took a cigarette from a platinum case. 'I wasn't an officer,' he said. 'I went into the Army a private, and I came out that way. I'm the only private they ever had.'

'They kept booking you in the stockade, I hear.'

'Yes, I learned a thing or two,' Marion said. 'You see, it's easy to kill a man. Easier to do that than chase after a roach and squash it.'

'Maybe you don't know all there is about it.'

But Marion was always ahead of me. 'You want a girl?' he asked abruptly. 'I'll get you a girl for nothing.'

'Not tonight,' I said.

'I didn't figure you would.' He had sensed what I was trying to keep from everybody. I had followed Pelley's troubles carefully, for we shared the same trouble. It had come on me shortly before I left Japan, and I had been helpless ever since. Once or twice, with girls I picked up in the bars of Desert D'Or, I had tried to cut my knot and only succeeded in tying it more tightly. 'I'm keeping myself for the woman I love,' I said to steer him away.

Love was the subject which steered Faye. 'You look,' he said to me, 'you take two people living together. Cut away all the propaganda. It's dull. The end. So you go the other direction. You find a hundred chicks, you find two hundred. It gets worse than dull. It makes you sick. I swear you start thinking of using a razor. I mean, that's it,' he said, waving a finger like a pendulum, 'screwing the one side, pain the other side. Killing. The whole world is bullshit. That's why people want a dull life.'

This was beyond me. I looked into his white-grey eyes, on fire with the argument, and said, 'Where do you end up with this?'

'I don't know,' he said, 'I got to work it out.' He had straightened up then, had looked at his watch as though to cover how surprised he was to hear himself talk for so long, and said quietly, 'When is Jay-Jay getting here? I have something to tell Dorothea.'

That was his other friend at The Hangover. Whenever Dorothea and Marion were not talking, he used the publicity man Jennings James for communications. Jay-Jay had managed to remain on good terms with them both. Years ago, he had been a legman for Dorothea, and he had known Marion as a boy. There was a tie between them; Marion tolerated him, he put up with Jay-Jay's speeches, his drunks, his depressions; he had something like affection for him.

No matter his red hair, Jay-Jay's tall skinny body and his skinny face with its silver-rimmed spectacles made him look like a bank clerk. Yet there was something childish about him. He lived in the past, and he loved to reminisce about those early days of the Depression when he was penniless in the capital and lived in a bungalow with two musicians, existing on oranges and the hope he could sell one of his short stories. Those were the good old days and now he did scattered publicity for Supreme Pictures, filing items with gossip columnists on whatever Supreme stars might come to town. I knew for a fact he supplemented his income by sending an occasional girl Marion's way.

With it all, he had a wistful charm. He would tell story after story in a slurred voice, often telling me, for I was the only one new enough to listen, that the great line, 'Men with lipstick on their mouths look like they just discovered sex,' credited to the movie star, Lulu Meyers, was in point of fact a sentence he had written for her. 'I'm sick of it,' Jay-Jay would say to me. 'Why, I remember when Lulu was married to Charley Eitel and thought brains was everything. I saw her walk into a room one night at a party with her face shining like she'd just discovered love or drunk some jungle juice. "Eitel has just given me my first acting lesson," she says, "and it was so stimulating." This after three years of making movies and seven starring roles, and I have to run interference for people like her.'

I think he was the first person in Desert D'Or to mention the name of Charles Francis Eitel. After that, it seemed as if everybody was always ready to tell some new story about the man. Eitel was a famous film director who was staying at the resort in the off-season, and he was one friend of Marion's who never came to The Hangover. Until I came to understand it better, I often thought that Marion kept the friendship just to provoke Dorothea, for Eitel had been in the news in the last year. I heard that he walked off a set one day in the middle of shooting a picture, and two days later he was called a hostile witness by an investigating committee of Congress. Dorothea was livid about Eitel. As a gossip columnist she had never grown to be nationally big, and finally had been bored by the work, but in the last year or two before she retired, the head of her column always featured the American flag next to her photograph, and her copy was filled with shadows of subversion in the movie industry. Even now she was very patriotic, and like most patriots she felt strongly and thought weakly, and so it was not easy to argue with her. I never tried, and I was careful not to mention Eitel unless I had to. Soon after I met him, I came to think of Eitel as my best friend at the resort, and I stopped her once in the middle of one of her tirades, said that he was my friend and I did not want to talk about him, and for a moment I thought she would tear into a rage. She came close, she came very close, her face flushed dark red and she let fly at me. 'You're the lousiest snob I ever met,' Dorothea shouted.

'That's right,' I answered her, and I didn't dislike Dorothea for the truth of it. 'I am a snob.'

'Well, swill in it,' she said under her breath, but Pelley was there passing a drink, and we didn't discuss Eitel.

'Just 'cause you're a rich man's son, and phony up to the ears,' Dorothea said, 'don't think you know all the answers.'

'All right. That's enough,' I muttered in my turn, and we let it lay.

But I was feeling satisfied. Dorothea's boasts were built on the considerable ground of her experience, and since she was always saying that she could tell on what side of the tracks a man was born, I had the thought that I wasn't too poor an impersonator.

4

I never knew my mother for she died too early, and my father, who gave me the princely name of Sergius O'Shaugnessy, stopped taking care of me when I was five years old, and surrendered himself to travelling from job to job. He was not a bad man in his own way, and the few times he visited the orphanage were events I remembered a long time. He would bring me a present, he would listen with sad eyes when I would ask him to take me with him, he would promise to return soon, and then he would disappear for another few years. It was not until I grew older that I realized he could never keep his word.

When I was twelve, I found out my last name was not O'Shaugnessy but something which sounded close in Slovene. It turned out the old man was mongrel sailor blood – Welsh-English from his mother, Russian and Slovene from his father, and all of it low. There is nothing in the world like being a false Irishman. Or maybe my mother was Irish. Once my father made that confession to me, he could never bring himself to add another detail. A working man all his life, he wanted to be an actor, and O'Shaugnessy was his fling. Before he was through, he played a number of places. He did the Merchant Marine, and he took his mouth organ on more than one freight train, and he even ran some rum until his luck ran out and they railed him into the state pen. When they let him out, he was good for washing dishes. I can say that he passed some of his character on to me. I was the biggest boy in the home for my age, but I was not what they call forward. At least, not then. When he died, however, I began to look for a new character. At fourteen you don't wear a name like Sergius easily – I had hidden it under a dozen nicknames, I had been Gus and Spike and Mac and Slim and I could name some others – but once he was dead, once I knew, and it took a long time to learn, that there were going to be no more visits and I was all alone, I began to call myself Sergius again. Naturally, I paid for it with a dozen fights, and for the first time in my life I was wild enough to win a thing or two. I had always been one of those boys for whom losing came naturally, but I was also rare enough to learn from winning, I liked boxing. I didn't know it then but it was the first thing I had found which was good for my nervous system. In the space of four months I lost three fights and then won all the others. I even won a boxing tournament the Police Department held. After that I'd earned my name. They called me Sergius.

I needed it, and I paid for it. My father left me a bum's inheritance; underneath his drunks and his last disappointed jobs and his shy hello for me, in all those boarding-house rooms where he watched the wallpaper curl and the years go down in one hash-house after another, he kept his little idea. There was something special about him, he had always thought, someday, somewhere . . .

Everybody has that, but my father had it more than most, and he slipped it on to me. I would never admit it to a soul, but I always thought there was going to be an extra destiny coming my direction; I knew I was more gifted than others. Even in the orphanage I had a lot of talents. They always gave me the lead in the Christmas play, and when I was sixteen I won a local photography contest with a borrowed camera. But I was never sure of myself, I never felt as if I came from any particular place, or that I was like other people. Maybe that is one of the reasons I have always felt like a spy or a fake.

Of course I had been faking all my life. At the children's home, I remember we used to go to a parochial school, and during class hours we were treated like everybody else. But the lunch period was a torture. They used to bring us sandwiches from the orphanage, and we were supposed to eat together in a corner of the lunchroom while the others looked at us. That didn't make it easy to become friends, and I remember one term when I did without lunch. On the first day I got to know a boy who lived down the street from the school in a two-family house. Today, I couldn't give his name, but for all those months I was sick he might discover I was from the home. Later, I realized he must have known all the time, but he was nice enough never to let me guess.

There are enough stories I could tell of those years, but it would be a mistake. I could go on forever about the orphanage, and how none of the Sisters were like one another, for some were cruel and some were peculiar, and two or three were very good. There was a nun named Sister Rose, and when I was a child I loved her exactly like a hungry child. She took special interest in me, and, with it all, since she came from a wealthy family, she spoke in a very clear way, and I used to have dreams at six or seven that when I grew up I would pay her family a visit and they would appreciate how good my manners were. She used to teach me Catechism in every way she could, and when I learned to read she would give me the lives of the saints and the martyrs. But I do not know how well that took, for my father gave me another catechism, and in his acquired brogue he would tell me to ask her about the life of Bartolomeo Vanzetti, and he would talk for hours about the martyrdom in Boston and how religion was for women and anarchism for me. He was a philosopher, my father, and afraid of Sister Rose, but he was the only one I ever knew who was nice to the hunchbacked boy who slept next to me, and that was a poor boy. He was ugly and he had body odour, and we used to kick him. The Sisters would always have to make him take a bath. Even Sister Rose could barely tolerate him, for nuggets would drip from his nose, but my father had pity on the cripple and used to bring him presents too. The last I heard of the hunchback, he was in prison; a feeble-minded boy, trapped while shoplifting.

It was quite a life in the orphanage, and after my father died I ran away from the home five times in three years. Once I stayed away for four months before they caught me and brought me back. Yet I would not even be telling a fact, for the fact would have to include what I learned and that would take too long. It's a trap to spend time writing about your childhood. Self-pity comes into the voice.

I would rather mention what I learned. I came out of the home when I was seventeen with one ambition. I had read a great many books, whichever ones I could, I read constantly when I was a boy – I would leave the lives of the martyrs and sneak away to the public library where I would read about English gentlemen, and knights, and adventure stories, and about brave men and Robin Hood. It all seemed very true to me. So I had the ambition that someday I would be a brave writer.

I do not know if this can explain why Charles Francis Eitel was my best friend for almost all the time I stayed in Desert D'Or. But then, who can explain friendship? The explanations cover everything but the necessity. Yet one thing I believe can be said. I had the notion that there were few kind and honest men in the world, and the world always took care to put them down. For most of the time I knew Eitel, I suppose I saw him in this way.

Days before I met him I had already heard his name with its odd pronunciation, 'eye-TELL.' As I have said, he was a subject for gossip in Desert D'Or. I even had a clue to explain Dorothea's state. It seemed that years ago she had an affair with him, and in some way it must have hurt. I gathered that the affair had meant something to her and very little to Eitel, but this isn't definite, and they had each had so many affairs. In all the time I knew them both I never heard them mention the few weeks or the few months when they had been together, and I would guess that its history was important now to nobody but Marion.

One night when I wandered over to have a drink at his house, he mentioned the director. 'There's a case,' he said. 'When I was a kid, I used to think' – and Faye laughed harshly – 'that Eitel was a god and devil all in one.'

'It's hard to think of you feeling that way about anybody,' I said.

He shrugged. 'Eitel would talk to me when he was dating Dorothea. I was such a freak of a kid. Even after he broke up with my mother, he used to invite me over once in a while.' Faye smiled at the hint of feeling in what he said.

'What do you think about him now?' I asked.

'He'd be all right,' Marion said, 'if he weren't so middle-class. Very nineteenth century, you know.' With a blank expression, he left me for a minute to search through the drawer of his aluminium and blond-wood desk. 'Here,' he said, coming back, 'take a look. Read this.'

He handed me a printed transcript of the testimony taken at the hearings of a Congressional investigating committee. It was a heavy pamphlet, and as I looked at it, Marion said, 'Eitel's dialogue starts on page eighty-three.'

'You sent away for this?' I asked.

He nodded. 'I wanted to have it.'

'Why?'

'Oh, that's just a little item,' Marion said. 'Someday I'll tell you about the artist in me.'

I read it through. The testimony of the director came to twenty pages, but it was my introduction to Eitel, and I think I ought to give a page or two which is typical of the rest. In fact, I read it aloud many times. I had brought a tape recorder with me to Desert D'Or, and I would study my speech and try to improve it. Eitel's dialogue was an opportunity for me, and although I cared little enough about politics, considering them a luxury like gentleman's ethics which I could not yet afford, I would always have a reaction from his words. It is not very neat to say but I felt as if I were speaking my own words, or at least the way I would have liked to say them into the eye of somebody who knew I had broken a regulation. So the testimony was not boring to me, and I took the idea while I read, that I had a lot to learn from Eitel:

CONGRESSMAN RICHARD SELWYN CRANE: . . . are you now or have you ever been, I want you to be specific, a member of the Party?

EITEL: I should think my answer would be obvious.

CHAIRMAN AARON ALLAN NORTON: Do you refuse to answer?

EITEL: May I say that I answer with reluctance and under duress. I have never been a member of any political party.

CHAIRMAN NORTON: There is no duress here. Let's get on with the thing.

CRANE: Did you ever know Mr —?

EITEL: I probably met him at a party or two.

CRANE: Did you know he was an agent of the Party?

EITEL: I didn't know.

CRANE: Mr Eitel, you seem to delight in presenting yourself as stupid.

CHAIRMAN NORTON: We're wasting time. Eitel, I'll ask you a simple question. Do you love your country?

EITEL: Well, sir, I've been married three times, and I've always thought of love in connection with women. (*Laughter*.)

CHAIRMAN NORTON: We'll have you up for contempt if you don't stop this.

EITEL: I wouldn't want to be in contempt.

CRANE: Mr Eitel, you say you met the agent in question?

EITEL: I can't be sure. My memory is weak.

CRANE: A film director has to have a good memory, I should think. If your memory is as bad as you claim, how did you make your pictures?

EITEL: That's a good question, sir. Now that you've pointed it out, I wonder how I did make them. (*Laughter*.)

CHAIRMAN NORTON: Very clever. Maybe you won't remember something we have on record here. It says you fought in Spain. Want to hear the dates?

EITEL: I went over to fight. I ended up as a messenger boy.

CHAIRMAN NORTON: But you didn't belong to the Party?

EITEL: No, sir.

CHAIRMAN NORTON: You must have had friends among them. Who incited you to go over?

EITEL: If I did remember, I don't know that I would tell it to you, sir.

CHAIRMAN NORTON: We'll have you up for perjury if you don't watch out.

CRANE: To return to a point of questioning. I'm curious, Mr Eitel. In the event of war, would you fight for this country?

EITEL: If I were drafted, I wouldn't have much choice, would I? May I say that?

CRANE: You would fight without enthusiasm?

EITEL: Without enthusiasm.

CHAIRMAN NORTON: But if you were fighting for a certain enemy, that would be a different story, wouldn't it?

EITEL: I would fight for them with even less enthusiasm.

CHAIRMAN NORTON: That's what you say now. Eitel, here's something we have in our files on you, 'Patriotism is for pigs.' Do you remember saying that?

EITEL: I suppose I did.

IVAN FABNER (Counsel for the Witness): May I interrupt on behalf of my client to state that I believe he will rephrase his remarks?

CHAIRMAN NORTON: That's what I want to know. Eitel, what do you say about it now?

EITEL: It sounds a little vulgar as you repeat it, Congressman. I would have put it differently if I had known some agent of your Committee was reporting what I said at a party.

CHAIRMAN NORTON: 'Patriotism is for pigs.' And you make your living from this country.

33

EITEL: It's the alliteration of the *p*'s which makes it vulgar.

CHAIRMAN NORTON: Not responsive.

CRANE: How would you put it today, Mr Eitel?

EITEL: If you ask me to go on, I'm afraid I'll make a subversive remark.

CHAIRMAN NORTON: I order you to go on. Just how, in what language, would you word it for the Committee today?

EITEL: I suppose I'd say that patriotism asks you to be ready to leave your wife at a moment's notice. Possibly that's the secret of its appeal. (*Laughter.*)

CHAIRMAN NORTON: Do you usually think with such noble sentiments?

EITEL: I'm not accustomed to thinking on these lines. The act of making motion pictures has little to do with noble sentiments.

CHAIRMAN NORTON: I'm pretty sure the motion pictures industry is going to give you plenty of time to think noble thoughts after this morning's testimony. (*Laughter.*)

FABNER: May I ask for a recess?

CHAIRMAN NORTON: This is a subversive committee, not a forum for half-baked ideas. Eitel, you're the most ridiculous witness we've ever had.

When I finished reading, I looked up at Faye. 'He must have lost his job in quick-time,' I said.

'He certainly did,' Faye murmured.

'But why is he staying in Desert D'Or?'

Marion grinned out of his private humour. 'You're right, man. This is no place to stay when you've lost your loot.'

'I thought Eitel was rich.'

'He used to be. You don't know how anything works,' Faye said dispassionately. 'You see, along about this time they started looking at his income-tax returns. By the time they got done, Eitel had to strip himself to pay the back taxes. All that's left is his house here. Mortgaged, of course.'

'And he just stays here?' I asked. 'He doesn't do anything?'

'You'll get to meet him. You'll see what I mean,' Faye told me. 'Charley Eitel could be worse off. Maybe he needed a kick in the pants.'

By the way Faye said this, I had a clue.

'You like him,' I said again.

'I don't dislike him,' Faye said grudgingly.

At the Yacht Club, a few days later, Marion introduced me to Eitel. By the end of the week, I suppose I was making a point of going to see him every day.

5

The open-air café of the Yacht Club wandered around the cabañas and the swimming pool, its peppermint-striped tables and chairs another throw of colour against the hotel foliage and the mountains beyond Desert D'Or. Almost always, I could find Eitel seated at a table for the siesta, a paper-bound manuscript open before him. Yet it was hard to believe the script could be important. No sooner would I come by than he would close the pages, order a drink, and begin to talk.

I was surprised when we were introduced. Although he was over forty and had a big reputation as a film director, Eitel was better known in other ways. He had been married several times, he was said to have been the cause of more than one divorce, and these were the least of the rumours. At different times I heard he was an alcoholic, a drug addict, a satyr; some people even whispered he was an espionage agent. Considering all this, it was unexpected to meet a middle-sized man with a broken nose and a wide smile. He had a large face to match his broad body, and his head was half bald, crowned with a circle of strong curly hair. He had eyes you noticed. They were bright blue, and when he smiled, they were alive, and his broken nose gave him a humorous look. But only his voice gave a hint of his reputation. It was a voice which had a hundred things in it, and a girl told me once she thought it was 'seductive.' He had a way of offering something and pulling it back; just when you thought he was laughing at you, he seemed to like you – about the time you decided things were going well, his voice would turn you away. I've taken a few punches on the head, but I still know voices, I've got a good ear, and Eitel's voice had more than one accent. I could hear New York in it, and the theatre, and once in a while if he was talking to somebody from those parts, a trace of the

South or the Middle-West came into it, and with all of that it was a controlled voice – most of the time he sounded like society. With the way he had of laughing at himself, he told me once that he picked up the English accent last of all.

A long description, I know, but I had seldom liked anybody so much. I felt that he was a man like me, only many times smoother and he knew more. Later I learned that a lot of people saw Eitel this way. Of all the rumours about him, and most people seemed to enjoy saying that his career was finished, I believed nothing. He drank a lot, but I never saw him drunk; his speech only became slow; that he took drugs was a little strong for me, and his reputation with women I would have been ready to share. More than once I studied the friendly attention he was able to give them.

All the same, he was forced to be a lonely man, and a good part of our friendship was due to the fact that I looked for his company. At least, I thought so. It was his habit to drive over to the open-air café in the early afternoon, and there, as I have said, he would drink, he would talk, he would look at his script. Once, he had been a great friend of the manager of the hotel, but now he was waiting for the day when he would be asked not to enter the Yacht Club. 'You see, years ago I loaned the manager some money, and he's the sort of man who boasts that he never forgets a favour.' Eitel grinned. 'Right now, I find that a nice trait of character. For some silly reason, I like this place.'

Many days, nobody besides myself would sit down at all and I would help him drink through the afternoon and into the night. It seemed he was never invited anywhere, or at least anywhere he wanted to go. Usually, Eitel would get restless after a time and I would go along with him on a round of the second-rate night clubs and bars of the resort. All those hours were the same. Drinking friends would be found and lost, a girl might be picked up and dropped again, once he almost got into a fight because a drunk insulted a bar girl who was sitting with us and yet it was a kind of occupation. On we would go, hiding from our insomnia, not even trying to sleep until the dawn lifted over the desert and along the rounds of our drinking he drove himself like a man getting over a broken marriage. I could see him waste a day and then a night and do no more than answer a letter.

I was told his story more than once, hearing it from former friends, false friends, and people who did not know him at all, but most of his story I got from Eitel directly, for one of his qualities was the ability to talk about himself with considerable masculinity of mind. He was the only son of an auto dealer in a big Eastern city, and his father was born of Austrian immigrant parents and started as a junk dealer. His mother was French. Eitel was the first of his family to go to college. It had been expected he would be a lawyer, but while he was at school he got interested in the theatre and quarrelled with his parents about his career. By the time he graduated, the argument was settled; his father had lost his money in the Depression. Eitel drifted around New York looking for work. He was not a good-looking young college graduate, and he was shy, and so he fell in love with the first girl who fell in love with him. She was studying to be a welfare worker, and she lived at home, and wanted to marry him to get out of her parents' house. It was natural they should feel they were very much in love. She was political, his wife, and through her, through her friends, he studied radical literature, he talked politics. His wife worked in a bookstore to support him, and he wrote plays, he acted where he could, he got opportunities to direct plays in small theatres and in the worst of the Depression his own career grew. He was hired to put on a play in a government-sponsored project, and it was a success. A lot of people heard his name for the first time. He was a playwright, a director, an actor; he was offered a career in the movies. So he had gone to the capital, and on a small contract to make cheap pictures, he had the good luck to be allowed an experiment. It was a cheap experiment, no more, and yet he wrote and directed one, then two, and finally three pictures which are considered powerful even today. I saw one of them reissued the year I got out of the orphanage, and although I suppose it was dated, I don't remember a better picture made about the Depression.

Eitel always remembered those pictures as the best eighteen months of his life. He had been an aggressive young man at the time, he told me, opinionated, dogmatic, and more than a little sure of himself, liking everybody a great deal on the flush of his success, but understanding them poorly. He was young, and

37

there were people who told him he was a genius. Of course, it was not so simple. Those three pictures, for all their history of being seen by college film societies and museums and cinema clubs, for their reputation to this day, even for their influence on the many directors who imitated his style, were still pictures which did not make money. Although he was given a better contract by another studio with large budgets and bigger stars, the stories were no longer his own. He continued to make pictures which were better than most; they even showed a profit. Yet he was becoming dissatisfied. It was the period of the Spanish Civil War, and what he could not put into his work, he tried to find in the work there was to be done on committees. He was still full of enthusiasm, he argued about Spain, he spoke at public meetings, he helped to gather contributions, and all the while he was losing his first wife. She was unhappy and she hated the capital. She felt he did not want her any longer, and it was true, he did not; he wanted a woman who was more attractive, more intelligent, more his equal; he wanted more than one woman. He saw so many in the capital that he could have, and it made him anxious to be free.

However, he felt guilty about his wife. He had needed her at one time and they had been good friends, she had taught him so much, and it was not her fault that now he knew more. He would think at times that his work was spoiled not only by the studio, but by himself. That was the trouble with their marriage, he would tell himself; he was too comfortable and too bored, his talent was not growing. So he decided to go to Spain.

He got to the front lines as a visitor. The year he spent there was wasted, and it was impossible to begin the movie he wanted to make. 'The war which put a finish to five hundred years,' he was fond of saying, and he and his wife went back to their marriage. He had his affairs, she had her affairs; they told each other about them, for they swore they must be honest with one another. Yet they quarrelled. He had been offered a big salary at Supreme Pictures, and he said that he should take it, she said that he should not; he was full of the premise that to make the movies he wanted, he had to be powerful in a studio. He made two bad pictures and one of them made a lot of money, and then his wife wanted a divorce, she had found somebody else. He had dreamed for years of such a solution, yet to his surprise, he could not let her go; they had one of those final reconciliations, and a half year later they divorced. Eventually she moved to another city and married a labour organizer and Eitel never saw her again. By now he could hardly remember her.

Next he married an actress from the social register. While it lasted, he made movies, many movies, he bought a fourteen-room house with a library, a wine closet, a gymnasium, a swimming pool. There was a four-car garage, a volleyball court, a badminton court, and a tennis court; vines grew on the terraces and a row of cypresses leaned toward the ocean, there was a kennel for a dozen dogs, a stable for two horses. That was his second marriage and he kept the house long after the wife. From the wife he had picked up what he wanted, and paid for it of course.

His second divorce coincided with his commission into the Army. In Europe, he made training films and combat films and travelled the cocktail circuit of generals and beauties and black marketeers, of politicians and movie producers and statesmen. He even made the last of his good films, a documentary on parachute troops so different from all the battles one saw on the screen that the Army never released it.

When Eitel came back from the war, he took on the last of his reputations. There was a year or two when he was supposed to have slept with half the good-looking women in the capital, and it was a rare week which did not have his name in one gossip column or another. His films made money and he was the highest-paid director at the studio, for he had the reputation of being able to get relatively superlative performances from relatively untalented actresses. But his style had changed. In the face of all the pictures he was not encouraged to make, he came to choose movies of intricate action and odd character until it became at last a trade-mark, and 'the Eitel touch' would guarantee a string of exotic murders. 'Audiences are made of sentimental necrophiles,' he said to me once.

Yet of all the time which passed in making money and spending it, in directing films which were a compromise – actors, story, and plot furnished by Supreme Pictures; atmosphere and master's touch by Charles Francis Eitel – it was his last year in the capital which concerned Eitel the most. Over and over he would return to it in conversation.

The last year began with his third divorce. He always married out of pity, Eitel said to me, and he had come to distrust pity. It was the sure sign of vanity. 'I'm the archetype of the John who marries five or six times because he just can't believe the poor girl will live without him.' The third wife had been beautiful, she was Lulu Meyers. 'You'll meet her sooner or later,' Eitel told me. 'She comes down here between pictures.' Lulu was very young, Eitel went on, he had really believed she needed him. 'It's subtle when a marriage ends. You always go hog-wild. And to make matters worse, I was on vacation at the time. I don't know why, I got into the most dreary affair with a Rumanian actress. She had had one of those horrible lives you can't even bear to think about. Her first husband, the young love, was killed in a street accident, her second husband stole her money. It was grim. Apparently she was well known in Rumania, and when the war came she was put in a concentration camp, although for all I know she could just as well have been a *collaborateur*. In any case, she came here with nothing but an atrocious Rumanian accent. It doesn't matter what kind of star you were in Rumania, there aren't many roles you can play when you're over forty, your looks are going and you have an accent with all the wrong sounds in it. She made some sort of living being technical advisor 'for films with a Balkan locale.'

We were sitting on the patio which opened from the living room of Eitel's house, and he stopped abruptly and made a face at the yucca tree turning blue in the twilight shadows. 'Sergius O'Shaugnessy,' he said with the comic pompousness he loved to give my name, 'what are you doing here in Desert D'Or? Just what the hell are you doing, you smart Mick?'

'Nothing,' I said. 'I'm trying to forget how to fly a plane.'

'Do you have money to do this forever?'

'For a year or so.'

'Then what?'

'I'll think about the next town when my money is gone.'

'That kind of remark makes me feel old-fashioned. You're really here to have a good time?' Eitel asked suspiciously. I nodded. 'Women?' he went on.

'If I can manage it.'

'Sergius, you're a twentieth-century gentleman,' he said, and we laughed at this.

'The worst thing about my Rumanian,' Eitel continued, as if to explain himself now that he had an idea of me, 'is that she had been beautiful once, and too many men had been in love with her. Now, I'm afraid, it was the reverse. She had lost her looks and so she adored me.' He couldn't stand her, Eitel explained, and therefore he felt obliged to be as nice as possible. 'An affair like that can go on forever. It went on for a whole year. I've never been the kind of man who can be faithful with any regularity. I've always been the sort of decent chappie who hops from one woman to another in the run of an evening because that's the only prescription which allows me to be fond of both the ladies, but I was faithful in my way to the Rumanian. She would have liked to see me every night for she hated to be alone, and I would have liked never to see her again, and so we settled for two nights a week. It didn't matter if I were in the middle of a romance or between girls, whether I had a date that night or not – on Tuesday night and Thursday night I went to her apartment to sleep. I can say, parenthetically, that she was passionate in a depressing way.'

'How can passion be depression?' I asked.

Eitel was kind about it. 'You're right, Sergius. It wasn't really passion, and that's why it left me low. She was hungry, that's all.' He started to pour himself a drink, and instead rattled the ice cubes in his glass. 'As I say, I believed I went to see her because I didn't want to hurt her. But, looking back, I can see I was wrong. I needed to see her.'

'I don't know if I follow you.'

He shook his head. 'Maybe I was in bad shape after Lulu moved out.'

'Some of the people here think you're still in love with her,' I said directly. I guess I believed this myself. I had seen Lulu Meyers not more than a year ago, but I had seen her when she passed for a minute through our officers' mess escorted by generals and colonels, and I had seen her again with ten thousand soldiers between us while she told her jokes and prattled a little song on an improvised overseas stage like some fairy princess of sex who had flown across the Pacific to anoint us with tiny favours, a whiff of her perfume, a lift she lost from her heel, a sequin from her evening gown. I even remembered having heard the name of her husband, and having forgotten it, and so the situation seemed impressive to be able to talk casually of her now.

'In love with Lulu?' Eitel asked. He began to laugh. 'Why, Sergius, our marriage was the meeting of zero and zero.' He poured his drink and took a sip before putting it down. 'When Lulu and I got married, I knew it could never last. That was what bothered me afterward. You begin to think you're a sleep-walker when you can't believe in your marriage on your wedding day. That's why I needed the Rumanian. My work was going to hell.'

It had come on him, after fifteen years and twenty-eight pictures, that he would never be powerful enough to make only those pictures he wanted to do. Instead, he would always be making the studio's pictures. He was not even surprised to decide that he had no real desire to make his own films. For better or worse, his true marriage was with the capital, and he knew nowhere else to go. Worse. The commercial reputation at which he had sneered was being lost. His last picture, *Love Is But a Moment*, had been an expensive failure, but the two which came before it had not been successful either. 'And then,' Eitel said, 'there was that Subversive Committee.' It had hung over him for months. There were so many petitions he had signed, so many causes to which he had given money, first from conviction, then from guilt, finally as a gesture. It was part of the past; he was indifferent to politics; yet he learned that in the next subversive hearings in the film industry he would be called, and if he were not ready to give the name of everybody he knew who had ever belonged to any of the parties and committees on the government's proscribed list, he could never work again in the capital.

He felt nothing for all those people he once had known; some he liked in memory, some he disliked, but it seemed ridiculous to end his career by defending their names with his silence and so indirectly defending a political system which reminded him of nothing so much as the studio for which he worked. Yet there remained his pride. One did not go crawling in public.

'It was horrible,' Eitel said. 'I couldn't make up my mind.' He smiled at the memory as if relieved it were gone. 'You can have no idea of the work I put in. I had no time to *ponder* the moral questions, I was too busy having conferences with my lawyer, my agent was taking soundings at the studio, my business manager was lost in sessions with accountants to review my income-tax returns. They analysed the situation, they refined it, they analysed it again. My expenses were high, they told me, my salary was a necessity, my capital had been drained in divorce settlements, and Supreme Pictures was not going to protect me from the Committee. What with my big salary, my agent was even convinced they had encouraged the Committee to start on me. It seemed that when one got down to it, I had very little real money. So they all advised the same thing. Co-operate with the Committee.' Eitel shrugged. 'I said I would. I was sick about it, but there it was. My lawyer and I started to spend hours going over what I would say. In the middle of it all I started changing my mind again. When I got down to the details it was just too unpleasant. I got the lawyer to draw up a different plan in case I would not co-operate. And all the while friends kept seeing me and giving advice. Some said I should talk, others told me to be an unfriendly witness, others came just to admit that they didn't know what they would do. I was finding it hard to sleep. What nobody took into account was the picture I was making. The studio had assigned me to film a musical, *Clouds Ahoy*. I couldn't have asked for anything worse. I hate musical comedies.'

Everything about the picture was wrong. His producer inter-fered on the set, there were visits by high studio executives who did not say a word. Delays came up which could have been avoided and others which could not; the star got sick, the colour film showed mistakes in lighting, Eitel had a fight with the cameraman, a grip was hurt, it was decided that changes had to be made in the script, the schedule fell days behind, and an expensive scene with extras, calculated to take a morning, went into the morning of the next day; everything was lax, and Eitel knew he was to blame. Each night for salt to his sores, he had to sit in a projection room and watch the rushes from the last week. The more he worked, the worse it got. The pace was too slow or too rapid, the comedy was not funny, the sentiment was pious, and the production numbers with their troops of dancing girls and their kaleidoscope of scenery looked like a battlefield after the war between the dance director and Eitel. Lost in the middle was 'the Eitel touch'; here and there a scene with studied composition, intricate shadows, and a patch of atmosphere. It went on like this for three weeks of shooting, until one morning, with the picture not half done, everything went wrong, and everybody, producer, director, actors, cameramen, and grips, dance director and chorus, milled over the sound stage. Eitel, his nerves out of control, walked off the set and left the studio. Immediately his contract was revoked by Supreme Pictures, and the next morning another director was given the thankless mission of finishing *Clouds Ahoy*. Eitel wasn't there to learn the news. When he quit the studio that morning, he was beginning to act a script of his own which, whether behind or ahead of schedule, took several days to unwind.

6

Eitel went directly back to his fourteen-room house, and told the butler not to answer the door. His secretary was away on vacation, and so he called his answer service and told them he was going to be out of town for the next two days. Then he sat down in his study and began to drink. His telephone rang all afternoon and the only sign of how much liquor he had swallowed was that the sound of the phone became funny.

The fact was that he could not get drunk. Too sobering was the other fact that in forty-eight hours he would appear before the Committee. 'I'm free now,' he would tell himself, 'I can do what I want,' and yet he was able to think of nothing but the damage of quitting the set of *Clouds Ahoy*. His contract with Supreme was ruined, no doubt of that. Still, if he co-operated with the Committee, he would probably find work at another studio. What it amounted to was that a fit of temper was going to cost him a few hundred thousand dollars over the next five years. 'It all goes in taxes anyway,' he caught himself thinking.

The night before the day he was due to testify, he still had not seen his lawyer, and spoke to him on the phone only long enough to say he would meet him at his office a half hour before the hearings started. Then Eitel rang his answer service and started to take the list of messages. In the thirty-six hours since he had left the studio, there had been more than a hundred calls, and after a while he became tired of it. 'Just give me the names,' he said to the operator, and forgot them even as she mentioned them. When the girl came to Marion Faye, he stopped her. 'What did Faye want?' Eitel asked.

'He didn't leave any message. Just a phone number.'

'All right. Thank you. I'll take that, and you give me the rest later, dear.'

Faye arrived an hour after Eitel phoned. 'Trying to get used to living alone?' he greeted Eitel.

'Maybe that's what it is.'

Marion sat down and tapped a cigarette carefully on his platinum case. 'I saw Dorothea yesterday,' he said. 'She's betting that you'll talk.'

'I didn't know people were betting on me,' Eitel said.

Faye shrugged. 'People bet on everything.'

'I wonder why.'

'It's the only way to know.'

'Well,' Eitel said, 'how are you betting, Marion?'

Faye looked at him. 'I put down three hundred dollars that Dorothea is wrong.'

'Maybe you'd better hedge that bet.'

'I'd rather lose it.'

Eitel tried to sit back in his chair. 'I've been hearing a great many stories about what you're doing in Desert D'Or.'

'They're true.'

'I don't like it.'

'We'll talk another time about that. I just wanted to tell you . . .'

'Yes, what did you want to tell me?'

Marion's voice was not completely in control. 'I wanted to say that if I lose my bet, that's the end with you.' The finality of his sentence made him look young.

'Marion!' Eitel said for want of anything better.

'I mean what I say,' Faye repeated.

'I've seen you three times in the last three years. Not much of a friendship to be lost there.'

'Knock off,' said Faye. His voice was throbbing.

The answer irritated Eitel. Years ago, Marion would not have spoken to him in this way. 'I've been wanting to talk about you,' Eitel said.

'Look,' Faye muttered, 'I know you, Charley. You're not going to name names.'

'Maybe I will.'

'For what? So they'll let you make some more crud?'

'What else is there?' Eitel said.

'Why don't you find out? That's what you've been wondering for the last fifteen years.'

'Maybe I was fooling myself.'

'It's a big future, isn't it? You'll just keep cooking slop till you die.'

Eitel was never certain what he would have done if Faye hadn't visited him, but the next morning, after a very bad night, he walked into his lawyer's office, gave his broad smile and said easily, 'I'm not going to give any names,' as if this had been understood from the beginning. 'Just keep me out of jail, that's all.'

'Sure you won't change your mind on the way over?' the lawyer asked.

'Not this trip.'

In the weeks that followed, Eitel would try to think about his hour before the Committee, for it stood well in his memory. He had acted as he might have hoped to act; he had been cool, his voice had never lost control, and for two hours, carried by his excitement, he dodged questions, gave neat answers, and felt inspired to ruin every retreat. When it was over, he faced a crowd of photographers, sauntered to his car, and raced away. It was one o'clock in the afternoon, but he was hardly hungry. Feeding on his dialogue, he went for a drive through the mountains, his nerves enjoying every sound of the tyres along the winding road.

That was finally spent. More numb than not, he crawled along a boulevard which went to the ocean, and cruised along the shore for miles. On a wide beach where the swell rolled in on long even waves, he stopped his car, sat on the edge of the shore, and watched the surfboard riders. They were all young, somewhere between eighteen and twenty-two, and their bodies were burned to a golden bronze, their hair was bleached by the sun. They sprawled on the sand, wrestling with one another, sleeping, watching the water a half mile from shore where the riders would stand up and balance themselves on the first rise of the swell. Their feet on the board, they would race ahead of the surf, their arms stretched. When they had run into the shallow and could stand no longer, they would jump free, and propping the board into the sand at the water's edge, would lie next to one another, the boys resting their heads on the hips of the girls. Eitel watched them, became absorbed in studying a tall girl with round limbs and round breasts. Not ten feet from him, she stood alone, brushing sand from her light hair, her back curled. She seemed so confident of her body and the sport of being alive. 'I must make love to that girl,' Eitel thought, and was struck by how exceptional it was to feel such an easy desire.

'Is it hard to learn how to ride these boards?' he asked.

'Oh, depends.' She seemed concerned with the sand in her hair.

'Whom could I get to teach me?' he tried again.

'I don't know. Why don't you try it yourself?' He could sense that she was not reacting to him, and it brought an uncomfortable tingling to the skin of his face.

'If you didn't help me, I'd probably drown,' he said with twinkling eyes and a voice to charm the dead.

The girl yawned. 'Get a board and somebody'll show you.'

A tow-head of nineteen with broad shoulders and powerful legs went racing past them and slapped her on the thigh. 'Come on in,' he called in a booming voice, his short chopped features a cut of healthy meat to match the muscles of his limbs. 'Oh, Chuck, wait till I get *you*!' the girl shouted, and ran down the beach after him. Chuck stopped, she caught him, and they struggled, Chuck throwing sand on her hair while she hooted with laughter. A minute later, running side by side, they dived into the shallow water, and came up splashing at each other.

'I was ready to do anything,' Eitel said to me, 'to tell her my name, to tell her what I could do for her.' He stopped. 'All of a sudden I realized that I was without a name and I couldn't do a thing for anybody. That was quite a sensation. All those years people wanted to meet Charles Francis Eitel, and to meet him, they had had to meet me too. Now there was only me.' He gave a self-amused smile. 'Those surfboard kids looked like you,' he said with his honesty, and I saw another reason why Eitel liked my company.

'Back I got into my gilt-chromed Cadillac, feeling like a little middle-aged man who decides to grow a moustache. When I reached home, there was a call from my Rumanian. She was still loyal.' Eitel shook his head at himself. 'After that girl at the beach, I knew I couldn't go on with the Rumanian. Yet I never liked her so much as I did at that moment. So I had enough sense to know I was about to get into something really impossible. I talked to my business manager and told him to put the house up for sale and pay the servants off, and I got on the plane for Mexico.' That evening on the flight south, he had glanced at the newspapers long enough to see that he was on the front page. 'How they must be hating me,' he had thought, and drifted into an exhausted sleep.

In Mexico, at a seashore resort which looked like nothing so much as Desert D'Or glued to the side of a cliff, the reaction followed him. There were hundreds of letters: a pamphlet from a vegetarian society, a Lulu Meyers Fan Club president who was happy Lulu had divorced him, anonymous letters, obscene notes, congratulations, even a personal letter from an anti-tobacco society which enclosed a news photo circled in red pencil of Eitel smoking a cigarette. 'Eitel among the cranks,' he thought, and turned to open the letter from his business manager which gave the disaster of the back income taxes.

'It wasn't too bad in Mexico,' Eitel said, 'but on the other hand it was terrible. You may not believe it knowing me now, but I used to be capable of a lot of work, and all of a sudden I didn't seem able to do anything.'

I nodded – besides everything else I had heard stories of Eitel working eighteen hours a day while making a picture.

'There was a week or two down there,' he went on, 'when I began to think I was in poor shape. With all I've done in my life it may sound odd to you, but I started to think of how in college I used to dream of spending years wandering around, picking up little adventures here and there. It's naïve of course but everybody has that ambition when he's young. Anyway, I married much too soon, and when I thought about it in Mexico, it seemed to me that ever since, I had always been mixed up in something I didn't exactly want. I began to think that the reason I acted the way I did with the Committee was to give myself another chance. And yet I didn't know what to do with the chance. Yes,' he said reflectively, 'that put me in bad shape.' Eitel smiled. 'Anyway, win or lose, I managed to stop brooding. I tried to stay away from the places where I might meet people

I knew, and I tried to think, and after a while I began to get interested in a little story I'd been saving for years.' He tapped the manuscript on the table beside him. 'If I can bring this off, it'll make a movie that can justify so much bad work.' He riffled the pages. 'Pity I had to come back.'

'You don't really seem to be doing much more here than you did in Mexico,' I said.

Eitel nodded. 'It's ridiculous, I know, but when you're my age it's not that simple to go looking for a new place. I wanted to be among people who knew me.' He smiled. 'Sergius, I swear I'll get down to work. This movie ought to be made.'

'Would anybody give you money?' I asked.

'That's not the main problem,' Eitel said. 'There's a producer I know in London. I don't like him much, but if I have to, I can work with him. We've corresponded. He's wild about my idea, and in Europe I can direct the picture under a pseudonym. All that's necessary is to write a good script.' He sighed. 'Only, it's not that simple. I feel as if I've been . . . amputated. You know, I haven't had a woman in three months.'

I understood Eitel even less when he told me these stories. I had always thought that to know oneself was all that was necessary, probably because I didn't know myself at all. I did not see how Eitel could talk about himself so clearly, and be able to do nothing with it. I even wondered why he didn't mind that I told him nothing further about me, and I had the feeling that our friendship was of very small size. Often, after I left him and went back to the house I rented on the edge of the desert, I would leave off thinking about Eitel, and I would be stuck in my own past. I wanted to talk to him, to try to explain things I could not explain to myself, but I couldn't do it. I can't remember ever talking about the orphanage, at least not since I went into the Air Force. I had such a desire to be like everybody else, at least everybody who had made it, and to make it, I boxed my way into the middleweight semi-finals of an Air Force enlisted man's tournament, and when that gave me the chance to go to flying school, I studied hours at night to pass the pre-flight examinations. Until I graduated, nothing seemed so important as to get my wings.

It is hard to say what being a flier meant. I had friends I

thought would last forever, and in combat, routinely, in the way it happened, I saved other pilots two or three times just as they did the same for me. There was a feeling for each other. We knew there was nobody like us, and for once in my life I thought I had found a home.

That home fell apart. I can even pick the day I remember best, and it did not happen in combat. Fighting an enemy plane was impersonal and had the nice moves of all impersonal contests; I never felt I had done anything but win a game. I flew a plane the way I used to box; for people who know the language I can say that I was a counter-puncher. As flight-time built up, I went stale, we all did, but it was the only time in my life when I was happy and didn't want to be somewhere else. Even the idea of being killed was not a problem for who wanted a life outside the Air Force? I never thought of what I would do afterward.

Sometimes on tactical missions we would lay fire bombs into Oriental villages. I did not like that particularly, but I would be busy with technique, and I would dive my plane and drop the jellied gasoline into my part of the pattern. I hardly thought of it any other way. From the air, a city in flames is not a bad sight.

One morning I came back from such a job and went into Officers' Mess for lunch. We were stationed at an airfield near Tokyo, and one of our Japanese KP's, a fifteen-year-old boy, had just burned his arm in a kettle of spilled soup. Like most Orientals he was durable, and so he served the dishes with one hand, his burned arm held behind him, while the sweat stood on his nose, and he bobbed his head in little shakes because he was disturbing our service. I could not take my eyes from the burn; it ran from the elbow to the shoulder, and the skin had turned to blisters. The KP began to get on my nerves. For the first time in years I started to think of my father and the hunchbacked boy and Sister Rose's lessons on my duty.

After lunch I took the Jap aside, and asked the cooks for tannic-acid ointment. There wasn't any in the kitchen, and so I told them to boil tea and put compresses to his arm. Suddenly, I realized that two hours ago I had been busy setting fire to a dozen people, or two dozen, or had it been a hundred?

51

No matter how I tried to chase the idea, I could never get rid of the Japanese boy with his arm and his smile. Nothing sudden happened to me, but over a time, the thing I felt about most of the fliers went false. I began to look at them in a new way, and I didn't know if I liked them. They were one breed and I was another; they were there and I was a fake. I was close to things I had forgotten, and it left me sick; I had a choice to make. My missions were finished, my service was over, and I had to decide if I wanted to sign for a career in the Air Force. Trying to make up my mind I got worse, I had a small breakdown, and spent a season in the hospital. I was not very sick, but it was a breakdown, and for seven weeks I lay in bed and felt very little. When I got up, I learned that I was to be given a medical discharge. It no longer mattered. Flying had become too difficult and my reflexes were going. They told me I needed eyeglasses, which made me know how to feel old at twenty-two. But they were wrong, and I did without the eyeglasses, and my eyes got better, even if the rest of me didn't. Resting in bed, I remembered the books I read when I could get away from the orphanage, and picturing what my life would be like outside the Air Force, I could feel an odd hope when I thought that maybe I would become a writer.

For such a purpose, Desert D'Or may have been a poor place to stay, and in truth, I hardly wrote a word while I was at the resort. But I was not ready to work; I needed time, and I needed the heat of the sun. I do not know if I can explain that I did not want to feel too much, and I did not want to think. I had the idea that there were two worlds. There was a real world as I called it, a world of wars and boxing clubs and children's homes on back streets, and this real world was a world where orphans burned orphans. It was better not even to think of this. I liked the other world in which almost everybody lived. The imaginary world.

But I write too much. In a few days the winter season began, and all of that routine I divided between Dorothea at The Hangover and Eitel at the Yacht Club was altered. Before the movie colony had been in Desert D'Or a week, what little story I have to tell was fairly begun.

Part Two

7

With the beginning of the season, there was some rain, not a great deal, but enough to put the desert flowers into bloom. Which brought the crowd from the capital. The movie people filled the hotels, and the season residents opened their homes. Movie stars were on the street, and gamblers, criminals with social cartel, models, entertainers, athletes, airplane manufacturers, even an artist or two. They came in all kinds of cars: in Cadillac limousines, in ruby convertibles and gold-yellow convertibles, in little foreign cars and big foreign cars. Then with the start of the season on me, I came to like the wall around my house which was always safe in the privacy it gave, and I would think at times how confusing the town must be to the day tourist who could drive through street after street and know no more of the resort than the corridors of an office building would tell about the rooms.

Eitel did not take to this invasion. He had come to prefer being alone, and was rarely to be seen at the hotel. One day when I stopped by his house, the phone rang in Eitel's bedroom. From the den I could hear him talking. He was being invited to visit somebody who had just arrived at the Yacht Club, and after he hung up, I could feel his excitement. 'How would you like to meet a pirate?' he said with a laugh.

'Who is it?'

'The producer, Collie Munshin.'

'Why do you call him a pirate?' I asked.

'Just wait until you meet him.'

But Eitel could not keep himself from saying more. I think he was irritated at how much pleasure the invitation gave him.

Munshin was the son-in-law of Herman Teppis, Eitel explained, and Teppis was the head of Supreme Pictures,

Munshin had married Teppis' daughter, and it had helped to make him one of the most important producers in the capital. 'Not that he wouldn't have made it anyway,' Eitel said. 'Nothing could stop Collie.' He had been, I learned, a little bit of many things, a salesman, a newspaperman, a radio announcer for a small station, a press-relations consultant, an actors' agent, an assistant producer, and finally a producer. 'Once upon a time,' Eitel went on, 'he was practically an office boy for me. I know the key to Collie. He's shameless. You can't stop a man who's never been embarrassed by himself.'

Eitel began to change his shirt. By the way he picked his tie, I knew he did not feel nearly as casual as he was hoping to feel. 'Wonder why he wants to see me?' he said aloud. 'I suppose he wants to steal an idea.'

'Why bother?' I asked. 'Nothing is cheaper than ideas.'

'It's his technique. Collie gets a feeling about a story. Not anything you can really name. Some cloud of an idea. Then he invites a writer who's out of work to come to lunch. He listens to the writer's suggestions, and they talk the thing up. The next day he invites another man to lunch. By the time he's talked to half a dozen writers he has a story and then he uses one of the peons he keeps locked in a hole to write the thing. When Collie is done, he can sell the story to the studio as his own creation. Oh, he's clever, he's tenacious, he's scheming . . .' Eitel ran out of words.

'What's to keep him from running the studio?' I asked.

'Nothing,' said Eitel, putting on a jacket, 'he'll run the world someday.' Then Eitel smiled. 'Only first he has to learn how to handle me. Sometimes I can set him back.'

As he closed the door behind us, Eitel added, 'There's another thing which might hold him up. He's having woman trouble.'

'Does he run around with so many?'

Eitel looked at me as if I had a lot to learn about the psychology of prominent men in the capital. 'Why, no,' he said, 'Collie has too many decisions to juggle, and that slows a man up, don't you know? Besides, it's not so easy to keep a harem when your wife is Herman Teppis' daughter. You don't even keep a fancy girl. Just a child in a cubbyhole and she's caused him trouble enough with H.T. It's some poor dancer. She's been his girl for several years. I've never met her, but Collie will be the first to tell you the trouble she gives him. It's a conventional relationship. She wants him to divorce his wife and marry her and Collie lets her believe that he will. Poor boy, he can't bear to let go of anything.' Eitel chuckled. 'Of course, the girl friend makes him pay. When Collie's not around, his little kitten will go for a romp. A couple of actors who've worked for me have been with her. They tell me she's extraordinary in bed.'

'Isn't that rough on him?'

'I don't know,' Eitel said, 'there are parts and parts to Collie. He enjoys being a martyr.'

'Sounds like a sad character to me.'

'Oh, everybody's sad if you want to look at them that way. Collie's not so bad off. Just remember there's nobody like him in the whole world.'

We came to Munshin's bungalow, and Eitel tapped the knocker on the pink-coloured door. After a wait I could hear somebody running toward us, and then it flew open, and I had no more than the sight of the back of a fat man in a dressing gown who went bounding away to the phone, the gown flapping against his calves while he called over his shoulder, 'Come in. Be with you in a minute, fellows.' He was talking in a high-pitched easy voice to somebody in New York, holding the receiver in his left hand while with his right he was neatly mixing drinks for us, not only carrying on his business conversation but opening a big smile across his face at the introduction to me. A little under medium height, with short turned-up features, he looked like a clown, for he had a large round head on a round body and almost no neck at all.

The drinks made, he passed them over with a wink, and his right hand free again, he began to tickle his thin hair, discovering a bald spot on his head and then putting it into hiding again, only to leave his head for his belly which he prodded gingerly as if to find out whether it concealed an ache. He certainly had a lot of energy; I had the idea it would be rare to see him doing one thing at a time.

Eitel sat down with a bored look and smiled at the producer's calisthenics. When the call was done, Munshin bounced to his feet and advanced on Eitel with an outstretched palm, a grin on his face. '*Charley!*' he said, as if Eitel had just come into the room and he was surprised to see him. 'You look great. How have you been?' Munshin asked, his free hand covering their handclasp. 'I've been hearing great things about you.'

'Stop it, Collie,' Eitel laughed, 'there's nothing you can steal from me.'

'Steal? Lover, I just want to steal your company.' He clamped a bear-hug on Eitel's neck. 'You look great,' he repeated. 'I've been hearing wonderful things about your script. I want to read it when it's done.'

'What for?' Eitel asked.

'I want to buy it.' He said this as if nothing was in the way of buying anything from Eitel.

'The only way I'll let you buy it is blind.'

'I'll buy it blind. If it's from you, Charley, I'll buy it blind.'

'You wouldn't buy Shakespeare blind.'

'You think I'm kidding,' Munshin said in a sad voice.

'Stop it, Collie,' Eitel said again.

As he talked, Munshin kept on touching Eitel, pinching his elbow, patting his shoulder, jabbing his ribs. 'Charley, don't show your script to anybody. Just work on it. Don't worry about your situation.'

'Get your greedy little hands off me. You know I'm going to make the picture by myself.'

'That's your style, Charley,' Munshin said with a profound nod. 'That's the way you always should work.'

He told us a joke, passed a bit of gossip, and kept his hands on Eitel's body in a set of movements which called up the picture of a fat house detective searching a drunk. Then Eitel walked away from him, and we all sat down and looked at each other. After a short silence, Munshin announced, 'I've thought of a great movie to make.'

'What is it?' I asked, for Eitel only made a face. The producer gave the name of a famous French novel. 'That author knows everything about sex,' Munshin said. 'I'll never be able to think I'm in love again.'

'Why don't you do the life of the Marquis de Sade?' Eitel drawled.

'You think I wouldn't if I could find a gimmick?'

58

'Collie,' Eitel said, 'sit down and tell me the story you really have.'

'I don't have a thing. I'm open to suggestion. I'm tired of making the same old stuff. Every man has an artistic desire in this business.'

'He's absolutely unscrupulous,' Eitel said with pride. Collie grinned. He cocked his head to the side with the cunning look of a dog who is being scolded.

'You're a born exaggerator,' Munshin said.

'You can't stop Collie.'

'I love you.'

Munshin poured another drink for us. Like a baby, his upper lip was covered with perspiration. 'Well, how *are* things?' he asked.

'Just fine, Collie. How are things with you?' Eitel asked in a flat voice. I knew him well enough to know he was very much on guard.

'Charley, my personal life is in a bad shape.'

'Your wife?'

Munshin stared into space, his hard small eyes the only sign of bone beneath his fat. 'Well, things are always the same between her and me.'

'What is it then, Collie?'

'I've decided to give the brush to my girl friend.'

Eitel began to laugh. 'It's about time.'

'Now, don't laugh, Charley. This is important to me.'

I was surprised at the way Munshin talked so frankly. He hadn't known me fifteen minutes, and yet he was as ready to talk as if he were alone with Eitel. I was still to learn that Munshin, like many people from the capital, could talk openly about his personal life while retaining a dream of espionage in his business operations.

'You're not really giving her up?' Eitel said lightly. 'What's the matter, has Teppis laid down the law?'

'Charley!' Munshin said, 'this is a personal tragedy for me.'

'I suppose you're in love with the girl.'

'No, I wouldn't say that. It's hard to explain.'

'Oh, I'm sure of that, Collie.'

'I'm very worried about her future,' Munshin said, his fingers prodding his belly again.

'From what I've heard about her, she'll get along.'

'What did you hear?' Munshin asked.

'Just that while she's known you, she's had her extra-curricular activities.'

Munshin's round face became tolerant and sad. 'We live in a community of scandal,' he said.

'Spare me, Collie,' Eitel murmured.

Munshin was on his feet. 'You don't understand this girl,' he said in a booming voice. I was left behind by the sudden transition. 'She's a child. She's a beautiful, warm, simple child.'

'And you're a beautiful, warm, simple father.'

'I've defended you, Charley,' Munshin said. 'I've defended you against stories which even you wouldn't want to hear about yourself. But I'm beginning to think I was wrong. I'm beginning to think you're nothing but rottenness and corruption.'

'Honest corruption. I don't play the saint.'

'I'm not claiming I'm a saint,' Munshin bellowed again. 'But I have feelings.' He turned in my direction. 'What do you see when you look at a fellow like myself?' he asked. 'You see a fat man who likes to play the clown. Does that mean I have no human sentiments?'

He was far from a clown at the moment. His mild high-pitched voice had swollen in volume and dropped deeper in tone. Standing over us, he gave me the feeling that he was a man of some physical power. 'All right, Charley,' he said. 'I know what you think of me, but I'll tell you something. I may be a businessman, and you may be an artist, and I've great respect for your talent, great respect, but you're a cold man, and I have emotions, and that's why you can't understand me.'

Through this tirade, Eitel had been drawing on his cigarette. Nonchalantly, he put it out. 'Why did you invite me over, Collie?'

'For friendship. Can't you understand that? I wanted to hear your troubles, and I wanted to tell you mine.'

Eitel leaned forward, his broad body hunched on itself. 'I have no troubles,' he said with a smile. 'Let me hear yours.'

Munshin relaxed. 'There are pluses as well as minuses to this affair. It's easy to sneer at the girl,' he said. 'I've sneered at her myself. When I first set her up, I thought, "Just another night-club dancer. A hot Italian babe with that hot Latin blood." Well, it's a story, Charley. She may not be so brilliant, and she's obviously from a poor background.' He looked at me. 'I've always been full of prejudices about women,' Munshin said humbly. 'You know I've wanted girls with some class and distinction to them and I'll admit it, it's what I still hold against Elena. She doesn't match up to the people I know. But that doesn't keep her from being very human.'

'Still, you're giving her the brush,' Eitel said. 'You're giving the brush to a very human girl.'

'There's no future for us. I admit it, you see, I admit my faults. I'm a social coward like everybody else in the industry.'

'So like all cowards you got tired of turning down her marriage proposals.'

'Elena's not a schemer,' Munshin said firmly. 'You want to know something? Just a couple of days ago I tried to give her a thousand dollars. She wouldn't take it. Not once did she ever ask me to marry her. She's not the kind who threatens. It's just that I can't stand the thought she has no future with me.'

'Herman Teppis can't stand the thought either.'

Munshin allowed this to pass. 'Let me tell you about her. She's a girl who's composed of hurts and emotion and dirt and shining love,' he said in the round categorical style of a criminal lawyer who wishes to attract all the elements in a jury. 'I had my analyst send her to a friend of his, but it didn't come off. She didn't have enough ego to work on. That's how serious the problem is.' Munshin held out a heavy palm as if to draw our attention. 'Take the way I met her. She was doing a fill-in number at a benefit I ran. I saw her in the wings, dressed up, ready to go on. A real Carmen-type. Only a Carmen shuddering with fright,' said Munshin, looking at us. 'She was practically clawing the hand off her partner. "There's a human being in torment," I said to myself, "a girl who's as wild and sensitive as an animal." Yet when she got up on the stage, she was all right. A good flamenco dancer. In and out, but talent. Afterward, we started talking, and she told me she couldn't even eat a piece of bread on a day she was working. I told her I thought I could help her with some of her problems and she was grateful as a puppy. That's how we started.' Munshin's voice became heavy with emotion. 'You, Eitel, you'd call that scheming, I suppose. I call it sensitivity and heartbreak and all kinds of hurts. She's a girl who's all hurts.'

As Munshin kept on talking, I had the idea he was describing her the way he might line up a heroine in a story conference, the story conference more interesting than the film which would come from it.

'You take the business of being Italian,' Munshin lectured us. 'I can't tell you the things I've learned, the human subtleties, and I'm a good liberal. For instance, if she was served by a Negro waiter, she always had the idea that he was being a little intimate with her. I talked to her about such problems. I explained how wrong it is to have prejudice against a Negro, and she understood.'

'Like that,' Eitel said, snapping his fingers.

'You stop it, Charley,' Munshin said, bobbing in his seat. 'You understand what I mean. She was ashamed of her prejudice. Elena is a person who hates everything that is small in herself. She's consumed by the passion to become a bigger person than she is, *consumed*, do you understand?' and he shook his fist.

'Collie, I really think you're upset.'

'Take her promiscuity,' Munshin went on, as if he had not heard. 'She's the sort of girl who would love a husband and kids, a decent healthy mature relationship. You think it didn't bother me, her seeing other men? But I knew it was my fault. I was to blame and I'll admit it freely. What could I offer her?'

'What could the others offer her?' Eitel interrupted.

'Fine. Fine. Just fine coming from you. I'll tell you, Charley, I don't believe in double standards. A woman's got just as much right as a man to her freedom.'

'Why don't we start a club?' Eitel jeered.

'I've gone to bat for you, Eitel. I pleaded with H.T. not to suspend you after *Clouds Ahoy*. Are you so ungrateful that I have to remind you how many times I helped you make pictures you wanted to make?'

'And then you cut them to ribbons.'

'We've had our disagreements, Charley, but I've always considered you a friend. I don't care what transpires between us today, it won't affect my attitude toward you.'

Eitel smiled.

'I'm curious.' Munshin put his hands on his knees. 'What do you think of Elena the way I've described her?'

'I think she's better than you deserve.'

'I'm glad you say that, Charley. It means I've been able to convey her quality.' Munshin paused, and loosened the cord of his dressing gown. 'You see, about an hour ago I told Elena we couldn't go on.'

'An hour ago!'

Munshin nodded.

'You mean she's here?' Eitel asked. 'Here in town?'

'Yes.'

'You brought her out here to give her the brush?'

Munshin started to pace the floor. 'I didn't plan it. A lot of times I bring her along on my trips.'

'And let her stay in a separate hotel?'

'Well, I've explained the situation.'

'When is your wife due?'

'She'll be here tomorrow.' Munshin blew his nose. 'I had no idea it would happen like this. For months I knew I couldn't go on with Elena, but I didn't expect it for today.'

Eitel shook his head. 'What do you want me to do? Hold her hand?'

'No, I mean . . .' Munshin looked miserable. 'Charley, she doesn't know a soul in this place.'

'Then let her go back to the city.'

'I can't stand the thought of her being alone. There's no telling what she'll do. Charley, I'm going out of my mind.' Munshin stared at her handkerchief which he kept wadded in his hand. 'Elena was the one who said we should break up. I know what it means to her. She'll put the blame on herself. She'll feel she wasn't good enough for me.'

'It's the truth, isn't it?' Eitel said. 'That's how you feel.'

'All right, I'm the rotten one. I'm no good.' Munshin came to a stop in front of Eitel. 'Charley, I remember you saying, it's your exact words. You said that when you were a kid you always wondered how to get a woman, and now you wonder how to get rid of one.'

'I was bragging.'

'Can't you sympathize?'

'With you?'

'Could you pay her a visit?'

'I don't know her,' Eitel said.

'You could be introduced as a friend of mine.'

Eitel sat up. 'Tell me, Collie,' he said, 'is that why you loaned me the money two weeks ago?'

'What money?' said Munshin.

'You don't have to worry about Sergius,' Eitel said, and he began to laugh. 'I'm ashamed of you. Two thousand dollars is a lot of money for Carlyle Munshin to pay to have a broken-down director take a girl off his hands.'

'Charley, you're a corrupt man,' Munshin said loudly. 'I loaned you that money because I consider you my friend, and I oughtn't to have to tell you that you could be more discreet. If word ever got around, I'd be in trouble up to here.' The producer held a finger to his throat. 'It's Elena I'm thinking about now. Let this boy be the witness. If anything happens to her, part of it will be your fault.'

'There's no limit to you, Collie,' Eitel started to say, but Munshin interrupted. 'Charley, I'm not kidding, that girl should not be left alone. Do I say I'm in the right? What do you want, my blood? Offer a solution at least.'

'Turn her over to Marion Faye.'

'You're a stone,' Munshin said. 'A human being is in pain, and you say things like that.'

'I'll see her,' I blurted suddenly.

'You're a beautiful kid,' Munshin said levelly, 'but this is not the job for you.'

'Keep out of this,' Eitel snapped at me.

'Even the kid here will go,' Munshin said. 'Charley, tell me, is all the heart cut out of you? Isn't there even a little bit left? Or are you getting too old to handle a real woman?'

Eitel lay back in his chair and stared at the ceiling, his legs spread before him. 'Okay, Collie,' he said slowly, 'okay. One loan deserves another. I'll get drunk with your girl.'

'You're a jewel, Charley,' Munshin said huskily.

'What if you-know-what happens?' Eitel drawled.

'Are you a sadist?' Munshin said. 'I don't even think of things like that.'

'Then what do you think of?'

'You'll like Elena and she'll like you. It'll make her feel good to know that a fellow with your reputation and your presence admires her.'

'Oh, God,' Eitel said.

The phone was ringing.

Munshin tried to say something more as if he were afraid Eitel might change his mind, but the noise of the telephone was too distracting. Obeying the irregular rhythm of the switchboard operator, it would stop, it would be silent, and then it would ring again.

'Answer it,' Eitel said irritably.

Munshin pinched the receiver against his jowl. He was preparing to make another drink, but the sounds he heard through the earpiece stopped everything. We listened to a woman who was crying and laughing, and her fright quivered through the room. There was so much terror in the voice and so much pain that I stared at the floor in shock. One cry sounded so loud in its loneliness I couldn't bear it.

'Where are you, Elena?' Munshin said sharply into the mouthpiece.

Some climax passed. I could hear the sound of quiet sobbing. 'I'll be right over,' Munshin said. 'Now, you stay there. You stay there, do you understand, Elena?' He had no sooner hung up the phone than he was drawing on a pair of trousers, fastening the buttons to a shirt.

Eitel was pale. 'Collie,' he said with an effort, 'do you want me to come along?'

'She's in her hotel room,' Munshin said from the door. 'I'll call you later.'

Eitel nodded and sat back. We were silent once Munshin was gone. After a few minutes, Eitel got up and mixed a drink. 'What a horrible thing,' he muttered.

'How does a man,' I asked, 'stay with a woman who is so . . . It's messy.'

Eitel looked up. 'A little compassion, Sergius,' he said. 'Do you think we choose our mates?' And, moodily, he sipped on his drink. 'I wonder if I'll ever know the answer to that one?' he said almost to himself.

Time passed, and we kept on drinking Carlyle Munshin's liquor. Slowly, the afternoon went by. It seemed pointless to remain there, just as pointless to move on. Outside, there would only be the desert sun. 'I'm depressed,' Eitel said with a broad grin after half a dozen drinks. I had the feeling his face was numb; slowly, with pleasure, he was patting the bald spot on his head. 'Wonder how Collie is making out?' Eitel said after another pause.

As if to answer, there was a knock on the door. I went to open it, and an elderly man shouldered me aside and walked into the living room. 'Where's Carlyle?' he asked of nobody in particular, and left me to follow behind him.

Eitel stood up. 'Well, Mr Teppis,' he said.

Teppis gave him a sour look. He was a tall heavy man with silver hair and a red complexion, but even with his white summer suit and hand-painted tie he was far from attractive. Underneath the sun tan, his features were poor; his eyes were small and pouched, his nose was flat, and his chin ran into the bulge of his neck. He had a close resemblance to a bullfrog. When he spoke, it was in a thin hoarse voice. 'All right,' he said, 'what are you doing here?'

'Do you know,' Eitel said, 'that's a good question to ask.'

'Collie's up to something,' Teppis announced. 'I don't know why he saw you. I wouldn't even want to breathe the air a subversive breathes. Do you know what you cost me on *Clouds Ahoy*?'

'You forget the money I made for you . . . Herman.'

'Hah,' said Teppis, 'now he calls me by my first name. They leave me and they go up in the world. Eitel, I warned Lulu against you. Marry a fine young American actress, a girl who's too good for you, and you just drag her name through the muck and the dirt and the filth. If anybody saw me talking to you I'd be ashamed.'

'You should be,' Eitel said. 'Lulu was a fine American girl,

66

and you let me turn her into a common whore.' His voice was cool, but I could sense it was not easy for him to talk to Teppis.

'You have a dirty mouth,' Herman Teppis said, 'and nothing else.'

'Don't speak to me this way. I no longer work for you.'

Teppis rocked forward and back on the balls of his feet as if to build up momentum. 'I'm ashamed to have made money from your movies. Five years ago I called you into my office and I warned you. "Eitel," I said, "anybody that tries to throw a foul against this country ends up in the pigpen." That's what I said, but did you listen?' He waved a finger. 'You know what they're talking about at the studio? They say you're going to make a comeback. Some comeback. You couldn't do a day's work without the help of the studio. I let people know that.'

'Come on, Sergius, let's go,' Eitel said.

'Wait, you!' Teppis said to me. 'What's your name?'

I told him. I gave it with an Irish twist.

'What kind of name is that for a clean-cut youngster like you? You should change it. John Yard. That's the kind of name you should have.' He looked me over as if he were buying a bolt of cloth. 'Who are you?' said Teppis, 'what do you do? I hope you're not a bum.'

If he wanted to irritate me, he was successful. 'I used to be in the Air Force,' I said to him.

There was a gleam in his eye. 'A flier?'

Standing in the doorway, Eitel decided to have his own fun. 'Do you mean you never heard of this boy, H.T.?'

Teppis was cautious. 'I can't keep up with everything.' he said.

'Sergius is a hero,' Eitel said creatively. 'He shot down four planes in a day.'

I had no chance to get into this. Teppis smiled as if he had been told something very valuable. 'Your mother and father must be extremely proud of you,' he said.

'I wouldn't know. I was brought up in an orphanage.' My voice was probably unsteady because I could see by Eitel's change of expression that he knew I was telling the truth. I was sick at giving myself away so easily. But it is always like that.

You hold a secret for years, and then spill it like a cup of coffee. Or maybe Teppis made me spill it.

'An orphan,' he said. 'I'm staggered. Do you know you're a remarkable young man?' He smiled genially and looked at Eitel. 'Charley, you come back here,' he said in his hoarse voice. 'What are you flying off the handle for? You've heard me talk like this before.'

'You're a rude man, Herman,' Eitel said from the doorway.

'Rude?' Teppis put a fatherly hand on my shoulder. 'Why, I wouldn't even be rude to my doorman.' He laughed and then began to cough. 'Eitel,' he said, 'what's happened to Carlyle? Where'd he go?'

'He didn't tell me.'

'I don't understand anybody any more. You're a young man, Johnny,' he said, pointing to me as if I were inanimate, 'you tell me, what is everything all about?' But long before I could answer that question, he started talking again. 'In my day a man got married, and he could be fortunate in his selection, or he could have bad luck, but he was married. I was a husband for thirty-two years, may my wife rest in peace. I have her picture on my desk. Can you say that, Eitel? What do you have on your desk? Pin-up pictures. I don't know people who feel respect for society any more. I tell Carlyle. What happens? He wallows. That's the kind of man my daughter wanted to marry. A fool who sneaks around with a chippie dancer.'

'We all have our peculiarities, Herman,' Eitel said.

This made Teppis angry. 'Eitel,' he shouted, 'I don't like you, and you don't like me, but I make an effort to get along with everybody,' and then to quiet himself down, he made a point of looking me over very carefully. 'What do you do?' he asked again as if he had not heard my answer. 'Are you an actor?'

'No.'

'I knew it. None of the good-looking clean-cut ones are actors any more. Just the ugly ones. Faces like bugs.' He cleared his throat with a barking sound. 'Look, Johnny,' he went on, 'I like you, I'll do you a good turn. There's a little party tomorrow night. I'm giving it for our people out here. You're invited.'

The moment he gave this invitation, I knew I wanted to go to his party. Everybody in Desert D'Or had been talking about it for the last few days, and this was the first big party at the resort which I had been invited to. But I was angry at myself because I was ready to say yes, and in that second I almost forgot Eitel. So I told myself that I was going to play it through, and if Teppis wanted to invite me, and I didn't know why, I was going to get him to invite Eitel.

'I don't know if I want to go alone,' I said to him, and I was satisfied that my voice was even.

'Bring a girl,' Teppis offered. 'You got a sweetheart?'

'It's not easy to find the right girl,' I said. 'I lost too much time flying airplanes.'

My instinct about Herman Teppis seemed to be working. He nodded his head wisely. 'I see the connection,' he said.

'I was thinking Charley Eitel could help me find a girl,' I added.

For a second I thought I had lost it and Teppis was going to fly into a rage. He glared at both of us. 'Who invited Eitel?' he said furiously.

'You didn't invite him?' I said. 'I thought maybe you did.'

With what an effort, Teppis smiled benevolently. 'Johnny, you're a very loyal friend. You got spunk.' In practically the same breath he said to Eitel, 'Tell me, cross your heart, Charley, are you a Red?'

Eitel didn't rush to answer. 'You know everything, Herman,' he murmured at last. 'Why ask questions?'

'I know!' Teppis shouted. 'I know all about you. I'll never understand why you made such a spectacle of yourself.' He threw up his arms. 'All right, all right, I know you're clean deepdown. Come to my party.' Teppis shook his head. 'Only do me a favour, Charley. Don't say I invited you. Say it was Mac Barrantine.'

'This is one hell of an invitation,' Eitel answered.

'You think so, well don't look a gift horse, you know what I mean? One of these days go clear yourself with the American government, and then maybe I'll work with you. I got no objection to making money with people I don't like. It's my motto.' He took my hand and shook it firmly. 'Agree with me, Johnny? That's the ticket. I'll see both you boys tomorrow night.'

On the drive back to Eitel's house I was in a good mood. Teppis had been just right for me. I was even overexcited, I kept talking to Eitel about how it had felt the time I took my first solo. Then I began to realize that the more I talked the more depressed I made him feel, and so looking for any kind of question to change the subject I said, 'What do you say about our invitation? Maybe there's going to be just a little look on people's faces when you turn up.' I started to laugh again.

Eitel shook his head. 'They'll probably say I've been having private talks with the Committee, or else why would Teppis have me there?' Then he grinned at the frustration of it. 'Man,' he said, mimicking me, 'don't you just have to be good to win?' But there was more than enough to think about in this thought, and neither of us said another word until we turned into his garage. Then Eitel stopped the car with a jerk. 'Sergius. I'm not going to that party,' he said.

'Well, if you won't change your mind . . .' I wanted to go to the party, I was ready for it, I thought, but it was going to be harder without Eitel. I wouldn't know anybody there.

'You did well, today,' he said. 'You go. You'll enjoy it. But I can't go. I've been a bus boy to Teppis for too many years.' We went inside, and Eitel dropped into an armchair and pressed his hands to his forehead. The script was on the end table next to him. He picked it up, rustled the pages, and dropped it to the floor. 'Don't tell anybody, Sergius,' he said, 'but this script stinks.'

'Are you sure?'

'I don't know. I can't get out of myself long enough to look at it.' He sighed. 'If I ever bring it off, remind me, will you, of this conversation? You see, I've been trying to remember if I was as depressed in the old days when the work would come out well.'

'I'll remind you,' I said.

A short while later, Munshin phoned Eitel. Elena was all right, he told him. She was sleeping. Tonight, he would take care of her. But for tomorrow he begged Eitel to show her a good time.

Eitel said he would. When the call was finished, his eyes were dancing. 'Do you know,' he said, 'I can hardly accuse myself of running after Teppis if I take Collie's girl along.'

'But what about the girl?'

'It could be the best way to get over Mr Munshin. She'll see that a stranger will do more for her in a night than he did in three years.'

'What are you up to?' I asked.

'Yes, I'm going to take her to the party,' Eitel said.

8

The Laguna Room at the Yacht Club which Herman Teppis had rented for his party was not a room at all. Painted in the lemon-yellow of the Yacht Club, it was open to the sky, and like the café, an amoebic pool strayed between the tables, rounded a portion of the dance floor, and ended behind the bar, a play of coloured lights changing the water into a lake of tomato aspic, lime jello, pale consommé, and midnight ink. On an island not twenty feet long, in the middle of the pool, the bandstand was set up, and the musicians played their dance numbers free of any passing drunk who might want to take a turn on the drums.

Since the party was given by Herman Teppis, the management of the Yacht Club had added some special old-fashioned effects. A big searchlight threw its column into the air. placed at such an angle as not to burn into the eyes of the guests, and a collection of spotlights and flood lamps was arranged to make it look like a party on a movie set, even to the expense of a tremendous papier-mâché camera on a wooden boom, directed by a bellhop wearing the outfit of a silent-film cameraman with the peak of his cap turned backward and a pair of knickers which reached his knees. All through the evening the camera was rotated on its boom, being lowered almost into the water or raised so high it threw a long shadow across the colours of the Laguna Room.

I had trouble getting in. Eitel had left earlier in the evening to meet Elena and had still not returned by eleven, so I decided to go alone, and I put on my Air Corps uniform with its ribbons. At the entrance to the Laguna Room, which was garnished with a gangplank, a man dressed like a purser stood checking the invitations. There was no record of my name on the guest list.

I said, 'Maybe I'm down there as John Yard.'

There was no John Yard on the purser's scratchboard.

'How about Charles Eitel?' I asked.

'Mr Eitel is listed, but you would have to come in with him.'

Yet it was the purser who discovered my name. In a last-minute addition, Teppis had recorded me as 'Shamus Something-or-other,' and so as Shamus Something-or-other, I got into his party.

Near the purser's stand, seated on two couches which faced each other, were half a dozen women. They were all dressed expensively, and their make-up, to make up for such faults as thin mouths, small eyes, and mouse-coloured hair, had curved their lips, slimmed their cheeks, and given golden or chestnut tints to their coiffures. Like warriors behind their painted shields, they sat stiffly, three and three, staring at one another, talking with apathy. I bobbed my head at them, not knowing whether to introduce myself or to move on, and one of them looked up, and in a voice which was harsh, asked, 'You under contract at Magnum?'

'No,' I said.

'Oh, I thought you were somebody else,' she said and looked away again.

They were talking about their children and I guessed, as Eitel later confirmed, that they were the wives of important men and men who wanted to be important, the husbands off in chase of one another through the Laguna Room while the women were left behind.

'What do you mean, California is no good?' one of them said fiercely. 'It's wonderful for children.'

When a man went by, they tried to pay no notice. I realized that in walking past with a clumsy smile, showing how I didn't know if I was supposed to talk to them or not, I had done the dirty service of reflecting their situation. A few other men came in after me, and I saw that they either walked by without a look, or stopped for a brief but wild gallantry which went something like this:

'Carolyn!' the man would say, as if he could not believe he saw the woman here and was simply overcome.

'Mickey!' one of the six women would say.

'My favourite girl,' the man would say, holding her hand.

'The only real man I know,' the deserted wife would say. Mickey would smile. He would shake his head, he would hold her hand. 'If I didn't know you were kidding, I could give you a tumble,' he would say.

'Don't be too sure I'm kidding,' the wife would say.

Mickey would straighten up, he would release her hand. There would be a silence until Mickey murmured, 'What a woman.' Then, in the businesslike tone which ends a conversation, he would say, 'How are the kids, Carolyn?'

'They're fine.'

'That's great. That's great.' He would start to move away, and give a smile to all the women. 'We have to have a long talk, you and me,' Mickey would say.

'You know where to find me.'

'Great kidder, Carolyn,' Mickey would announce to nobody in particular, and disappear into the party.

All through the Laguna Room, wherever there was a couch, three wives were sitting in much that way. Since a lot of the men had come without women, the result was that men got together with men, standing near the pool, off the dance floor, at the café tables or in a crowd near the bar. I picked up a drink and wandered through the party looking for a girl to talk to. But all the attractive girls were surrounded though by fewer men than squeezed up to listen to a film director or a studio executive, and besides I did not know how to get into the conversations. They were all so private. I had been thinking that my looks and my uniform might not do me any harm, but most of the girls seemed to like the conversation of fat middle-aged men and bony middle-aged men, the prize going to a German movie director with a big paunch who had his arms around the waists of two starlets. Actually I wasn't really that eager. Being stone sober, the fact was that it was easier to drift from one circle of men to another.

In a cove of the bar formed by two tables and the tip of one of the pool's tentacles, I found Jennings James telling a joke to several feature actors of no particular celebrity. Jay-Jay rambled on, his eyes blurred behind his silver-rimmed glasses. When he was done, other jokes were told, each more stray than the one which went before. I quit them after a while, and Jay-Jay caught up to me.

'What a stinking party this is,' he said. 'I'm supposed to work tonight, show the photographers a good time.' He coughed with stomach misery. 'I left all those photographers over at the canopy table. You know it's the truth about photographers, they'd rather eat than drink.' Jay-Jay had an arm on my shoulder, and I realized he was using me as an escort to reach the men's room. 'You know the line of poetry, "Me thought I saw the grave where Laura lay"?' he started to say. But whatever it was he wanted to add was lost, and he stood looking at me sheepishly. 'Well, that's a beautiful line of poetry,' he finished, and like a kid who has clung to the back of a streetcar while it climbs the hill, and drops off once the top is reached, Jay-Jay let go my arm and, listing from the change in balance, went careening to the urinal.

I was left to stand around the edge of one group or another. A director finished a story of which I heard no more than the last few lines. 'I sat down and I told her that to be a good actress, she must always work for the truth in what she's playing,' the man said in a voice not empty of self-love, 'and she said, "What's the truth?" and I said it could be defined as the real relation between human beings. You saw the performance I got out of her.' He stopped, the story was over, and the men and women around him nodded wisely. 'That's wonderful advice you gave her, Mr Sneale,' a girl said, and the others murmured in agreement.

'Howard, tell the story about you and Mr Teppis,' one of them begged.

The director chuckled. 'Well, this story is on Herman, but I know he wouldn't mind. There are enough stories on me in my dealings with him. H.T.'s got an instinct which is almost infallible. There's a reason why he's such a great movie-maker, such a creative movie-maker.'

'That's very true, Howard,' the same girl said.

I moved on without listening any more and almost bumped into the subject of the story. In a corner, off on a discussion, were Herman Teppis and two other men who were not too different from Teppis. They had been pointed out to me already as Eric Haislip, head of Magnum, and Mac Barrantine from Liberty Pictures, but I think I would have guessed in any case, for the three men were left alone. If I had drunk my liquor more slowly, I might have felt the social paradox which allowed only these men to be able to talk without the attention of a crowd, but instead I placed myself at the elbow of the producer named Mac Barrantine. They continued their conversation without paying any attention to me.

'What do you think you'll gross on *The Tigress*?' Eric Haislip was saying.

'Three-and-a-half to four,' Herman Teppis said.

'Three-and-a-half to four?' Eric Haislip repeated. 'H.T., you're not talking to the New York office. You'll be lucky to get your money out.'

Teppis snorted. 'I could buy your studio with what we'll make.'

Mac Barrantine spoke slowly out of the side of a cigar. 'I claim that you just can't tell any more. There was a time when I could say, "Bring it in at one-and-a-half, and we'll gross a million over." Today, picture-making is crazy. A filthy bomb I'm ashamed of makes money, a classical musical comedy vehicle like *Sing, Girls, Sing* lays an egg. You figure it out.'

'You're wrong,' Herman Teppis said, prodding him with a finger. 'You know the trouble? People are confused today. So what do they want? They want a picture that confuses them. Wait till they get really confused. Then they'll want a picture that sets them straight.'

'Now you're required to show them real things on the screen,' Eric Haislip sighed.

'Real things?' Teppis exploded. 'We bring real things to them. Realism. But because a fellow in an Italian movie vomits all over the place and they like it in some art theatre that doesn't even have air-cooling, we should bring them vomit?'

'There's no discipline,' Mac Barrantine said. 'Even a director, a man with a high-powered tool in his hands. What does he do? He runs amuck like a gangster.'

'Charley Eitel cut your throat,' Eric Haislip said.

'They all cut my throat,' Teppis said passionately. 'You know something? My throat don't cut.' He glared at them as if remembering times when each of them had tried to treat him to a razor. 'Bygones. Let it be bygones,' Teppis said. 'I get along with everybody.'

'There's no discipline,' Barrantine repeated. 'I got a star, I won't mention her name. She came to me, she knew that in two months we were starting production on a really big vehicle for her, and you know what she had the gall to say? "Mr Barrantine, my husband and I, we're going to have a baby. I'm six weeks along." "You're going to have a baby?" I said. "Where in hell's your loyalty? I know you, you're selfish. You can't tell me you want the heartache of bringing up an infant." "Mr Barrantine, what should I do?" she bawled to me. I gave her a look and then I told her. "I can't take the responsibility for advising you what to do," I said, "but you damn well better do something."'

'She's going to be in the picture, I hear,' Eric Haislip said.

'Of course she's going to be in the picture. She's an ambitious girl. But discipline and consideration. Do any of them have that?'

Eric Haislip was looking at me. 'Who are you? What do you want here, kid?' he asked suddenly, although he had been aware of me for several minutes.

'I've been invited,' I said.

'Did I invite you to sit on my lap?' Mac Barrantine said.

'You'd be the first,' I muttered.

To my surprise, Teppis said, 'Leave the boy alone. I know this boy. He's a nice young fellow.'

Barrantine and Haislip glowered at me, and I scowled back. We all stood nose to nose like four trucks meeting at a dirt crossroad. 'The youth, the young people,' Teppis announced. 'You think you know something? Listen to a young fellow's ideas. He can tell you something. This boy has a contribution.'

Barrantine and Haislip did not seem particularly enthusiastic to hear my contribution. Conversation ground along for several minutes, and then they left on the excuse of filling their drinks. 'I'll call the maître dee,' Teppis offered. They shook their heads. They needed a walk, they announced. When they were gone, Teppis looked in a fine mood. I had the suspicion he had come to my defence in order to insult them. 'First-rate fellows,' he said to me. 'I've known them for years.'

'Mr Teppis,' I said irritably, 'why did you invite me to your party?'

He laughed and clamped a hand on my shoulder. 'You're a clever boy,' he said, 'you're quick-tongued. I like that.' His hoarse thin voice drew a conspiratorial link between us whether I wanted it or not. 'You take the desert,' he confided to me, 'it's a wonderful place to make a human being feel alive. I hear music in it all the time. A musical. It's full of cowboys and these fellows that live alone, what do you call them, hermits. Cowboys and hermits and pioneers, that's the sort of place it is. Fellows looking for gold. As a young fellow, what do you think, wouldn't you like to see such a movie? I like history,' he went on before I could answer. 'It would take a talented director to make such a story, a fellow who knows the desert.' He poked me in the ribs as though to leave me breathless and therefore honest. 'You take Eitel. Is he still hitting the booze?' Teppis said suddenly, his small flat eyes studying my reaction.

'Not much,' I said quickly, but my look must have wandered because Teppis squeezed my shoulder again.

'We got to have a long talk, you and me,' Teppis said. 'I like Charley Eitel. I wish he didn't have such a stain on his character. Politics. Idiotic. What do you think?'

'I think he's going to make the best movie of his life,' I said with the hope I could worry Teppis.

'For the art theatres,' Teppis stated, and he pointed a finger to his brain. 'It won't be from the heart. You're too fresh for your own good,' he continued with one of his fast shifts, 'who's interested in your ideas? I'll tell you what the story is. Eitel is through.'

'I disagree,' I said, cheered to realize I was the only one at this party who did not have to be polite to Herman Teppis.

'You disagree? What do you know? You're a baby.' But I thought I understood what went on in him, the fear that he might be wrong chewing at the other fear he might make a fool of himself by considering Eitel again. 'Now listen, you,' he started to say, but we were interrupted.

'Good evening, daddy,' a woman said.

'Lottie,' Teppis said moistly, and embraced her. 'Why didn't

78

you call me?' he asked. 'Ten o'clock this morning and no call from you.'

'I had to miss it today,' said Lottie Munshin. 'I was packing for the trip.'

Teppis began to ask her about his grandchildren, turning his back almost entirely on me. While they spoke I watched Carlyle Munshin's wife with interest. She was one of those women who are middle-aged too soon, her skin burned into the colours of false health. Thin, nervous, her face was screwed tight, and in those moments when she relaxed, the lines around her forehead and mouth were exaggerated, for the sun had not touched them. Pale haggard eyes looked out from sun-reddened lids. She was wearing an expensive dress but had only succeeded in making it look dowdy. The bones of her chest stood out, and a sort of ruffle fluttered on her freckled skin with a parched rustling movement like a spinster's parlour curtains. 'I was delayed getting here,' she said to her father in so pinched a voice I had the impression her throat was tight. 'You see, Doxy was littering today. You know Doxy?'

'It's one of the mutts?' Teppis said uncomfortably.

'She took the state-wide blue ribbon for the class,' Lottie Munshin said. 'Don't you remember?'

'Well, that's good.' Teppis coughed. 'Now, why don't you leave those dogs out of your mind for a couple of weeks, and you take a good vacation. You relax. You have a good time with Collie.'

'I can't leave them for two weeks,' she said with something like panic. 'Salty litters in the next ten days, and we have to start training Blitzen and Nod for the trials.'

'Well, that's fine,' Teppis said vaguely. 'Now, there's a fellow I got to see, so I'll leave you in the company of this young man. You'll enjoy talking to him. And Lottie, you remember,' he said, 'there's more important things than those dogs.'

I watched him walk away, nodding his head to the people who swarmed to greet him, carrying them one at a time like parasite fish. One couple even moved off the dance floor and came hurrying toward him.

'Do you like dogs?' Lottie Munshin asked me. She gave a

short rough laugh for punctuation, and looked at me with her head cocked to one side.

I made the mistake of saying, 'You breed them, don't you?'

She replied; she replied at length; she insisted on going into details which led into other details, she was a fanatic, and I stood listening to her, trying to find the little girl who had grown into this woman. 'Collie and I have the best ranch within the county limits of the capital,' she said in that pinched voice, 'although of course keeping it up devolves upon me. It's quite a concern, I can tell you. I'm up at six every morning.'

'You keep an early schedule,' I offered.

'Early to bed. I like to be up with the sun. With such hours everybody could keep themselves in fine condition. You're young now, but you should take care of yourself. People should follow the same hours animals do, and they would have the natural health of an animal.'

Over her shoulder I could see the dance floor and the swimming pool, and I was pulled between my desire to quit her for people who were more interesting, and my reluctance to leave her alone. While she spoke, her bony fingers plucked at her chin. 'I've got a green thumb,' she said. 'It's an unusual combination. I breed dogs and things grow under my thumb. Sometimes I think my father must have been meant to be a farmer because where else could it have developed in me?'

'Oh, look. There's your husband,' I said with relief.

She called to him. He was some distance away, but at the sound of her voice he looked up with an exaggeration of surprise which betrayed he was not surprised at all, and came moving toward us. As he recognized me his expression changed for a moment, but all the same he shook my hand warmly. 'Well, we meet again,' he said broadly.

'Carlyle, I meant to ask you,' Lottie Munshin went on in a worried voice, 'are you going to try that favourite-food diet?'

'I'll give it a look,' he said in a bored tone, and caught me by the arm. 'Lottie, I have something to talk over with Sergius. You'll excuse us.' And with no more than that he steered me under a yucca tree, and we stood in the harsh shadow made by a flood lamp above the fronds.

'What are you doing here?' he asked.

80

Once again I explained that I had been invited by Herman Teppis.

'Eitel, too?'

When I nodded, Munshin burst out, 'I wouldn't put it past Eitel to bring Elena here.' As he shook his head with indignation, I began to laugh.

'It's a rotten party,' I said, 'it needs some kicks.'

Munshin surprised me. A calculating expression came over his face and suddenly he looked like a very tough clown to me, a clown who in a quiet private way knew more than a few corners of the world. 'It would be worth a lot of money to know what's in H.T.'s head,' he muttered to himself, and walked away leaving me beside the yucca tree.

The party was becoming more active. People were going off by couples, or coming together at one centre of interest or another. In a corner a game of charades was going on, the dance floor was nearly filled, a well-known comedian was performing for nothing, and an argument about a successful play almost killed the music of the rumba band. A drunk had managed to climb the boom which supported the papier-mâché camera, and he was quarrelling with the cameraman who was trying to get him to go down. Nearby his wife was laughing loudly. 'Ronnie's a flagpole sitter,' she kept announcing. The swimming instructor of the hotel was giving a diving exhibition in a roped-off portion of the pool, but only a few were watching her. I had a couple of drinks at the bar, and tried to work into one circle or another without success. Bored, I listened to a folk singer dressed like a leatherstocking, who sang old ballads in a quavery twang which could be heard above the dance orchestra. 'Isn't he talented?' a woman said nearby.

I felt a tap on my shoulder. A blond man whom I recognized as the tennis professional of the Yacht Club smiled at me. 'Come on over,' he said, 'somebody would like to meet you.' It turned out to be the movie star, Teddy Pope. He was a tall man with an open expression and dark-brown hair which fell in a cowlick over his forehead. When I came up with the tennis player, he grinned at me.

'Isn't this party a dog?' Teddy Pope said.

We all smiled at one another. I could think of nothing to say.

Beside Pope sat Marion Faye, looking small and bored. He only nodded at me.

'Do you know roulette?' the tennis player asked. 'Teddy's an *aficionado*.'

'I've been trying to get a system,' Teddy said. 'I had a theory about the numbers. But mathematically it was too much for my low intelligence. I hired a statistician to try to figure it out.' He grinned at me again. 'You a weight-lifter?' Teddy asked me.

'No. Should I be?'

This turned out to be very amusing. Pope and the tennis player and Marion Faye shared a long run of laughter. 'I can bend an iron bar,' Teddy said to me. 'That is, if it's a slim enough iron bar. I just stay in weight-lifting to keep from getting fat. I'm getting so fat now.' He pinched his belly to give a demonstration and was able to show an excess of flesh no thicker than a pencil. 'It's disgusting.'

'You look in good shape,' I said uncomfortably.

'Oh, I'm pudgy,' Pope said.

'Weight-lifting ruined your forehand,' the tennis player said.

Teddy Pope made no answer. 'I can see you're a flier,' he said. 'Is it true that most of you live for drinking and sex?' He leaned back and smiled at the sky. 'Oh, there's a beauty,' he said as a girl passed. 'Would you like to meet her? Marion says you're a little shy.'

'I'll make out.'

'Why don't you help him, Teddy?' Marion jeered.

'I would just be a drag,' Pope said.

'Sit down, Sergei,' said the tennis player.

'No. Well, you see,' I said, 'I promised to bring a drink to somebody.'

'Come back if you get bored,' Teddy said.

I was approached beneath another yucca tree by a little bald-headed man in a sky-blue tropical suit who had a tall red-headed girl by the hand. 'Ah, there you are, I missed you before,' he said briskly. 'I'd like to introduce myself. I'm Bunny Zarrow, you may have heard of me. Actor's representative.' I must have looked at him with surprise, for he added, 'I see you were talking to Mr Teppis. May I ask what you were talking about?'

'He wanted my advice on a movie.'

'That's interesting. That's unusual. And what is your name?'

'John Yard,' I said.

'You're under contract, I take it?'

'Of course.'

'Well, a contract can sometimes be bettered. I wish I could place your name. I will say this is neither the time nor the opportunity, but you and I must have lunch to discuss it. I'll call you at the studio.' He pointed to the girl beside him. 'I'd like you to meet Candy Ballou.' The girl yawned and then tried to smile. She was very drunk.

Bunny drew me aside. 'Let me give you her phone number. She's a charming outgoing girl.' He blinked his eyes. 'I'm glad to do you a favour. If I weren't so overworked, I would keep her number, but it's a shame to keep such a girl to myself.' He returned me to Candy Ballou and placed our hands together. 'Now, kiddies, I'm sure you two have a great deal in common,' he said, and left us looking at one another.

'Would you want to dance?' I asked the red-headed girl.

'Don't panic, love-bucket.' She said this as if it were a passing word, and then opened her eyes to focus on me. 'What studio you at?' she blurted.

'That's just a joke, Candy,' I said.

'A joke on Zarrow, huh?'

'That's right.'

'What do you do?'

'Nothing,' I said.

'No dough. I might have known.' She swayed her body to the rhythms of the rumba music and yawned fiercely. 'Oh honey,' she said in a little broken voice, 'if you had class you'd help me to the ladies' room.'

On my return from that errand with no more for company than a new highball, I saw Eitel come in at last. He was with a girl. Elena, I knew.

9

She was a near-beauty. Elena's hair was a rich red-brown and her skin was warm. She walked with a sense of her body, and I had always been drawn to that in a girl since my first year in the Air Force when like every other fly at an enlisted men's dance, I would cock my hat and try to steal prizes like Elena with my speed. Although she wore a lot of lipstick, and her high heels would have satisfied a show girl, there was something delicate about her and very proud. She carried herself as if she were tall, and her strapless evening gown showed round handsome shoulders. Her face was not exactly soft, but it was heart-shaped, and above a tender mouth and chin, the nares of her long narrow nose suggested ample aptitude to me. Munshin's description seemed passing poor.

Except that she was obviously not at ease. As I watched Eitel lead her into the mouth of the party she reminded me of an animal, ready for flight. Their appearance at the party had set off a ripple of confusion, and very few of the people who saw him knew what to do. There were several who smiled and even said hello, there were some who nodded, and even more who turned away, but I had the feeling they were all frightened. Until they knew the reason why Eitel had been invited, they could only feel the panic that whatever they did could be a mistake. It was grim the way he and Elena were left to cross the floor of the party without catching anybody to accompany them, and I saw Eitel stop finally at an empty table near the pool, set out a chair for Elena, and then sit down himself. From a distance I had to like the way he succeeded in looking bored.

I went up to their table. 'Can I join you?' I said clumsily.

Eitel gave me a quick grateful smile. 'Elena, you must meet Sergius, he's the best person here.'

'Oh, shut up,' I told him, and turned to her. 'I'm awfully sorry, I didn't catch your last name,' I said.

'It's Esposito,' Elena muttered, 'an Italian name.' Her voice was just a little hoarse, and surprisingly deep, which made it considerably less useful to her than her face, but it was a voice which had muffled strength in it. I had heard accents like that since I was a kid.

'Doesn't she look like a Modigliani?' Eitel said enthusiastically, and then added, 'Elena, I know you've been told that more than once.'

'Yes,' Elena said, 'that is, someone once told me. As a matter of fact it was your friend.'

Eitel passed over the reference to Munshin. 'But where did you get those green eyes?' he teased her. From the angle where I sat, I could see his fingers tapping restlessly on his knee.

'Oh, that's from my mother,' Elena said. 'She's half Polish. I guess I'm one-quarter Polish and three-quarters Italian. Oil and water.' We all worked a little to laugh, and Elena shifted uncomfortably. 'What a funny subject,' she said.

Eitel made a play of studying the Laguna Room and said, 'What do you think this party needs?'

'What?' I asked.

'A roller coaster.'

Elena burst into laughter. She had a nice laugh which showed her white teeth, but she laughed too loudly. 'Oh, that's so funny,' she said.

'I love roller coasters,' Eitel went on. 'It's that first drop. Like the black hole of death. There's nothing to compare with it.' And for the next two minutes he talked about roller coasters, until I could see by the look in Elena's eyes how alive he made the subject seem. He was in good form, and to draw him out, Elena was a good listener. I found myself thinking that she was not stupid, and yet she would only answer with a laugh or some little remark. It was the style of her attention. Her face gave back the shadow of everything he said, until Eitel was carried away. 'It proves an old idea of mine,' he said. 'One gets on a roller coaster in order to feel certain emotions, and I wonder if it's not the same with an affair. When I was younger, I used to think it was ugly, even unclean I suppose, that a man who thought he was in love would find himself using the same words with one girl after another. Yet there's nothing wrong about it really. The only true faithfulness people have is toward emotions they're trying to recapture.'

'I don't know,' Elena said. 'I think a man like that wouldn't be feeling anything for the woman.'

'On the contrary. At that moment, he adores her.'

This confused her. 'I mean,' she interrupted, 'you know it's . . . oh, I'm not sure.' But she could not let it pass. 'A man like that isn't relative to the woman. He's detached.'

Eitel looked pleased. 'You're right,' he reversed himself. 'I suppose it's the proof of how detached I am.'

'Oh, you can't be,' she said.

'I certainly am,' he smiled, as though to flag an advance warning.

It must have been hard to believe. His eyes were bright, his body leaned toward her, and his dark hair looked charged with energy. 'Don't judge by appearances,' Eitel began, 'why I can tell you . . .'

He broke off. Munshin was coming toward us. Elena's face lost all expression, and Eitel began to smile in an unnatural way.

'I don't know what it is you got,' Collie boomed, 'but H.T. told me to come over and say hello. He wants to talk to you later.'

When none of us answered, Munshin contented himself with staring at Elena.

'Collie, how are you?' Eitel said finally.

'I've been better.' He nodded his head. 'I've been a lot better,' he said, continuing to look at Elena.

'Aren't you having a good time?' she asked.

'No, I'm having a rotten time,' Munshin answered.

'I was looking for your wife,' Elena said, 'but I don't know who she is.'

'She's around,' Munshin said.

'And your father-in-law? He's here, I heard you say.'

'What difference does it make?' Munshin asked with a moist look as if he were really saying, 'Someday you won't hate me any more.'

'Oh, yes, no difference at all. I wouldn't want to embarrass you,' Elena said, her voice all but out of control. It gave a hint of how badly she would act in a quarrel.

'I met Teddy Pope tonight,' I interrupted as best I could. 'What is he like?'

'I can tell you,' Eitel said nimbly, 'he's been in several of my pictures. And you know, I think he's really sort of decent as an actor. Some day he may be very good.'

At that moment, a beautiful blonde girl in a pale-blue evening gown came up behind Munshin and covered his eyes with her hands. 'Guess who?' she said in a throaty voice. I had a glimpse of a little turned-up nose, a dimpled chin, and a pouting mouth I had seen before. At the sight of Eitel she made a face.

'Lulu,' Munshin said, half rising from his chair, and not knowing if her interruption had helped the situation or made it worse, he hugged Lulu with fatherly arms, smiling at Elena and Eitel, while with his free hand visible only to me, he patted the small of her back as though to tell her she might do worse than to hug him again.

'Miss Meyers, Miss Esposito,' Eitel said smoothly, and Lulu gave a passing nod to Elena. 'Collie, we have to talk,' Lulu said. 'I have something I definitely want to tell you about.' Then she gave a sweet smile to Eitel. 'Charley, you're getting fat,' she said.

'Sit down,' Eitel offered.

She took a chair next to him, and told Munshin to sit on the other side. 'Isn't anybody going to introduce the Air Force?' she asked directly of me, and when that was done, she made a game of studying my face. I forced myself to stare her down but it took something out of me. 'What a pretty boy you are,' said Lulu Meyers. She could not have been much more than twenty herself.

'She's great,' Munshin said. 'What a tongue.'

'Would you like a drink?' I asked Elena. She hadn't said a word since Lulu had come, and by comparison she did not seem as attractive as I thought her before. Maybe aware of this herself, she picked nervously and savagely at the cuticle on her nail. 'Oh, yes, I'd like a drink,' Elena agreed, and as I started away, Lulu handed me her glass. 'Get me a small Martin, will you?' she asked, turning violet-blue eyes on me. I realized she was as nervous as Elena, but in a different way; Lulu made herself sit easily in the chair – I had learned the same trick in flying school.

When I came back, she was talking to Eitel. 'We miss you, old ham,' she was saying. 'I don't know anybody I'd rather get drunk with than Eitel.'

'I'm on the wagon,' Eitel said with a grin.

'You're on the wagon as far as I'm concerned,' Lulu said with a glance at Elena.

'I hear you're going to marry Teddy Pope,' Eitel answered.

Lulu turned on Munshin. 'You tell H.T. to lay off the drums,' she said, and nipped her cigarette to the floor, grinding it out with a quick impatient motion. I had a peep at her legs and her little feet covered by silver slippers. Those legs were as familiar as the contour of her mouth, each drawn on one's memory by a hundred photographs, or was it a thousand? 'Collie, this propaganda has got to stop, I tell you.'

Munshin gave his sheepish smile. 'Now, you relax, doll. Who's forcing you into anything?'

'I approve of Lulu marrying Teddy,' Eitel drawled.

'Charley, you're a troublemaker,' Munshin said quickly.

Elena and I looked at each other. She was trying very hard to be a part of this, her eyes following everyone who spoke, her smile forced as if she didn't want to seem ignorant. Probably I was acting the same way. We sat at opposite flanks of the conversation, no more than social book-ends.

'I'm serious,' Lulu said. 'You can tell Mr T. I'll marry this pretty boy first,' and she inclined a finger toward me.

'You haven't proposed yet,' I said.

Elena laughed with enough pleasure to have said it herself. Again her laugh was too loud, and the others stared at her.

'Don't panic, love-bucket,' Lulu said with an authority the red-headed girl, Candy Ballou, had not been able to muster. She held her empty glass up for us all to see and poured its last drop on the floor. 'I'm sad, Collie,' she announced and laid her head on Munshin's shoulder.

'I saw your last picture,' Eitel said to her.

'Wasn't I just awful in it?' Lulu made a face again. 'They're ruining me. What did you think, Eitel?'

He smiled noncommittally. 'I'll talk to you about it.'

'I know what you'll say. I was performing too much, wasn't I?' She raised her head and pinched Collie on the cheek. 'I hate acting.' And with hardly a pause she leaned forward to ask a question. 'What do you do, Miss Esposo?'

'Esposito,' Eitel said.

Elena was uncomfortable. 'I've been . . . not exactly, a dancer, I guess.'

'Modelling now?' Lulu said.

'No . . . I mean, of course not . . .' Elena was not altogether helpless before her. 'Different things,' she finished at last. 'Who wants to be a skinny model?'

'Oh, I'll bet,' Lulu said, and spoke to me again. 'You the latest tail on Eitel's old tattered kite?'

I could feel myself turning red. Her attacks came so fast that it was a little like waiting for the sound to stop in musical chairs. 'They say you're through, Charley,' Lulu went on.

'They certainly do talk about me,' Eitel said.

'Not as much as you think. Time passes.'

'I'll always be remembered as your second ex-husband,' Eitel drawled.

'It's a fact,' she said. 'When I think of Charley Eitel, I think of number two.'

Eitel smiled cheerfully. 'If you want to put on the brass knuckles, Lulu, just give the word.'

There was a moment, and then Lulu smiled back. 'I'm sorry, Charley, I apologize.' She turned to all of us, and in that husky voice which went along so nicely with her blonde hair and blue eyes, she said, 'I saw an awful picture of me today in the papers.'

'Lulu,' Munshin said quickly, 'we can rectify that. The photographers will be working soon.'

'I won't be mugged with Teddy Pope,' Lulu declared.

'Who's forcing you?' Munshin said.

'No tricks, Collie.'

'No tricks,' Munshin promised, wiping his face.

'Why are you perspiring so?' Lulu asked, and then broke off to stand up. 'Jay-Jay!' she cried aloud, and opened her arms. Jennings James, who had just walked toward us, wrapped her to his skinny body in a parody of Munshin's bear-hug. 'My favourite girl,' he said in his high Southern voice.

'That was a bitchy release you had on me day before yester-day,' Lulu said.

'Honey, you're paranoidal,' Jennings James told her. 'I wrote it as a work of love to you.' He nodded to all of us. 'How are you, Mr Munshin?' he said. The trip to the men's room seemed to have revived him.

'Take a chair, Jay-Jay,' Munshin said, 'this is Miss Esposito.'

Jennings James bowed formally to her. 'I love the dignity of Italian women, Miss Esposito.' His freckled hand smoothed his red hair. 'Are you going to stay with us long in Desert D'Or?'

'I'm going back tomorrow,' Elena said.

'Oh, you're not,' Eitel said.

'Well, I'm not sure,' Elena corrected herself.

A waiter brought ice cream. It was melted on the plates and only Elena took a dish. 'This is soft ice cream, isn't it?' she said. 'That's the expensive kind, I've heard.' When everybody looked puzzled by the remark, Elena became a little desperate in the attempt to prove it. 'I don't remember where I heard, but I did see it advertised, soft ice cream, I mean, or maybe I was eating it, I don't know.'

Eitel came to her aid. 'It's true. Duvon's in the city features a sort of melted ice cream. I've had it myself. But I don't think this is Duvon's, Elena.'

'Oh, no, I know it isn't,' she said quickly.

Jay-Jay turned back to Lulu. 'Honey, we're ready for the pictures. Those photographers have finished grossifying them-selves, and it all waits on you.'

'Well, let it wait,' Lulu said. 'I want another drink.'

'Mr T. asked me specially to get you.'

'Come on, let's go,' said Munshin, 'everybody.' I think he included Elena, Eitel, and myself to prevent Lulu from deciding she wanted to stay with us. Once on his feet, Munshin took her arm and started along the edge of the pool past the dance floor toward a group of photographers I could see gathered near the papier-mâché movie camera.

Jay-Jay brought up the rear with me. 'That Esposito dame,' he said, 'she's Munshin's little gal, I hear.'

'I don't know,' I said.

'Oh, man, she's a dish. I never got my hooks into her, but I know some who have. When old Charley Eitel gets done with Esposito, you ought to spend a couple of delicious hours with her.' He then started to give me the details of how good she was supposed to be. 'And she looks like a sweet kid, too,' he added gallantly. 'It's hard for a girl living in the capital. I don't hold it against any of them. Why, Teppis himself, that son of a bitch . . .' But Jay-Jay had no time to finish the sentence for we had come up to the photographers.

I could see Teddy Pope moving in from another direction. The tennis player still was with him, and they were laughing at some private joke. 'Lulu, honey,' Pope said, and held out his hand to shake hers. They touched fingertips and stood side by side.

'Now, fellows,' said Jay-Jay, springing forward and talking to the three photographers who stood phlegmatically in front of the camera boom, 'we want some human interest stills. Nothing elaborate. Just how cinema folks live and entertain each other. You got the idea.' People were coming over from various corners of the Laguna Room. 'Honeybun, you look lovely,' Dorothea O'Faye called out, and Lulu smiled. 'Thank you, sweetie,' she called back. 'Hey, Teddy,' a man said, 'have your autograph?' and Teddy laughed. Standing before an audience, his manner had changed. He seemed more boyish and more direct. 'Why, here comes Mr T. now,' he said aloud, and showing a crack disdain to those who could see it, he began to clap his hands, and at least a dozen of the people near him, trapped into obedience, applauded as well. Teppis held his arm aloft. 'We're taking some pictures tonight of Teddy and Lulu, not only for interest on their picture, or should I say *our* picture, *An Inch From Heaven*, but as a symbol, as I would call it, of tonight and the kind of good time we've had.' Teppis cleared his throat and smiled sweetly. His presence had succeeded in drawing even more people, and for a while the scene was busy with the flash-bulbs of the cameras, the shifting of positions, and the directions given by the photographers. I saw Teppis in place between Teddy and Lulu, Lulu between the two men, Teddy and Lulu together, Teddy and Lulu apart, Teppis holding Lulu's hand in a fatherly way, Teppis photographed with his hand on Teddy's elbow. I was struck by how well they did it, Teddy smiling, happy, healthy, and Lulu sweet, Lulu demure, Lulu ready, all with an ease which balanced the pride of Herman Teppis. It was just about perfect. Teddy Pope turned his face to every instruction of the photographers, his voice had sincerity, his smile seemed to enjoy his surroundings. He waved his hands in the air like a prize-fighter and gave a play of having wrenched his shoulder from the exercise; he put his arm around Lulu's waist, he bussed her cheek. And Lulu with a cuddling curving motion slipped against his side. She seemed to bounce when she walked, her shoulders swayed in a little rhythm with her hips, her neck curved, her hair tumbled in gold ringlets over her head, and her husky voice laughed at everyone's jokes. I thought she was about as beautiful as any girl I had ever seen.

When the photographers were done, Teppis made another speech. 'You never know. We're a big family at Supreme. I'll tell you something. I don't think these two kids were acting.' And with a hand against each of their backs, he pushed them together until they had to hug each other in order not to trip. 'What's this I hear, Lulu?' he said aloud to the laughter of the guests, 'a little ladybug has told me you and Teddy are dear friends.'

'Oh, Mr Teppis,' Lulu said in her sweetest voice, 'you should have been a marriage broker.'

'It's a compliment. I take it as a compliment,' Teppis said. 'A producer is always making marriages. Art and finance. Talent and an audience. Are you all having a good time tonight?' he asked of the guests watching, and I listened to more than one answer that a good time was being had. 'Treat the camera boys,' Teppis said to Jay-Jay, and walked off with Lulu on his arm. The crowd faded, the photographers were left to pack their equipment. Beside the pool I saw Teppis stop to talk to Eitel, and while he spoke he looked at Elena.

I could see that Teppis recognized her name the moment Eitel introduced her, for Teppis' reaction followed quickly. His back stiffened, his ruddy face seemed to swell, and he said something, something to the point, since Eitel and Elena turned away immediately.

Alone with Lulu, Teppis was mopping his forehead with a silk handkerchief. 'Go dance with Teddy,' I heard him say hoarsely as I approached. 'Do it as a favour for me.'

Because of the crowd I could no longer see what had happened to Eitel.

Lulu caught my eye. 'Mr T., I want to dance with Sergius first,' she said with a pout, and slipping away from Teppis she put her hand in my palm and drew me to the dance floor. I held her tightly. The liquor I had been drinking all evening was finally beginning to do its work.

'How long will it take,' I said in her ear, 'before you start to look for Teddy?'

To my surprise she took this meekly. 'You don't know what I'm up against,' Lulu said.

'Why? Do you know?'

'Oh, don't be like that, Sergius, I like you.' At the moment she seemed no more than eighteen. 'It's harder than you think,' she whispered, and by the softness with which she held herself, I found it hard to believe in the first impression she made on me. She seemed young; spoiled maybe, but very sweet.

We danced in silence. 'What did Teppis say to Eitel?' I asked finally.

Lulu shook her head and then giggled. 'He told Charley to get the hell out.'

'Well, then I guess I have to go too,' I told her.

'You weren't included.'

'Eitel is my friend,' I said.

She pinched my ear. 'Wonderful. Charley will love that. I have to tell him when I see him.'

'Leave with me,' I said.

'Not yet.'

I stopped dancing. 'If you want,' I said, 'I'll ask Mr T. for permission.'

'You think I'm afraid of him.'

'You're not afraid of him. You'll just end up dancing with Teddy.'

Lulu began to laugh. 'You're different from what I thought at first.'

'That's just liquor.'

'Oh, I hope not.'

Reluctantly, in a sort of muse, she allowed me to take her from the dance floor. 'This is an awful mistake,' she whispered.

Yet Lulu was not exactly timorous when we passed Teppis. Like a promoter who counts the seats in the house, he stood near the entrance, his eyes adding up the scene. 'Girlie,' he said, gripping her by the arm, 'where are you going?'

'Oh, Mr T.,' Lulu said like a bad child, 'Sergius and I have so much to talk about.'

'We want to get some air,' I said, and I took the opportunity to give him back a finger in the ribs.

'Air?' He was indignant as we left. 'Air?' I could see him looking for the ceiling of the Laguna Room. Behind us, still in operation, the papier-mâché camera rotated on its wooden boom, the searchlights lifting columns to the sky. A pall lay over the party. The zenith had passed, and couples were closed into tête-à-têtes on the couches, for the drunken hour had come where everything is possible and everybody wants everybody; if desires were deeds, the history of the night would end in history.

'You say to Charley Eitel,' Teppis shouted after me, 'that he's through. I tell you he's through. He's lost his chance.' Giggling at the sound of his rage, Lulu and I ran along the walks and over the little trellised bridges of the Yacht Club until we came to the parking circle. Once, underneath a Japanese lantern, I stopped to kiss her, but she was laughing too hard and our mouths didn't meet. 'I'll have to teach you,' she said.

'Teach me nothing. I hate teachers,' I said, and holding her hand, pulled her behind me, her heels clicking, her skirt rustling in the promising tap-and-whisper of a girl trying to run in an evening gown.

We had an argument over whose car to take. Lulu insisted on using her convertible. 'I'm cooped up, Sergius,' she said, 'I want to drive.' 'Then drive my car,' I compromised, but she would have no other way than her own. 'I won't leave,' she said, driven to a pitch of stubbornness, 'I'll go back to the party.'

'You're frightened,' I taunted her.

'I'm not.'

She drove badly. She was reckless, which I expected, but what was worse, she could not hold her foot steady on the pedal. The automobile was always slowing or accelerating and drunk as I was she made me aware of danger. But that wasn't the danger I was worrying about.

'I'm a nut,' she'd say.

'Let's park, nut,' I would answer. 'Let's cut the knot.'

'Did you ever go to the crazy doctor?' Lulu asked.

'You don't need him.'

'Oh, I need something,' she said, and with a wrench, gravel stinging our fenders, she brought the car off the shoulder and on the road again.

'Let's park,' I said.

She parked when she would have it. I had given up hope. I was prepared to sit politely while she skidded us off the highway and we rolled and smacked at seventy miles an hour through the cactus and desert clay. But Lulu decided we might just as well live a little while longer. Picking a side road at random, she screamed around the turn, slowed down once it was past, drifted along, and finally pulled off in some deserted flat, the night horizon lying all around us in a giant circle.

'Lock the windows,' she said, engrossed in pressing the button which raised the canvas top.

'It'll be too hot,' I argued.

'No, the windows have to be closed,' she insisted.

All preparations spent, she turned in her seat and took my kiss. She must have felt she had let loose a bull, and in fact she had; for the first time in almost a year I knew that I would be all right.

Yet it was not so easy as that. She would give herself to my mouth and my arms, she would be about to be caught, and then she would start away, looking fearfully through the car window. 'There's a man coming,' she would whisper, her nails digging my wrist, and I would be forced to lift my head and scan the horizon, forced to stop and say, 'There's no one around, can't you see?'

'I'm scared,' she would say, and give her mouth to me again. How long it went on I do not know, but it was a classic. She coaxed me forward, she pushed me back, she allowed me a strip of her clothing only to huddle away like a bothered virgin. We could have been kids on a couch. My lips were bruised, my body suffered, my fingers were thick, and if I succeeded finally in capturing what clothing she wore beneath her evening dress, pushing it behind me in the seat like a mad jay stuffing its nest, I still could not inspire Lulu to give up her gown. Though she allowed the most advanced forays and even let me for one, two, and then three beats of the heart, she sat up with a little motion that pushed me away, and looked through the windows. 'There's someone coming. There's somebody on the road,' she said, and pinched me when I tried to come near her.

'This is it,' I told her, but for all I told her, high-water mark had been reached. For another hour, no matter what I did, how I forced, how I waited, and how I tried, I could not get so close again. The dawn must have been not too far away when exhausted, discouraged, and almost indifferent, I shut my eyes and murmured, 'You win.' With a weary hand I passed over my cache of her door-prizes and lay back against the seat.

Tenderly, she kissed my lashes, her fingernails teased my cheek. 'You're sweet,' she whispered, 'you're really not so rough.' To revive me, she pulled my hair. 'Kiss me, Sergius,' she said as if I had not yet done anything at all, and in the next minute while I lay back on the seat, not believing and almost dumb to her giving, I was led to discover the mysterious brain of a movie star. She gave herself gently to me, she was delicate, she was loving, loving even to the modesty with which she whispered that this was all very unplanned, and I must be considerate. So I was obliged to take the trip alone, and was repaid by having her cuddle in my arms.

'You're wonderful,' she said.

'I'm just an amateur.'

'No, you're wonderful. Oooh, I like you. You!'

On the way back I drove the car while she curled beside me, her head on my shoulder. The radio was on and we hummed to the music. 'I was crazy tonight,' she said.

I adored her. The way she had treated everybody when I met her made this even better. For on that long drive she took me before we parked, I had told myself that absolutely I had to succeed with her, and the memory of this feeling now that I had succeeded was fine. Maybe it was no more than that enough time had gone by, but I felt all right, I felt ready – for what, I hardly knew. But I had made it, and with what a girl.

Lulu was tense when we kissed good night outside her door. 'Let me stay,' I said.

'No, not tonight.' She looked behind her to see if the walks were deserted.

'Then come to my house.'

She kissed me on the nose. 'I'm just beaten, Sergius.' Her voice was the voice of a child.

'All right, I'll see you tomorrow.'

'Call me.' She kissed me again, she blew a kiss as she disappeared through the door, and I was left alone in the labyrinth of the Yacht Club, the first sun of a desert morning not far away, the foliage a pale-blue like the pale-blue of her gown.

It may sound weird, but I was so excited with enthusiasm that I had to share it, and I could think of nobody but Eitel. It did not even occur to me that he might still be with Elena, or that as the ex-husband of little Lulu, he would not necessarily find my story a dream. I don't know whether I even remembered that Lulu had been married to him. In a way, she had no existence for me before tonight, and if she seemed bigger than life, she was also without life. How I loved myself then. With the dawn spreading out from me until it seemed to touch the Yacht Club with its light, I began to think of those mornings when I was out on a flight which started in the darkness of the hangars, the syrup of coffee on my tongue, the blast of my plane flaring two long fires into the night. We would take off an hour before dawn, and when morning came to meet us five miles high in the air with the night clouds warmed by a gold and silver light, I used to believe I could control the changes of the sky by a sway of my body as it was swelled by the power of the plane, and I had played with magic. For it was magic to fly an airplane; it was a gimmick and a drug. We knew that no matter what happened on ground, no matter how little or confusing we ourselves could be, there would always come those hours when we were alone in formation and on top of life, and so the magic was in the flight and the light made us very cool, you know? and there was nothing which could happen once we were down which could not be fixed when the night went into the west and we ganged after it on our wings.

I had been careful to forget all of this. I had liked it too much, and it had not been easy to think that I probably would never have any magic again; but on this dawn with the taste of Lulu still teasing me, I knew that I could have something else, and I could be sad for those airplanes I deserted because there was something to take their place.

Thinking this, or thinking of such things, I started up the path to where I parked the car. Halfway, I sat on a bench underneath a bower of shrubbery, breathing the new air. Everything had come to rest around me. Then in a cottage nearby I heard sudden brawling sounds, a mixed dialogue or two, and a door in the wall opened and Teddy Pope lurched out, wearing a sweater and dungarees, but his feet were bare. 'You bitch,' he shouted at the door.

'Stay out,' came the voice of the tennis player. 'I don't want to tell you again.' Teddy cursed. He cursed at such length and in so loud a voice that I was sure everybody sleeping nearby must be reaching for their pills. The door to the bungalow opened again, and Marion Faye came outside. 'Go beat your meat, Teddy,' he said in his quiet voice, and then he stepped back inside and shut the door. Teddy turned around once and looked past me with blank eyes which took me in, or maybe he didn't see anything at all.

I watched him stagger along the wall, and in spite of myself I followed at a distance. In one of the minor patios of the Yacht Club where a fountain, a few yucca trees, and a hedge of bougainvillea set up an artificial nook, Teddy Pope stopped and made a phone call from an outdoor booth set under a trellis of rambler roses. 'I can't go to sleep like this,' he said into the receiver. 'I've got to talk to Marion.' The voice at the other end made some answer.

'Don't hang up,' Teddy Pope said loudly.

Like a night watchman making his rounds, Herman Teppis came into sight along one of the walks. He approached Teddy Pope, came up beside him, and slammed the receiver on its cradle.

'You're a disgraceful human being,' Herman Teppis said, and kept on down the walk without saying another word.

Teddy Pope wobbled away and came to rest against a joshua

tree. He leaned on it as if it were his mother. Then he began to cry. I had never seen a man so drunk. Sobbing, hiccuping, he tried to chew on the bark of the tree. I backed away, I wanted nothing so much as to disappear. When I was out of sight, I heard Pope scream. 'You bastard, Teppis,' he cried out into the empty dawn, 'you know what you can do, you fat bastard, Teppis,' and I could picture his cheek on the joshua tree. I drove slowly home, making no attempt to find Eitel after all.

Part Three

10

Women who have come to know me well have always accused me sooner or later of being very cold at heart, and while that is a woman's view of it, and a woman can rarely know the things that go on inside a man, I suppose there is a sort of truth to what they say. The first good English novelist I ever read was Somerset Maugham, and he wrote somewhere that 'Nobody is any better than he ought to be.' Since it was exactly what I was thinking at the time, I carried it along with me as a working philosophy, but I suppose that finally I would have to take exception to the thought because it seems to me that some people are a little better, and some a little worse than they ought to be, or else the universe is just an elaborate clock. Nonetheless I can hardly claim that I am the most warmhearted man-and-jack to come sauntering down the pike.

Among the different people each of us has in himself is the gossip columnist I could have been. Maybe I would have been a bad columnist – I'm honest by inclination – but I would have been the first who saw it as an art. Quite a few times I have thought that a newspaperman is obsessed with finding the facts in order to tell a lie, and a novelist is a galley-slave to his imagination so he can look for the truth. I know that for a lot of what follows I must use my imagination.

Particularly for Eitel's affair with Elena Esposito. I have to wonder a little if I am the one to write about it. I have picked up something of an education since I was in Desert D'Or, but Eitel is very different from me, and I do not know if I can find his style. Yet imagination becomes a vice if we do not exercise it. One of these days I am going to write a book about a town I visited for twenty minutes, and if I do it well enough, everybody will believe I lived there for twenty years. So there is no use in making apologies – I have the conceit that I *know* what happened, and at the least everybody in Desert D'Or knew that their affair began well.

When Teppis told him to leave the party, it put Eitel in a good mood, for to find his self-respect Eitel usually had to do something which was of no advantage for himself. On the walk to the car, with Elena on his arm, he was pleased enough to be giving imitations of the people they had talked to at the party. 'I love the dignity of Italian women,' he said, mimicking Jennings James, and Elena, breathless from laughter, could only plead, 'Oh, stop!'

Once they arrived at his house, she went in with him quite naturally. He made two drinks and sat beside her on the couch, thinking that nothing could be more of a tonic for her than to make love gently, showing the affection he felt. Yet his pulse was quick. 'I think I've seen you before,' he said after a silence.

Elena nodded. 'You did. But you weren't even looking at me.'

'I don't believe that's possible,' he said with his best smile.

'Well, it's true.' She nodded seriously. 'I used to do wardrobe work at Supreme. One time I brought up a couple of dresses for you to look at, and you didn't even see me. You just looked at the dresses.'

'I thought you were a flamenco dancer.'

Elena shrugged. 'I wanted to be. Once in a while my agent would get me a job for a couple of nights. But no career to speak of.'

Her words gave him a picture of the men through whom she must have passed: would-be agents, unemployed actors, real-estate operators with a one-room office, musicians, a man or two with a name for a one-night stand, a man perhaps with a name like his own.

He disliked mentioning Munshin but he was curious. 'Collie said he met you at a benefit.'

She laughed. 'That's Collie's story. He likes to build things up. Why he never even saw me dance. He used to make me feel too inhibited.'

'Then how did you meet?'

'Collie wasn't like you. He noticed me.' Her green eyes teased him. 'I had to take some costumes into Collie's, too, and what

104

with one thing and another, Collie finally took me to dinner.'
She sighed. 'You know what I hold against Collie? He got me to
quit the job, and then he put me in an apartment. He said he
couldn't keep on seeing me if I worked at Supreme.' She gave a
wry twist to her childlike mouth. 'So that's how I got kept. I
guess I'm lazy.'

Eitel was studying her face, considering Elena as a possibility
for a small role in his film. She would not do. He could tell that
at a glance. There was the sad fact that her nose was too long
and the sensuality of her nostrils would be exaggerated by the
camera.

He changed the subject. 'Have you ever done any skiing?'
Eitel asked.

'No.'

'We must do it sometime. There's nothing like skiing,' he said
as though in an hour they would be on a plane to a ski resort.

'I haven't done anything much.'

'I bet you have,' Eitel said, his voice low from the nearness of
their bodies. 'I've always thought that everything you learn is
done by fighting your fear.'

They each sat sipping their drinks. 'I think I can get some
Spanish music on the radio,' Eitel said. 'Would you dance for
me?'

'Not tonight.'

'But you'll dance for me sometime?'

'I don't know,' she said.

'I'd love to see you. I hear you do a great flamenco.'

'You're just being nice.' Her hand was playing nervously with
his. After a minute or so, she leaned forward with a sad little
smile and kissed him.

In no time at all, they were in the next room. Eitel was
amazed. How much she knew, he thought numbly, how very
much she knew. With the exception of a moment when she tried
to hold him off, and cried out, 'No, no,' to which he answered
not brutally, 'Oh, shut up,' only adding to her excitement by the
words, he had never had a woman give so much the first time.
For Eitel, who had decided more than once that when all was
said, not too many women really knew how to make love, and
very few indeed loved to make love, Elena was doubly and

indubitably a find. He had blundered on a treasure. It was one of the best experiences of his life. Long after his enthusiasm had passed, and he catered to her with the art and technique he had been at such competitive turns to pick up, he could picture Munshin's round face and its unhappy look. '*Et tu*, old friend,' Munshin would be saying, and it gave Eitel new appetite. She caught every improvisation, she stimulated others – he was a ferment of invention. Eitel always felt that the way a woman made love was as good a guide to understanding her character as any other way, and from the distance of an inch Elena was a woman of exceptional beauty. Never had he seen such a change. Where she was timid with people, she was bold with him – where crude in her manners, subtle with intuition. So it went, her energy almost ruthless in its call on him. When at last they were done and Eitel could glow from a show of skill more valuable to him than the pleasure itself, they lay side by side smiling at each other.

'You're . . .' she started to say at last, and ended by using an odd word. 'You're a king,' Elena said. And with a groan she turned away from him. 'I just never . . . you see . . . it never happened like this.'

Since the day on the beach with the girl and her surfboard, he had begun to doubt himself. As he had grown older he had become more sensitive to the small ways in which women refused his body even as they accepted it, and this had made him fragile. He had thought that in a few more years this part of his life would be gone.

It was nice to believe Elena then, not only because it was nicer than to think she usually made such a speech, but from an instinct now finely tuned after many such remarks made to him by women who were more or less honest, by women who had loved him, and by women who wished to use him. He had heard it so many times, and not without justice, for satirically he considered this his true art. 'To be a good lover,' I had heard him say, 'one should be incapable of falling in love.' But he believed her out of something more. To give herself as she had given was past flattery. It was not the sort of thing one could deliver at will. In the course of the years he had had affairs which had been hardly despicable, pearls as he would think of them drily, but never, no, not ever, had the first night opened such an extravaganza. It was not so bad, he thought, to be called a king by a girl who must be on speaking terms with everything from an acrobat to a tango dancer. Loving himself, loving her body as it curled against him, he closed his eyes thinking with drowsy contentment that if he usually wanted nothing more than to quit a woman once they were done, now he not only wished to sleep the night with Elena but to hold her in his arms. He fell asleep a happy man.

In the morning, both were depressed. They were strangers after all. Eitel left her in bed and put on his clothes in the living room. The ice-cube bucket held an inch of water, and he washed it out, poured some liquor neat, and cleared his throat. When Elena came out in her evening gown, her face without make-up, her long hair hanging forlornly over her cheeks, he was almost forced to laugh. If she had been beautiful the night before, she looked sullen at this moment and not at all attractive.

'Let's have breakfast,' he said, by an effort smiling at her, and when she nodded, he began to scramble some eggs and put the coffee on.

'After we get a little food in us,' he called from the kitchen, 'and feel human, I'll take a drive out to your hotel and bring you some clothing. It'll pick you up.'

'I'll get out. You don't have to worry about me,' she said in a surly voice.

'I'm not talking about that.' She had sensed he would just as soon be rid of her, and he was moved to be kind. 'I want you to spend the day with me,' he said quickly.

She softened. 'I'm always in a bad mood in the morning.'

'Oh, so am I. We're alike, I tell you.' And on an impulse he reached to kiss her. She offered her cheek.

Over breakfast, given the stimulation of coffee, his humour improved. 'How would you like to take a swim at the Yacht Club?' he asked.

'There?'

He nodded, he could see she was wondering how it would be to appear at the pool. So many strangers would see her with Eitel the morning after the party.

'I don't think so,' she said.

'We'll shock them.' He was in clownish good spirits. 'If Teppis comes along, we'll push him in the pool.'

'He's an awful man,' Elena said. 'So cruel. The way he talked to you.'

'It's the only language he knows. He doesn't use words. He just throws out language to convey emotion.' Eitel laughed. 'Now, there's a man who's all emotion. Not like me.'

'You're full of emotion,' she said, and then looked at her plate in embarrassment.

A bad mood slipped over Eitel. He had not answered Teppis properly. There were any number of things he *might* have said, but he had thought too long and then merely smiled and walked away with her.

'I just remembered something,' he told her, starting himself up again. 'I know a water hole in the desert. It's kind of pleasant. Lots of cactus. Even a tree, I think. Why don't we go swim there?'

Despite signs to the contrary, she was still his sullen little Italian. 'I guess I'll take the bus home today,' she said quietly.

'Oh, you're out of your mind.'

'No, I want to go home.' He noticed she did not dwell on how little she could expect there. 'You've been very nice,' she added clumsily, and began to shiver.

'Look, Esposito,' he began in a light tone, but tears came into her eyes, and she left the room. He could hear her close the bedroom door.

'Stupid,' Eitel said aloud. He hardly knew if he meant Elena or himself.

He was thinking that she had given herself to him in order to humiliate Munshin. Now, the next day had come and she had only humiliated herself. He went to the door, opened it, and sat down beside Elena on the bed. 'Don't cry,' he said tenderly to her. She was dear to him suddenly. He liked her ever so much. 'Don't cry, little monkey,' Eitel said and stroked her hair. It let loose a watershed of tears from Elena. He held her in his arms, a little amused, a little bored, and yet not without sympathy. 'You're very sweet,' he said into her ear.

'No . . . you're so nice to me,' she sobbed.

After a time, she got up to examine herself in the mirror, made a small sound of horror, and whispered to him, 'Once I get my other clothes, let's go to the pool.'

'Oh, you're a terror,' he said, and she hugged him hungrily.

'Please don't look at me,' Elena said. 'Not until I fix myself.'

He obeyed her. Given the key of Elena's room after she confessed her room would be messy, and he swore it was a matter of indifference to him, Eitel went for a quick drive through Desert D'Or and found her hotel. Her room was not a large room, and its window looked on an airshaft, the only airshaft in Desert D'Or, he thought. She had brought but one suitcase, a shabby piece of luggage, yet she had managed to strew its contents over every piece of furniture. She was certainly sloppy, and as a hint to the standards of the hotel, the chambermaid had done no more than make the bed. Sadly, Eitel studied the disarray. She was so messy, he thought, tossing a slip on top of a rumpled blouse in order to clear a space for himself. He sat down on the chair he had cleared, and lighting a cigarette, said to himself, 'I'll have to get around to putting her on the bus tonight.'

Put her on the bus, he did not. The afternoon turned into fun. If no one came to their table to talk, it suited his mood exactly. Ever since he had awakened, his temper was shifting between melancholy and excitement. It satisfied him somehow that the news of his quarrel with Teppis had spread so quickly. Let him be all alone, he thought; let *them* be all alone, Elena and himself. 'Fresh beginnings,' Eitel repeated to himself all day like the line of a song which one cannot get out of mind.

He was very pleased with Elena. Her body, which he had not had time to study, was delightful in a bathing suit. He felt a slow warmth sitting in the sun, able to know that in a few hours he would have her all over again. It was pleasant beyond pleasure to put off that moment. She had a merry laugh today. Her soft mouth widened, her beautiful white teeth gleamed to his sight, and he discovered that he was trying to make her laugh. She was aware of how people looked at them, she was not at ease, far from it, and yet unlike the night before at the party, she succeeded in showing some poise. He had to value the dignity with which she listened to him, her eyes alive to the meaning of what he said. 'I could make something of this girl,' he thought.

It would not be so difficult. He could teach her to speak without moving her hands, he could direct her deep voice away from its vulgarities. Eitel was in love with the afternoon. Everything was so perfect. 'Charles Francis against the world,' he thought with cautious irony, but it could hardly trap his exuberance. He found himself thinking of those years when he had been in college at an Eastern university which had put the crown to his parents' ambition; and with a shock – it was truly so long ago – he remembered how clumsy he had been in his late adolescence. With what hunger he had watched, and with what hatred, while healthy students paraded their dates through the doors of all those fraternity houses to which he had never been invited; what contempt he had felt for his own dates in college – town girls, working girls, an occasional night with some unattractive student from the neighbouring college for women. He had left school with the fire of knowing that the world saw him as homely and insignificant, and maybe that had been the spur to make those early movies. If it was true, then his success had come from hunger and from anger, and in those years at the capital, while his hunger had been fed and his anger mellowed into wit, he had spent his urge and been admired and lost the energy of his talent. Sitting beside Elena, thinking of how he was back where he had begun, he had a hope that his talent would return. She would help him, he could live with such a woman now. She was warm, and she had given him so much last night. How necessary that had been for his confidence. 'You're wonderful,' he said to her like a boy and was even more taken by the doubt with which she took his praise. She was sensitive. That he had decided beyond a doubt. Of her own accord she began to talk about Munshin, and he enjoyed the way she saw him. 'He's not a bad man,' Elena said. 'He thinks he would like a woman to be really in love with him. I was mean. I made him think I loved him.'

Her honesty drew Eitel. 'Collie thought you loved him?' he asked.

She surprised Eitel by what she said next. 'I don't know. He's sharp. You know he has a lot of understanding of relationships.'

'Yes, indeed.'

'My analyst thought I should try to make a go with him.'

'You're finished now?'

110

'I stopped going to the analysis. I don't think I made the right kind of transference.' It seemed odd, somehow, to hear such words from her mouth. 'You know,' she said, 'my doctor was like Collie to me.' A devil shone in her eyes for an instant. 'I think I used to go out and get in some of the nutty things I did with men, just so I could be more unusual to my doctor.' She giggled. 'You know, so he'd write me up as a case of something.'

Eitel tried not to wince at her language. 'How did Collie take all this?' he asked.

'I hate him,' she said suddenly. 'He'd have forgiven me if I'd, you know, maybe let him watch. He's such a hypocrite,' she said furiously, and squeezing Eitel's hand, added, 'I don't know how I could have stayed with him so long.'

Eitel nodded. 'Collie wasn't so nice when it came to divorcing his wife.'

'Oh, it was impossible. I'm disgusted with myself.' She fingered her mouth vacantly. 'He's a funny man, Collie. He's so full of guilt and anxiety.'

'That blasted jargon again,' Eitel said to himself. It carried unpleasant connotations from other affairs. So many of his women had been in analysis, and they had carried gossip back and forth: what Eitel had said about the analyst; what the analyst had said about him. A modern *ménage à trois*.

But Elena was off on her own thoughts. 'Collie is very complicated,' she told Eitel. 'He wants to think he's unselfish, and he also wants to think he's no good. The only time he's happy is when he feels both things at the same time. Does that make sense? I mean, I don't know, I don't know how to say things.'

She was priceless, thought Eitel. 'Couldn't put it better myself,' he said lightly.

'I don't really hate Collie,' she added, 'I'm just ashamed.'

'Why?'

'Because . . .' Her nervous fingers tore cuticle from her nail. He would have to correct that habit, Eitel was thinking.

'Because you know you're better than he is,' Eitel said with a smile.

'Well, I don't know.' An impish look peeped out of her green eyes. 'I guess it's what I do mean,' she said, and laughed again.

'You're wonderful,' Eitel said.

'I'm having such a terrible time today,' Elena smiled.

That night was like the night before, even better perhaps, for he had been wanting her all day, and besides he found her more likeable. Once again he could marvel at Elena. She had the lusts of a bored countess, and what had he been looking for so long, if not for that? The doubt whether they could repeat themselves or had only enjoyed an accident was now answered for him. 'It's never been like this,' she said to him, and when he nodded, she shook herself with wonder. 'Something has happened to me.' Nestling closer she whispered, scratching a first pinprick of jealousy in him, 'I was almost always acting with other men.'

It had happened before. He had had women who gave him their first honest pleasure, and he had taken all the bows for his vanity, but he had never met so royal a flow of taste. It was remarkable how they knew each other's nicety between love-making and extravagance. It had always been his outstanding gift, or so he felt, to be able to know a woman, and he had the certainty at little instants that he could discover every sympathetic nerve. 'The onanist at heart,' he had thought, and made love to a woman with care enough to have made love to himself. But Elena carried him to mark above mark. Her face was alive, she was alive, he had never been with anyone who understood him so well. The balance was perfect, without any bother that too little had been done or relatively too much.

Eitel fell into a deep sleep. Like most cynics he was profoundly sentimental about sex. It was his dream of bounty, and it nourished him enough to wake up with the hope that this affair could return his energy, flesh his courage, and make him the man he had once believed himself to be. With Elena beside him he thought for the first time in many years that the best thing in the world for him was to make a great movie.

Down one could go, very far down, but there was a bottom. Himself, wasted beyond wasting, and this girl he knew hardly at all. Together each of them would make something of the other. He felt full of tenderness for Elena. She was adorable. Her back was exquisite. 'Wake up, little monkey,' he whispered to her ear.

Through the day he toyed with the thought that she should come to live with him. He was far too careful to give her such an idea before he was certain of it. But time passed well. They were now in the stage of talking about past affairs, a subject which always drew Eitel. He found that Elena not only loved to gossip, but was moved by the mention of complications.

'Do you know what I mean by a sandwich?' she asked.

He did. She insisted he give the details and listened like a child to a fairy tale, hugging herself while he told the story. 'Maybe we can do something like that,' she offered.

'Maybe.'

'Oh, what a crazy conversation.' But she was a greedy rabbit for more carrots. Her heart-shaped face dimpled with interest, she wanted to know if he had ever been to a ball.

'I've more or less stayed away from that,' Eitel said. He went on, however, to tell her that he knew people in Desert D'Or with whom it was possible. Was she interested?

She was interested. They must do it sometime. 'I've been, you know, sometimes with women,' Elena confided. 'And once . . .' It seemed she also had stories. She was vague about it. 'Collie wanted to kill me when I told him. He found that one hard to forgive.'

'You little demon. You did it just so you could tell him.'

'Well, he had to pry it out of me.' She giggled. 'I'm awful.'

'I'm wondering how you would describe me,' Eitel said.

'I wouldn't talk about you,' she said. 'Never. I couldn't.' He looked away, but the question came. 'Why?' she asked, 'would you talk about me?'

'No, of course not,' Eitel told her. 'Absolutely fantastic,' he could hear himself saying, 'the best woman I ever had.' He slapped her bottom. 'You're a funny monkey.' Before he realized it, his voice said, 'And who do you love now?'

'You,' she said, and then looked away. 'No, I don't. I don't love anybody at all.'

'You feel on your own?'

'Yes.'

'It's a good way to feel.' With hardly a pause he went on to tell a new story. Cosily the day went by, and only at its end did they begin to talk about what she would do. Elena still insisted she would go back to the capital tomorrow, and Eitel said he would not let her. At the end of an hour of such argument, he said in full enthusiasm, 'Let's live together.'

To his surprise she seemed more troubled than pleased. 'I don't think so,' she said quietly.

'Why?'

She tried to give her arguments. 'I've been with one man for so long . . .'

'Not really,' Eitel interrupted.

'Well, now I'm free of Collie, and I don't want to start . . . that is, not yet. I want to see if I can live by myself.'

'You're not giving the real reason.'

'Yes, I am,' she said, and looked at him. 'Besides it wouldn't work with you.'

'Why not try?'

Elena became agitated. 'Sure, why not try? What can you lose?'

Annoyed, he was about to say, 'What can *you* lose?' but he kept silent.

They settled on a compromise. Elena would stay in Desert D'Or and they would see each other when they felt like it, even every day if so it worked out.

'You can do what you want,' Elena said, 'and I'll do what I want.'

'Perfect,' Eitel said. 'If you need a loan of any money . . .'

'I've got enough to get on by myself for a while,' she said modestly.

It was really better than he could have expected. To have her, and to have his privacy too. She was wise, he thought, she knew how not to spoil things. Eitel insisted on paying a week in advance for her room, and that night he saw Elena to the hotel and slept alone. The moment she was gone he knew he had been looking forward to this. There came a time in every affair when he wished to be by himself; fortunately she had the sense to understand this.

Eitel fell asleep thinking how easily sleep came now. But in three hours he was awake, and could not close his eyes again. The long wait from early morning to the dawn brought all of his life back before him, until no one had ever seemed quite so useless to him as himself. The smell of Elena's body clung to

114

him still, somehow was penetrated into the cave of his throat. The tension of his nerves became acute; his limbs might have been on a rack. It was too late for a sleeping pill, and in this condition he would need several. Eitel got out of bed and began to drink. But it did little good, no more than to keep him from feeling worse.

He found that he was juggling with the idea of calling Elena to come to his house. The thought of having her with him was more than pleasant; it seemed a necessity; he did not want to wait by himself for the dawn. So he picked up the phone, dialled the number of her hotel, and asked the desk to ring her room. There was a long ten seconds in which she did not answer, time enough for him to learn by the pressure on his heart of what a crisis it would be if she were out at this hour. Then she answered. He could not be certain but he had the feeling Elena was pretending drowsiness.

'Oh, darling,' she said, 'is something the matter!'

'Nothing.' He cleared his throat. 'It's just that I want to hear your voice.'

Her answer came softly back to him. 'But, Charley, at this hour?'

Eitel lit a cigarette, and made his voice casual. 'Listen, you wouldn't want to come over here now, would you?'

She did not answer right away. 'Honey, I'm tired,' Elena finally murmured.

'Oh, well, forget it.'

'You're not angry?'

'Of course not,' Eitel said.

'I'm so sleepy.'

'I shouldn't have called you. You go back to bed.'

'I missed you tonight,' Elena said. 'But it'll be nice tomorrow.'

'Tomorrow,' he repeated, 'I missed you too,' and sat looking at the phone. Somehow, he could not rid himself of the idea that there had been a man in her room.

To his amazement, Eitel discovered that he was jealous, he was jealous of Elena. It had been so many years since he felt jealousy that the emotion was interesting, indeed any kind of emotion was interesting. Nonetheless, he began to feel some fine tortures. The thought of Elena giving her sounds of pleasure to someone else crawled on his flesh.

Eitel fought one of those heroic battles of the night which leave not a single corpse in the morning; a dozen times he reached out his hand to the phone and then drew it back. By the insight of jealousy, the radical tool of the emotions, Eitel worked into the honest earth of all those giggling anecdotes she had told, so he had no more than to think of a man she had mentioned, and her chance comment, 'Boy, was I drunk,' to dig into the centre of how she had given herself, acting he knew, bleating, crying, purring, all of it alone and drink-inspired, his imaginative eye gouged by the chisel of jealousy – these orgiastic pictures were arousing him as well. The man she had been with, trust that man not to have known she was acting, and off on an exploration by herself, and so that man would boast afterward of just what she had said and what she had done. It was too much for Eitel. If he had listened in the past to confessions by other mistresses and seen it as a closed rehearsal of the comic and the entertaining, the scurry beneath the stone, he could by now have murdered every one of the men Elena had known. They did not appreciate her and that was their crime; they did not appreciate her any more than she could appreciate herself – like all jealous lovers Eitel thought Elena took scandalous care of his property. She was only what he could make of her, and if he were jealous of her past it was because what she had done before could be understood only as something she was doing now. Those words she might once have whispered to some other man lived now only to deny the fire of what she whispered to him. Like an ice pick to the breast, he heard his own words about her. 'When Collie's not around, his little kitten will go for a romp. A couple of actors who've worked for me have been with her. They tell me she's extraordinary in bed.' He could have wrung her throat because she had not waited for him; why hadn't she known she did not need to act for he would come to join her? Gone was the close reason which said that you got on a roller coaster in order to feel. He considered it a crime she had ever enjoyed even a moment with some other man.

The next few days were unbearable. He spent his time waiting for Elena to arrive, and when she came to his house, he would

116

take her with a hurry he had believed gone forever. When she was absent he would drink, he would sit at the Yacht Club, he would go for a drive, he would pass her hotel, he would circle the town in order to pass her hotel again. When I visited him for the first time since the party, he was pent with energy. In an hour he told me one story after another, acting all the parts and creating person after person by no more than a move of his hands. I had put off seeing him. I had been slow after all to tell what happened with Lulu, afraid it might hurt our friendship, but he shook with laughter when I confessed the fact, congratulated me, gasped, 'I knew it would happen. By God, I knew it would happen.'

'But how?'

'Oh, you know. I set something off in her. I had the idea, I just had it that now she was ready for a rough-and-ready with a gentleman sword.'

'A gentleman sword? Why I have a gutter psychology,' I said. But I was pleased. 'Tell me,' I added casually, 'what is Lulu like?'

Unable to sit still, he sprang to his feet and paced about. 'Oh, no! Oh, no! You don't think I'm a Collie Munshin, do you? Discover her for yourself.' And then he did the unexpected thing of slapping me powerfully on the back. 'How we're to be pitied,' he cried theatrically.

At the end of a week, just when he was thinking his jealousy was wrong, or to describe it right, just at that time when his jealousy had begun to ebb and he kept it alive for the pleasure of watching the pain, believing he could end it on notice, Eitel learned that Elena had been unfaithful to him.

She came into his bungalow quietly, she kissed him absent-mindedly, she was sweet and a little distant. 'I met an old friend of mine today,' she said after a while, 'somebody who knows you, too.' When he did not answer, his heart beginning to pound, Elena said, 'It was Marion Faye.'

'Marion Faye. How do you know him?'

'Oh, I knew him years ago.'

'He's an old friend of yours?' Until now, Eitel had managed to hide his jealousy, but the effort was going to be too much. 'Tell me,' he said, 'were you shopping for prices?'

Her eyes were wary. 'What are you talking about?'

'Marion Faye is a pimp.'

'I didn't know that. Honest I didn't.' Elena's face became expressionless. 'Oh, my God. He's just an old boy friend.'

'And now he's a new boy friend?'

'No.'

'You just talked to him?'

'Well, a little more than that.'

'You mean a lot more than that?'

'Yes.'

Eitel felt gleeful. If his knees were numb, his tongue was sharp. 'Obviously, I haven't been enough for you.'

'How you talk.'

'Still, you had something left in reserve.'

'No. I wouldn't say that.'

'Just threw a party for Auld Lang Syne?'

'You're enjoying this,' Elena said, 'you're making fun of me.'

'Forgive me for hurting you.' He restrained a desire to clap his hand to his forehead. 'Elena!' he exclaimed, 'why did you do it?'

Her face took on defiance. 'I felt like it. I was curious.'

'You're always curious, aren't you?'

'I wanted to see . . .' she stopped.

'I know. You don't have to tell me. I'm an expert on female psychology.'

'You must be an expert on everything,' Elena said. She stopped and began again. 'I didn't know, and I wanted to find out if . . .'

'If this blossoming of the flesh was something you could cultivate only with me, or whether any old lad would do. Is that it?' From far away, Eitel was offended by the way he was speaking.

'Something like that.'

'Something like that! I'll kill you,' he roared hopelessly.

'I had to find out,' Elena muttered.

'What did you find out?'

'That's what I wanted to tell you. I felt like a statue with him.'

'Only you didn't act like a statue with him.'

'Well . . . I thought of you all the time.'

'You're a pig,' he said to her.

'I'll go if you want me to go,' she said stiffly.

'Stay here!'

'I think we'd better quit now, you and me,' Elena said. 'I'll pay you for my hotel room . . . I'll owe it to you.'

'And where will you get the money? From Faye?'

'Well, I didn't think of asking him,' she said, 'but now that you mention it . . .'

To his surprise, Eitel began to shake her. Elena started to cry and he released her and walked away. His body ached.

'You don't care about me,' she said. 'You don't really care. Just your pride is hurt.'

He tried to calm himself. 'Elena, why did you do it?'

'You think I'm stupid. Well, maybe I am stupid. There's nothing interesting I can tell you. I'm just a game for you.' Her weeping increased. 'You're too intelligent for me. All right.'

'What has this got to do with it? I think you're smart. I've told you.'

Again she was defiant. Her little heart-shaped face tried to show indifference. 'When a woman's unfaithful, she's more attractive to a man.'

'Stop reciting your lessons,' Eitel shouted. In a kind of frenzy, he caught her to him. 'You idiot!'

'It's true. It is true. It's not lessons. I know.' The pain in her face was momentarily real to him. She was right. If her flesh were tainted, she had never seemed more pure to him, nor ever so attractive. 'You idiot,' he repeated, 'don't you understand? I think I love you.' From the paralysed centre of his mind came the thought, 'You're in the soup now, friend.'

'You don't love me,' she said.

'I love you,' he amended.

Elena began to weep again. 'I worship you,' she sobbed. 'Nobody ever treated me the way you do.' She was kissing his hands. 'I love you more than I ever loved anyone,' she said with final abandon.

So their affair really began, and Elena consented to live with him.

11

In the first weeks of living together, Elena's eyes never left Eitel's face; her mood was the clue to his temper; if she was gay it meant he was happy; if Eitel was moody, it left her morose. No one else existed for her. I do not like to put things so strongly, but I believe it is the truth.

From what Eitel had been able to learn of Elena's life – he was always vague about the details – he found out that her parents owned a candy store in the centre of the capital, and their marriage had been miserable, her father an ex-jockey with a broken leg, a vain little man, a bully; the mother a petty shrew, a calculator, another bully. She had coddled Elena and scolded her, made much of and ignored her, given her ambitions and chased them away. The father, cheated of his horses, ridden with five children, had disliked her – she was the youngest and she had come much too late. There were brothers and sister, uncles and aunts, cousins, grandparents, family parties where they all got together and fist fights started. The father was good-looking, he was a dandy, he could not be alone with a woman without trying to make love to her, but he was also moral, he told others how to live. Her mother was a flirt, she was greedy, she was jealous; she was sick that life had left her in a candy store.

'You see, she was so funny to me,' Elena would tell him, 'she would take me when I was a kid and say, "If you don't do nothing else, get off this goddamn street." But then five minutes later, she'd slap me so hard I'd almost fall down. And sometimes when I wouldn't do what they said, they would tell me that I wasn't really their daughter, but that they had bought me from somebody, and they were going to send me back. Oh, it was bad, Charley.' As a child, Elena would cry silently while the mother and father yelled insults at one another. Her childhood had been spent listening to their jealous quarrels.

Elena had had the courage to leave home before she was twenty, and she had moved into a furnished room, and from there, through the friends she had, girls who worked at Supreme, young unemployed actors, ageing college boys who went to night school, Elena had learned to go bohemian, that was the word she used. So she had taken night courses, and studied dancing and worked as a model in art schools and as a hatcheck girl in restaurants with coloured plastic tables and imitation wood-panelled walls. Then had come Collie, and a furnished apartment near the studio.

Eitel would grow tender when he would think of her life. She had opened his sympathy in a way nobody had for years. She had come out of nothing, and with such pain, such waste, such backward looks. Even now, though she had not seen her family ten times in the last six years, she was always thinking about them. She had an aunt who sent her all the news. That was the only tie, and Elena always answered with long letters, eager to hear that this relative was married, that cousin was sick, her brother was trying to get on the police force, her sister was studying to be a nurse; Elena told him these items about people he would never see. She could not go back to her family – that was the short of it. They would take her, but she did not want to pay the price. The last time she had visited her parents, they had found nothing to say to one another and had sat down to dinner. In the middle of the meal her parents had started to yell at her for the way she lived and Elena fled the house.

Now, she was Eitel's responsibility, without family and without friends. Collie had taken care to wean her from everybody she knew, and for that matter Elena made friends poorly. If she could chat easily with Eitel, often going on like a child from one subject to the next, she was stiff in company the few times they went out. But Eitel hardly cared these days what people were saying about him, and they were not invited out that much. Three days after Elena moved in, the gossip column of the weekly sheet in the resort had an item:

What's this we hear about Red-tainted Charley Eitel doing a boudoir Pygmalion with the former protégée of a certain extra-but-big producer???

Whether it was coincidence or not, he was asked about this time not to come to the Yacht Club any more, and I could measure the meaning of that by the way Lulu would go into a fury every time I visited them. Eitel only laughed when I told him. 'Deep-down, Lulu's admiring you,' he said with a grin. 'Tell her she's welcome to come over.'

That was the night he told me his theory, and although I do not want to go into theory, maybe it is a part of character. I could write it today as he said it, and I think in all modesty I could even add a complexity or two, but this is partly a novel of how I felt at the time, and so I paraphrase as I heard it then, for it would take too long the other way. Eitel made references to famous people and famous books I never heard about until that evening although I have gotten around to reading them since, but the core of Eitel's theory was that people had a buried nature – 'the noble savage' he called it – which was changed and whipped and trained by everything in life until it was almost dead. Yet if people were lucky and if they were brave, sometimes they would find a mate with the same buried nature and that could make them happy and strong. At least relatively so. There were so many things in the way, and if everybody had a buried nature, well everybody also had a snob, and the snob was usually stronger. The snob could be a tyrant to buried nature.

Meanwhile, the days passed quietly, and the nights followed one another with the lamp on the bed table throwing a golden light. Eitel was making the trip he had begun so many times and quit as often and was now making again. For he thought that Elena was soft, she was tender, she was proud when they made love, and she was more real to him as a woman who had come from a fantasy than as a girl with a history. The act was now quiet to them, it was tender – that was the emotion he felt over and over – their first nights together which he had thought so extraordinary seemed like no more than a good hour in a gymnasium compared to what they had now. And Eitel felt changes in his body race beyond the changes in his mind, as though all those nerves and organs which he had tired almost to death were coming back to life, carrying his mind in their path, as if Elena were not only his woman but his balm. He had the hope that he would keep this knowledge of her, that the old snob would not come back to torture him with her little faults, her ignorance, her inability to be anything but his mate. He would stay with her in his house, he would refresh himself, he would do the work which had to be done, and then he could go out to fight.

Eitel loved these weeks. He felt as if he were in the good days of convalescence when appetite comes back and each day one is stronger. He would spend hours at a time on the patio of their bungalow, thinking, daydreaming, storing strength. And at night, full of the warmth of the sun, they would lie in bed, delighted with each other, caught each time with surprise at how they had forgotten how nice it was, every moment seeming more perfect than the one before. 'Poor memory is so indispensable to passionate lovers,' Eitel would think with a smile.

He felt at times that he lived in an opium dream, for nothing was very real to him except to wait for night, when easily led by each new wish, waiting for the pleasure itself, they would come together, they would explore a little further, he would come back with more. Over and over he would remind himself that nothing lasted forever, and the tenderness he enjoyed so much might not be equally attractive to her – their first few nights together had been, after all, quite a different kind of thing – but Elena had a spectrum of fancies as complex as his own, and so he had the faith these days that they would continue to change together.

They had their quarrels, of course, they had their troubles, but they enjoyed them. Elena had insisted that he let his cleaning woman go because she could do the housework. Pleased by her offer, knowing he should save money, Eitel had agreed. Only Elena was a poor housekeeper, and the messiness of the house irritated him. Their fights followed a predictable routine – making breakfast could end in a crisis – but for Eitel these fights were new, they were fun; in the past, arguments with his women had ended in chilly silence, and so he could enjoy these quarrels. He would criticize Elena for something, and she would lose her temper. She hated to be criticized.

'You're tired of me,' she would say, 'you don't love me.'

'You don't love me,' he would tell her. 'The moment I hint you're not perfect, you could take a butcher knife to me.'

'I know. You think I'm not good enough for you. Remember

that thing in the papers? You tell me I don't love you because you don't love me. It's all right. I'll leave.' And she would make a move to the door.

'For God's sake, come back,' he would command her, and five minutes later the scene would be forgotten. He understood. He knew that in back of all this, she did not believe in her happiness, she waited for it to end at a sudden blow, and judged the danger not by the quarrel but by the way he made up the quarrel. It was exhausting to him at times, it was annoying, he sometimes felt as if he had asked a subtle animal to share his house. Her concern for what he thought was so intense that he knew nothing to measure it by.

They had only one jealous quarrel, and it was Eitel who started it. In a bar, they ran into Faye, and he sat at their table, he was pleasant to Elena, and as they were leaving she invited him to come over to their house. Eitel was fairly certain she was indifferent to Faye, but when they were home he accused her of wanting Marion, feeling all the while he talked that it was not true, that with her odd capacity to love, infidelities did not remain with her, not even the picture of them. Such pictures were left for Eitel, and he guarded them like a curator. If he had only one real treasure of his own, there were all the ones he had borrowed from Munshin. So Eitel forced himself to be hurt with the sense that to lose his jealousy was to lose his knowledge of how she could hurt him, blessed woman who could cause him pain after so many dozen who caused him nothing.

It was not for this alone he loved the situation. He saw it now that he had one true love – those films which had flowered in his mind and never been made. In betraying that love he had betrayed himself. Which led into another theory. The artist was always divided between his desire for power in the world and his desire for power over his work. With this girl it was impossible to thrive in the world except by his art, and for these weeks, these domestic weeks when all went well and the act of sitting beside her in the sun could give him a sense of strength and the confidence of liking himself, he would feel indifference to that world he had found so hard to leave. To quit it by the bottom – that was nice, it gave a feeling there was fruit to life. And he was warmed by the knowledge that he was good for Elena, that for the first time in was-it-forever? somebody improved by knowing him, someone grew, he did not spoil all he touched. So he could see their affair hopefully. He would teach her all the small things, that was nothing. What was more important, she understood the rest. Eitel could see her becoming one day the wise mistress of his home, confident in herself and what she could give to him. So, at the end of fantasy, was his return to the world after all.

He was always making references to the future, he would talk of what they would be doing together a year from now, two years from now. As if a slave to his tongue, she would listen helplessly while he wrapped the net around them. 'Let's go to Europe sometime, Elena,' he would say. 'You'd love Europe.' She would nod. 'You know when the picture is finished,' he would go on, 'then maybe . . .'

'Maybe what?'

'I don't offer you anything now, do I?'

She would be upset. 'I don't think about it. Why do you?'

'Because you're a woman. You have to think about it.' He would be furious suddenly. 'I know all these people, sitting around, waiting for us to break up.'

'They're squares. I don't think about them.' Somewhere she had picked up the word, and it served for her shield. When he was jealous he was being square; when she was nothing she was at least not square. 'If I left you because you wouldn't marry me,' she said quietly, 'it would mean I didn't really love you.'

He adored her for that. She did possess dignity. If he could make his film, he would do well by her. No matter what, he would treat her well. He promised that to himself. All this while, ideas formed for that movie with which he had teased himself so many years, and for the script which he had begun several times in the last months. There were nights when he would lie awake in the excitement of creating whole passages of dialogue, whole scenes, and he would hear Elena murmur in her sleep as he turned on the lamp and scribbled still another item into the notebook he kept on the bed table. The notebook was filling quickly now, and he had the hope that finally he was ready, he could succeed. With the pride that other people might feel for their children, Eitel was in love with his creation, impatient for all the months he had to work before he had a script, and then money, and then his production.

One night his feeling for the picture came to such a point that he sat down and wrote an outline, pressing into it by the choice of his language all the enthusiasm he could no longer contain. And some of his doubts. He showed it to me the next time I came over to visit.

I will try to sketch the tale of a modern saint. A man who has risen in the world by profiting on the troubles of others. He will have a famous television programme where people are selected to tell their problems and he will give them the advice an audience wishes to hear. Through the seasons my hero will market sentiment and climb the heights of his own career while the anonymous ones, the faces which visit his programme, stammer their laments and disasters about the parents who are incurably ill and the children who run away, the cripples who are dying for love and the lovers who spurn the cripples, and always there, and never named, will be the sensual envy of jealousy, the jealousy of the desperate. Jealousy for the missing husband, the lecherous wife, the fast sister, the weak brother. All of them, and my hero gives them advice on his enormous programme and converts their suffering to theatrical material.

I will have to make it clear that this is a fairy tale. For we will come to the moment when my hero cannot bear to listen to these stories any more. Rich through the suffering of others, that suffering swallows him. There is no more than a little door opened to his heart but through that door floods the gulf of the world's pain. My hero tries to give genuine advice to his supplicants, and thereby destroys the interest of his programme. So, brouhaha, pressure from the front office, storms and alarums and excursions until the *explosion* and the programme is gone. Only the smoke.

Then my hero goes down to the bottom of the world and he wanders through the slums and the soup kitchens and the dreary cheap saloons, all the black shadow and grey light of the city where he has been king, trying to bring comfort to the people he sees and so saying the wrong comfort for he has taught dishonesty and they must turn on the honest man, until in the anger of his chain of defeats he turns on them, he destroys himself with some pathetic violence, his sainthood remembered only by the despairing round of his sins.

If I work it well enough there's a beauty beyond the picture, the beauty of a man who opens himself to an ocean of pity and there is drowned. Scathe the world with this mirror of itself, the hypocritical world, the brutal world. Gone is the idea that the evils of life exist so that man may destroy them.

My favourable comment: If I do it well enough, the hero can be truly beautiful, and the picture a masterpiece.

My adverse comment: One doesn't usually make a masterpiece by beginning with that idea. Am I just playing with the enthusiastic emotions of the night?

C.F.E.

I gave it back to him and told him I thought I saw what he meant, and he nodded and said, 'Of course in two pages it's all a little ridiculous, but I do have a *vision* of it.' He laughed at the word. 'Elena thinks it's beautiful, but she's prejudiced.'

'Don't joke about it,' Elena said from across the room.

The devil in Eitel pushed him a little further. 'Do you know, Sergius,' he said with one of his ambiguous smiles, 'Elena thinks I have you in mind as the model for this improbable hero of mine.'

'Now, keep quiet,' Elena said, not looking in my direction.

'Listen, Charles Francis,' I said, pretending to be indignant, 'I'd pose for a weight-lifter's magazine before I'd model for your hero. What a future for me!'

We all laughed, and I kept my eye on Elena, beginning to think for the first time that Eitel might have more of a woman on his hands than he would always be ready to realize. Though we had never made much about it, Elena and I liked each other, we had things in common – my first girl friend had been a Greek and her father had owned a fly-specked hash-house. So before two minutes went by, I was not surprised that Elena's eyes met mine. We laughed in private, just the two of us, while Eitel looked puzzled. I think that was the moment Elena and I made an instinctive agreement that we would be friendly about the little thing we felt and never go near one another, at least not so long as her life was running parallel to Eitel.

'Let's go over to that nice little bar,' Elena said to him.

They had taken the habit of going to a little French bar a few doors from their house, and I would often find them there. It was a new place, and the only entertainment was accordion music. The musician was not very good, and yet I used to think that the melody of the accordion wound itself into their affair, its

127

breathy notes leaving the whisper of the *bal musette*: 'Life is sad, life is gay, life is gay because life is sad,' soft as the music of an old song, and I believe it turned Eitel back on those movies he made when he was young. He was getting ready to begin work again. For a change, he was busy, he wrote letters to his business manager, calculated the money he still had left, and with a kind of pleasure at the modesty in which they lived, announced to Elena that possibly they would have enough for three more months. Afterward, he could sell his car and sell the mortgage on the bungalow. That much was left from fifteen years. Yet it did not leave him depressed.

One night in his house with the accordion washing through the desert air, he showed for Elena and himself, on his own projector, a print in sixteen millimetre of one of his early films. It was very powerful, he felt; a picture about jobless people with the ideas of a young man and the enthusiasm of twenty years ago, but still it was so good that he knew why he had not looked at it in a long time, and while the camera and the actors went their short course, he watched with an aching heart, excited with the artist's self-love for what he had done, suffering from the dull fear that he could never do it again, and yet caught by the sudden enthusiasm that he could do more, that he could do everything. And all the while he wondered at the young man who had made such a film. 'I didn't know a thing when I made those pictures,' he said to Elena, 'and yet somehow I knew more. I wonder where it's hiding in me.' Elena kissed him when the movie was done. 'I love you,' she said. 'You'll do a wonderful strong movie like this again.' And Eitel, frightened beyond fright, knew his vacation was over, and he must begin again that script, that skeleton of an art work he had until now been unable to create.

12

I had never known a girl like Lulu, nor had I ever been in such a romance. Of course I had had my share of other girls – one doesn't go through the Air Force without learning something about women – but I had always been a poor detective and ladies were way ahead of me.

Yet I think Lulu would have had her surprises for any man. I couldn't tell from one hour to the next if we were in love or about to break up, whether we would make love or fight, do both or do nothing at all. The first time I saw her again, she was with friends and never let me be alone with her; the next day she came to visit my house and not only made it easy, but told me she was in love. Naturally, I told her the same. It would have been hard not to, and for sure I was in love if love is the time to do nothing else. Before she left, we had a quarrel; we would never see each other again. A half hour later she telephoned from the Yacht Club and burst into tears. We loved each other after all.

It was out of control, beyond a doubt. I was able to discover emotions I never knew I owned, and I must have enjoyed it as much as Lulu. So I thought by virtue of the things we did I would put my mark on her forever. What she may have intended as a little dance was a track and field event to me, and I would snap the tape with burning lungs, knotted muscles, and mind set on the need to break a record. It was the only way I could catch her and for three minutes keep her. Like a squad of worn-out infantrymen who are fixed for the night in a museum, my pleasure was to slash tapestries, poke my fingers through nude paintings, and drop marble busts on the floor. Then I could feel her as something I had conquered, could listen to her wounded breathing, and believe that no matter how she acted other times, these moments were Lulu, as if her flesh murmured words more real than her lips. To the pride of having so beautiful a girl was added the bigger pride of knowing that I took her with the cheers of millions behind me. Poor millions with their low roar! They would never have what I had now. They could shiver outside, make a shrine in their office desk or on the shelf of their olive-drab lockers, they could look at the pin-up picture of Lulu Meyers. I knew I was good when I carried a million men on my shoulder.

But if I caught her in bed, I caught her nowhere else. There were days when Lulu told me to leave her alone, there were other days when she would not let me quit her for a minute, but the common denominator was that I had to follow every impulse. I could go over at noon to her suite in the Yacht Club after a summons by phone; she would be decided that we go horseback riding in the desert. I would arrive to find her still in bed. Breakfast had not yet come, would I have coffee with her? The moment room service left a tray, Lulu told me she wanted a Stinger.

'I don't know how to make Stingers,' I would answer.

'Oh, sweetie, everybody knows how to make a Stinger. There's brandy, crème de menthe. What did you do in the Air Force, milk a cow?'

'Lulu, are we going horseback riding?'

'Yes, we're going horseback riding.' She would hold up a mirror, study her face with the stare of a beauty-parlour oper-ator, and stick out her tongue at the reflection. 'Do I look good without make-up?' she would ask in a professional tone which allowed no nonsense.

'You look very good.'

'My mouth's a little too thin.'

'It wasn't last night,' I would say.

'Oh, you. A corpse could satisfy you.' But she would hug me matter-of-factly. 'I love you, darling,' she would say.

'Let's go horseback riding.'

'Do you know, Sergius, you're neurotic.'

'I'm neurotic. I can't stand to waste a day.'

'Well, I don't feel like getting on a horse,' Lulu would decide.

'I knew you wouldn't. I didn't want to either.'

'Then why did you wear jodhpurs?'

'Because if I didn't wear them, you would want to go.'

'Oh, I'm not like that.' Sitting in bed, she would hug herself, her beautiful face arched above her cool throat. 'Honest, I'm not.'

The phone would ring. It would be a call from New York. 'No. I'm not marrying Teddy Pope,' she would say to a columnist. 'Of course, he's a son of a bitch. Yes, say we're good friends and that's all. Goodbye, sweetie.' She would hang up, she would groan. 'That stupid press agent I've got. If you can't handle a gossip columnist what kind of press agent are you?'

'Why don't you let him try?'

'He's beyond hunger.'

So it would go. About the time I was past being exasperated she would begin to dress. The coffee was cold she would tell me and call room service for more. I would lose my temper. I was definitely leaving I would tell her. She would run after me and catch me at the door. She knew I was willing to be caught. 'I'm a bitch, I tell you,' she would say. 'I was trying to get you mad.'

'You never came near.'

'You'll end up hating me. You will. Nobody likes me who really knows me. Even I don't like myself.'

'You love yourself.'

She would grin delightfully. 'It's not the same thing, Sergius, let's go horseback riding.'

Finally, we would go. She was always dawdling or at a gallop. One time we were riding around an abandoned wooden fence and she told me to jump it. I told her I wouldn't because I was a bad jumper. It was an honest estimate. I had been riding for a month.

'The lousiest stunt man will fall on his ass for fifty bucks,' she said, 'but you won't try anything.'

Actually, I wanted to jump. I had the anticipation of falling and Lulu nursing me. That was a part of our affair which had never been tried. When I took the jump, and I thought it was a good one, I turned around for her applause and saw her trotting away in the opposite direction. For all I knew she hadn't even looked. After I caught up to her, she turned on me. 'You're a baby. Only a second-rater would take a stupid dare like that.'

We rode back without a word. When we reached the Yacht Club, she went into her cabaña, came out in a bathing suit, and talked to everybody but me. The only time our eyes met, she held out her glass as she had done the night of the party, and said, 'Sugar, get me a small Martin.'

Her caution when our affair began was often a chore. She used to come to my house on foot, or she would admit me to her room only after dark. 'They'll crucify me when they find out,' she would complain, 'look at Eitel,' that way comparing me to Elena. About his affair she was furious. 'Eitel never had any taste,' she would say. 'Any tramp who tells him he's terrific can always sell him a ticket to her favourite charity.' And once when we met them on the street, she was hardly easy on Elena. 'I bet she has dirty underwear,' Lulu said. 'You watch. She's going to be as fat as a bull.' When I argued that I liked Elena, Lulu became sullen. 'Oh, sure, she's the underdog,' Lulu snapped. Yet, a few hours later, she said to me, 'You know, Sugar, maybe it would have been better if I had to struggle. Maybe my character would be better.' Her finger to her chin, she asked, 'Am I really a bore?'

'Only when you're vertical . . . says the Irish in me.'

'You'll pay for that.' And she chased me around with a pillow. When she had finished pounding me, she made me lie down beside her. 'I'm awful, but Strongarm O'Shaugnessy, I want to be good. It was terrible with Eitel. He would laugh at me and some of his friends were intellectually very overbearing.' She giggled. 'When I was with Eitel, I used to study to be an intellectual.'

If she had been decided to keep our affair a secret, she changed her mind one day by sitting on my lap at the Yacht Club pool. 'You ought to try Sugar some time,' she said to several of her woman friends, 'he's not bad at all.' Which depressed me. Because I knew if I was really good, she wouldn't give her friends a clue. For a few days she couldn't walk in public without my arm around her. Pictures were taken of us by night-club photographers. I got up one morning to find Lulu by my bed, a gossip column in her hand. 'Look at it. How awful!' she said to me. I read the following:

132

Atom Bomb Lulu Meyers and the potential next Mr Meyers, ex-Marine Corps Captain Silgius McShonessy, scion of an Eastern-or-is-it-Midwestern fortune, are setting off those Geiger counters in Desert D'Or.

I don't know if I was more pleased or more horrified. 'Don't they ever get a name right?' I blustered. Lulu began to tickle me. 'You know that's not bad. They could have been a lot nastier,' she said. 'Atom Bomb Lulu Meyers. Do you think people really think of me that way?'

'Of course they don't. You know your press agent wrote it.'

'I don't care. It's still interesting.' Like so many name-people in Desert D'Or, it didn't matter to Lulu that the news came from her. Seeing the printed lines made an alchemy; I know our affair was more real to her. 'Geiger counters,' Lulu said thoughtfully. 'that's a smart line, publicity-wise. Oh, he's a good press agent. I'm going to call him in a day or two.'

Now that our romance was publicly big, or better, torrid, Lulu started to confuse people again. 'They make Sugar sound so good in the newspapers,' she said one night to some people in a bar, 'that I'll really try him. I really will, Sugar.' And she gave me a sisterly kiss. Older sister.

We soon found something new to fight about. I discovered that to make love to Lulu was to make myself a scratch-pad to the telephone. It was always ringing, and no moment was long enough to keep her from answering. Her delight was to pass the first few rings. 'Don't be so nervous, Sugar,' she would say, 'let the switchboard suffer,' but before the phone had screamed five times, she would pick it up. Almost always, it was business. She would be talking to Herman Teppis, or Munshin who was back in the capital, or a writer, or her director for the next picture, or an old boy friend, or once her hairdresser – Lulu was interested in a hair-do she had seen. The conversation could not go on for two minutes before she was teasing me again; to make love and talk business was a double-feature to her.

'Of course I'm being a good girl, Mr Teppis,' she would say, giving me the wink. 'How can you think these things of me?' As the end in virtuosity, she succeeded one time in weeping through a phone call with Teppis while rendering a passage with me.

I would try to get her to visit my place but she had grown an aversion. 'It depresses me, Sugar, it's in such bland taste.' For a while everything would be bland. Her own place was now spoiled by that word, and one day she told the management to have her room suite redecorated. Between morning and evening its beige walls were painted to a special blue, which Lulu claimed was her best colour. Now she lay with her gold head on pale-blue linen, ordering pink roses and red roses from the telephone; the florist at the Yacht Club promised to arrange them himself. She would buy a dress and give it to her maid before she had even worn it, she would complain she had not a thing to wear. Her new convertible she traded in one afternoon for the same model in another colour, and yet the exchange cost her close to a thousand dollars. When I reminded her that she had to drive the new car slowly until it accumulated the early mileage, she hired a chauffeur to trundle it through the desert and spare her the bother. Her first phone bill from the Yacht Club was five hundred dollars.

Yet when it came to making money she was also a talent. While I knew her, negotiations were on for a three-picture contract. She would phone her lawyers, they would call her agent, the agent would speak to Teppis, Teppis would speak to her. She asked a big price and got more than three-quarters of it. 'I can't stand my father,' she explained to me, 'but he's a gambler at business. He's wonderful that way.' It came out that when she was thirteen and going to a school for professional children in the capital, Magnum Pictures wanted to sign her to a seven-year contract. 'I'd be making a stinking seven hundred and fifty a week now like all those poor exploited schnooks, but daddy wouldn't let me. "Free-lance," he said, he talks that way, "this country was built on free-lance." He's just a chiropodist with holdings in real estate, but he knew what to do for me.' Her toes nibbled at the telephone cord. 'I've noticed that about men. There's a kind of man who never can make money for himself. Only for others. That's my father.'

Of her father and mother, Lulu's opinion changed by the clock. One round it would be her father who was marvellous. 'What a bitch my mother is. She just squeezed all the manhood out of him. Poor daddy.' Her mother had ruined her life, Lulu explained. 'I never wanted to be an actress. She made me one. It's her ambition. She's just an . . . octopus.' Several phone calls later, Lulu would be chatting with her mother. 'Yes, I think it gives me hives,' she would say of some food, 'glycerine, will that do, mommie? . . . He's what? . . . He's acting up again . . . Well, you tell him to leave you alone. I wouldn't put up with it if I were you. I would have divorced him long ago. I certainly would . . .

'I don't know what I'd do without her,' Lulu would say on hanging up the phone, 'men are terrible,' and she would have nothing to do with me for the next half hour.

It took me longer than it need have taken to realize that the heart of her pleasure was to show herself. She hated holding something in. If Lulu felt like burping, she would burp; if it came up that she wanted to put cold cream on her face, she would do it while entertaining half a dozen people. So it went with her acting. She could say to a stranger that she was going to be the greatest actress in the world. Once, talking to a stage director, she was close to tears because the studio never gave her a part in a serious picture. 'They ruin me,' she complained. 'People don't want glamour, they want acting. I'd take the smallest role if it was something I could get my teeth into.' Still, she quarrelled for three days running, and how many hours on the telephone I could never guess, because Munshin who was producing her next picture would not enlarge her part. Publicity, she announced, was idiotic, but with her instinct for what was good to an adolescent, she did better than co-operate with photographers. The best ideas always came from Lulu. One sortie when she was photographed sipping a soda she shaped the second straw into a heart, and the picture as it was printed in the newspapers showed Lulu peeping through the heart, coy and cool. On the few times I would be allowed to spend the night with her, I would wake up to see Lulu writing an idea for publicity in the notebook she kept on her bed table, and I had a picture of her marriage to Eitel, each of them with his own notebook and own bed table. With pleasure, she would expound the subtleties of being well photographed. I learned that the core of her dislike for Teddy Pope was that each of them photographed best from the left side of the face, and when they played

135

a scene together Teddy was as quick as Lulu not to expose his bad side to the camera. 'I hate to play with queers,' she complained. 'They're too smart. I thought I had mumps when I saw myself. Boy, I threw a scene.' Lulu acted it for my private ear. 'You've ruined me, Mr Teppis,' she shrieked. 'There's no chivalry left.'

For odd hours, during those interludes she called at her caprice, things had come around a bit. To my idea of an interlude which must have left her exhausted, she coached me by degrees to something different. Which was all right with me. Lulu's taste was for games, and if she lay like a cinder under the speed of my sprints, her spirits improved with a play. I was sure no two people ever had done such things nor even thought of them. We were great lovers, I felt in my pride; I had pity for the hordes who could know none of this. Yes, Lulu was sweet. She would never allow comparison. This was the best. I was superb. She was superb. We were beyond all. Unlike Eitel who now could not bear to hear a word of Elena's old lovers, I was charitable to all of Lulu's. Why should I not be? She had sworn they were poor sticks to her Sugar. I was even so charitable that I argued in Eitel's defence. Lulu had marked him low as a lover, and in a twist of friendship my heart beat with spite. I stopped that quickly enough, I had an occasional idea by now of when Lulu was lying, and I wanted to set Eitel at my feet, second to the champion. It pleased me in my big affair that I had such a feel for the ring.

We played our games. I was the photographer and she was the model; she was the movie star and I was the bellhop; she did the queen, I the slave. We even met even to even. The game she loved was to play the bobby-soxer who sat with a date in the living room and was finally convinced, always for the first time naturally enough. She was never so happy as when we acted at theatre and did the mime on clouds of myth. I was just young enough to want nothing but to be alone with her. It was not even possible to be tired. Each time she gave the signal, and I could never know, not five minutes in advance, when it would happen, my appetite was sharp, dressed by the sting of what I suffered in public.

To eat a meal with her in a restaurant became the new torture.

It didn't matter with what friends she found herself nor with what enemies, her attention would go, her eye would flee. It always seemed to her as if the conversation at another table was more interesting than what she heard at her own. She had the worry that she was missing a word of gossip, a tip, a role in a picture, a financial transaction, a . . . it did not matter; something was happening somewhere else, something of importance, something she could not afford to miss. Therefore, eating with her was like sleeping with her; if one was cut by the telephone, the other was rubbed by her itch to visit from table to table, sometimes dragging me, sometimes parking me, until I had to wonder what mathematical possibility there was for Lulu to eat a meal in sequence since she was always having a bit of soup here and a piece of pastry there, joining me for breast of squab, and taking off to greet new arrivals whose crabmeat cocktail she nibbled on. There was no end, no beginning, no surety that one would even see her during a meal. I remember a dinner when we went out with Dorothea O'Faye and Martin Pelley. They had just been married and Lulu treasured them. Dorothea was an old friend, a dear friend, Lulu promised me, and before ten minutes she was gone. When Lulu finally came back, she perched on my lap and said in a whisper the others could hear, 'Sugar, I tried and I couldn't make doo-doo. Isn't that awful? What should I eat?'

Five minutes later she outmanoeuvred Pelley to pick up the check.

13

In time, I came to meet a lot of Lulu's friends. The one who counted the most was Dorothea O'Faye Pelley, and my nights at The Hangover began again. Some few years ago when Dorothea had the gossip column, Lulu was one of her favourites, and the friendship remained the same. Of all the people Lulu saw, and they were numerous enough, it was only with Dorothea that I ever knew her to relax. On the hours we spent visiting, Lulu would put herself on a hassock near Dorothea's feet and listen to what was said, her face set between her hands. Since Lulu was now more of a name than Dorothea, it must have been startling for any new visitor to find her set in place between the real-estate operator and the drunk O'Faye, but I know if Lulu had tried to match Dorothea, they could hardly remain friends.

For me, Dorothea's charm had turned, and the better I came to know her the less I was impressed by her. I had come to realize it was court procedure for everybody to expose their lives to Dorothea. She liked nothing better than to discuss their problems, and she always gave the answer which fixed her friends at The Hangover. So, for example, Jay-Jay parading his loves:

He had a girl friend I never saw. She was supposed to have saved him from the needle – he had been on mainline, Jay-Jay would explain – and his girl had taken him through the cure, the two locked in a room for a week. He was over it now and he would never go back so long as he had his girl. She was a true diamond.

'Only you don't want to marry her,' Dorothea would say.

'Well, now, that's it, I don't,' Jay-Jay would admit. 'I got to marry her, she's put in five years on me, but I got a wandering eye. I can't think about nothing but cheating on her.'

'With that face she has,' Dorothea would snort, 'I'd cheat on her myself.'

Jay-Jay would laugh as hard as any of the others. 'Oh, I pick them, I can really pick them,' he would say, and then with a seriousness which begged to be thrown on its back, he would add, 'A lot of the time like now, when I think about her, I think I'm really in love, so help me.'

Pelley would cough. Madame's maid to Dorothea, he would say sternly, pompously, 'If a man's really in love he wants to get married,' and Dorothea would chuckle with her heavy laughter. 'How's that other bag you're running around with?' she would ask.

'You mean the one that looked like she was sucking a fig?' Jay-Jay would ask, and shake his head. 'I gave her up before she could wear me down.' Jay-Jay would smile. 'I got another gal now,' he said, 'she's crazy. Sweet little kid with two little girls. Roberta, her name is, Bobby. Her husband and her has broken up and she wants to become a call girl. Man! I could be a call girl before she could.'

'Man, you could,' I thought, but you can't say everything.

This sort of story brought Marion Faye to mind, and Dorothea's pleasure was spoiled. Maybe Jay-Jay wanted to spoil it.

Sooner or later, it would be my turn. Dorothea had come to the conclusion that I was good for Lulu, and so it became one of her projects to better my life. Dorothea always had a job for me – she knew a columnist who would take me on as a leg-man, there was a studio where she could arrange a place as assistant to a very big director, there was a businessman who could groom me for a spot – I only had to say yes. I would try to turn the conversation, I would be flippant, I would be dull. Once, I even threw her a bone. 'It's all right, Dorothea,' I said, 'one of these days I'll go respectable.'

To everybody's surprise, Lulu came to my defence. It was the only time she ever crossed Dorothea. 'Leave him alone, sweetie,' she said. 'Sergius is respectable now. If he gets a job, he'll be a dupe like everybody else.' That ended it for a few days and I was left in peace without a career.

Lulu's dilemmas were dilated at length. She loved to give Dorothea each new bulletin on the progress of Herman Teppis'

139

desire to marry her off to Teddy Pope, and it became one of the jokes at The Hangover. Lulu was always wondering how she could entertain Teddy's friends. 'They'll have to know who I am,' she would say, 'I mean, how will they be able to tell I'm not in drag?'

'Just leave off the make-up, dearie,' the drunk O'Faye would lisp with a lopsided smile.

'Oh, God,' Lulu said to the laughter of the court.

'Oh, God, my eye,' said Dorothea on this night, 'if you don't want to marry Teddy, you better do something. Herman Teppis is one man who really tops me.'

'Why don't you marry Sergius?' Pelley asked, and I knew Dorothea had instructed him.

''Cause he won't have me,' Lulu said, and showed her pretty teeth.

Such talk left Lulu more tense than ever. She was beginning to suggest these days that we ought to get married, and I think she never found me so attractive as when I would turn her down. The thought of marriage left me badly depressed. I could see myself as Mr Meyers, a sort of fancy longshoreman scared of his wife, always busy mixing drinks for Lulu and the guests. I suppose what depressed me most was that I was forced to think about myself and what I wanted, and I was not ready for that, not by far. Once in a while, depending on my mood and my general estimate of my assets, I would think of becoming everything from a high-school coach to a psychoanalyst, and several times I found myself thinking vaguely of a career in the FBI or more easily being a disc jockey with one of those sinuous lines of patter which mean so many things to so many people who stay up late at night. Once in a very great while, with a lack of ambition as cheerful as a liver complaint, I would remember that I wanted to be a writer, but like all my other inspirations, the central urge was not there – the only hint could be that I wanted to find some work I liked.

But talk of marriage was the death of enjoyment for me. Lulu and I had come to the point where we fought more often than not, and the fights had taken on some bitterness. There were times when I was sure we had to break up, and I would look forward with a sort of self-satisfied melancholy to the time when

I would be free. In fact, I felt it would be easy to give her up. That much confidence is banked when a woman wants to get married.

Other times I have to admit she could make me miserable. No sooner would she ask me to marry her, no sooner would I turn her down, than she would tell me how attractive she found other men, especially for those qualities in which I was considered lacking. One man was sharp, another masterful, a third suave – she was always enjoying the theory that to have such an affair would pass the same qualities over to her. At times like that, I would have to admit I was in love with her, for I used to look for her faults, even feel a false relief at each fault I discovered, as if I believed I could thereby reduce her to size.

Of course it didn't work. Preparations on Lulu's new picture were moving and she decided to go to the capital for a few days to sit in on some conferences. Each of us looked forward to the separation. She was always saying she was bored with Desert D'Or, and I felt how nice it would be to remain in my house, read a book for once, relax and see nobody. The desert dust was probably gathering on my camera and tape recorder. I needed to think, I thought slowly in those days. I found myself remembering the pleasures of loneliness, thinking that if loneliness was difficult well then so was love, until I would wish Lulu off to the capital in order to leave me at rest.

Once she was gone, I could not get myself together; the book I read only underlined my restlessness and the days went with nothing done. I was so used to fighting her that I could spend a morning talking to myself about whether or not to take a walk. While she was gone, we were always on the phone. I called her up to tell her I loved her, she called me back half an hour later and we had the same conversation again. So, like old gypsies who make a sign a hundred times a day, we swore we loved each other. A day earlier than she planned, she ran back to Desert D'Or, and we had a royal tourney that night. 'You carry me so far,' she said. 'Sergius, it's just the best.' This she told me many times. By morning she was down and so was I. We had overdone it. Once we were dressed, Lulu told me she could smell herself. 'I have the most awful body odour, Sugar.'

'All I can smell is your perfume.'

'No, you have no sense of smell. I tell you, I know it's there. That happens to people. They suddenly develop terrible smells and they have them for the rest of their lives.'

'Where do you pick up these witches?'

'I know someone it happened to. Sugar, I have to take a bath.'

She bathed, she came out of the bath, she bathed again. She got me to powder her; she had now decided the smell was somewhere in the room. 'Oh, it's awful,' she cried aloud.

For several days she was taking baths all the time. Then she decided she had breast cancer, she ordered me to search for a lump. I told her to see a doctor. Instead, she went to see Dorothea, and came back afraid of something else. 'When I get older, my breasts are going to droop: she said sadly. 'There's no way I can stop it. Will you promise to be careful when you touch them, Sugar?' She burst into tears. What was the matter, I asked. Nothing was the matter. Something must be the matter; I made her tell me. It was disclosed that Lulu had always planned to have an operation to raise her breasts once they began to sag. But, today, she had seen Dorothea's breasts, and Dorothea had had such an operation.

'They're so unattractive,' Lulu said miserably. 'They're square.'

'They aren't.'

'But they are. She showed me. They're square. I feel like it's happened to me.'

'Well, it hasn't . . . yet.'

'You don't know anything. You're just a brute.'

As the starting date to the shooting of her next picture came nearer, was only a few weeks away, her nervousness got worse. One day she declared she was going to take acting lessons. 'I'm going to begin from the very beginning. I'm going to learn how to walk. And to breathe. I've never been properly trained, Sergius, did you know that?'

'You'll never take lessons,' I snapped at her.

'Of course I will. I'm going to be the greatest actress who ever lived. That's what nobody understands.'

I learned later that this was partly the result of bad studio publicity. I felt her pain as she showed me a news photo of herself. She was bruised by the photo. 'Look at Tony Tanner,' she said, 'he looks better than me, and he's just a feature actor. I dislike him intensely.' She was so bitter. 'They ought to shoot the photographer,' she said. 'Haven't they any brains, releasing such a still?' Lulu wanted to call Herman Teppis. 'I'll put it up to him. I'll say, "Mr Teppis, they're ruining my face, and it isn't fair." It isn't. They're plotting against me 'cause they hate me at the studio.'

'When did you meet Tanner?' I asked.

'Oh, he's a nothing. He's going to be with Teddy Pope in my next picture. They're coming out here soon to do publicity with me.'

'You don't look so miserable with his arm around you,' I commented.

'And you're a fool,' Lulu said. 'Why, that's just publicity. I can't stand him. He's an ex-pimp, that's all he is. He and Marion Faye used to go around together, only he's even worse than Marion. I think they're both despicable.'

'Marion isn't that simple,' I said to irritate her.

'Yes, dear Marion. He's a homo like you,' Lulu said. 'Why don't you go see your homo friend again?'

'Just because I don't want to marry you doesn't make me a three-dollar bill,' I said.

'Poor Dorothea,' Lulu said out of nowhere.

It piqued Lulu that I saw so much of Marion Faye. I had taken the habit of visiting him in those early-morning hours after I had been with Lulu and she wanted me to go home. I could never explain to myself what I looked for in Faye. I even wondered about Lulu's interpretation, trying to catch some fear which might prove her correct. If I looked in deep enough I could catch anything – there were some little memories from the orphanage – but I think maybe what I looked for at Faye's was something else entirely. Marion had not changed a bit; in everything he said was contempt for me and Lulu. And it was for this reason, I think, that I went to see him. I have noticed more than once how people in an affair surround themselves with friends who like their affair or dislike it altogether, in order to see outside themselves the faces of their own feelings. For example, Eitel looked for me since I liked Elena and so helped Eitel to like his affair, just as I hunted out Marion to keep me from marrying Lulu for I was always being weakened by her constant attacks, her declarations of helplessness, my sneaking sense of my own helplessness, and perhaps worst of all, the steady hurrah and approval which Dorothea made the court pay to our romance, the outside pressure to love being stronger finally, I decided, than love itself, until I was forced to wonder if people would ever be in love if there weren't the other people to say that love they must, and I was sure that Lulu and I marooned on a desert island would mumble over whose turn it was to catch the fish, and leave love to the people on the ocean liners which passed just out of sight.

I say, therefore, it was probably for that, that I saw Marion so often. Still, we did not talk so very much about Lulu and me. There is probably no passion greater than the philosopher looking for an audience, and Marion seemed decided to make me his audience. I didn't have to be surprised that we ended by Marion talking about himself. Somewhere, he had picked up a line in a book he had read: 'There is no pleasure greater than that obtained from a conquered repugnance,' and as an example, he would talk to me about his sessions with Teddy Pope.

'All right,' he would say, 'take my life with the girls. When I gave Teddy his first smile, I figured I'd hate it and have to work. Then that way I could really make it. Only it didn't turn out just so. You see what I caught is that deep down I'm half queer anyway, so it wasn't repugnant. I was doing the whole thing backward.'

'I saw you once with Pope,' I said.

'Cruelty, yes. That's where I did being homo. You see, cruelty is repugnant to me. When I tell Pope he's disgusting and repulsive, and all he wants is for me to give him the time of day because he's willing to do all the loving, deep down he's nothing but a sweet little flower waiting to be stomped, well at times like that I have to force myself to be cruel, but afterward I feel fine. Almost, that is. I've never made it all the way, not in anything in life.'

'You know,' I said, 'you're just a religious man turned inside out.'

'Yes?' murmured Faye. 'You have a brain like a scrambled egg.'

'No, look,' I said. 'Take your formula and change one word.'

'What word?'

'Listen: "There is no greater pleasure than that obtained from a conquered vice."'

'I have to think about that,' he said, and he was angry. 'What an Irish cop you are,' he said with cold admiration.

Two nights later, he answered me. 'I think I've worked it out,' he said. 'Nobility and vice – they're the same thing. It just depends on the direction you're going. You see, if I ever make it, then I turn around and go the other way. Toward nobility. That's all right. Just so you carry it to the end.'

'And what's in the middle?' I asked.

'Slobs.' He snuffed the ember of marijuana on the edge of his lip, and put the remains back in the jar. 'I hate slobs,' he said. 'They always think what they have to think.'

Self-swindles roiled Faye; in this sense he was absolutely opposed to the human race. Through the course of the nights we spent in talk, I came to know him better, and he grew less of a mystery to me although I never thought I understood him. But at least I got a picture of how he spent his time when I wasn't there, and in those stories he fed me to make a point, I came to have an idea of the kinds of things he would do when I was not there, and from the vague notion of how he spent his afternoons – for he was seldom up before twelve – passing through the larger hotels to take a drink at the bar and drum up assignments for his girls, I saw past the rounds of the gamblers, the oilmen, the actors down for a night, and the politicians from the capital, into some of the smaller corners. He didn't go to bed before dawn, and it was his habit to keep the last two hours of the night for studying odd books, laying new arrangements of his Tarot cards, and thinking about the little things, or so he would put it. For the evening and the night, that layover between the work of afternoon and the solitude of early morning, he took whatever happened, and I learned finally that it was usually something new which happened, so for a night he could be busy with the hysterics of one of his girls, for another be the host to mobsmen or hoods, for a third be away at that business he despised – it was become so routine – of working a new girl in, for the fourth, like the flip of a coin, make his appearance at Dorothea's, for the fifth drive to the capital to hear some new musicians, or as easily drive in the other direction across the state line to one of the gambling cities of the desert. He could visit friends like Eitel, he could drop in on Teddy Pope or the friends of the set, he could even catch a movie or a drink in a bar, but by three o'clock or four, he was home. Out of all this, there are twenty stories I could tell about him, but I pick the one which most applies, I think.

This passed in the not so early morning, shortly after I left his house one night. He was sitting there alone, the deck of the Tarot out, when the telephone rang. He was used to this no matter how it annoyed him; his profession surrounded him with people who thought it was important to talk to him right away, and although he was equally sure that there never was a call which could not wait a week or more, he took the irritation as one of the wastes of his work.

So Faye answered the phone, and was hardly surprised when it was Bobby, Jay-Jay's girl, who had been working for him just ten days.

'Marion, I had to phone you,' she said.

Conversations at four in the morning always began that way. 'Charmed,' Marion said. 'I thought I told you not to call me after three.'

'I had to. Please, Marion.'

He smiled to himself. 'How'd it go?' he asked. When his girls called this late, it usually meant they had been humiliated and wanted to complain. Once in a while, one of his more talented girls would have come across something unusual, and would be anxious to learn what he thought of it, but he could hardly believe, however, that this had happened tonight.

'That's what I mean,' Bobby said, 'it was so extraordinary and unexpected.'

'Then tell me about it.' He was the father of the garter girls and he had listened to children's stories so long that he was ill.

'I can't tell you over the phone.'

No girl ever could, he thought. 'All right, tell me tomorrow.'

'Marion, this is a special favour, I know . . . but could you come over and see me tonight so I can tell you?'

Bobby was something to resent. She had the wheedling

146

watered charm of a small-town beauty and she tried to use it on him. 'Knock off,' he said into the phone.

'Well, can I come see you?'

'Yes, tomorrow.'

'Marion, our mutual acquaintance gave me five hundred dollars.'

'Congratulations.' But he was interested. He could not understand it.

'Will you come see me now?' she asked.

'No.'

'Can I come see you?'

'If you don't take too long.'

'But I can't, Marion. I let the baby sitter go when I got home.'

He had, of course, not forgotten. There were the two babies in the bedroom of that tiny four-room cottage.

'Get the sitter back,' he said patiently into the phone.

'I don't know how I can, Marion.'

'Then leave it until tomorrow.'

There was a pause. He could almost hear Bobby's little brain with its quick calculations. Finally, she gave a girlish sigh. 'All right, Marion, I'll get her somehow.'

'You be over soon,' he said, 'or I might go to sleep,' and he set the phone down.

While he waited, he put on a dressing-gown. The marijuana in his jar was low and he told himself to pick up more tomorrow, debating whether to make a new stick or not. Marijuana gave him no pleasure. He never got a lift from it. The drug made him cold, his temples even felt as if ice had been laid to them. Once in a while it got to be too much for him.

Still, he smoked it. Now and again it placed him in deep mental states. If a thought came up which should be written down – something for example which could seem as clear at night and as mysterious in the morning as 'The three eyes of love' – he would discover that his brain watched the thought, and the thought watched his hand, and his hand the pencil, the pencil the paper, until the paper stared back at him with a hostile grin. 'You're flying, man.' He had tried to go on from marijuana. There had been a period a few months ago when he moved on to mainline, but the results had been impossible.

There was a knock and Bobby came in. It was known that his door was never locked, and this was one of his disciplines. There were enough people he had to be afraid of, things he had done one way or another, and he was full of fear. Many nights he lay awake listening to the desert sounds, the rare animals, the wind, the noise of automobiles, his heart beating from anger at his fear. For punishment he never used the bolt. The thought that he must never lock his door had come on him one night in a sweat-soaked bed, and he revolted at the idea. 'Oh, no,' he said aloud, 'do I have to do *that*?' and in the act of pleading leniency for himself, had made it impossible to lock his door again.

Bobby kissed him on the cheek. It was one of the mannerisms of call girls who had no talent. They loved to act like sorority queens, and he would watch how each new one would pick up the affectations of the others.

'It was a wonderful night, Marion,' Bobby said.

'Sure,' said Marion, 'you made five hundred.'

'Oh, it wasn't that. He was so nice to me. He called it a loan. Do you know, Marion, if I ever hit it,' Bobby promised, 'I'm going to pay him back.' She wandered around the room, looking at him, moving a little restlessly from chair to chair. Bobby was tall and a bit thin for a call girl and she had a wan demure expression which was out-of-date. 'What a wonderful pad you have here,' she said.

He rented the house furnished, and he never felt it had a great deal to do with him. The modern furniture meant as much to his eyes as stones and cactus on the desert flats. 'How'd it go?' he asked. He was not really curious; Marion had collated so much information about everyone in Desert D'Or that a new figure could hardly alter the statistics. He asked out of the onerous duty of the specialist.

'Well, it was wonderful. I was really living,' Bobby said.

This, Marion could doubt. His taste, lately, had been for frigid women, but he had found her less than frigid; the act was a nightmare to her, and what was most disgusting, she didn't even know what she thought about it. There had been a stiff little-girl smile on her mouth. 'Living it high,' Marion said.

'I was sent.'

'Yes,' Marion said. 'Eitel's got lots of technique.'

'It wasn't technique. I think Charley has a crush on me. You don't know how sweet he is.'

'He's a sweet guy,' Marion said.

'It was so funny when he saw the kids. Veila woke up and began to cry, and he held her and rocked her. I could swear there were tears in his eyes.'

'This is before he paid you?'

'Yes.'

'Well, what do you know?' said Marion.

'You're not being nice,' Bobby said. 'You don't understand. I had the blues today. I was thinking that maybe I couldn't make it so well for this kind of work, and Charley Eitel gave me a terrific-type lift. He makes you feel like you're . . . something.'

'When did he say he'd see you again?'

'Well, he didn't say exactly, but the way he smiled when he left, I know it won't be but a day or two.'

'Five hundred,' Marion said. 'Figuring it one-third to me, two-thirds to you, you owe me one huudred and sixty-seven. I can make change.'

Bobby was surprised. 'Marion,' she said, 'I thought I only owed you seventeen dollars. After all, he was supposed to leave just *fifty* dollars, wasn't he?'

'One-third, two-thirds. That's how it's done.'

'But I didn't have to tell you how much he gave me. You're penalizing me for being honest.'

'Baby, you felt like shooting your mouth off. That's what you're paying for. Vanity. It's all vanity. I have vanity that I want to be paid.'

'Marion, you don't know what the extra money means for my children.'

'Look,' he said, 'you can go and drown them. That's all right with me.'

He was wondering if he ought to hit her. This was something he seldom did, but she irritated him. She was such a small-town girl, and masochist on top of it. She believed she had come down in the world. Of such characters, he thought, was his stable made. It would be a mistake to hit her. Bobby would enjoy herself for a week.

'Marion, I feel as if there's something I ought to tell you.'

149

'Why don't you stop announcing everything you have to say?' he snapped.

She went right on. 'I think I've got a strong crush on Eitel,' she said, 'and it's brought up a certain dilemma you ought to know about, Marion. I don't think I'm made out to be a party girl.'

'Sure you are. I never met the chick who wasn't.'

'I was thinking that if it takes with Charley Eitel and myself, that well, what I would like is to leave this and all this work as being just a little episode when I was on the rocks. I mean, think of the kids.' Bobby put a hand on his shoulder. 'Marion, I hope you won't be disappointed and think you wasted time on me. You see I really have a very strong crush on Charley. An experience like tonight doesn't happen that often. With the money he gave me, less the seventeen dollars that belongs to you, I mean, out of fifty, I could get everything sort of straightened out.'

He didn't listen to her. Marion was thinking of the parakeet she kept, and how she would stand in front of the cage in the shabby living room of her cottage, lisping to the bird in baby talk, and he wondered if he were up on marijuana for he was thinking that Bobby's bird talked to her, and now the bird who was Bobby talked to him in the pad of his cage.

'Look,' Marion said abruptly, 'you think Eitel has a hurt for you?'

'I'm sure he does. He couldn't have acted that way otherwise.'

'But he didn't say when he'd see you again?'

'I just know that it's going to be soon.'

'Let's find out,' Marion said, and reached for the phone.

'You're not going to call him now,' Bobby protested.

'He won't mind getting up,' Marion said, 'he'll just take another sleeping pill.'

Over the line he could hear the phone ring and ring again. After a minute or more, there was the sound of the receiver going over with a crash, and Marion smiled to himself at the thought of Eitel groping on the floor in the darkness, half dumb with sleep, half dumb with Nembutal.

'Charley,' Marion said brightly, 'it's Faye. I hope I didn't disturb you.' Bobby had snuggled next to him to hear the responses.

'Oh . . . it's you . . .' Eitel's voice was thick. There was a pause, and over the wire Faye could feel how Eitel tried to find himself. 'No, no, it's all right. What's it about?'

'Can you talk?' Marion asked. 'I mean like is your friend around?'

'Well, in a manner of speaking,' Eitel said.

'You're still asleep.' Marion laughed. 'You just tell your friend I called to give you a tip on a horse.'

'What horse?' said Eitel.

'I'm talking about a date of yours named Bobby. You remember Bobby?'

'Yes. Of course.'

'Well, I mean like she just left here, and she was talking about you.' He kept his voice as neutral as a referee. 'Charley, I don't know what you got,' he said, 'but Bobby digs you. Man, she really digs you.'

'She does?'

He was still groggy, Marion thought. 'Now, look, Charley, try and concentrate 'cause I have to make arrangements.' His voice very distinct, he asked, 'When would you like to see Bobby? Tomorrow night? Night after?'

This would wake Eitel up. As if the phone were an antenna, he felt sleep vanishing, the line becoming clear, and Eitel tense and nervous and wide-awake before him. Maybe it was ten seconds until the answer came.

'When?' Eitel repeated. 'Oh, God, never!'

'Well, thanks, Charley. You go to sleep. I'll get you a different kind of chick next time. Give my regards to your friend.' And with a look, Marion put the phone down.

'He was asleep,' Bobby said. 'He didn't know what he was saying.'

'I'll call him again.'

'Marion, it wasn't fair.'

'Sure, it was fair. Did you ever hear of the unconscious? That's what he was talking from.'

'Oh, Marion,' Bobby whimpered.

'You're tired,' he told her, 'you better get some sleep.'

'He meant the things he said when he was with me,' Bobby blurted out, and began to cry.

It took him fully ten minutes to bring her around and send her home. At the doorway, with a sheepish smile she handed him one hundred and sixty-seven dollars, and he patted her and told her to rest. When she was gone he wondered if he should have kept her a little longer, and wished that he had. Life was a battle against sentiment, and to exercise Bobby while she still cherished the wound of being in love with Eitel would have been novel.

Woman's vanity. He wanted to crush it like a roach, and was wistful he had taken too much tea. When he was on tea it was impossible to make love, his body was numb. A pity, because it would have been exactly right to burn into her brain the seed of what she had never possessed: one grain of honesty. She had never loved Eitel, Eitel had never loved her, not for thirty seconds. No one ever loved anyone except for the rare bird, and the rare bird loved an idea or an idiot child. What people could have instead was honesty, and he would give them honesty, he would stuff it down their throats.

It occurred to him that he had missed a perfect chance with Bobby. What he should have done, what he had never thought of doing, was to ask her to stay. There was a business she claimed was loathsome, and he could have kept her at it for ten or twenty minutes while nothing happened, nothing at all. Why hadn't he thought of that sooner? and knew it was his pride that held him back. There was the danger of Bobby talking.

Suddenly, he decided to be without pride. He could do it. He could be impregnable if sex was of disinterest to him and that was how to be superior to everybody else. That was the secret to life. It was all upside down, and you had to turn life on its head to see it straight. The more he thought of what he could have done with Bobby, the more frustrated he became. There was still time to call her, he could call her back, he smiled at the idea of the baby sitter who would be hired for the third time.

Yet, thinking of the lesson he should have given Bobby, he found to his surprise that no matter the marijuana, he was no longer numb, and so it was now ridiculous to phone her, he would only teach the opposite: Bobby would decide she loved him instead. Faye didn't know if he wanted to smash his fist through a wall or burst out laughing.

'Hey, Marty, how you doing, kid?' a voice said.

He realized he was standing in the middle of the floor with his eyes closed, his fists pushed with all their force into the pockets of his dressing-gown. 'Well, Paco, what do you say?' Faye asked quietly.

'I'm flying, Marty, I'm flying.' Paco looked at him like a foundling come out of the storm, a skinny Mexican boy of twenty or twenty-one with a long face and large eyes. They were feverish now, and Marion knew why he had come. Paco needed a fix. He strutted, he was jaunty, he waved his hands, he was holding himself together by the most intense effort of will.

'You know what I was thinking,' Paco went on in the same bright voice, 'I haven't seen Marty in a while, tail-hound Marty, the kid who helps out a kid . . .'

'What are you doing down here?' He knew Paco from the capital; there had been a time when he went around with the club to which Paco belonged.

'Here? Here? I been here a day. This town is for birds.'

'It's a town,' Faye said.

Paco had been the sad one in the club. He was worth nothing in a fight, he was funny-looking, he was a natural to play patsy and punk. Still, nobody bothered him for he was considered a little crazy. That was the thing about Paco. He was the only one in the club who would do things no one else would ever think to do. Once he picked up a scissors and stabbed the club leader because the club leader had been talking about Paco's sister.

Marion had not seen him in a long time. Paco had been picked up in a robbery and had lived a term in state prison. The fact he dropped in like this after an absence of two years did not startle Faye. Such things were always happening to him.

'I hear you're peddling gash,' said Paco, 'you got some gash for me?'

It was weird. Paco was neurotic, Faye thought, a pimply dreamy kid, begging for dough. In his family his mother hounded Paco, he used to call her dirty names; in the clubhouse he would lie around for hours reading comic books; once he announced he wanted to go to the South Seas. Even at the age of seventeen, tears came into his eyes at a harsh word. And now he was a junkie, and he needed a fix. Sudden compassion for Paco burned Faye's eyelids. The poor slob of a *pachuco*.

'You're on a horse, aren't you?' Faye asked.

'Marty, I kicked the habit, so help me, but I'm sick now, this boy's sick, it's part of the cure, I need a little.' Paco beamed. 'Fifty bucks, Marty, and I got enough for a week. I sail, and then I kick the habit.' When Faye didn't answer immediately, Paco went on. 'Twenty-five, that holds me. Marty, I got to get out of this town. It disgusts me. I'll go nuts here.'

He could give him a hundred, and then Faye caught himself thinking of the pistol he kept in his bureau drawer, and the automatic in the glove compartment of his car. From the judge Faye could never escape, there came the decision: 'Give him nothing at all.' His compassion was not pure; he was a little afraid of Paco. Even of Paco! he told himself.

'No,' Faye said, 'no loan.'

'Ten bucks. I need a fix. Marty!'

'*Noda.*'

'Five bucks. Jesus God.' Paco had begun to come apart. He sweated abominably and his poor sad pimply face was unbelievably ugly. In another minute he might faint or throw up.

Faye was almost sick with pain and excitement. He fought his compassion with the fury of a man looking for purity. 'Get out, Paco,' he said gently.

Paco sat down on the floor. He looked as if he were ready to chew on the rug, and from what seemed an infinite distance, Faye remembered Teddy Pope and the joshua tree, and thought with a pang that to make it, maybe one had to be a slob and suffer like Pope or Paco. Was that why he had tried to get on mainline? So that he could crawl on his hands and feet and bark like a dog?

'*Chinga tu madre,*' Paco was singing at him.

He had to get the *pachuco* out of here. But where? There was only the police station. Faye shrugged. A month from now, two months from now, it was possible he could be beaten up by Paco's friends for leaving a junkie with cops. Of course, he paid the police protection, they could handle it quietly. But the police themselves would give Paco a fix, they would have to. They would send him to the county farm of the capital all fixed up. So, no matter what, Paco would get his horse.

For an instant Faye thought of killing him. Only that was killing a zero, and if he were to kill somebody there should be a score. However, he had to do something with Paco. But what? He could take him in his car and leave him on the road. People would find him, they would drop him at a hospital, they would fix him there. Whichever way he considered it, Paco was going to get his fix.

Now Paco was threatening to kill him. Only a junkie would tell you he would kill you while he lay flat on his face.

'Why don't you knock over a store?' Faye said.

'What store?' said Paco hoarsely.

'You don't think I'm going to have it on record that I told you the store?'

This thought revived Paco. If he robbed a store there was money, and with money there was horse. So Paco got to his feet and staggered to the door. Possibly he could hold himself together for another hour. In his own body, Faye felt how Paco's head was bursting.

'I'll kill you soon, Marty,' Paco said from the door with his swollen tongue and his aching mouth.

'Come around and we'll have a drink,' said Faye.

Once the sound of Paco's footsteps had disappeared down the sidewalk of the empty street with its modern homes and its cement-brick fence, Faye went into the bedroom and put on a jacket. He felt as if he were close to bursting. There was no pressure in all the world like the effort to beat off compassion. Faye knew all about compassion. It was the worst of the vices; he had learned that a long time ago. When he was seventeen, he had spent a day out of curiosity begging money on the street. There had been nothing to it; the only trick was to look people in the eye and then they could never turn you down. That was why bums made so little – they couldn't look people in the eye. But he could, he had stared into a hundred faces, and ninety had blanched their little bit and given him back some silver. It was fear, it was guilt; once you knew that guilt was the cement of the world, there was nothing to it; you could own the world or spit at it. But first you had to get rid of your own guilt, and to do that you had to kill compassion. Compassion was the queen to guilt. So screw Paco, and Faye burned for that sad pimply slob.

It was impossible to sleep. Instead, he went to the garage, got into his little foreign car, and raced it down the street, cashing a tight smile at the thought of how he might be waking people. To the east, ten miles perhaps, there was a small rise; it was nothing, but on all those roads which were laid in lines across the mesa of the desert it was the only one which had a view. There was a dirt track over the mountains, but he could never reach that summit in time. The dawn would be coming very soon and he wanted to see it and look into the east. There was Mecca. Faye raced his car until its light chassis quivered like a bird whose wings are clipped, giving all of himself to the task, looking for the peace which comes from curious contests, the ice-cream-eating derby, the public-speaker's symposium, the apple-polisher's jubilee.

He made the rise in time to see the sun lift out of the table of the east, and he stared into that direction, far far out, a hundred miles he hoped. Somewhere in the distance across the state line was one of the great gambling cities of the South-west, and Faye remembered a time he gambled around the clock, not even pausing at dawn when a great white light, no more than a shadow of the original blast somewhere further in the desert, had dazzled the gaming rooms and lit with an illumination colder than the neon tube above the green roulette cloth the harsh dead faces of the gamblers who had worn their way through the night.

Even now, there were factories out there, out somewhere in the desert, and the tons of ore in all the freight cars were being shuttled into the great mouth, and the factory laboured, it laboured like a gambler for twenty-four hours of the day, reducing the mountain of earth to a cup of destruction, and it was even possible that at this moment soldiers were filing into trenches a few miles from a loaded tower, and there they would wait, cowering in the dawn, while army officers explained their purpose in the words of newspaper stories, for the words belonged to the slobs, and the slobs hid the world with words.

So let it come, Faye thought, let this explosion come, and then another, and all the others, until the Sun God burned the earth. Let it come, he thought, looking into the east at Mecca where the bombs ticked while he stood on a tiny rise of ground trying to see one hundred, two hundred, three hundred miles across the desert. Let it come, Faye begged, like a man praying for rain, let it come and clear the rot and the stench and the stink, let it come for all of everywhere, just so it comes and the world stands clear in the white dead dawn.

Part Four

14

Eitel did not go to sleep after the telephone call from Marion Faye. Elena had stirred just long enough to ask who was on the phone, and when he gave the answer Faye had been considerate to provide – that it was a tip on a horse, no more, no less – Elena grumbled drowsily, 'Well, they have some nerve. My God, at this hour,' and fell back to sleep. In the morning she would not remember, he knew, for she often had such conversations in the dark.

So it was hardly the fear of Elena learning about Bobby which kept Eitel awake now. Still, the longer he thought about it the more convinced he became that Bobby must have been with Marion while they talked. He knew Faye; Faye would not have called otherwise, and Eitel thinking of how he had groaned, 'Oh, God, never!' was sick at the thought Bobby might have overheard. In a day or two he could have paid the girl a visit, he would have known how to tell her that he would not see her again. He could even have left a present, not five hundred dollars this time, but something.

Abruptly, Eitel decided that he must have been out of his mind. After all these months of trying to remember that he was not rich any more, he had seen fit to throw away five hundred dollars on a ridiculous, sentimental, and sickly impulse, and thinking of that, Eitel knew no matter how long he lay in bed, the next day was ruined for work. Pressed next to Elena, trying to soothe himself by the warmth of her body, his memory, like a battered drunk at the end of a spree, groped over the events of the last six weeks.

Was it just so short a time ago that he had started work on his movie script? He had been in the state of mind of the gambler who puts all he owns on a single bet, so desperate to win that he comes to believe the longer the odds against him the better his chance. Yet now, remembering that confidence, he thought that he had not had such very good luck. Finally, it was his own fault, finally it was always one's own fault, at least by Eitel's standards, but still things could have gone a little better. Six weeks ago, just the day before he was ready to begin writing, the world did not necessarily have to come knocking on his door, he did not have to be paid an unexpected visit.

Yet the world had come. It came in the shape of a man named Nelson Nevins, who had worked as Eitel's assistant for several years, and now had his own reputation as a director. Eitel despised Nevins' work; it was tricky, dishonest, and with pretensions to art – in short all the blemishes he found in so much of his own work. What irritated him most about the visit was that Nevins had come to gloat.

Eitel and Elena spent an hour with him. Nevins had been in Europe for a year, he had made a picture there, it was the best he had ever done, he assured Eitel. 'Teppis cried when he saw it,' Nevins said. 'Can you believe that? I didn't believe it myself.'

'I never used to believe it when Teppis would cry over my pictures,' Eitel said languidly, 'and I was right. He calls them degenerate now.'

'Oh, I know,' Nevins said. 'He always cries. But that's not what I mean. He really cried. You can't fool yourself on something like that.' Nevins was plump, he wore a grey flannel suit and a knit tie. He smelled of expensive toilet water and his nails were manicured. 'You should have been over in Europe, Charley. What a place. The week before the Coronation was fabulous.'

'Oh, was there a coronation?' Elena asked. Eitel could have throttled her.

'You know the princess is just fascinated by movie stars,' Nevins went on, and Eitel had to listen. Nevins had been here, he had been there, he had slept with a famous Italian actress.

'How is she?' asked Eitel with a smile.

'There's nothing fake about her. She's beautiful, intelligent, alive. One of the wittiest women I ever met. And in the hay, oh, man, she's genuine.'

'I think it's terrible how men talk about women,' Elena

offered, and by an effort Eitel kept himself from saying, 'Don't feel obliged to join every conversation.'

Minutes went by and Nevins continued to talk. He had had a most marvellous twelve months. It was the best period of his life, he would admit. There had been so many people he had met, so many fantastic experiences he had had; there was the night he got drunk with a distinguished old boy from the House of Lords, the week he spent with the highly placed American statesman who wanted Nevins' advice on the delivery of his speeches – all in all it had been a diverting year. 'You ought to get to Europe, Charley. Everything's happening over there.'

'Yes,' said Eitel.

'I hear you expect big things from this movie you're on.'

'Little things,' Eitel said.

'It's going to be marvellous,' Elena said in a dogged voice.

Nevins glanced at her. 'Oh, I'm sure,' he said. It chafed Eitel to see how Nevins looked at Elena. He was polite and rarely talked to her. Nevins seemed to be saying, 'Why do you have to go to such lengths, old man? There are all those amazing women in Europe.'

When he left, Eitel walked him to his car. 'Oh, by the way,' Nevins said, 'don't mention I was here. You know what I mean.'

'How long are you going to be in town?'

'A couple of days only. That's the worst of it. I'm very busy. I guess you are, too.'

'The script will have me working.'

'I know.' They shook hands. 'Well,' said Nevins, 'give my regards to your lady, what is her name again?'

'Elena.'

'Very nice girl. Give me a ring and maybe we can find the right sort of place to have lunch.'

'Or ring me.'

'Of course.'

After Nevins had driven away, Eitel hated to go back in the house. He was met by Elena in a tantrum. 'If you want to go to Europe, you can go right now,' she said in a loud voice. 'Don't think I'm holding you back.'

'How you talk. At the moment I can't even get a passport.'

'Oh, so that's it. If you could get a passport, you'd take off in five minutes, and tell me to kiss your ass.'

'Elena,' he said quietly, 'please don't shriek like a fishwife.'

'I knew it,' she said between her sobs. 'It was just a question of time, just waiting for the trigger to explode.'

He could be distantly irritated by her use of metaphor. 'All right, what are you so upset about?' he said in a weary voice.

'I hate your friend.'

'He's not worth hating,' Eitel said.

'Only you think he's better than you are.'

'Now, don't be ridiculous.'

'You do. That's what's so awful. You call me a fishwife 'cause you can't screw a princess the way he did.'

'He didn't screw a princess. It was just an actress.'

'You'd like to be over in Europe right now. You'd like to be rid of me.'

'Stop it, Elena.'

'You stay with me 'cause I'm somebody you can feel superior to. That's how you get your opinion of yourself. By what other people think of you.'

'I love you, Elena,' Eitel said.

She did not believe him, and all the while he comforted her, all the while he said that a thousand Nelson Nevinses were not so important to him as even one unhappiness for her, he hated himself that it was not true, hated the pang of jealousy, call it more properly the envy he felt that he was being forgotten, and men who had been his assistants went to coronations and slept with women who were more famous than any he had known in a long time. 'Will I never grow up?' he asked himself in despair.

It was such bad luck. For the first time in several weeks, he was in a serious depression, and over and over he would complain to himself, 'Did Nevins have to come today? Just when I was ready to begin.' All that evening he studied Elena, studied her critically, and when she could feel his attention on her, she would look up and ask, 'Is anything the matter, Charley?' He would shake his head, he would murmur, 'Nothing's the matter. You look beautiful,' and all the time he would be telling himself that she was such poor material, she had such a distance to go. He knew by a dozen signs she gave that she was inviting him to make love again tonight, and he dreaded it a little and proved to be right, for afterward he found himself more depressed. It was the first time Elena had failed for him, and yet it was at that moment she said, 'Oh, Charley, when you make love to me, everything is all right again.' And with eyes that longed for the safety of innocence, she asked him timidly, 'Is it really the same for you?'

'Why more than ever,' he was obliged to say, and so with quiet and private defeat upon defeat, his mood turned on him still again and he felt lonely indeed.

Next day, by an act of will, he set to work. It was the third time he had started this script in fifteen months, not to mention the half-dozen occasions over the last ten years, and he was hoping that he was finally ready for the task. He had spent so many years thinking about this story, and in the last weeks at Desert D'Or since he had been living with Elena, he had outlined every scene, he knew exactly what he wished to do. Yet as he worked he found that he kept seeing his movie as someone like Nelson Nevins might see it. No matter how he tried, and there were days when he drove himself into exhaustion, sitting before his desk twelve and fourteen hours, the work would always turn into something shoddy or something contrived, into something dull, into something false. Afterward, tired and irritable, he would lie inertly beside Elena, or rouse himself long enough to take her perfunctorily, no more he often thought than a quick coup to stun his brain.

Certain nights with his desire to understand himself, he would draw even more deeply from his depleted energy, he would gamble for knowledge by taking several cups of coffee and drugging them with sleeping pills, until like a cave explorer he would be able to wander into himself, the thread of his escape a bottle of whisky, for with the liquor he could always return when what he learned about himself became too large, too complex, too directly dangerous. And next day he would lie around, dumbed by the drugs. 'I even compete with the analysts,' Eitel would think, 'how competitive I am,' and feel that no one could help him but himself. For the answer was simple, he knew the answer. This movie of his was dangerous, he had so many enemies, they were real enemies – no analyst could banish them.

Had he been so naïve as to think he could make his movie while men like Herman Teppis sat by and applauded? He needed energy for it, and courage, and all the wise tricks he had learned in twenty years of handling the people who worked for him, and to do that, to do all of that, perhaps a young man was needed, someone so strong and simple as to believe the world was there for him to change it. With rage he would think of all the people he had known through the years, and their contempt for the film. Oh, the film was a contemptuous art to be sure, a fifteenth-century Italian art where to do one's work, one had to know how to flatter princes and lick the toes of *condottieri*, and play one's plots and intrigue one's intrigues, and say one's little dangerous thing, and somehow delude them all, exaggerate one's compromises and hide one's statement until if one were good enough, one could get away with it, and five centuries later, safe in a museum, the tourists would go by and say obediently, 'What a great artist! What a fine man he must have been! Look at the mean faces of those aristocrats!'

No, the work would not go well, and the more he tried to exercise his will, the less the story would return to him. Each day, despite himself, he would find that he was weighing the consequences of every line, thinking of all the censors in all the world, and so he could not get rid of the technique he had spent fifteen years in learning. He could only work in that technique, choosing a bag of tricks one day, floundering in a bog of blunders for the next. During three weeks Eitel spent all his energy on the script and in certain ways they were the worst three weeks of his life. They seemed more than a year, because all his experience told him that the script was very bad; the little surprises, the bonuses, the unexpected developments of plot and character were simply not coming to him, and he had been so certain his work would go well. Somehow he had never believed that this script would be beyond his courage, no more than a boy expects his future to be made of defeat and failure.

One way or another he had had the idea that this picture was going to be his justification. Back perhaps so far as the Spanish Civil War, certainly through all of the cocktail parties and the jeep rides and the requisitioned castles which had been the

Second World War to him (excepting that visit to a concentration camp which had terrified him deeply because it matched so exactly his growing conviction that civilization was capable of any barbarity provided only that it be authoritative and organized), along all of that uneven trip from one beautiful woman to another, there had been the luxury of looking at his life as wine he decanted in a glass, studying the colour, admiring the corruption, leaving for himself the secret taste: he was above all this, he was better than the others, he was more honest, and one day he would take his life and transmute it into something harder than a gem and as imperishable, an art work. Had he been afraid to try, he would think, for the fear that his superiority did not exist? The manuscript lay like a dust-rag on his desk, and Eitel found, as he had found before, that the difficulty of art was that it forced a man back on his life, and each time the task was more difficult and distasteful. So, in brooding over his past, he came to remember the unadmitted pleasure of making commercial pictures. With them he had done well, for a while at least, despite all pretences that he had been disgusted, and looking back upon such emotions, concealed so long from himself, Eitel felt with dull pain that he should have realized he would never be the artist he had always expected, for if there were one quality beyond all others in an artist, it was the sense of shame, of sickness, and of loathing for any work which was not his best.

Yet he knew his situation was a little unreal to him. That was true of all his life, all of it was unreal to him. Could there possibly have been a time when he had been so young as to break his nose trying out for the college football squad because he wished to demonstrate to himself he was not a coward? Had there been that other time in Spain when he had volunteered as a rifleman, and for three disastrous weeks had lived in a shelled village on the bank of a river with an exhausted Anarchist brigade, discovering that he was braver than he thought, for he had held himself together even after the front had collapsed, and it had been necessary to make a sad escape across the Pyrenees into France. Where had it all gone, the good along with the bad? It was not true, he would think, that as one grew older the past grew clearer. The past was a cancer, destroying memory, destroying the present, until emotion was eroded and the events in which one found oneself were always in danger of being as dead as the past.

Still, the time had come to face himself, to take account, and go on into new work. Only Eitel could not think of other work to do. Most remarkable cancer! It not only erased the past and stunned the present but it ate into the future before he could create it. So for days after he stopped believing in his script, he continued to work at it, carrying a quiet depression to dull his work and even his effort and move him from one day into the next.

Under such a burden, he was growing critical of Elena's faults. He would wince as he watched her eat, for she waved her fork, her mouth often full as she spoke. He had tried to correct her. She would listen with sullen eyes these days, she would promise to try, and with her stubborn insight would never learn at all, as if she were saying to him, 'If you really loved me, I would learn everything.'

It was maddening to him. Didn't she realize how much he wanted her to learn, did she desire no more than that the son of the junk dealer marry the daughter of the candy store keeper? His parents were dead now, but there had been years when he was young and had to fight his battles against them, against the bonds of his mother's love and the force of his father's contempt that he had a son who wasted time in the theatre and was supported by his wife. So, all the while, he would suffer at her clumsiness.

Since he had been in Desert D'Or, particularly since the party at the Laguna Room, the number of people who sent him invitations had become fewer and fewer. Socially, his life was now all but empty, and he found Elena and himself restricted to a small group whom he called the *émigrés*. They were writers and directors and actors and even a producer or two who had refused, as he had refused, to co-operate with the Subversive Committee. Years ago many of them had bought winter homes in Desert D'Or, and like Eitel they had come here now for refuge. The social life he was obliged to share with them, since they were invited nowhere else in Desert D'Or, was hardly satisfying to him, however, and he hated the thought of being classed with the *émigrés*.

Elena liked them no better. 'Boy, are they pompous,' she said to him once.

'You're right on the nose,' he smiled.

'Pompous men are always full of self-pity,' she added now that he had encouraged her.

Eitel agreed. Most of the *émigrés* he found dull, one or two were pleasant, but as a group they bored him. Eitel was always bored by people who could enter a discussion only so far, and then could go no farther, because to continue would mean that they would have to give up something they had decided in advance they would continue to believe in. Besides, he knew them so well; even years ago they had bored him when he had belonged to their committees. And these days he found them so eager to believe he was a great artist who refused to compromise with the vultures – exactly the modest picture they had of themselves.

Of course in the years after he took his name off committees, they had been the first to pass ugly gossip about him, and so he could hardly be impressed with the adulation they gave him now. If anything, the women were more irritating to him than the men; since his first wife he had never been partial to women who were too directly political. Yet no matter how he disliked the *émigrés* and their wives, he found himself wishing that Elena was not so ignorant of everything they talked about.

If the conversation was even medium clever Eitel knew the evening was ruined for her. Elena would be grim, she would sit among the others with a smile stitched to her face. When she tried to say something, and that was rare enough, he would feel that everybody was suffering. Someone, for example, might tell a joke, others would laugh, and Elena would repeat the last line and then explain it. 'He didn't really want to,' Elena would say, 'isn't that funny?' When they got home from such an evening, she would be in a bad mood. 'No, don't talk to me,' she would say as he would start a careful lecture. 'It's my fault, I know it is, I just don't want to talk about it.'

'Elena, you can't hope to be smarter than everybody, you know.'

Recollecting the details of the evening, she would cry out, 'But I'm stupider,' and fling herself on a couch to stare at the wall. 'It's you,' she would say bitterly five minutes later, 'don't put the blame on me. If you like those women so much, go get one of them. You're not stuck with me.' Sometimes she would begin to cry.

One night, in contrast to the usual drama with which she announced she would leave him, Elena said quietly that it would be better if they broke up. 'I could live with an ordinary man. I could be happy with somebody else,' she said.

'Of course you could,' he soothed her.

'Even some of those pompous friends of yours.'

But he began to laugh, and gave one of his imitations. 'Years from now,' he said in the voice of a public speaker, 'when credit is given the struggle for peace in this country, they won't forget the courageous stand which individual statements of principle – no matter how unco-ordinated like Charley Eitel's here – made on the consciousness of the American people, who let us not forget are under their collective hysteria a deeply peace-loving and progressive nation.'

'Oh, sure they're silly,' Elena said, 'and they're all afraid of their wives, but a couple of them are real men, maybe.'

'Yes,' he drawled, 'they have the strength of big-breasted women.'

She laughed unhappily. 'I'm going to leave you some day, Charley. I mean it.'

'I know you do, but I need you.'

Her eyes filled with tears. 'I wish I could be better,' she said.

Finally, he came to restrict himself to seeing the few people with whom Elena felt comfortable. I was one of them, and on those nights when Lulu and I were fighting, I would visit Eitel and Elena. With me, Elena could be gay, she could be silly. We spent evenings, the three of us, listening for the most part to Eitel's stories which he told with happy flourishes. On those evenings he would seem content with her, and she would glow with love for him. It was all fine until the morning; then work began again and his depression with it. At such moments, deep in the frustration of writing his film, Elena seemed a poor companion with whom to take in the Coronation. 'Hello, your duchess,' he could hear her stammer.

15

About this time Collie Munshin flew up to Desert D'Or and spent his first evening in the resort with Eitel and Elena. Collie's explanation that he had come for a week's vacation to think about a picture he was going to produce did not sound very convincing to Eitel, but in any case, whatever Collie's reasons, he repeated the visit on the following evening. The next day Collie was over for late-afternoon drinks. In my absence – Lulu and I had gone on a gambling binge to one of the towns across the state line – Munshin became the friend of the family.

They were cosy, the three of them. Now that Munshin had lost Elena, everything Elena did delighted him. In the middle of talking to Eitel about productions and budgets and temperaments and rivalries, at exactly those moments when Elena would begin to feel most excluded, Munshin would beam at her and say, 'Doll, you're ravishing.'

But these were only preliminaries. It took Collie less than an hour to become personal. 'I hate civilization,' he said after the first silence.

'Why?' asked Eitel obediently.

'Because here we are with the most involved and intricate relationships, and what do we do? We talk about trivia.'

'What else is there to talk about?' Elena asked.

He turned to her. 'Elena, you can't know the emptiness you've left in the way I live. I don't exist for you any more.' He took a swallow of his drink. 'There's a savage core to women. I'm convinced of it.' His voice became resonant, and Eitel had an idea of the rhetoric to come. 'You women forget things the way a man never could,' Collie declared. 'I can imagine what you've said about me, Elena, and it's true, it's all true no doubt, you're a sensitive person, but did either of you ever think it was painful to me, and that it's me who remembers the good things, not you, Elena, the solid things that existed between us, yes, even the passion, the passion, do you hear, Eitel?'

'Collie,' Eitel asked, 'do you really think you can brag in this house?'

'Treat me like a human being,' Munshin roared, and added in a tiny voice, 'I'm bleeding.'

'You can afford to,' Eitel said. 'You have lots of blood.'

He knew however that Collie had been successful. What woman could not forgive an old lover who claimed to suffer? Once Collie had made his speech, Elena became vivacious, she started to tease Collie with a sharp little malice Eitel had never noticed before. Elena began to chat, she laughed her merry laugh, she put little questions to Collie. 'I read in the papers,' Elena would say, 'that your wife won a prize for the dogs.'

'Yeah, Lottie took it again.'

'I bet you got a big kick out of it,' Elena said.

Collie loved it. Each time Elena attacked him, the moist sheepish look would appear in his eyes. 'I deserve it,' he would seem to say. 'Don't think I don't know.'

At night when they went to sleep, Elena kept saying, 'I feel so good tonight, Charley.'

She could not keep her mood however. As they were turning over in bed, she said thoughtfully to Eitel, 'You know, Collie doesn't care about me. It's you he's interested in.'

Drunk with the admiration of another man for her, Eitel did not want his moment spoiled. 'You're silly,' he said.

'No,' she said almost sadly, 'now that it's over, Collie likes to talk about what he lost.' She surprised him by what she said next. 'Charley, if he should start telling you things about me, don't believe them. You know how Collie gets carried away when he tells a story.'

'What could he possibly tell me about you that I don't know?'

'Nothing,' Elena said quickly, 'but you know how he is. He lies. I don't trust him.'

Still, Munshin's daily visits became something they waited for. After the depression of working, it was pleasant to spend a few hours this way, the three of them married in the most agreeable fiction: Eitel and Elena ten years together and Collie

172

the bachelor friend. It was so agreeable that for the first time in all the years he had known Munshin, Eitel decided that he liked him. He had almost come to the conclusion that Collie was changing. At the very least he was the only executive at Supreme who had the courage to see him regularly. It was hard to resist this sort of attention.

Yet Eitel was still suspicious; he could not understand why Munshin had come to Desert D'Or. Therefore, it was to Eitel's surprise that he found himself telling Collie the story of his movie. It was on the fourth visit the producer made, and they stayed up late. After Elena had gone to bed, Collie began to talk about his own problems. It was part of the technique Collie used to borrow ideas, but Eitel did not resent it this time. Collie was being frank and even confessed he was in trouble on a picture and asked Eitel's advice.

Finally, it was Eitel's turn. Munshin sighed, he squirmed his heavy bulk in the chair and said, 'I don't suppose you want to tell me, Charley, but I was wondering how things are going with your script.' His high-pitched voice was gentle.

Eitel thought of lying. Instead, he answered, 'It's going very badly.'

'I figured it that way,' Munshin said. 'Charley, you're used to working with people. If you want to tell me about it, maybe I can make a contribution.'

'Or steal my story.'

Collie smiled. 'I got an idea I couldn't steal this one even if I wanted to.'

Eitel was wondering why he felt tempted. Collie could not possibly like his story and yet it might prove fruitful. Perhaps in Munshin's reaction he might find new ideas. Eitel did not really know why. 'You're trying to kill it,' he said to himself.

To tell a story was a talent he had discovered years ago, and this time he told his story well, too well indeed; he felt even as he was talking that if the story were as important to him as he had believed, he should not be able to offer it so easily. It took a sort of life as he continued to speak, it was better than anything he had written for it, and all the while Collie provided a fine audience. Munshin was known for the way he could listen to a story; he would exhale his breath heavily, he would cluck his tongue, he would nod his head, he would smile in sympathy: Collie could always leave the impression that he had never listened to a better story. From experience, Eitel knew how little this meant.

When he was done, Munshin sat back and blew his nose. 'It's a powerhouse,' he said.

'You really like it?'

'Extraordinary.'

All this meant little. Collie's criticism would come later. 'I believe,' he went on, 'that this can make the greatest picture in the last ten years.'

'Not with the script I have.'

'You can't have a script for this. You need a poem.' Munshin fingered his belly. 'That's the one weakness,' he sighed. 'I don't say I'm sure, Charley. If anybody can surprise me, it's you, but can you put poetry on the screen?'

Eitel did not know if he was satisfied or disappointed. 'Collie, why don't you say what you really think?'

It took ten minutes for Munshin to come to the point. 'I'll tell you,' he said at last, 'I like it. I like stories that are offbeat. But no one else would like this property because they couldn't understand it.'

'I disagree. I think it would be amazing how many people would like it.'

'Charley, you don't understand the story yourself. You're a director, but you're not thinking in terms of film. You're concrete and this is mystical. I know why you've had trouble working. You're trying to write a script which violates everything you know about film-making.'

'Of course. You know what I think of film-making.'

Munshin put his hand on Eitel's arm. 'I love this story,' he said, 'and I know what it suffers from. At least I think I do.'

'What?'

'There's no rooting interest.' This was the death sentence. 'Charley, it's too hip. It's a whorehouse. Your hero is a creep. A character who's making thousands of dollars a week on TV, and he decides to give it up. For what? To go out and help people? To end suffering? They'll laugh your picture off the screen. You

174

think an audience wants to pay money to be told this character is better than they are?'

Eitel did not bother to argue. With each word Collie had been burying his hopes. The masterpiece was impossible, he felt suddenly. That must have been why he told it to Munshin, to learn it was impossible, something he had probably always known, but he needed someone to tell him. Perhaps, now, he would not waste his effort. Relief came over Eitel, an old relief; he was rid of a burden.

'You know,' said Munshin, 'I see a way to make this property successful. It needs a handle, that's all.' One of Collie's fat arms went up into the air. 'Let me think about it a little.' But Collie would do his thinking aloud. 'Eitel, I have it,' he said. 'The solution is simple. You need a prologue to the picture. Let your hero start as a priest.'

'A priest!'

'You haven't been using your head. A priest takes you off the hook. I'm surprised you didn't think of it yourself.' Collie was talking rapidly now, the story being teased by his producer's mind, nimble as the fingers of a puppeteer. In the beginning Eitel's hero ought to study to become a priest. Personality-wise, he would have everything, Munshin stated, charm, intelligence, poise – everything but the most important thing. 'The guy's too cocky,' Munshin said. 'I see a terrific scene where the principal or the head monk or whatever they call him at a priest school, a kind of wise old priest-type Irishman, calls in Freddie' – one of Munshin's habits when telling a story was to call the hero 'Freddie' – 'and tells the kid that it's no go, he doesn't think Freddie ought to become a priest, not yet. Scholastically, he says, the kid's got everything. He's tops in Church History, in Holy Water, in Bingo Management, he's A plus in Confessional Psychology, but he doesn't have the heart of a priest. "Get out in the world, son, and learn humility," the old priest says. Do you see it now?'

Eitel saw it. He had no need to listen. 'Let's take it from Freddie's point of view,' Munshin said with the pleasure of a man digesting a good meal. 'If you want motivation for Freddie, you can present the priest as a sort of father-figure to him. The kid takes the advice like a rejection. He's bitter. He feels unloved.

So what does he do? He goes out from the priest school, and one way or another – we'll work it out – he gets into television, a bitter kid, the kind who plays the angles. Yet at the same time we can drop hints that he's feeling full of guilt for the slop he feeds people. And all the while his career is going up like a sky-rocket.' Munshin interrupted himself, holding his hands forward expressively. 'You build him up as a heel, and then you give the switch. Something happens to give him humility. I don't know what we can find, but I wouldn't even worry about it. Something with a crucifix or a cross. Show a Christ motif on the screen and who cares about motivation? The audience will buy it. Once Freddie starts his binge-sequence, we can give him a *Wanderjahr*, stumbling around bums with tears in his eyes, lots of business where he just loves everybody. I'm telling you even the kids will stop eating their popcorn. You get what I mean. I don't even have to elaborate it. At the end . . .' Freddie did not have to die in the gutter, Collie explained; he could go back to the seminary and be accepted. An up-beat ending. 'Something with angels' voices in the background. Only not full of shit.'

Munshin was so excited he could not sit still. 'This story's got me,' he said as he walked back and forth. 'I won't be able to sleep tonight.'

Eitel laughed. 'Collie, you're a genius.'

'I'm serious, Eitel, we have to do this picture. H.T. will love it.'

'I could never do it.'

'Of course you could.'

'I don't approve of the Church,' Eitel said.

'You don't approve of the Church? Baby, when I was a kid in the slums, one cut above a hoodlum, I used to spit on the street when I passed a church. What's that got to do with it?'

'Well, for one thing, you know and I know the Church might just have a little bit to do with these subversive committees.'

'If they weren't interested, somebody else would be. Charley, I've been a liberal all my life, but for God's sake keep politics out of this.'

'Let's leave the story,' Eitel said, 'for tonight.'

'For tonight we'll drop it. All right. But you think about what I said, Charley. I swear, I want to do it with you. This property is a gold mine.' He patted Eitel's shoulder. 'You don't realize what you have here,' Munshin said again before he left.

Eitel never found out whether Collie could sleep that night, but it was certain he did not. Everything seemed turned on its head. The professional in Eitel lusted for the new story; it was so perfect for a profitable movie, it was so beautifully false. Professional blood thrived on what was excellently dishonest, and Collie had given him the taste of that again.

In the morning when he tried to work, he found that his mind was fertile with ideas for what was already titled Masterpiece-Sub-Two. Had the story to which he had given such pain disappeared already? Was his dislike of the Church unreal, was he himself unreal? He was even wondering what financial terms he could make with Munshin. 'I won't appear before the Committee again,' he found himself thinking, 'I'll do the script black market first, no matter how much I lose that way.' And all the while he was wondering how serious Collie had been.

Munshin did not visit them that day, and when Eitel called the Yacht Club, he learned the producer had taken a plane to one of the gambling resorts. So it was clear enough. Collie could afford to wait twenty-four hours and let him worry. It was an obvious tactic, but Eitel was still uneasy.

Early evening Marion Faye stopped by their house. Eitel and Elena were used to seeing him once or twice a week; the tension which had existed for a time after Elena's episode with Marion was now less noticeable. Lately, Eitel had even enjoyed Faye's visits.

Marion had a habit of appearing at odd times; a week might go by without even a telephone call and then he would show up suddenly. It may have been the marijuana, but Faye was capable of sitting in their living room for half an hour without saying a word, sometimes not even answering their few polite questions. Then he would get up and go out the door.

Other times, he would talk a lot, and once in a while he might give them glimpses of his charm. It was extraordinary, Eitel often thought. When Marion was pleasant he seemed more than pleasant; the relief one felt helped to exaggerate his amiability.

Curiously, he was often nice to Elena. He would even flirt. Nights when Faye had been attentive, she would preen a little bit and tease Eitel once Marion was gone. 'Oh, would he love to cause trouble between us,' Elena might say.

'I've never seen him so interested in a woman.'

Elena would become sullen again. The compliment had been too direct. 'He would just like to make me one of his prostitutes.'

'That's ridiculous.'

'It's not ridiculous. That's what he thinks of me. I don't like him,' Elena said.

'Never think too poorly of yourself,' Eitel said angrily.

He was so anxious for Elena to grow. Once, just once, she had a success on one of the evenings at the *émigrés*. Someone put an *alegrías* on the phonograph, and Eitel saw her dance her flamenco. Her head was proud, her teeth white, her skin golden, and she danced with a kind of scorn, her skirts flying, her sharp little heels beating out the rhythm with a precision, a fury, and a confidence that had him watching her in admiration. Then she became too drunk and stopped dancing, but the glow he felt at her triumph lasted through the night. In the morning he scolded her for not practising dancing, and for a few days she began to do exercises, she even talked about trying to find a night-club career again. But in watching her practise he knew she would never be a professional, and he had a picture of how unhappy she must have been in those shoddy engagements her agent had been able to get for her, no more than an excuse for drinks between two stripteasers. Probably everyone talked while she danced.

No, she could never grasp the first requirements for a professional. No matter one's mood, there was always a minimum to the performance. One was never terrible. Elena could not be like that. Watching her work, he knew she was gifted, but she had the wild gifts of the amateur. No wonder she took her talents to bed; love was for amateurs. So he knew, although he hated to believe it, that the more he wanted to make of her, the less she would become. She had only her own cry, 'Love me, really love me, and maybe I can do what you want.'

Faye told him as much. The night Eitel spent waiting for a phone call from Munshin, Marion stayed for hours. At the beginning of the evening, while Elena was in the kitchen making coffee, Eitel told him about Munshin's idea for his story, sensing uneasily even as he spoke that he wanted Marion to encourage him.

'It sounds like one of Collie's contributions,' Marion said.

'I find it so awful that I'm half intrigued,' Eitel murmured.

'Don't like being out of things, do you?' Marion said, and was silent until Elena came back into the room. He remained silent, and it made Elena uncomfortable. When, finally, Faye mentioned a new girl he had taken on whose name was Bobby, Elena was eager to hear everything about her. To each detail Faye offered – that Bobby had tried modelling, that she hoped to be an actress, that she had been married and divorced and had two children – Elena would listen with absorption.

'But how did she get started?' Elena interrupted. 'I mean what was she doing before?'

'How do I know?' Faye said. 'She sold ties at a hatstand, or she took photographs in a night club. What does anybody do?'

'No, I mean, how did she make up her mind to go into it?'

'Do you think it's complicated? Jay-Jay took her over the bumps, and then I talked to her.'

'But how did she *feel*?' Elena insisted.

'How would you feel?' Faye said.

Elena giggled for her answer. 'It's terrible,' she said to Eitel. 'I guess a girl like her gets started because she can't have a decent relationship with a man.'

'And *you* can,' Faye said. Eitel knew the signs. Marion was becoming ugly.

'Yes, I can,' Elena said. 'Don't you think so?'

Faye laughed. 'Sure I do. Just find the right man. That's every girl's trouble.'

'What do you mean by that?' Elena said.

Eitel smiled. 'He means, get rid of me.'

'Marion hates you, Charley.' She made this announcement defiantly as if they both would turn on her. Eitel could only laugh. For years he had protected himself with that laugh. 'Is she right, Marion?' he said lightly.

Faye inhaled on his cigarette and then flipped it into the fireplace. 'Sure, I hate you,' he said.

'But why?'

'Because you might have been an artist, and you spit on it.'

179

'And what is an artist?' Eitel asked. He felt a pang at the venom in Faye's voice.

'Do you want to start a discussion?' Marion jeered. 'I thought I wouldn't have to tell you what it is.'

'I'm sorry you see it this way,' Eitel said. He had a feeling of loss that Marion no longer respected him. 'Another protégé gone,' he told himself drily.

'If you feel that way about Charley,' Elena said, 'why do you come here all the time?'

Faye stared at her as if she were a specimen. 'Do you mean that,' he asked, 'or do you say it because you think maybe I'm right?'

'I think you're . . . Get out of this house!' Elena shouted at him, and like all commands which have no threat, she could only carry it out by leaving the room herself.

'What in the name of heaven did you have to say that for?' Eitel groaned.

'Because,' Faye said, 'I see more in that little chick than you do.'

'Ah, well, I expect you're right,' Eitel said coolly, and went to the bedroom. Elena was in tears; he had known as much. She would not listen to him, she only lay on the bed. 'You shouldn't let anybody talk to you like that,' she sobbed. 'And they shouldn't talk to me that way either.' He reasoned with her – Marion had not meant what he said, his nerves were tense, she should not have asked so many questions. Hopelessly, Eitel continued. All the while he knew that what he was really trying to do was convince her that Marion was wrong; they would not break up, he would always take care of her.

At a given moment, Elena turned on him. 'You think so much of your friend out there. You ought to know the kind of friend he is.'

By the way she said it, he knew there was more to follow. 'What are you talking about?' Eitel asked.

'Every time your back is turned, Marion says he wants me to go live with him.'

'Did he say that?'

'He even said he loved me.'

If Eitel was startled, he could tell that he was also pleased.

Let someone else care for her, and perhaps his own responsibility was less. 'Then can't you understand why Marion was so nasty?' he heard himself asking.

'Aren't you even angry?'

'Elena, let's not make too much of it.'

'You're cold, Charley,' she said.

'Oh, come on back. You can't really be angry at Marion if he has a crush on you.'

Finally she consented to say good night. Sheepishly, with red-rimmed eyes, she came back for a moment and smiled at Marion. 'You're beautiful, sweetie,' Marion said, and threw her a dry kiss. 'What I mean is, you're better than all of us.'

When Elena had gone to bed, and they were alone, Marion's mood was bad. 'Why won't you believe I love her?' Eitel said to him.

'What do you want me to say? I'll say it.'

'You see something in her yourself,' Eitel went on. 'You said so. She has such a need for dignity,' he exclaimed.

'Dignity!' Marion leaned forward as though to drive himself through an obstruction. 'Charley, you know like I know, she's just a girl who's been around.'

'That's not true. That's not all of it.' And Eitel was offended at the calmness of his voice. 'If I loved her, I wouldn't talk to him now,' he thought.

'You can do anything with Elena,' Faye said almost dreamily. 'She's the kind of girl you could wipe your hands on.' He stared into space. 'Provided you lead the way. You got to lead that girl, Charley. That's what she's got.'

Eitel made one more attempt. 'In certain ways she's the most honest woman I've ever known. My God, her parents brought her up with a meat cleaver.'

'Absolutely,' said Faye. 'Do you know why you stay with her?'

'Why?'

'Because you're scared, Charley. I'll bet you've been faithful.'

'I have.'

'And you're the one who used to say that faithfulness is an outrage to the human instincts.'

'Perhaps I still believe that.'

'You're really scared. You're even scared to take one of my girls.'

'I've never been interested in call girls,' Eitel said.

'What are you trying to tell me? That it's a matter of taste?'

As Faye spoke, Eitel felt again something of the rage he had known during the first weeks at Desert D'Or when he had come to realize that the kind of women he once had known would never enter an affair with him now, certainly not the ambitious ones, nor the young ones, nor the ones he might desire; for him had been left only the wives of the *émigrés* and those second-rate call girls and downright prostitutes so low in the scale of Desert D'Or that he would still be important to them. Or was Faye right? Was he frightened even of such women? As he thought these things, Eitel had a glimpse of the contempt he felt for Elena. But instead he answered, 'If you think so little of my girl, why are you interested in her?'

'I haven't figured it out yet. It must be the animal in me.' Faye yawned and got up. 'Do yourself a favour,' he said as he was about to leave, 'ask Elena if she ever did it for money.'

Eitel felt an unmistakable thrill. 'What do you know?' he asked.

'I don't know, Charley. I just got an instinct for this.' And Faye sauntered out the door.

Eitel didn't have a chance to ask Elena until the following afternoon. She was asleep when he went to bed and awake before him in the morning. No call came through from Munshin, and while Eitel tried to work, desire for Elena teased him powerfully. In the middle of the afternoon, they had an exciting half-hour, doubly exciting for Elena, he knew, because his desire seemed so spontaneous. Afterward, it seemed harmless to ask her the question. Had she ever taken money? Well, never exactly, she told him, except for once. Except for once? he had said, and how was that? That was a funny time, Elena reminisced. How had it happened? he asked, his chest frozen. Well, there had been a man, and he had wanted to, and she had refused, and then the man had offered money, twenty dollars he had offered.

'So what did you do?' Eitel asked.

'I took it. It made the man seem exciting to me.'

'You're a dirty little girl,' Eitel said.

Elena's eyes were alive. 'Well, you know I am,' she said. 'You are too.'

'Yes.' The worst of it was that these stories aroused him so.

'I enjoyed spending the twenty dollars,' Elena went on.

'It didn't bother you?'

'No.'

'It bothered you,' Eitel insisted.

'Well, I did get hysterical the next night, but I'm so loused up anyway.' Her face became distant for a moment. 'Charley, let's not talk about it. When I was sixteen, I used to worry I would end up a whore.' Then she laughed as if to chase all memory away, and sat on his lap. 'You remember when we were talking about two girls?' Eitel nodded. 'Well, maybe we can find a girl sometime. It would have to be the right kind of girl though. The kind I wouldn't be jealous of.' Elena laughed at herself. 'Isn't it terrible talking like this and planning?'

He squeezed her to him, feeling so many things he could never have told her, excitement at the memory of himself with two women, sensuous pain that she had sold herself for twenty dollars, and with it all, concern, a concern for Elena which almost forced the tears to his eyes. What would happen if he didn't take care of her?

A little later they decided to go for a swim. While they were having a drink he remembered that Collie was still missing. It was so easy to believe anything; equally possible that they would never see Collie again, or instead see him that night. Playfully, Eitel flipped a coin in the air, and it came down tails. 'I'll never see him again,' he told himself, and the thought was not pleasant. Did it mean he had decided to depend on Collie?

What for superstition? The coin was wrong and Munshin came to their house that evening. It took hours before Elena would go to sleep, and not a word was said about movie scripts. When she finally left them, Munshin became reflective. 'We're in a fantastic occupation,' he said.

Eitel had no patience for this. 'How's the head monk?' he asked.

Munshin smiled. 'Charley, I hope our little conference the other night was productive.'

'It gave me an idea or two.'

'I'm still wild about it,' Munshin said. 'I haven't felt enthusiasm like this in years.' Collie often said such things; he would use them as a way of passing from one subject to another. '"What are you gambling here for?" I said to myself last night. "The real gamble is back with Eitel in Desert D'Or."'

'Where's the gamble?' Eitel said. 'Last time we talked you seemed to think the story couldn't miss.'

'Charley, let's not negotiate at arm's length. We're each too smart for that. Your story, even with my contribution, is a gamble. It's straight gamble all the way down the line.'

Eitel made a small performance of mixing a drink. 'Maybe we ought to drop the idea then,' he said.

'Cut out the sparring, Charley.' Munshin was nibbling on his upper lip with all the pleasure of a fat little boy. 'I've given a lot of thought to this. Lover, if you want to go it alone, the suggestion I made is yours, and I hope it helps you to pull down a fortune for the script when you want to sell it.'

Eitel made a bored face. 'You know very well, Collie, that nobody in the industry will go near me.'

'All you got to do is clear yourself with the Government.'

'Just that little thing. I have my pride, Collie.'

'Then you ought to work with me.'

'Maybe there are other possibilities.'

'Who are you kidding? If you want to make it in Europe, you got to get a passport.' Munshin beamed. He had a better deal worked out, he said. Eitel would do the script, and he would contribute editorial advice, and when it was done – did Eitel think he could do it in twelve weeks? – Collie would present it to Teppis as his own screenplay. He didn't have to remind Eitel, he went on, what a Munshin original was worth.

'You ought to be able to get between seventy-five and a hundred thousand for it,' Eitel said.

'Charley, why talk about money now?'

'Because I want to know how we'll split.'

Munshin pursed his lips. 'Charley, talking like this is not your style at all.'

'It may not be my style, but I want ten thousand dollars in advance, and I want us to divide three-quarters to me, one-quarter to you.'

'I'm bewildered, Charley,' Munshin said. 'I don't understand your point of view.'

'Make an effort.'

'You make the effort. What's in this for me except worries? If Teppis ever found out I was working with you, he'd hand me my head. You think I'd take a chance for a lousy few bucks?'

'Plus the prestige of a Munshin original.'

'Not worth it.' Munshin shook his head. 'No, Charley, no. I see it the other way. Since you're short of ready money, I'll give you twenty-five hundred for the script, and then we'll split three-quarters to me.'

'Collie, Collie, Collie.'

'We'll also forget that loan I gave you.'

'Don't think I don't know why you gave it to me.'

They went on for another hour before the rough treaty was drawn. Later – Munshin explained he would have to discuss it with his lawyer – they might or might not draw up a contract, and the best way to pay Eitel would have to be devised for income-tax purposes. But these were details; they could trust each other.

The perfect contract, Eitel thought. Collie would have the money, and he would have photostats of the script in his own handwriting. He took the best terms he could get. Collie would give him four thousand dollars for writing the script, two thousand tonight, two thousand when it was done. If the script was not sold it would belong to Munshin; if it was sold, Collie would take two-thirds of the sale price. Subsidiary rights would belong to Collie, but he would make certain Eitel got a percentage. It was a simple arrangement: Eitel would do the work and Collie would get the money. In return, if Eitel would co-operate with the Subversive Committee, Collie would do his best to have him direct the picture. They might even share credit for the story.

'So now,' Eitel thought bleakly, 'I'm one of the peons Collie keeps locked in a hole.' He was furious. Collie knew people; all of Collie's peons were honest; he would never make an arrangement like this with a man he could not trust. 'After all these years I'm still honest,' Eitel said bitterly as Collie passed over twenty one-hundred-dollar bills. The bargain was made. Eitel felt a tingling in his hand.

Yet if he thought their business was finished for the night, he was to learn that it had only begun. Collie went off on a long account of how he had met Lulu in the gambling casino. 'She was with that man, your flier friend. What's his name?'

'Sergius.'

'That's right, Sergius.' Collie sighed. 'He's a nice kid. Not as smart as he thinks.'

'Perhaps.' Eitel merely waited.

'Charley,' Munshin said, 'I could cry every time I think of how you ruined your career.'

Eitel refused to answer.

'Did you have to flaunt Elena under H.T.'s nose the night he gave the party?' Collie asked. 'You don't know what a mistake that was. Why do you think he invited you in the first place?'

'I've never understood why.'

'Charley, for all your intelligence and all your perception, you've always treated H.T. the wrong way. H.T. wants to act like a father to people, and you never give him a chance. Two hours before that party started, before I even knew you were invited, he said to me, "I want to do a rehabilitation on Charley-boy." Those were his words.'

'No less!' Eitel finished his drink and poured another. 'I suppose he was going to take me off the black list?'

Munshin nodded wisely. 'He would have fixed it so you testified in secret session. Nobody would ever have known what you said.'

How clever they were, Eitel thought. A secret session, a few lines in the back of a newspaper, and he could have his career again. The word would be put out for the gossip columnists to be kind.

'H.T.'s a hard man,' Munshin said, 'but he's a lonely man. Deep down, he misses you. He gave that invitation to the party because he had an idea for a picture that only you could make.'

'Sergius told me,' Eitel said. 'A desert musical.'

'Baby, you're wrong. You don't understand H.T., I keep telling you.' Collie stuck out a finger. 'What he had in the back of his mind was to make a picture about Sergius O'Shaugnessy.'

This was worth a drink. 'I'm blind,' Eitel said, 'I don't see it.'

'You're just rusty. The beau is a war hero with ten planes to his credit.'

'Three planes, Collie, not ten. If you ask Sergius, maybe he'll tell you it almost made him a mental case.'

'Sue me if I built it up a little,' Munshin said. 'The essence of the yarn is not how many planes, but the fact that Sergius is an infant who was left on the steps of an orphan asylum. Movie-wise, could you have anything more viable?'

'It sounds revolting.'

'Take the girl who's his mother,' said Munshin. 'I see her cast as a bobby-soxer. It's got a perfect beginning. You could open on her setting a two-month-old baby on the steps of this orphan home and ringing the bell. Then she runs away crying. Somebody opens the door, an old janitor say, and there's a note pinned to the baby's diapers. This was H.T.'s idea. "I wish I could give my baby a family name," the note says, "but since I can't, please call him Sergius because that's beautiful."' Munshin's face showed the delight of a man who stares at the Kohinoor diamond. 'How can you miss?' he said. '"Sergius, because that's a beautiful name." Take it from there. He goes on to become a war ace. The orphan is a hero.'

Eitel could well believe it. Once, twice, three times a year Herman Teppis would get an inspiration, and then it was up to somebody to develop a movie from his idea. The origins could consist of less than 'the orphan is a hero'; years ago, Teppis had called Eitel one morning and said, 'I have a movie in my mind. *The Renaissance*. Make that movie.' He had managed to divert Teppis to another director, and the movie as it was finally made had another title, but the inspiration had been enough to keep people at Supreme worried for a year. When all was said, it was as good a way to make movies as any other; most of Teppis' inspirations showed a profit.

'What do you think?' Munshin asked.

'This story has nothing to do with Sergius. I don't understand why you even want to bother to buy the rights from him.'

'He could never sue us. That's not the point. Only look at the story. It stinks. Nobody would believe it unless you could build around a real-life person. That's what got H.T. excited. The publicity values.'

'I don't believe Sergius will give you the rights,' Eitel said.

'You think so,' said Munshin, 'I think differently. There's twenty thousand dollars in it for him.'

'Then why don't you have a talk?'

Munshin sighed. 'It's too late. You know how H.T. is with his enthusiasms. He wanted you to make the picture because Sergius would co-operate with you. Now it's all ruined. You had to insult H.T. gratuitously.'

'Collie, why are you bringing up old history?'

'Why? I don't know.' Munshin put a finger in his ear and rubbed vigorously. 'Maybe it's because I have an idea in the back of my mind,' he announced. 'If we could get the kid to okay this project, I feel, Charley, that I could still talk H.T. into letting you direct it.'

Eitel laughed. 'In other words you want me to prove to Sergius that it's a good idea.'

'I want you to help me and to help yourself as well.'

'Everybody benefits,' Eitel said. 'Sergius is rich again, I direct, and you bring back what H.T. sent you here for.'

'If you want to put it that way, yes.'

'What if H.T. won't let me direct?'

Munshin looked the least bit tentative. 'I've been thinking about that,' he said. 'What we might be able to do in that case is change the terms of our agreement on your script. I don't want you left out in the cold.'

'How lucky we're partners already,' Eitel said. Collie was marvellous, he decided. He had come to Desert D'Or because H.T. had told him to buy the life of Sergius O'Shaugnessy. But if Collie went down to the market, it was to borrow with one hand while he sold with the other. So it did not matter what happened now: Collie could hardly lose. Eitel found himself wondering how many other deals Collie had made this week.

'Sergius doesn't want your twenty thousand dollars, does he?' Eitel asked abruptly.

'We left it an open question.'

'What did you do, discuss it over a roulette wheel?'

'It's as good a place as any.'

'And is Lulu working on Sergius too?'

Collie had to smile. 'Well, it's a little complicated. H.T. is just morbid on the subject that she should get married.'

'To Teddy Pope?'

Collie nodded. 'The thing is, however, given favourable circumstances, I believe H.T. could see his way clear to Lulu marrying Sergius.'

'What a beautiful end to the movie.' Eitel roared with laughter. 'For a fat man, Collie,' he managed to say at last, 'you can certainly squeeze into a lot of narrow places.'

Munshin laughed with him. They sat in Eitel's living room, laughing and laughing, but Collie was the first to finish. 'I'm crazy about you, baby,' he said, wiping his eyes, 'you're the only character I know who can see through me.'

'That is a compliment,' Eitel said genially.

'You'll give me a hand with Sergius, won't you?'

'No,' said Eitel, 'I won't lift a finger.'

16

Munshin let out a surly belch. 'I figured that would be your reaction,' he said, and he leaned forward in his chair. 'What would you say, Charley, if I tell you that I think you owe me something?'

Eitel knew he was getting drunk; he was aware suddenly of his anger. 'I don't owe you anything,' he said, and his voice throbbed. 'Not after the pennies you just bought me with.'

Munshin nodded confidently. 'Yes, I know. I'm no good. I'm a cheap crook to you. But if you could think for two minutes of anything but yourself, maybe you'd realize that you don't' – Munshin held up a finger – 'begin to appreciate my feelings in this.'

'I appreciate them perfectly,' Eitel said. 'You want help on one of your manoeuvres.' The easy rhythm of the whisky had been spoiled, and his mind was clear again, too clear – it was trying to be ready for anything Collie might be preparing. 'Munshin, don't you ever rest?' Eitel said irritably.

'Listen, Charley, call me any kind of monster you want, but just remember I'm the only monster in that lousy cut-throat studio who cares two bits about what happens to you.' Munshin's voice was taking on new tones with every phrase. 'So don't play around with me. I wouldn't want to find out which one of us has got the muscle. Because, whether you want to believe it or not, I care about you, Charley.'

Eitel laughed, but his laugh was slightly high in pitch to his critical ear. He was furious at the self-betraying affection he felt for Munshin, and so he said, 'Yes, I see a successful producer crying his heart out.'

'Damn you, Eitel,' Munshin said in a low tone, 'I didn't say I'm sobbing myself to sleep over you. I said I cared a little.'

Eitel made himself sit back in his chair, and he extended his legs. 'Well, Collie,' he said, 'that I might buy.'

'Eitel, trust me for the premise of this hour. There are too many other characters in the world to fight. I don't want to fight you.'

'Then let's not talk about Sergius.'

'What if I say to you that I understand how you feel about the kid? Believe me I do understand it. I don't care how much slop I've jammed up the hole of more than one cruddy and delirious piece of film product, I am still sentimental enough to think that everybody's got to be an altruist about one person in the world. One person anyway. So you can be an altruist about Junior. I won't fight you anymore.'

Eitel took a long careful swallow of his drink. He was beginning to feel better. 'I'll tell you a secret,' he said. 'We'll get along if you cut down the length of your speeches.'

Munshin smiled tolerantly at the reprimand. 'Then listen to this. I want you to tell me in all objective seasoned honesty, because that you owe me, Eitel; honesty you owe me: just tell me how you think Sergius would develop if I can talk him into going in Uncle Herman's direction.'

'Uncle Herman?' Eitel asked. 'Uncle Herman *Teppis*?'

Collie grinned. 'Please don't say it so loudly.'

They laughed together as at an old family joke.

'Why, Collie,' Eitel said, 'this is turning out to be a good drunk.'

'Tell me about Sergius, lover.'

'As a demonstration of my intelligence?'

'You know what I think of your intelligence. Do you want me to get down on my hands and knees?' Munshin said with a growl. 'What do you think I'm here for?'

Eitel tasted his liquor carefully. It came over him that for the first time in some weeks he was conceivably out of his depression. 'I have a little love for you, too, Collie,' he said slowly, 'and you're far from the dullest gentleman and wrestler I've ever had to deal with, but I think you're underestimating Junior.'

'Are you sure you're not being a proud father?' Munshin passed one of his heavy hands along his dark jowl. 'Sergius is just a lucky opportunist to me.'

'After all these years, do you still believe in luck?'

'Luck, I believe in. To make a right connection at a good time? That's luck I can believe in. And your friend is a very lucky operator.'

'No, it's never so simple.' Eitel touched the bald spot on his head. 'I don't know if I really ought to talk about him, Collie, but – ' Eitel sighed, as if to surrender to the attractions of conversation. 'You're right, I do like him. He was a friend during one of my plague months, and I wouldn't want to see him develop into a bad piece of work.'

'Where is all this development?' Munshin asked. 'The kid will have twenty thousand dollars as consolation when Lulu tells him how real it's been, and goodbye.'

Eitel paused significantly. 'You know, you'd do better to think of his possibilities as a movie actor.'

'A movie actor, you say?' And Munshin's face became grave.

'Yes. He's five years short of the theatre, but there is something about his personality which is potential box office. I don't say he'll make a good screen actor, because for the life of me, I don't know whether he has real talent. But, Collie, if my opinion is worth anything, that boy has a *wide* appeal.'

'Now that you mention it, there is a certain something about him,' Collie said in a speculative voice.

'Definitely. You don't think Lulu would blow her time with a boy who had nothing?'

'What I don't understand after all this,' Collie said, 'is why you're not in a hurry to encourage him to listen to me. I thought the guy was your friend.'

'I don't know if he's right for it. If he doesn't have talent, or if he doesn't care about such things, and he becomes too popular too quickly, he could turn out to be a pompous snot. I can see him growing into the kind of actor who's read a hundred pages of Proust, and will take any celebrity aside at a party to tell him that he hates the acting profession because it kept him from being a great writer. And then of course every ambitious stock girl who's ready to have lunch in his dressing room will get the lecture how the director on the picture is an idiot and doesn't know the difference between The Method and Coquelin.'

'What projection you have,' Munshin said. 'I didn't even know the athlete could read.'

'Yes, indeed. He doesn't know it, but he wants to be an intellectual. I'm seldom wrong on such predictions. Why, he hates intellectuals like a small-town slick writer.'

'Very interesting,' Collie said. 'Do you want to know how I read him? Given a full expansion of his potential – if he has potential – I see him growing into a super-Western type. The whole bit. He'll put hair tonic on his chest, and he'll kick you in the crotch if it's a fight to the death. I'll say something worse. I sense ugliness in that kid. He could end up an amateur actor and a professional vigilante who starts gossip-column posses to hunt down subversives like you.'

Eitel shrugged unhappily. 'Well, I don't know that I disagree with you. That's possible, too. This particular light-heavyweight can go in any one of a hundred directions. It's why I find him interesting.'

Collie nodded. 'You may have a taste for hipsters, but they're just psychopaths to me.'

'Don't put labels on people,' Eitel snapped.

'This is getting us nowhere. I'm curious, Charley. Do you still think after all we've said about Sergius, that he won't come to terms with me?' Collie smiled. 'Not even a little chance?'

'I have to admit that I don't know. If Sergius is bitched enough on my ex-Goddess to be ready for Uncle Herman, then you're going to have an actor who'll need a secretary for his fan mail.'

'Eitel, I have news for you,' Collie said abruptly. 'H.T. thinks Sergius is fan mail too.'

Eitel smiled at the connection. 'Well, Collie, when thieves agree . . .'

'You give me a pain in the ass. If you weren't so pure, I could pull off a masterpiece. How I would love to ream H.T. with Sergius as the bait and you as the hook.' Munshin nodded at the decisive beauty of the project. 'Charley, what would you think of signing a peace pact with me? Maybe it's the good whisky, but I'm beginning to believe we could be friends.'

The intrusion of politics on friendship shivered Eitel's mood again. 'Don't you think I've sold enough of myself for one night?' he said coldly.

'Sold what? Eitel, in my book you're still an infant prodigy.

You don't begin to know what's in my mind. I know I'm very drunk, but do think of this: *H.T. is not going to be in control of the studio forever*.' Collie gave the sentence in a whisper which vibrated through the room. 'We could make an interesting team, you and me. You're one of the few directors who was never a cheap operator. And I *worship* real class, Charley. If I had top say in the studio, I can assure you that within reason I would let you make the kind of pictures you want to make.' His voice trailed off as if he regretted the timing of the proposition.

'Collie, we could have made a team,' Eitel admitted, and then shook his head in a small imperative motion as if to destroy the possibility forever. 'But you did too many unpleasant things to too many pictures I cared about for me to forget so quickly.' A forgotten hatred came back to his voice. 'And the worst of it was that you weren't even right as a businessman so much of the time. They're just beginning to find some of the nuances I wanted to do five years ago.'

'Stop living in the past!' Munshin looked at him levelly. 'Brother, can't you believe that maybe I want to change, too?'

Eitel gave the lonely smile of a man who has ceased to believe in the honesty of others. 'You know,' he said, 'it's not the sentiments of men which make history, but their actions.'

Munshin looked at his watch, and got out of his chair. 'All right,' he said, 'since that's the way you think, I'll give you evidence of good faith. Forget the two thousand dollars I'm supposed to pay you on finishing the script. You can have it tomorrow. I'll send it over by messenger.'

Eitel stared coldly at him as if he were a monster after all. 'Still playing with pennies, aren't you, Collie?'

The fatigue of a twenty-four-hour working day came into Munshin's voice. 'Eitel, you're quite a man with the needle,' he said, swaying a little on his feet. 'Because you're right. I do think in pennies. But, you see, one thing Elena and I have in common is that my folks ran a candy store too. A crummy one with a numbers man to come around for the daily collections. It does things to the shape of your character that a café-society toff like Charles Francis Eitel could never begin to understand.'

'Sometime I'll tell you about me,' Eitel said almost gently.

'Sometime. I hope so, Charley.' They shook hands formally.

'Let me send that messenger in the morning. As a favour to me.' Munshin sighed with considerable force and liberty. 'What a night this has been!'

Eitel was in a good mood when he went to sleep and he awakened in the same good mood. His sleep had left him in a state of well-being. His stomach, which was usually sensitive until late in the afternoon, accepted his breakfast and coffee with appetite. His satisfaction lasted until the moment he realized he would have to tell Elena that the script was no longer his own.

She was upset, and all the while he was explaining that working for Collie meant nothing, it was merely that he needed time and money was time, he knew that last night, far at the back of his thoughts, he had been dreading to tell her. 'Nothing is changed really, darling,' he said. 'I mean this script I do for Collie will be so different from my own that I'll be able to do the other one later.'

She looked gloomy. 'I didn't know you were close to being broke.'

'Very close,' he said.

'Couldn't you have sold your car?' she asked.

'Is that a solution?'

'I just hope you didn't give up too soon.' Elena sighed. 'I don't know about these things. Maybe you're right.' She was convincing herself even as she spoke, and all the time he knew that she did not believe him; at bottom nothing fooled her. 'I'm sure the new one will be good,' she said, but she was silent all day.

The work on Munshin's script went smoothly. Years ago, Eitel had defined a commercial writer as a man who could produce three pages in an hour on any subject assigned. That was the way it went with the new masterpiece. There were hitches, there were delays, there were mornings when he could not start, but over the whole, what amazed him, annoyed him, and pleased him, was how easy the writing had become. Where he had written scenes many times only to decide that the latest version was worse than the previous failure, now ideas flowed, sections fitted together, and walls of plot grew to support one another. Eitel knew nothing about the Church, and yet Freddie's scenes in the seminary were good, they were commercially good, they boiled with movie ingredients. What did one have to know about the Church? There was a fine wit to the old priest, and Freddie was properly arrogant. One could rely on the stenographic code of the film which would say: Here is a heel, but it is a Teddy Pope heel, and regeneration is on the way.

Eitel began to enjoy himself by the time he started writing about Freddie's success on the programme. To the sugar of the seminary Eitel added the vinegar of television, and knew as he worked that the scenes which came later could not fail. A little syrup, a little acid, and lots of heart. These were the cup-cakes which won Hercules awards, and it was fine to be working again with cynical speed.

Munshin would telephone almost daily from the capital. 'How is Freddie coming?' he would ask.

'Freddie's fine. He's really alive,' Eitel would say, and think that no problems about character could exist any longer; Freddie was now an actor, any actor with a skier's body, a sun-tanned face, and cartloads of heart.

'How's Elena?' Munshin would ask, and answer himself by saying, 'That's great, that's great,' even as Eitel was muttering, 'She's fine, thank you, she says to send a kiss.'

Only that was hardly true. If Eitel was in good spirits these days, Elena was not, and her depression wore against his optimism. For the first time since he had been living with Elena he found himself repeating the emotions of many old affairs. The time had come to decide how he would break up with her. This was always delicate, but with Elena he would have to be more than subtle. No matter how he might dislike her these days for her sullenness, her vulgarity, her love itself, he was always aware that it was his fault. He had begun the affair, he had insisted on it, and so he ought to hurt her as little as possible. At the same time he did not want to end it immediately; that would be too disturbing to his work. The proper time was in a month, two months, whenever he was finished; and in the meantime, adroitly, like fighting a big fish on slender tackle, he must slowly exhaust her love, depress her hope, and make the end as painless as the blow of the club on the fatigued fish-brain. 'My one-hundred-and-fourteen-pound sailfish,' Eitel would think, and what a match she gave him. He was cool as any good fisherman.

'I'm the coolest man I know,' he would think, and with confidence, aloofness, and professional disinterest he manoeuvred Elena, he brought her closer to the boat. There was always the danger she would slip the hook before he pulled her in, and so the battle was wearying. He could not let her realize how his attitude had changed; she would force a fight which would go too far; that was her pride; she would not stay a moment once she knew he did not love her, and he had to struggle with temptation not to reel in line too fast, too soon.

He had wrapped his work about him and it gave the distance he needed, the coldness, the lack of shame. He would be far away from her, he would eat a meal without speaking, his eyes on a book, he would sense how despair swelled in her, fatiguing love, fatiguing spirit, and at the moment when he would feel that she could stand it no longer, 'We can't go on like this' about to burst from her mouth, he would confuse her completely.

'I love you, darling,' he would say out of a silence and kiss her, and know her bewilderment had seated the hook more firmly.

'I was just thinking you were sick of me,' Elena would answer, uncertain tears in her eyes.

The hook had to be seated over and over; she had resources for such a struggle; he would be amazed at times how she read his mind, the two of them sitting over a drink, chatting about nothing while his thoughts were working on the problem of being free. He might even be telling her how pretty she looked that evening, and the child's eyes would stare back at him, the open green eyes, and she would say, 'Charley, you want out, don't you?'

'What gives you these ideas!' he would say, pretending to be angry, fighting the single word 'Yes!' which twitched at his nerves, so much did he want to say it. But that would be fatal, for however it ended the damage would be too great. Either she would leave him and he would be unable to work just when he had found his rhythm; or what was worse, the calculating numbness he had been at such ends to cultivate in himself would disappear and he would be open to her pain, there would seem nothing more terrible in all the world than that she should suffer, and so the fish would be free, it would be no longer a fish, it would be Elena, and he would have to start all over again. So he must be patient, he must be cold, and all the while he must act, manufacturing warmth he did not feel.

He had come to the conclusion that to be able to end this affair, he must understand it first. Why should a second-rate man spend so much time on a fifth-rate woman? It was not logical. Second-rate men sought out second-rate women; the summits of society were inhabited by such people, and why had he deserted his caste? But he knew the answer or thought he did; there was always Faye's mocking presence, and the words he had said a week ago, 'You're scared, Charley, you're really scared.' Was it true? In the last two years he had performed badly with many women. Those were the laws of sex; borrow technique in place of desire, and sex like life would demand the debt be paid just when one was getting too old to afford such a bill. If he had clung to the Rumanian, he was chained to Elena. Could the fishing contest be another joke he played on himself, and would he never let her go, not so long as his delicate manhood depended on her? He had come to resent the attraction of their love-making. The confusion these days was that often he enjoyed her as much as ever, and in his sleep, he would sometimes be aware that he was holding her and whispering love-words to her ear.

In the past his pleasure had been created by the situation; a rendezvous with a woman in a hotel room had more charm than to take her to his home. Now, his life seemed stripped of interest. The inevitable progress of a love affair, Eitel thought. One began with the notion that life had found its flavour, and ended with the familiar distaste of no adventure and no novelty. It was one of the paradoxes he had cherished. The unspoken purpose of freedom was to find love, yet when love was found one could only desire freedom again. So it was. He had always seen it as a search. One went on, one passed from affair to affair, some good, some not, and each provided in its own way a promise of what could finally be found. How sad to finish the journey and discover that one was unchanged, that indeed one was worse; still another illusion was lost. He had merely succeeded in spoiling the memory of his old affairs. Elena stimulated his perception of what it meant for a woman to desire a man, and with his vulnerability to being found unattractive, he wondered how he could make love now to someone else. It was true; he was frightened; and he brooded for such comforts as the blessing of living alone. He had come to desire an affair with a woman for whom he cared nothing, an affair simply exciting, exciting as the pages of a pornographic text where one could read in safety and not grudge every emotion the woman felt for another man. It was the only sort of affair for which he was suited, he told himself, and instead he was locked in Elena's love. He could not even manage to have some trivial affair, for he had neither time enough nor money and Elena could never be deceived three times a week. It was true, Eitel would think, marriage and infidelity were wed, and one could not exist without the other. Many nights he sat in the living room with Elena and felt if he did not quit her for an hour, he would leave her forever.

The visits of Marion Faye made these feelings more intense. Eitel tried to say to Marion, 'But she loves me. Don't you understand why I feel responsible?'

'She doesn't love you,' Faye said. 'She wouldn't know what to do if she didn't think she was in love with somebody.'

'You give her no credit,' Eitel insisted, but something turned in him. How loathsome was the thought that she didn't love him.

'When a man gets older,' Faye said, 'there comes a time when he can be a sport with only one woman.' He smiled. 'For instance my stepfather, Mr Pelley.'

'Maybe one of these days I'll ask you for a girl,' Eitel heard himself say.

'What's the matter? You getting tired of the circus?' Faye said, and Eitel could imagine what Elena's night with Marion must have been. 'Let's make it for this evening,' he said.

'What will you tell Elena?'

'I'll tell her something,' Eitel snapped, and his date with Bobby was arranged.

He told Elena that Collie wanted him for a conference on the script and that they were going to meet in a town midway between the capital and Desert D'Or. That was easy enough. For one night almost any excuse would do, and the arrangements made with Marion, he drove out to the bar where Jay-Jay was waiting for him, trying not to think about Elena alone in the house. She hated to be alone, starting at noises, oppressed by the silence of the desert, careful to lock all the doors and windows.

Jay-Jay was drunk already. He was crazy about Bobby, he told Eitel, she was a good little girl. She had registered already in a hotel room and would be waiting for them. So they went off together, Jay-Jay stopping long enough to buy a bottle, and then they went on to meet her. As luck would take it, the hotel where Bobby had rented a room was the one in which Elena had waited for Collie, and with the sour bite of memory Eitel was forced to think of the morning he had come here to pick up her clothing.

As soon as he was introduced to Bobby, he was convinced it was a mistake. If he had a type, Bobby was certainly not it; her eyes seemed to say, 'I wish we didn't have to meet under such circumstances.' This would be another of Faye's jokes.

The three of them sat around in the hotel room, Jay-Jay passing the bottle while they dipped into a melting bowl of ice cubes. Bobby was shy. She would keep her head turned to Jay-Jay, talking to him about friends Eitel did not know, saying Larry had lost a roll at poker dice, and Barbara was pregnant again, and Dan was marrying a bar girl in the capital, and Lillian had her band organized but no good contracts, and on it went; Eugene was doing female impersonations and Renee had another crush. Eitel listened, watching Jay-Jay with amusement, for Jay-Jay was so warm, he liked Bobby so much, he would cluck his tongue at other people's troubles and give Bobby passing compliments. 'You're the loveliest, sweetie,' Jay-Jay said, and Bobby smiled. 'I adore this man,' she told Eitel.

'It's a romance,' Jay-Jay said and looked at his watch. He would have to be moving on, he told them. Eitel knew where; in the course of an evening Jay-Jay might arrange three or four introductions for Marion. As he was about to leave the room, he motioned to Eitel. 'Sweetie, you got to excuse us,' he said, 'Charley's promised me a tip on a horse.'

'If it's a good bet, let me in,' Bobby chimed, and Eitel smiled. 'Jay-Jay and I only bet losers,' he said.

In the hotel corridor, Jay-Jay swayed slightly. 'Charley,' he muttered, 'she's a good kid, she's all right, Bobby. Only I ought to tell you, she's kind of cold, can't help it, one of those. But you don't have to worry 'cause she'll do anything you want.' In a quick résumé, Jay-Jay explained exactly what was 'anything.' Eitel listened with distaste. 'Poor Jay-Jay, he's worse than me,' Eitel thought, and gave him a farewell tap on the shoulder.

Back in the room Bobby continued to chat in her bright little voice. 'Jay-Jay's a wonderful person,' she said to Eitel. 'Do you know anyone nicer?'

'Hard to say,' said Eitel.

'When I get the blues he's always very kind and considerate. Sometimes I wouldn't know what to do without him.'

'Do you have the blues often?'

'Well, the last couple of months have been very hard. You see, I just got divorced a little while ago.'

'And you miss your husband?'

'It isn't that. He was hard to take. But I don't care how old-fashioned this sounds, you need a man in the house, don't you think so?'

They had to get out of the hotel room, Eitel thought: it was stifling to remain here. 'I've seen you somewhere before, haven't I?' he said, as he had said once to Elena.

Bobby nodded. 'You did, Mr Eitel.'

'Recently?'

'Well, maybe it was two years ago. You see, I was an actress. I still am, of course. I think I'm good, really I do, people have said I have talent, but you know, no pull.' She sighed. 'Anyway, my husband knew a producer who owed him a favour, and so I was able to get an extra card. Once I was an extra in a crowd scene in one of your pictures.'

'Which one?' he asked.

'*Flood on the River*.'

'Oh that,' Eitel said.

'No, Mr Eitel, really I think it was a wonderful picture. You're a wonderful director.' She looked carefully at him, and then said with energy, 'I'm so happy to meet you at last.'

She had a personality which was interchangeable with a thousand other actresses. It was obvious she had been taught that an actress must use her personality, and so she was forever

201

using it, forcing her wan face and soft voice into artificial enthusiasm, artificial disgust, artificial gaiety.

'You enjoyed working with me?' he offered.

'It was an awful day for me,' Bobby said despondently.

'Why?'

'Well you see, I was such a crazy kid. I mean . . . oh, I don't know, I had – all kinds of ideas. I thought if I could get my face in the camera, maybe somebody would recognize me.'

'You mean some studio executive would say, "Who is that girl? Send for her!"'

'That's right.' Bobby sipped her drink reflectively. 'What a nut I was,' she said in a tone which was both cheerful and valiant. 'I remember at the end of the day, a woman who'd been an extra for years came up to me and told me not to get up front so much. "They won't hire you, honey, if your face gets too familiar to audiences," she said to me and she was right.' Bobby laughed nervously. 'So, you see, no stardom.'

'Unhappily, I'm afraid your friend was right about not working close to the camera if you're an extra.' The conversation reminded him of things Elena had said the night he met her, and he felt low. How could he ever possibly make love to Bobby?

It was obvious Bobby expected him to make the first move. She was so green. He held out an arm to her, and she put her hand in his, and sat timidly on his lap. After he kissed her, he knew he had to get out of this room. Her lips were stiff and frightened, and her body had a rigidity he understood only too well.

'Look,' he said, 'couldn't we go someplace else? Hotel beds always look like cadavers to me.'

She laughed and seemed a little more relaxed. 'I don't know,' Bobby said doubtfully. 'You see, we could go to my house, but it's nothing much. I hate to show you what a mess it is.'

'I know it's more pleasant than this place.'

'Oh, it's comfy all right, but you see, Mr Eitel . . .'

'Charley.'

'Well, Charley, my two little girls are there.'

'I didn't know you had children.'

'Oh, yes. They're wonderful kids.'

That was the answer, Eitel thought. He would go home with

her, he would talk a while, he would pay her and excuse himself on the plea that the children made him uncomfortable. 'Let's go,' he said softly.

On the drive across town, she continued to chat. There were times, she told him, when she was sick of everything. She had had such a rotten time in the capital. If she ever got a little bit ahead, she thought she would go back to her home town. She knew a fellow there who still wanted to marry her, children and all; they had been sweethearts in high school. He knew her mother and father who were the sweetest people in the world. Only she had been so stupid, she had married a musician. 'That's advice I can give anybody,' Bobby said. 'Never follow a man who blows a horn.'

In her tiny furnished four-room bungalow with its cheap wrought-iron furniture, one red sofa and two green armchairs, and the mounted photographs of her parents and children on the wall, he did not feel a great deal better. Bobby was making drinks, the baby sitter had left, and somewhere, probably in the kitchen, she had turned on the radio. Directly across from where he sat was a spindly lamp and next to it, a bird cage with a parakeet. If she ever prospered as a call girl, she would move to another house, the furniture would be changed, there might even be a maid, but the bird would remain with her. He felt unaccountably sad for Bobby, so sad that tears came to his eyes; only Marion could find joy in making Bobby one of the girls.

She had come back with a drink for him, and because she did not know what to do, she was talking to the bird. 'Pretty Cappy, pretty Cappy,' she lisped, 'do you love me, pretty Cappy?' The bird was silent and Bobby shrugged again. 'I never can get Captain to make a sound when company's around.'

'Let's dance,' Eitel said.

She did not dance well, she was rigid. Nothing with her body would come easily. When the number ended, she sat down on the couch beside him and they began to neck. It was all wrong; she kissed with the tense activity of a fifteen-year-old, and it seemed as if their lips never quite met. He would have to get out of here, Eitel told himself again.

At that moment the baby began to cry. 'It's Veila,' Bobby whispered with relief and she sprang away and tiptoed into the bedroom. He hardly knew why, but he followed her and stood beside Bobby as she rocked a one-year-old child in her arms. 'She's wet her pants,' Bobby said.

'I'll hold her while you change the diaper.'

He had always been indifferent to children, but his mood made him vulnerable to the baby he held in his arms. He passed through one of those drunken moments when years, decades, and lives seem to balance on the edge of alcoholic wisdom, and all is understood, forgiven, and put away. With whisky, the squire to love, he could love Veila for this instant, see her life as it must be, or see another life, or ten lives, or see himself at the age of one and Bobby as a child and Elena as a child, a little monkey-faced Italian child with surprising green eyes, so different, so familiar, to the tiny blonde package in his arms. Would Elena be like Bobby in another few years?

Bobby had taken the child from him and was fixing the diaper. As she worked, she looked up at him, and to his horror he knew there were tears in his eyes again.

'Veila had pneumonia last month,' Bobby said, 'so I have to take special care of her now. God, those doctor bills.'

Eitel was mourning the death of the unwritten hero; buried by Freddie; no, buried by himself. All the troubles of the world had been borne by a character in his mind, and now they were borne no longer. 'Poor baby, she must have been very sick,' he said, and he turned away and went back to the living room. He had to control himself; these were whisky tears. And all the while, tearing as the rupture of flesh, tore the thought: when Elena becomes like Bobby, how will men treat Elena?

So from nowhere, or so it must have seemed, he heard himself calling to Bobby, 'May I give you a loan?' Since the night he made the contract with Collie, he had been going around with a thousand dollars in his wallet. She had come back to the living room then and stared at him quizzically, almost warily. 'No, look,' said Eitel, touching a hand to her cheek, 'this is for nothing, this is a loan.' And pulling out the wallet, he drew three, then four, then five one-hundred-dollar bills and folded them into her fingers.

She squealed. 'Why, I could never . . . Charley, I could never pay you back.'

'Sure you can. It doesn't matter how long it takes. Someday you'll hit it, and I'll be happy to find the money drop in on me just when I need it.'

'But I don't understand.'

He wondered if he had ever been as sentimental in his life. 'No, look,' he said again, like an adolescent enraged at existence, 'it all stinks, do you understand? Let this be a present. That's how things should be. Some people have given me more,' he said finally, inarticulately.

He had been ready to go then. At that moment he wanted nothing more than to leave the house, leave the present, leave his minor miracle.

But Bobby was overcome. She would not let him go, and made him sit beside her on the couch.

Glowing from his generosity, he was still doubtful of his motive. 'How much I paid to avoid a fiasco,' he thought, and then gave himself up to necking with Bobby again. It was better than before, she wanted to please him, and so, inevitably, they set about fulfilling the purpose of the evening. But it did not go as smoothly as that, for with an air close to panic she begged him to allow her a few more minutes, and the sight of her thin boy's body and her grateful inept kisses damped any promise he might have felt. Then it became necessary to choose one of the items from the schedule of crossed pleasures Jay-Jay had offered, and with the aid of that, and the aid of every relevant memory, they succeeded the two of them, he was able, and for five minutes, the sweat on his back, the sweat on his face, he pretended to be happy and finished with a smile.

Bobby was delirious, or at least she presented the face of delirium. Something had happened to her apparently, a tremor of sensation perhaps which had wormed free out of a frozen wilderness. 'Oh, you're wonderful,' she said, 'it was marvellous.' And on she went, babbling a little, trying by language to swell that tremor into a lion of passion. It was impossible, he thought, he could not have been wrong. Almost to the end she had borne him with a cramped smile and eyes which she turned away. He had never felt so lonely in his life as when he had made love to her, and now she was trying to believe they had had a triumph.

'Darling Charley,' she was saying, kissing his eyelashes, fondling his hair.

She was close as a sticky jelly, and it took him half an hour to leave her. At the end, just as they kissed good night, Bobby looked at him with shining eyes and said, 'When will I see you again?'

'I don't know. Soon,' he said, and disliked himself for a liar.

When he got back to his house, he scrubbed himself with a rough washcloth and took Elena in their bed, hugging her to his chest until she purred that he was breaking her, and he gave himself to her, crying, 'I love you, I love you,' her body a cove where he could bury himself. Then he took a sleeping pill and drifted into unconsciousness until Faye's call awakened him.

Now it was morning and everything in the last six weeks took its turn at tormenting him. He suffered these sleepless hours the way men with shattered bodies fight for the time which will be the end of their pain. So Eitel fought for the minute when Elena would wake up and he would no longer be alone. But while he waited, he could only think that if Elena had lied to him the way he had lied to her, had been with another man, washed, and come to his bed, he could have strangled her. It was ridiculous. One could not compare the pleasure he had found with Bobby to the pleasure Elena gave him. Still, someone watching Bobby and himself might have thought he found pleasure; considerately, he had uttered sounds of enjoyment. That was meaningless, it came from him, but the thought of Elena uttering such sounds with another man . . . that was odious. Abruptly, he recognized how completely he must own her.

'I'm willing to grant her no life at all,' Eitel said to himself, and with a sickly perspiration could only think, 'How I'm deteriorating, oh how I'm deteriorating.'

17

Munshin was telling part of the truth. He had talked with me for a few hours in the roulette den where Lulu and I spent our time during our trip away from Desert D'Or. Maybe we came back the night Eitel was visiting Bobby; at any rate I missed nearly all of what was happening, and I knew nothing about Eitel's new script or that Collie had seen him so often.

I was too busy. Lulu had suggested one afternoon that we get into her car, pack a picnic supper, and travel three hundred miles across the state line to her favourite gambling hole. Since Lulu did not know how to drive below ninety on the desert roads, and I liked a hundred, the picnic was not so impossible as it sounded. As things turned out, however, we ate the sandwiches she brought at two in the morning, and we would have needed a fifty-gallon drum of coffee to supply us while we stayed.

I had gone ready to gamble. The fourteen thousand dollars with which I came to Desert D'Or was half gone already, and I had the idea it was time to make more. I was ready to win a lot or lose a lot, and I did both before we were through. We arrived with only a few hundred dollars between us, but Lulu had standing credit, and I borrowed from it until I knew we were going to stay and then cashed in my account from the bank in Desert D'Or.

For twelve days we gambled, and we might have gambled for thirty more if Collie had not come to bother us, betting through the long working day of the gambler, from ten at night to nine in the morning, and for that stretch of time there could have been a heat wave for all we knew or an earthquake or even a war; we worked all night, we tried to sleep through the day, and at mealtime Lulu would be counting the serials on dollar bills to find her lucky number for the night while I would be busy covering page after page with astronomical computations so I could find a system for roulette. I came up with one just as I was beginning to lose interest, and it was exactly the system of a man who has given up; with thirty thousand dollars of capital, I could be sure of making a hundred dollars a night, or at least fairly sure; the odds were two hundred and fifty to one in my favour; but if I lost, I lost everything, all thirty thousand. I explained it to Lulu, and she made a face. 'You have ice water for blood,' she snapped at me.

Lulu played like a one-man band on amateur hour. She would have her lucky number or two numbers or ten, and she would play her combination only long enough to desert it and pick another, any number, the count of people at the table, or the string of buttons on the croupier's vest, and then she would swoop off into red and black or odd and even, make a stand on double-zero, and come flying back to two, three, seven, or eleven, as if a pair of dice were interchangeable with a roulette cloth, cleaving to two and three during what she called the 'evil hours,' seven and eleven when things went well. If she won a bet she squealed with delight, if she lost she groaned, and sometimes she was so confused, for she could never remember the odds, nor even the idea of the game, that a winning bet on red would grow for several rounds until she finally noticed it with a gasp of surprise, or just as often never knew how much she finally lost because she forgot her chips too long. With it all, she tipped the croupiers, how she tipped them and to everybody's irritation would come out ahead more often than not. Watching her gamble made one believe in the lion and the lamb. Roulette was her passion Lulu would say to anyone who listened, but she gambled with the passion of a child for a dessert or a dixie cup.

She certainly irritated me. I was professional no more than Lulu, but I had talent – at least I thought so – and I was serious. Gambling was hard work to me, and I was always going with a dozen calculations at once, listing every number which came up on the wheel that night and marking it red or black, odd or even, adding a Roman numeral to denote its third of the cloth, trying all the while in the stew of five half-developed systems to know how the imbalance was moving; was it red now or was it black which must be ready to have its run or the law of averages would be sadly maimed?

Every once in a while I would start to see myself in that big room with its Louis the Fourteenth chandeliers hanging in no apology over the fluorescent lights of the game tables while the modern bar that went along one wall was deserted except for the tourists who came to get drunk, to drop their thirty dollars, and to sport the worried leer of the Anglo-Saxon in a tropical brothel. Then, looking at the hundreds of people in the room, listening to the hush, and the dry popping sounds of the ball going and goggling its route against the wheel, I would be startled to discover myself as if I were all of a sudden undressed, and for a moment I would seem weird, life would seem weird. For money was usually real to me, I had had so little of it, and even in Desert D'Or, like a rube who got rich, it was not an easy thing for me to buy an eighty-dollar jacket or order a five-dollar meal. Once, I have to admit, I swept that poker game in Tokyo, but I was low then, I was ignorant, I was lucky as Lulu, and now with a coldness that looked me in the eye when I would start to think of the size of the room rather than the spin of the wheel I would put up twenty dollars, forty dollars, eighty dollars, and double it a few times again, the amounts no more than figures on my pad, the sign of talent; there was the cold gambler in me.

Talk of my talent, I ended by losing a lot of money. There is no point in going into how I would feel afterward on winning nights and losing nights. The common denominator was the same; I wanted to go back for more, sure if I had won that my new system had shown itself, sure even more if I lost that the mistakes I made were now taken into account and the error would be fixed tomorrow. Win or lose, I controlled the situation with my mind, I was superior, I understood; that is the sweet of gambling; and so, long description is unnecessary – all real gambling is more or less the same. Why tell how my seven thousand dollars went to five, and the five, eight, and how eight thousand dropped to three, nor the interesting hours of that night when three thousand became ten thousand and went back to five again? What counts is that I came back to Desert D'Or with a third of the money I had when I left, the itch for gambling gone with the cash.

But while it lasted, it was an itch. Lulu and I took adjoining rooms in an air-conditioned hotel, and there were heavy drapes on the window to give us night when it was day. Those rooms were made for sleeping, and sleep we did, swimming along in the light slumber of people suffering from fever. In all those days we did not make love once; Lulu could have been a goat or a wagon of hay for all I cared, and she cared less. We lived together, we ate together, we gambled together, and we slept next door to one another. We had never been so polite.

As I have said, it could have gone on for a month, but Collie came to bother us. It happened after we had been gambling only a few days, and nothing he said at the time seemed very pressing. A stranger might as well have come up from behind and said I had inherited a million dollars. 'Fine,' I would have told him, 'but have you noticed that seventeen has come up three times in the last twelve plays? There's a mint to be made on that number.'

Collie put it on the table; he told me that once I gave the rights, a signature, no more, he would give me ten thousand dollars. When I showed no interest, saying to him, 'Oh, man, just take my life and forget it. I'm looking for another,' it set off a kind of compound interest in Collie, until by degrees the ten thousand dollars was doubled. Lulu teased him, and I said that I never made up my mind in a hurry. He gave up without even my word to give an answer, and after he left we forgot about him for a day or two, but I heard him later on the phone to Lulu, and whatever they talked about, and I can guess that Herman Teppis was the subject, he made his impression. Lulu began to sweat free of the long fever; she was getting critical of me again. By the night we left, we were tired of gambling; something had filled its space.

On the drive home, there was a fight. 'Naturally you don't want to think about the future,' Lulu said.

There was nothing I wanted to think about less.

'You're bland, do you know that, Sergius?'

'I don't want a slob movie made out of my name.'

'A slob movie! If you really loved me, you'd want to get married instead of treating me this way. With twenty thousand dollars you'd have financial security.'

'A lot of security,' I said. 'Twenty thousand dollars would buy your toenail polish.'

She was so angry she ran the car on the shoulder of the road and had to twist it back. 'You don't love me,' she said. 'If you did, you would listen to me.' We continued the quarrel for half the drive. Then Lulu had an inspiration. 'You're right, Sergius,' she said, 'twenty thousand dollars isn't enough.'

'Rat-feed,' I said cautiously.

'But I know a way you could make more.'

'How?'

Her face became hard as though she were considering which dress to wear. 'Sugar, I want you to tell me exactly what H.T. said to you the day he invited you to the party.'

'Oh, now look !'

'Sergius, I'm serious. You tell me every word.'

While I talked, she listened with a little air of triumph, nodding her head at certain details. 'Of course that's it,' she announced when I was done. 'I tell you, Sugar, I can see right into H.T.'s mind. What he's thinking is that maybe you could act in your own picture. You could be the star.' She put a hand on my arm as I started to laugh at her. 'Now be serious!' she cried. 'It's obvious H.T. is behind Collie in wanting to make this picture. H.T. likes you. He thinks you have sex appeal.'

'Did you give him a run-down on me?'

'I just know. If we play our cards right, H.T. will agree to everything you want.' She nodded her head at the thought. 'If you're a star, Sugar, then we each have financial independence, and we can get married.'

'I don't know how to act,' I said.

'There's nothing to learn.' And she gave me a talk. The way Lulu described it, nothing was easier than to act. A good director would draw out my qualities. 'If you're wooden,' Lulu said, 'he'll make it seem like sincerity. If you're self-conscious, he'll know tricks to make you look like a small-town boy. And if you ruin a scene . . . well, you know, they always shoot protection. With the way they work, you could walk through the part.'

'This is the end,' I told her. 'I don't want to be an actor.' But as if to hint I was a liar, my heart began to beat.

'Wait till Collie gets ahold of you,' she said.

Lulu was not wrong. Two days after we returned to Desert D'Or, the producer flew down to see us and slammed me into a conference. To my surprise, for I always thought people found it hard to understand me, Collie wasted no time in dissecting my character. 'Look, Sergius,' he said in the first hour we were alone. 'I know you, and I'm going to tell you frankly. You're a sick boy. You got many qualities of character which could amount to something, honesty, integrity, bravery, desire, durability, heart' – he rattled these off like a recipe – 'but they don't mesh. You don't click. Nothing's working in you.' On he went, stabbing for the centre of me. 'I'm older than you, Sergius,' he said, 'and I can tell what's at the bottom of your attitude. You're afraid things will change. You're not happy with Lulu and yet you hold on to her. What really scares you is that one of these days she's going to take off for the capital on her new picture and hook up with some other guy. You know something? I don't blame her. You're afraid to move back, you're afraid to move forward. You just want to sit still. Only it's not possible. How much money do you have left?'

'Three thousand,' I found myself admitting.

'Three thousand. I can see you pinching it, trying to keep up with Lulu, hoping the character next to you will pick up the check. You can carry three thousand, maybe you can carry it ten weeks. And then what? You're broke. Do you understand that? What are you going to do next? Bum around here, take a job as a car-hop? Kiddo, don't look smug. I'll blast your smugness. Do you know what it's like to go to a new town without a cent?'

'Yes, I know what it's like,' I said.

'Once you knew it, but now you've had a taste of something else. You think you're going to enjoy goosing waitresses when you've been boffing the best? Brother, I can tell you, once you've been bed-wise with high-class pussy, it makes you ill, it makes you physically ill to take less than the best. There's nothing worse,' Munshin promised.

He had succeeded. He made a puncture. For the first time the four thousand dollars I lost became real to me, and I saw their loss as the loss of future time. Munshin had figured it well; I had been spending, I never knew how, several hundred dollars a week, and by his words, weeks went away, fifteen weeks, sixteen weeks, I saw suddenly that I had very little time left at the resort, and I had no idea where to go, and what to do about Lulu.

Now Munshin changed his tactics. Like an advertising executive, he worked first with fear and then with hope. 'I know how you feel about the movie industry,' he said. 'You think it's phony, you don't like the movies they make, the lies they hand out. Should I tell you something? It's disgusted me, too. There's hardly a day goes by I'm not disgusted to the breaking point. It disgusts every man in the industry who wants to be a part of something serious and important and progressive. These people exist, they work, they make up three-quarters of the industry, four-fifths, and you'd be amazed at the quality of some of the product. I tell you the industry is more than just an entrée into something ridiculous and corrupt. It's a chance to fight, an opportunity to grow!' And Munshin threw out his arms like an expanding world creating space. 'Sergius, you've been thinking along the lines that you'd be trading your soul for a bag of loot. You're a child,' he growled at me. 'This is your opportunity for the real money, kiddo, and dignity and importance. So you start as an actor. I don't like actors myself. But you can go into anything from there, production, direction, even writing although I don't advise it. But you'll meet the people who count, you'll have opportunities. You'll get an education and you can use one. What the hell do I have to break my heart arguing with you for? Sergius, I know you. Get yourself in gear and you could be a full-fleshed articulate guy benefiting the world, benefiting yourself, that's your type if you give yourself a chance. What, do you think it's purer in any other line of work? Why you have no idea of how we're planning to show up that orphan asylum where they pushed you around.'

Maybe this was the one mistake Collie made. Without warning, I lost my temper. 'Show up that orphan asylum?' I yelled. 'Munshin, you're a damn liar.'

He looked delighted at having aroused an outburst, and this made me even angrier. 'Progressive? Important people?' I babbled at him. 'Serious?'

'Cough it up, kid,' Munshin said agreeably.

'It's all bullshit,' I shouted. 'War, marriage, movies. I mean take religion,' I said, not even knowing how that had come into it, 'suppose there's a God and imagine what *He* thinks seeing people get in the same room and get down on their hands and knees, I mean just look at the idea of sticking kids in an orphan asylum, did you ever think of how crazy that is, I mean a man and a woman for instance making legal arrangements to live together all their lives?' I must have sounded insane to him. 'You're fun of bullshit, too, Munshin.'

'Oh, oh, oh, another anarchist,' Munshin groaned. He stretched out his arms. 'You know something?' he asked, beginning all over again, 'anarchists make talented people. Maybe I think the way you do, deep down. I know Charley Eitel does.'

His easy voice made me feel ridiculous. 'Have a drink, Sergius,' Munshin smiled, and I knew then how easy it was for him to start tantrums like mine.

After hope comes sentiment. So the world has been sold ten times over. 'The only real appeal I know,' Munshin said, 'is to your best instincts. I think you ought to act in this picture, but there's something bigger than that. You can help a friend.'

'Eitel?' I asked. I hated the way I continued the conversation as if nothing had happened.

'Exactly. He's the only man who could direct you properly. I know I could sell H.T. on that. Do you understand what it would mean to Eitel?'

'He wants to work by himself,' I said.

'Nonsense. I've known Charley Eitel for years. Do you realize the talent he has? I wish you could have seen how Eitel at his best could take mediocre talent and weak scripts and make films that had a beauty to them. His talent is rotting away now because his talent is to work with people and be loved and admired. You could put him back where he belongs.'

'You mean I could put him back where you'd like to have him.'

'Listen, you have a brain like a muscle. I understand Charley Eitel better than he understands himself. Everything is closed to him now. You can't begin to appreciate the interrelations of film-making, the finances. H.T. has a big thumb, big enough to blacklist him at any studio in the world, and it's only Herman

Teppis who can lift that black list. You're the boy I can use to convince H.T. that he should take Eitel back.'

'Even if I went along with you, it wouldn't be that easy.'

'Everything is easy,' Munshin said. 'When H.T. wants a picture, and I can make him want this picture, he'll cut off his arm before he'll be stopped. He'll even take Eitel.'

'I'd like to see you put that in writing.'

'Did you just come out of the woods?' Collie asked. 'Fifty lawyers would have a stroke. You can trust me. I want Eitel back more than you.'

'Why? You know, I wonder about that,' I said to him.

'I don't know why, brother,' Collie answered with a big grin. 'Maybe I ought to talk to my analyst.'

'I'd like to talk to Eitel,' I said.

'Go ahead. Ruin it. Charley Eitel is all pride. You think you can go to him and ask what he wants? You got to beg him to do your picture.'

'I don't know what to say,' I said finally. What an answer!

'Say yes. You'd agree right now if you weren't so stubborn that you hate to contradict yourself.'

Munshin had to be back in the capital by morning, and at last he quit me, leaving the promise he would call. I can say that he kept his word. Between Lulu's emotional blackmail and Collie on the phone I didn't have a moment to think.

I had been tempted more than once to sign the papers Munshin would hand me, but it wasn't stubbornness alone which held me back. I kept thinking of the Japanese KP with his burned arm, and I could hear him say, 'Am I going to be in the movie? Will they show the scabs and the pus?' The closer I came to wanting the contract, the more he bothered me, and all the while Collie would go on or Lulu would go on, painting my career with words, talking about the marvellous world, the real world, about all the good things which would happen to me, and all the while I was thinking they were wrong, and the real world was underground – a tangle of wild caves where orphans burned orphans. Yet the more they talked, the more I wanted to listen to them, and I didn't know what to do. I didn't know what was right, and I didn't know if I cared, and I didn't even know if I knew what I wanted or what was going on in me.

No matter what Collie said, I ended by going to see Eitel. I had to; I no longer knew if it was more selfish to refuse Munshin than to sell my expensive history to Supreme Pictures.

Eitel refused to talk about it at first. 'You see,' he said, 'I promised I wouldn't mix in it.'

'To Collie?' I asked in surprise.

'I'm sorry, Sergius. I can't say.'

'You're my friend,' I told him. 'Don't you think this is more important to me than it is to Collie?'

Eitel sighed. 'I suppose I knew,' he said, 'that I couldn't stay out of this.'

'Well, what do you think I should do?'

He smiled sadly. 'I don't know what you should do. Did it ever occur to you that as you get older, it gets more difficult to give advice?'

'Sometimes I think that no matter what, you still have to do something,' I told him.

'Yes. In my day it used to be dialectics.' He nodded his head at this as if deciding whether to absorb it or throw it away out of hand.

'Tell me,' I asked, 'what kind of picture do you think would come out of this?'

'Sergius, let's not be naïve,' he snapped. 'It will be a picture and it will have lots of beautiful photography about airplanes shooting at airplanes. What kind of pictures do you think Collie makes anyway?'

'And what about the plans Collie has for you?' I asked.

He shrugged. 'I know those plans,' Eitel said. 'If your picture is going to be made, and they want me for it, I wouldn't have an easy time deciding.' He held a finger to his nose as though to stop me because he wanted to say more. 'Sergius, I don't think it will be very nice if you use me as the excuse. You see, you may be doing me no favour.' Then he stared into my face for a long time, and he looked stern. 'Are you sure,' he said at last, 'that you don't want the career . . . and the money . . . and the rest of it? Are you sure you don't really want to be an actor?' And he went on to tell me about his talk with Collie.

As he spoke, I felt a touch of sickness. It was no more than a turn in my stomach and an instant when I felt pale, but I had one of those hints of what cold and violent ambition had been stifling in me for so many years, and it was as if deep inside two powerful hands fought each other forward and back, locked in a test of strength which left room for little else. 'You see,' Eitel was saying into my ear, 'it took me until now to realize I wanted such things very much, and that was why I stayed in the capital.'

I could hardly answer him. I sat there sick at what I had found. 'You're right,' I said, and I suppose my voice shook, 'I guess I was trying to put it off on you.'

'Maybe you were,' he said, and then leaned forward. 'I'll tell you a little of what I think. I think you should pass this offer by if there's something you want to do more. But that is what you have to know.'

I nodded at this. 'What do you think of me being a writer?' I asked slowly.

'Well, Sergius, that's hard to say.'

'I know. I brought something along I wrote a couple of weeks ago. It's a poem. Just a stunt.' I had hoped I wouldn't have to show it – I had written it after waking up from a dream – but I reached into my pocket and handed him a piece of paper. 'I like to play with words,' I mumbled.

'Sergius, do shut up, and let me read your masterpiece.'

This was the poem:

THE DRUNK'S BEBOP AND CHOWDER

Shirred athe inlechercent felloine namelled Shash
Head tea lechnocerous hero calmed Asshy

Befwen hes prunt cuddlenot riles fora lash
Whenfr hir cunck woodled lyars arfordelay?

'Yi munt seech tyt und speets tytsh'
'I-uh wost tease toty ant tweeks tlotty'

'And/or atuftit n pladease slit,'
'N ranty off itty indisplacent,'

'Frince Yrhome washt balostilted ina lady.'
'Sinfor her romesnot was lowbilt inarouter dayly.'

When he finished it, he laughed. 'It's amusing, I guess. I realize how much you're under the influence of Joyce.'

I knew I was going to make a fool of myself, but for once I didn't care. 'Who's Joyce?' I asked.

'James Joyce. You've read him, of course?'

'No. I think I heard the name though.'

Eitel picked up my poem and read it through again. 'Isn't that odd?' he said.

There was one thing I wanted to take home with me. 'You think I'm talented?' I asked.

'I'm beginning to have that suspicion about you, yes.'

'Okay,' I nodded, 'I guess . . . well . . .' So much talk was coming up in me, so much enthusiasm. I felt as old as a ten-year-old boy, and it was a relief to feel that way with somebody I could trust. 'Do you mind if I talk about why I never thought of being a professional fighter?' I asked him.

'I always thought it was because you didn't want to get your brains scrambled.'

'Well, yes,' I said, 'do you know that's exactly it. I was afraid of that. How did you know?'

He only smiled.

'Charley, I was afraid all the time. There are fighters like that, you know and some of them even get to be halfway competent, but that's not the way to be. Not to go in scared every time.'

'Maybe the boys you fought felt the same way.'

'I suppose some of them did. But I didn't know that then.' I shook my head. 'Besides, there's something worse. After a while I realized I had no punch. A counter-puncher who doesn't have a punch fights all night and he takes too much punishment.' I whistled. 'I can hardly tell you how I hated to admit to myself that I had no real punch. No *real* punch.'

'Yes, I know.'

'Once, I had a punch,' I said to him. 'It was the Quarter-Finals fight in the Air Force tournament. The word we had around the Base was that if a man reached the Semi-Finals, he had a good chance for flying school. So I was pressing for that fight, and I almost got knocked out. I don't remember a thing, but my second told me that I caught the other dupe with a beautiful combination when he was coming in to finish it off.

And they counted him out, and I didn't even know until it was all over. Then in the Semi-Finals I took a beating. I got stomped. But they say that sometimes a fighter is dangerous when all that's left is his instinct sort of, because he can't think his fight any more. It seems to come from way inside, like you're a dying animal maybe.'

'And what is your instinct now?' Eitel asked.

'I can't help it. I guess I want to be a writer. I don't want somebody else to tell me how to express myself.'

'Trust your instinct,' Eitel said, and made a face. 'How optimistic I am at bottom. Do what you think, Sergius.'

Somehow, I had known Eitel would help me to refuse the offer. On the way back, knowing my decision was made, I discovered I was feeling fairly well. I knew that my decision didn't mean very much; if my movie was not made then others would be made, but at least my name would not be used. I suppose what I really was thinking is that I would always be a gambler, and if I passed this chance by, it was because I had the deeper idea that I was meant to gamble on better things than money or a quick career. I had a look then into the kind of vanity I shared with Eitel. Each of us judged himself hard, for strong in us was the idea that we must be perfect. We felt we were better than others and therefore we should act better. It is a very great vanity.

By evening my fear had come back, physical fear with a dry throat and a hot heart. I was scared and there was no check on it, because I knew my mind was made up and I would not change it now. I even forced myself to tell Lulu. I expected anything from her, tantrums, fights, maybe even the announcement that she wouldn't see me any more. Instead she surprised me. She was silent for a long time, and then she said, 'You didn't want to do it, did you, Sergius? I knew, honey. I knew you were unhappy.'

At that moment I was full of pity for her. She looked so small, so blonde, so disappointed and frightened, and yet she would not try to argue with me. Suddenly I felt Lulu was really very frail and I loved her. My anger was gone. She had given me the best she could, and I could love her; how can there be love

219

without some weakness? All I knew was that I wanted to give her all I had, and it hurt that I had so little.

'I love you, baby,' I said to her.

Tears came into Lulu's eyes. 'I love you, too,' she whispered. 'I know that now.'

'Oh, listen,' I said, 'listen, let's get married.'

'How?' she said hopelessly.

'No, look, it's not that hard. Let's go away. Give it up. Give up the movies. Maybe you can act on the stage, and I'll do something, I swear I will.'

Lulu began to cry. 'It's not possible, Sergius,' she said.

'It is. You hate the movies. You told me so.'

'I don't really hate them,' she said in a little voice.

'Then we'll live where you say. But marry me.'

She tried to nod. This was just what she had wanted a month ago, but once we want more, we can hardly want less. 'It couldn't work, Sergius.'

I didn't know if it could. While we sat holding one another I tried to find a way, and in my enthusiasm it did seem possible. 'Let's try,' I said at last.

'Kiss me, darling,' she said.

We hugged each other very hard, and while she cried she kissed my eyes and nose with long wet kisses. 'Oh, Sergius, let's just go on like this for a while and not worry, and then we'll see.'

What she said made me afraid again, and it was a tangible fear, as if the moment I left her room the burned corpses of half the world would be lying outside the door. We started to make love, and I couldn't think of her or of myself or anything but flesh, and flesh came into my mind, bursting flesh, rotting flesh, hung on spikes in butcher stalls, flesh burning, flesh gone to blood.

All the while Lulu and I were caressing each other I could think of nothing else, and although I tried up to the end I knew it was no use. Her body was frightening to me. 'No, I can't, I just can't tonight,' I said to her in panic, and she must have known it already for she did nothing except to touch my face, easily and gently.

'My poor baby,' Lulu said, and held me against her breast. 'What's the matter, my darling? I do love you.'

I had a horror I would start crying, and I couldn't trust myself to speak. We weren't inches apart and yet I had the feeling I had to reach out to her across a great distance. 'Everything's the matter,' I said, and perspiration covered my body.

'Tell me, tell me, I don't care what it is.'

I did tell her, or at least I tried; for half an hour, maybe it was an hour, maybe more, I told her all the things I never told anybody else, the operations I had flown and their names, those box-office names military press agents would put on them until they sounded like night-club acts, 'Operation Castanet,' and 'Punchbowl,' and 'Red Hot Mama,' and how red the fires had been which our planes sowed, and how cruel was jellied gasoline – a blob on a man and the man was the fire, fire hot enough to melt the skull. So I told her what I thought the corpses looked like, for we were never encouraged to get up to visit the front, but I could know how dead Oriental Villages looked the following day, staring their blind eye into the air like the sour black ash of a garbage dump, and all the while we flew and we would drink and there were the geisha houses and the poker games and the taste on one's tongue of being up at four in the morning ready for a flight, and the long conversations about parties and girls where nobody ever knew who knew the most, and the arguments about the technical performances of airplanes and which plane was better, and what was a career in the Air Force. I tried to tell it all to her, about the Japanese KP, and how I came not to like the fliers I knew, until finally there had come the time when I could no longer go to the geisha girls, so nice, so feminine, because flesh was raw, flesh was the thing one burned in the real world, and in a kind of sweat at myself, I would yell into the pressure of my brain, 'I enjoy it. I enjoy the fire. I have the cruelty to be a man.' So I had been without a woman and without love until the night I met her, she had been the first in over a year, and that had meant more, it had meant so much more than anything which had happened to me ... except that now my sickness seemed to have returned.

'Oh, my baby, oh, my darling,' Lulu said, 'if I could only chase it away.' And with a little air of tender child's amazement, as if she had never considered this before, she said, 'You've been hurt even more than me.' She was good that night, and as we

221

lay together hour after hour my fear went back where it had come from, but it was weaker when it left. I could feel her body again, I could come to touch it and to sense it and to know it was beautiful until the moment when caught by the curve of her belly, loving the touch of her hips and so fond of the wink of her breast, I was able to take her again. It was the best night we ever had, for I loved her and I think she loved me. We passed into each other, and long afterward lay looking at one another and smiling. 'I love you,' I kept whispering to her, and her eyes filled with tears. 'I feel like a woman for the first time,' she said. Yet, before I left, our mood changed again. If I had loved her earlier in the evening, I loved her more now, I had never loved her more, and yet it was with bitter love, with a feeling of loss. For each of us knew that there was nowhere to go after this night.

My instinct was good. By the next day I had lost her sure enough. We had lost what we had had. We were close no longer and we could rarely lift above the sad depression which hangs upon people who still feel emotion and know the emotion has no future. We did what she said, we went on the way we had before, we even made believe there was nothing the matter. And all the while I was mourning our one fine hour.

We made the rounds, we had our little fights, we even made love, and the while we were waiting. The date when she would have to begin work on her new picture came closer, and as if that were the first of a whole series of dates which meant ends to different things – the day she left for the capital, the day I drew my last money from the bank, the day I would have to leave Desert D'Or – we never talked about it. Once she told me that Teddy Pope and Tony Tanner would be down soon at the resort for publicity photos with her, and she even bothered to explain the movie. The new picture would be a triangle. Teddy Pope was to get her in the end, but through the middle of the film she was to think she was in love with Tony Tanner. 'I don't want you to be silly about it,' she said to me. 'Naturally, I have to be seen all the time with Tony and Teddy. The studio wants a lot of advance publicity on this picture.'

'I guess I won't be seeing much of you.'

'That's so ridiculous. You can be with us all the time. It's just that when they take pictures, it would be better if you sort of dropped into the background.'

'I'll carry my trap door,' I said.

'You're just a baby.'

When Teddy and Tony arrived, our life changed. Instead of going to Dorothea's, we made a tour of the supper clubs and the night clubs, Teddy going as escort to Lulu while Tony Tanner and I would follow behind. A week went by of watered whisky, dim rooms, and the curving walls and scalloped arches of Desert D'Or architecture. We made quite a quartet. Publicly the romance between Teddy and Lulu was sounded again, and there must have been a hundred pictures taken of them looking into each other's eyes, holding hands, or dancing together. Yet when we were seated and no photographers were around, Teddy Pope gave his attention to me and Tony Tanner would go into long conversations with Lulu. At dawn when we separated, Lulu and I would be alone for an hour or two. I had never seen her so happy. Lulu was enchanted to be divided into three.

'I wonder which girl you like,' I said to her after an evening and she answered too quickly, 'The one with you, of course. What a bore that Tony is.'

Tony was good-looking. Naturally. He was tall and big-muscled and he had dark hair which ran in rolling waves. He had a dimple in his chin. He was twenty-five but he still walked with a swagger, and he used the aggressive style of some comedians with little of the humour. I was prejudiced, that I knew, but he irritated me. 'Hey, boy chicks,' he would say, 'let's play the mouse into the next hole,' which was a way of saying that we should move on. Lulu laughed at almost everything he said. He had picked up several kinds of talk and he whipped them like a rug-beater. 'Sugarboy,' he would say if I started to argue with him, 'don't swallow your words. Discussion is for squares.' To a woman's nervous giggle, he would answer, 'Lady, oil that libido.' Maybe it will help you understand him if I mention that he was friendly when I was alone with him. The only half hour we ever spent that way, he was full of admiration I was a flier. 'You guys,' he said, nodding seriously, 'I mean, you really had it rough. I was overseas on an entertainment junket, so in my own small way I know what it is.'

'Yes,' I said, 'in your own small way.'

'It makes me feel ashamed and like nothing when I talk to guys like you. Why . . .'

'I understand you know Marion Faye,' I interrupted.

'That bastard. A couple of bimbos I used to have around did a little work for him, so the word's out I pimped. That's the kind of thing that happens just when you're starting to make it big in the industry.'

'You want to make it big, don't you?' I asked.

He looked at me cautiously as though he didn't know if it was important for me to like him. 'What else?' he asked. 'Don't you?' Then his mouth turned. 'I never will, though. I'll never make it, laddie.'

'You never know. You might just make it.'

'I got a scandal. There was this screwball I used to live with, and she was nuts about me. Only she was hopeless. I carried her as long as I could, and then I told her to hang up. You know what? She killed herself. Believe it or not, I wanted the best for that little chick. What a break. They say I drove her to it.'

The moment Tony Tanner was not alone with me, his style would change. Before an audience, he was always on the attack. He and Lulu would have fancy exchanges. 'You're a bland boy,' she tried once on him.

'Bland? Honey, I'm mellow.'

Lulu laughed. 'I bet you faint on the doorstep.'

'Your sweet little doorstep?' Tony fingered his hair. 'Let me in, and I'll demolish the house.' He talked so loudly that people at the nearby tables turned around. Tony winked at them and their eyes went back to their plates. 'You darlings,' he said to them.

'Oh, God,' Teddy Pope groaned. These days it was his habit to sit morosely.

'What's the matter,' said Tony, 'you bleeding?'

'I wish you were a Bimmler already,' Pope told him. 'It would make things more relaxing.'

'I have news for you,' Tony said, 'you know how much fan mail I got last week?'

Teddy yawned and turned away. 'It's such a pity you're afraid of me,' he said in my ear. His manner went through several mutations. On the first evening he teased me. 'You're still a shy aviator, I see,' he said. Then he yawned again. 'Forgive me. I forget you're in love.'

Things improved a little. After a few nights he was even friendly. 'When you're over thirty, as I am,' he said once, 'you'll understand that you can't have romance unless it's against the conventions.'

In the meantime, somehow or other, Tony and Lulu were talking about Messalina. 'Messalina had nothing on you, mouse,' Tony was saying.

'I like you, Tony,' said Lulu. 'You're so crude.'

'I'm tattooed. Try me.'

That was about the way it went. To help my mood I discovered after several days that Desert D'Or gossip was putting Tony in Lulu's bed, and Teddy in mine. 'Now that we're lovers,' Teddy said with a grin one night, 'let me warn you that I have a bad character.' He made a play of telling me the story of his life. 'My mother's a very sad person,' Teddy said. 'Father died when I was a kid, and then she was always introducing me to a new uncle. I guess I panicked. Today, what I would like is for something to happen where I could be true to myself. A moment of dignity.'

'You don't mean it,' I said to him.

Teddy looked at me. 'Sergius, you don't like me,' he said.

'I don't feel anything one way or the other.'

'Yes, you do. I make you uncomfortable. I make a lot of people uncomfortable, but that's no reason for them to feel superior.'

'You're right,' I said to him. 'I'm sorry.'

'Are you really sorry?'

'Yes,' I said. 'Everybody has the right to love the way they can.' I meant it. I suppose I couldn't have meant anything more, but it must have sounded superior. Teddy exhaled smoke in my face, and said, 'I hate to camp. But for some reason you bring it out in me.'

'All right kids, break it up,' Tony Tanner yelled. 'Lulu can't even hear me whisper in her ear.'

'Let's go outside and have a little talk,' I said to Tony.

'Talk before an audience,' he answered. 'It stimulates me.'

225

'You're very stimulating. With a crowd around you,' I told him across the table. He was about twenty pounds heavier than me, and he was conceivably in good shape, and I was not, but I had no worries about what was going to happen. All the pleasure of boxing was in my fingers. Like nearly everything else, good boxing is what is done with the rhythm and even more what is done just off the rhythm. I was so nicely ready that I was hoping Tony was good – I wanted it to go on for a while. 'Tell you what, man,' I said, 'you going outside or you going to sit here and let me give the talk?'

But Lulu put an end to that. 'You stop it, Sergius,' she snapped at me. 'You're brutal. You're practically a professional prize-fighter.'

'Well,' said Tony, relaxing, 'you didn't mention that detail, did you?'

I didn't know where I was and who seemed worse to me – Tony, Lulu, or myself. I couldn't even think of anything to say. But I have to give credit to Tony – he knew what to say.

'Why not go outside?' Tony said. 'Only when you take care of me, you better take good care, because if you don't kill me I've got a couple of friends who will be looking around for you.'

'Oh, let's go,' I said, starting to get out of my chair.

And Lulu stopped us again. That was a night. I can't know about the others, but I sat around drinking for hours and all the adrenalin I didn't use was burning in me. 'Look, like let's forget it, man,' said Tony at the end of the evening, and I felt so stupid and so worn out that to tell the truth, I even shook hands with him.

For a week the four of us endured each other, and then it was time for Tony and Teddy to go back to the capital. Lulu was in a bad mood the night they left. I took her afterward to one of the clubs but she was restless. 'I can't stand Tony,' she said. 'It's the reaction setting in. I hate his vulgarity, don't you, Sugar? He makes me vulgar too. That's what's so disgusting.'

In the following nights we returned to The Hangover. The routine was picked up again. We played Ghost, and we heard the words of Martin Pelley telling us how perfect was Dorothea. There was a change in Lulu, however. Her rudeness to me had come back, and she was listless and mean in bed. A depression thick as a fog bank settled over her.

To change Lulu's mood, Dorothea hired a projectionist one night, and we were shown two of Lulu's movies. As films I thought they were bad, and Lulu's acting was bewildering. There were a few scenes where she did the character called for by the plot, there were others where she was herself, and there were many scenes where she showed faces new to me. Yet she did something in and around the character, and what she did was a triumph for her – she was more beautiful than she ever seemed before. A girl somewhere between a child and a woman danced through the film. She had a naïve chastity which coaxed a man to find his opposite. Her husky little voice curled through a run of private humours. I sat beside her in the den while the film was projected, and felt she watched a vision. Little sounds came from her throat, her lips opened and closed, her body swayed slowly back and forth. She studied herself with an admiration, a pain, and a kind of awe.

She took a drink afterward, she listened with a half-smile to the praise of Dorothea's friends, she remembered to thank them, she even managed to stay for another half hour. When we got home, she was hysterical.

'It's awful, it's awful,' she wept.

'What's awful?' Before my eyes I could still see that silver image of Lulu, more troubling to her, more real, than anybody she had ever known.

'Oh, Sergius,' she cried, 'for the rest of my life I have to go downhill.'

As in all such moments, everything seemed to happen at once. The phone was ringing. It was Tony calling from the capital. Lulu sobbed into the mouthpiece, she hung up, she started to cry again. After half an hour of soothing her, she said in a broken voice, 'Sergius, you have the right to know. I slept with Tony Tanner.'

'But where? When?' I cried aloud, as if to learn that was most important of all.

'In a telephone booth.'

Saying these words, she became helpless with grief. He had humiliated her, she manged to tell me. 'I'll never be anything good,' she wept into the darkness, for I had turned off the lights and sat beside her, smoking a cigarette by the edge of the bed.

Next day she left Desert D'Or and went to the capital. She had to be there for her picture, she told me. Her picture was not scheduled to start for another ten days, but it was urgent that she leave. For a week I tried to reach her by telephone, but she never answered the messages and she was always out.

18

One night while they were lying in bed, Eitel noticed that
Elena's thighs were beginning to show dimpled hollows. It was
the only blemish on her skin, and yet it depressed him deeply.
Afterward, he could not take his eyes away. He had to let her
go, he would tell himself. There was no future with him, and she
had left only a few years of youth.

How he hated himself. He would look for comfort in the
thought that he was the only one who would feel such a sense of
responsibility for her. But then Eitel was forced to remind
himself that it was he who had begun the affair and made it
what it had become and therefore he could not escape it. What
would become of her? When she loved she kept nothing with
which to bargain and so she would always lose. There would be
many men after him, many loves, each more impossible than the
one before. If she never grew up, there would be drink or, in
contrast, dope – no need to become melodramatic, he would tell
himself – and yet what would become of her? Once again he was
filled with compassion and writhed because the compassion was
for the image in his mind. Toward the body sleeping beside him
he felt nothing. That body only hindered his limbs, he could not
really believe in the painful existence of that body.

Yet he felt her desperation. She slept restlessly; night after
night she would wake in terror from a dream and shudder next
to him in the darkness. A robber was trying the door, she would
say, or she had heard someone in the kitchen. Every story she
read in the newspapers of a rape or a murder was repeated in
her fear.

'A man followed me today,' she would tell him.

'Of course he did. You're an attractive woman,' Eitel would
say irritably.

'You didn't see the look on his face.'

'I'm sure he wanted to cut off your head and stuff you in a gunny sack.'

'That's what you'd like to do to me.' She looked bitterly at him. 'You're a good time Charley. You only like me when I'm in a good mood.'

The truth of this piqued him. 'You're the good time Charley,' he told her. 'When I say nice things, then you love me.'

'You're so superior,' Elena said. 'But you don't know what goes on in my head.'

After half an hour, he uncovered her latest secret. She wished to become a nun.

'Are you crazy?' he asked her. 'You'd make a honey of a nun.'

'A nun is never alone,' Elena said.

He was put in depression by her words. It was true, he thought, he ruined everything he touched. If someone lived with him and loved him, he provided her with nothing but loneliness. 'Nuns always have company,' Elena said in a stubborn voice.

A few days later she began wondering whether to cut her hair. She returned to the subject over and over. Would he like it? Did he think she would look good in short hair? What did he think? Should she do it? And Eitel, pretending to be interested, ended finally by beginning to think perhaps she should cut her hair. Her hair was one of her best features, but in the course of an evening it became dishevelled. It was so difficult for her to be neat.

'Will you still love me if I cut my hair?' Elena would ask, and then decide, 'No, you won't.'

'If my love depends on a haircut, you might as well find out now,' he would say, and wonder if she was right.

'Yes, I ought to find out,' she would repeat.

Ever since the night he had come back from Bobby's house, he had known that the effort to free himself of Elena had been premature. So, with a sadness that haunted him, for he had no idea if he was sad for Elena or sad for himself, he would say to her over and over, 'I know that I offer you nothing,' as if by saying it often enough, he could beg from the demon he saw judging him, one whisper of grace. 'You do try,' the demon might say, 'you are not completely dishonest.' But if he was

230

always telling Elena that he offered her nothing, he was attracted to another idea. On those long sleepless nights, he would think that to be fair he must marry her; somebody had to marry her. Otherwise, he could hear the complaint of all her future lovers: 'Munshin didn't want to, and Eitel didn't want to, so why should I?' The only answer was for them to get married, and he would consider just how he would ask her, and how afterward he would arrange the divorce. He would make it clear to Elena; they would get married in order to get divorced. That way she could probably find somebody else. As the former Mrs Eitel, the divorced wife of an ex-director, it was better than Miss Esposito. So he would be married a fourth time – how much did that cost him? – and she . . . she would feel that a man had cared enough to give her his name. How idiotic. But it would have meaning for Elena. If she could play her cards right . . . only Elena would never be able to do that, she could not play her cards at all. In a fury at her, he would stare at the ceiling and wonder if he would ever be able to make Elena see it the way he saw it. So days passed, and Eitel worked on his script, and found no satisfaction at how well it went.

One afternoon while he was in the middle of work, there was a phone call from Lulu. Her picture had been postponed a week, and she had decided to visit Desert D'Or for a night. To celebrate Dorothea was giving her a party. 'Charles, you're the one who's got to be there,' Lulu said over the phone. 'I think I came back just to talk to you.'

Eitel said, 'I hear you've broken up with Sergius.'

'Yes, it was sort of hectic, but now I think the wounds are healed.'

'I'm sure yours are,' Eitel said.

'Stinker.'

'Did you say the party is being given by Dorothea?'

'Charley, it's perfectly all right. Dorothea really wants you to come. I can't say more, but believe me, there are reasons.'

The party was a party like many others. He was not surprised to find The Hangover decorated for the evening, nor to see fifty people jamming the den with the promise of another fifty to arrive. Lulu happened to be in the foyer and took them directly to Dorothea who was installed on a bar stool to greet her guests.

'Goddamnit,' said Dorothea, 'every time I see poor Charley Eitel at a party, people introduce us.'

'Once the two of you get to know each other,' Lulu said, ignoring Elena, 'it'll be a romance.'

'It *was* a romance,' Dorothea said and gave her heavy chuckle. She squinted at Elena and added, 'Have a good time, sweetie.'

They wandered through the den and spent some time talking to Dorothea's husband. Martin Pelley was delighted with Elena and kept drawing Eitel aside to inform him what a wonderful girl he had. 'She's a great kid,' Pelley said. He called to her. 'Elaine,' Pelley said, 'you're marvellous, you're sweet.'

Elena flushed and looked nervously at the press of people in Dorothea's den. 'It's a very nice party, I think,' she said.

'You know, I've been wondering about the two of you,' Pelley went on. 'Everybody's wondering. When the hell are you going to get married?'

Elena's face was without expression. Pelley clapped Eitel on the back. 'A nice restful girl like this. You ought to marry her.'

'She won't have me,' Eitel said.

'I'm going to get a drink,' Elena said, and walked away.

'This is a great night,' Pelley went on, and bent over to whisper with drunken intensity, 'You ought to marry Elena.'

'Yes,' Eitel said. Pelley annoyed him. He was like every married man.

At the party they played Ghost, they played charades, a nest of men surrounded the slot machines in the hall between the den and the living room and played them continuously, feeding their quarters under the sign which read: *Dorothea O'Faye Retirement Fund.* Eitel lost sight of Elena. With gusto, he entered a game of charades and was easily the best man on his team. After an hour or two – he had lost count – he wearied of it, aware suddenly that he was drunk. Across the room he could see Elena standing uncomfortably at the edge of a group, but he had no thought of going to her rescue. Later, he watched Marion Faye talking to her but it did not bother him. Nothing would come of that.

A man Eitel recognized immediately came up with Dorothea and said hello. The moment he heard the voice, he had a feeling of dread. It was Congressman Richard Selwyn Crane of the

Subversive Committee, and Eitel had dreamed about Crane; often in the middle of a nightmare he could see Crane's youthful face with its grey hair and ruddy cheeks, hear the Congressman's soft voice. 'I'll allow you two characters to discover each other,' Dorothea said, and left them alone.

'Quite a party tonight,' Crane said, 'but then Dorothea always gives a good party.'

In the days when she had her column, it was regular once a week to find a reference to Crane; he was a great Congressman, Dorothea would tell her readers, and add that of all her friendships there was none she treasured more.

'I'm not familiar with Dorothea's parties,' Eitel said. He spoke carefully, concerned to control his emotion.

'You'd like her if you knew her,' Crane said intimately. 'Dottie . . . well, Dottie's an old trouper. Theatre people like you always take to such a girl.' A caterwaul of laughter from the charade players made Crane wince humorously. 'Mr Eitel,' he said, 'I'd like to talk to you. Could we go upstairs?'

Eitel looked at him dumbly. When he could think of no answer to make – there were so many contradictory ones to choose from – he merely nodded, his heart beating, and followed down the hall. They ended in a maid's room upstairs. There was a bottle on the table, and an unopened pack of cigarettes next to the ash tray.

The Congressman sat down on the bed and motioned Eitel to the single armchair in the room. Below them, partially muted, they could hear the eager avaricious noise of the party. 'I've been wanting to talk to you for a long time,' Crane said.

'So I see,' Eitel answered with a look at the whisky on the table.

Crane sat back and studied him thoughtfully. 'Mr Eitel,' he said, 'I know you don't like me, but the curious thing is that the day I questioned you, I had the feeling we could be friends under other circumstances.'

'Isn't it unwise for you to be seen with me?' Eitel interrupted. His pulse had calmed, but he felt honour-bound to keep his expression fixed.

'There's always danger in politics,' Crane said, 'but I don't believe this would be misunderstood.'

233

'In other words the Committee knows you're seeing me.'

'They know I'm interested in your case.'

'Why?'

'We all feel it's a shame.'

'Oh, now really!'

'Mr Eitel you probably have the idea we're interested in persecuting people. It happens not to be true. I personally can say I'm concerned enormously with the safety of this country, but none of us want to hurt people needlessly. You'd be amazed at the good work we do with some of the witnesses. I might say that it's always been my belief there's an uplifting element to all work. My father was a country preacher, you see,' he added intimately, and when Eitel failed to smile, Crane nodded coldly.

'At the time you appeared,' he went on, 'we had information that you were a card-carrying member. Since that time we've learned otherwise.'

'Then why doesn't the Committee say so?'

'Is that a reasonable demand?' Crane asked. 'You said some pretty potent things.'

'I don't understand why you're interested in me.'

'We feel you could help us. If we were to go over some of your former associations, it's possible you'd discover you have information you're not even aware of.'

'Are you offering a secret session?'

'I can't speak for the Committee, but that's part of what I see for you.'

The temptation of a secret session had been in his mind, Eitel knew. Perhaps that was why he could not bring himself to be gracious. 'Crane, if I should testify,' he said, 'what will you do about the newspapers?'

'We don't control them. You may smile, but we feel we've been misrepresented by them.' Crane shrugged. 'Perhaps you could get your lawyer or your public relations man to give a cocktail party. I understand it's a fine way to soften up the press. Of course, I'm no expert on these matters.'

Eitel did smile. 'Congressman, it's hard to think of you as an amateur.'

'Mr Eitel,' Crane said, 'I don't know if there's much point in going on with our talk.'

'A politician must be used to a few insults,' Eitel said, 'particularly at the beginning of his career.'

Crane chose to laugh. 'Why do you resist me?' he said warmly. 'I just want to help you.'

'I much prefer to help myself,' Eitel said, and then looked at him. 'You talk to your Committee. It's barely possible we can make some arrangement. Provided the session is secret of course.'

'We'll think about it,' Crane said, 'and let you know. I'm flying back to the East tomorrow, but here's my office number any time you want to phone.' He smiled, patted Eitel on the back, and told a joke about a secret agent who masqueraded as a woman at a banquet. Then they went down to join the party. In the den they separated, and Eitel worked himself into a corner and began to drink again. He hardly knew if he was in a good mood or a savage mood.

Marion Faye stopped by to talk. 'You lost me a girl,' he said.

'Elena?' Eitel said.

'Bobby.' Marion sipped at his cigarette. 'I set up a deal with Collie Munshin when he was here last week.'

'What does Collie want with her?'

Faye shrugged. 'He doesn't. He wants her as a stock girl at Supreme.'

'The poor kid.'

'She'll love it,' Marion said. 'A career.' He smiled. 'You know, Don Beda is here tonight.'

'Isn't he supposed to be in Europe?' Eitel said.

Marion ignored this. 'Don told me he digs Elena. He wants you to meet his wife and see if you dig her.'

'I thought Beda was divorced,' he said to Faye.

'He's married again. Wait till you see his chick. An English model, don't you know?'

Beda's marriages were famous; no one could understand them. He had been married at different times to an actress, a coloured singer, a Texas oil heiress with a European title – that had been a particular scandal – and to the madam of what was reported to be the most expensive brothel in South America. With it all, Beda had the reputation of giving the wildest parties in New York. They were legend; they were parties carried to conclusion; of the hard core who remained after the orchestra had gone and the curious and the college boys in for a weekend, everybody who stayed got around to everybody. There was even a kind of chic to saying, 'I was at one of Beda's parties. Left early of course.'

The other fifty people had arrived by now and the press in the den was so great that Faye and Eitel stood breathing in each other's faces. Somewhere, somebody was trying to sing a ditty and Eitel wondered how many meetings had been arranged by Dorothea tonight. He hated matchmakers, he thought dizzily, overwhelmed by the crush of people and the liquor he had drunk. 'I don't know,' he said, 'I think I'd just as soon not see Beda tonight.'

That was going to be impossible. Beda was working his way toward him, was shaking his hand. 'Charley, you old ham,' he smiled.

The odd thing about Beda was that he looked like a satyr. He was handsome and a little heavy with a small scar on his cheek, a black moustache, and eyes which protruded; he carried himself with the confidence of a man who knows that people talk about him, and it was his boast that he would invite anybody to his parties. 'You could never guess some of the long-shots who've come in,' he would say with a laugh. 'It's my money brings them,' and then everyone would roar despite the fact that Beda was very wealthy. Eitel had told Elena about him once and she had been fascinated. 'What does he do?' she had asked.

'Nobody knows. He's a mystery. He's made a fortune on the stock market, or at least they say so. I've heard he owns hotels, or maybe it's night clubs. And then he seems to have something big to do with something or other in television.'

'He sounds like he has fifty fingers,' Elena remarked.

'Yes. He really is hard to figure out.'

At his elbow, Beda was saying, 'Charley, that's a lovely girl you have.'

Eitel nodded. 'I hear you're married again.'

'Inevitably,' Beda said, pointing to a tall woman in a red dress with chiselled features and a blank, haughty expression. 'I've known them all,' he smiled, 'but Zenlia is the most. I had to steal her from a certain fat king.'

'Very beautiful,' Eitel said. At the moment, drunk, close to being sick, he thought she was as beautiful as any woman he had ever seen, and it was such expensive beauty. To his annoyance he saw that Marion had slipped away.

'Well, man, do we connect?' Beda said. More and more he had come to talk this way. When Eitel had first known him ten years ago, Beda had been literary and even had a reputation as an essayist on various esoteric subjects. Beda had been living in the capital with his first wife, the actress. He was not so well known in those days and Eitel thought of him as a bit of a maverick, for Beda was using his own money to produce and direct a movie. When it came out it was a failure financially and critically, a movie with too much atmosphere and hints and allusions which no one could follow, all in all a poetic movie. Still, Eitel thought Beda had talent.

But who could remember him for his talent? One night on an evening at Beda's house, Beda had offered him his wife. Eitel had been out with a girl he barely knew and Beda suggested they switch for the night. It had been agreeable to all four, and Beda's wife had said to Eitel, 'I'd like to see you again.' So Eitel remembered it as an interesting night. It was Beda who had stayed away from him after that.

'Charley, I said, "Do we connect?"'

'What do you mean, do we connect?'

'I swear you're drunk.' Beda looked at a woman who had been staring at him curiously and when he winked, she turned away in embarrassment. 'Oh, God, the tourists,' he said. 'They're ruining Desert D'Or. Zenlia was tired of New York and I promised her we'd find a ball here. "In the sun?" she asked,' and Beda began to chuckle. 'Look, Charley, you know we always dig each other's taste. I've got a good idea of what Elena's like. It's that coarse sullen thing in her, just a touch of bawd and lots of energy. Am I right?'

They might have been discussing a local peasant wine. 'You're not quite right,' Eitel said, 'there's more than energy to Elena.' He did not know if he was defending her, or telling tales out of school. 'Life gets confusing,' he had time to think.

'More than energy,' Beda repeated. 'She *knows*, doesn't she, Charley?' he asked, and answered himself, 'Yes, now it comes through. She's a very sensitive girl.' He laughed. 'Charley I tell you we have got to get together. We'll all know more when we're done.'

'Stop pushing science,' Eitel wanted to say, but did not trust the inspiration. Using his drunkenness, he smiled enigmatically at Beda. 'You know, Don,' he drawled, 'in every gourmet there's a lost philosopher.'

'Ha, ha. Ha, ha. As Munshin says, "I love you."'

When Beda continued to grin at him, Eitel finally said, 'Elena's complicated.'

'What kind of talk is that?' Beda looked around the room. 'I don't know anybody who isn't complicated. Why don't we skip and go to my place?' When Eitel did not answer, Beda began to count. 'There's the four of us,' he said, 'you, me, Zenlia and Elena, and then Marion and a couple of his brood, have you seen them here? – one of them's very nice – only Marion could bring a call girl to Dorothea's party, and then I was thinking of Lulu, and any odd jacks I could invite. I'd love to proposition Dorothea, she's gotten so respectable.'

'Dorothea wouldn't go.'

'How about Lulu?'

'No, Lulu would turn you down too,' Eitel said to gain time.

'You positive?'

'She thinks,' Eitel said, 'about things like raids.'

'Well, the rest of us then.'

Eitel started to back out of the corner. 'Not tonight, Don,' he said, 'really not.'

'Charley!'

What sort of apology could he give? 'Don, you'll have to excuse,' he said lamely, 'but I'm under the weather tonight.'

Beda looked at him carefully, eyes twinkling. 'You want to make it another night for the four of us?'

There was a card Eitel kept turning over in his pocket. Whose was it, he wondered, and then remembered. It was the card of Congressmann Crane. 'I don't know, I don't think so,' Eitel said. 'If I change my mind, I'll give you a ring.'

'I'll call *you*,' Beda emphasized, and let him slip away. In the upstairs bathroom, all the while Eitel was throwing up he had the kind of clarity which comes at such times. Everything had gained its proportion and was remote. 'Do I really want to say

238

no to Crane?' he thought to himself and then he retched again and added reflectively, 'Why is my brain always so alive when I'm too drunk ever to do anything about it?'

Once he got downstairs he pushed his way to the bar and swallowed some aspirin before taking a drink. A little business-man from Chicago named Mr Konsolidoy started to talk to him, and wanted Eitel's advice on how much it would cost to make a documentary film about his business. It was yoghurt manufac-ture, Mr Konsolidoy explained. 'I want something cheap but with distinction.'

'That's the way to want it,' Eitel said and poured another drink. Everything was idiotic, absolutely everything. 'Can you smell the vomit on my breath?' he said sombrely.

There was a familiar rustle behind him, and Lulu kissed his cheek. 'Charley, I've been looking for you all evening. Isn't it wonderful the way Crane took such an interest in you?' Eitel nodded and Mr Konsolidoy saluted them. 'My friend,' he said to Eitel with the pride of a courtier who has learned a foreign phrase, 'I'll leave you now to romance your doll.'

'Who's that?' Lulu said.

'That's a man who wants me to direct a two-million-dollar epic.'

'Charley, I'm glad for you. What's he offering?'

'Half a grand.'

Lulu looked at him sideways and then laughed. 'You had me,' she said, and put a hand on his shoulder. 'Charley, are you in the mood to listen tonight?' Before he could answer she went on, 'I have the feeling that you're the only one who could understand how I feel right now.'

'Why me?' he asked.

'Because, Charles, I was very much in love with you once. And you hurt me. I've always thought it's the people who can hurt you who understand you the best.'

He was drunk in a way where nothing seemed to help. It could hardly matter whether he took more whisky or not; he would remain dizzy and oppressed and his stomach would be threatening.

'Yes, Lulu, it was the same for me,' he said. He could say anything, he felt.

'We were silly, weren't we?'

'Silly.'

'You know I'm in love again.'

'With Tony Tanner?'

She nodded. 'I think it's for real this time.' When he did not answer, she went on, 'Everybody's against us. I'm the only one who understands a certain side of Tony.'

'What a marvellous way to describe being in love,' Eitel said.

'I'm serious, Charles. There's a lot of potentiality in Tony. Underneath, he's more sensitive than you think, and I like that combination in a man.'

'What combination?'

'Why, crude and sensitive. Tony's a funny mixture of the two. If I can give him some polish, he's going to be a very interesting person. *You* ought to understand,' she said.

'But when has all this happened?'

'In the last ten days,' Lulu said. 'By the way, it was a ball from the start. Tony's a walking encyclopaedia. And you know what's funny, I didn't even like him at first.'

People were milling around them, and the noise of the party swelled against his ear. He was admiring a quality Lulu and he had in common. They were both adept at nodding to friends in such a way that no interruptions came.

'And Sergius?' he asked, 'did you invite him tonight?'

She nodded. 'Of course I did.' Lulu shook her head. 'Only he's probably sulking at home.'

'You thought you were in love with him two weeks ago.'

She smiled. 'Oh,' she said, 'he has so much to learn,' and she put a hand on his arm again. 'Charley. I wish you understood that I want only the best to happen for you. Really, you're one of the nicest people I've ever known,' she continued, her eyes moist. 'I've even come to see what you see in Elena. I think I like her.'

'So you're in love with Tony?' he repeated.

'I'm practically positive I am.'

'You must want me to kill it for you.'

'Oh, you're drunk.'

'No, I'm just wondering why you didn't bring him along?'

'Because . . . I wanted to get away a little to think about him. And now I miss him.'

She was so lovely to look at, Eitel was thinking. All the while they were talking, Lulu's violet-blue eyes smiled at him, they smiled their nuance, they seemed to say, 'You and I may pretend, but we also remember.' He felt like a middle-aged lush. Could it have been only a year ago, two years ago, that they had been married and everyone felt he married beneath himself? Now, she was beyond him, and new generations had come, Tony Tanner who once waited hours outside his office for a chance to say hello. 'You going to Europe soon?' he asked out of a silence. But of course she would be going to Europe soon. Let there be an important enough party and she would be on her way.

'The wild thing,' Lulu said, 'is I don't think Tony is in love with me.'

'That's all right. He will be if you make him respectable.'

'You're getting old and sour, Charley.'

The worst of it, Eitel thought, was that he wanted her so much. He wanted her more than he ever had when they were married. Across the room, he could see Don Beda talking to Elena, and he knew that if he were to slip out of the party with Lulu, it was likely that Elena would leave with Beda and Beda's beautiful wife.

'What are you thinking?' Lulu asked sharply.

He could feel himself swaying on the tips of his toes. 'I was just deciding,' Eitel said, 'that it's impossible to remember what an ex-wife's body looks like.'

Lulu laughed. 'What happened to those pictures you took?'

'Oh, they're destroyed,' he said.

'I don't believe you, Charles.' In a casual caress, she pinched the lobe of his ear between her fingers. 'I suppose this is very wormy,' she said, 'but I don't mind the idea that there are pictures of me, just a few of course.'

'Lulu, let's leave the party,' Eitel said.

'What for?'

'You know exactly what for.'

'And leave Elena behind?'

He hated her for asking that. 'Yes, and leave Elena behind,' he said, and felt as if he had committed sacrilege. The sacrilege was that it had been so easy to say.

'Charles, I think you're very attractive tonight, but I want to remain faithful to Tony.'

'Balls.'

'You're mean to ask me. I have to learn one thing at a time.'

'Let's get out of here,' Eitel said. 'I'll show you a new encyclopedia.'

Then he was aware of Elena at his shoulder. It was impossible to know if she had overheard what he said, but in fact it didn't matter. He had been leaning toward Lulu in a way that was unmistakable.

'I want to go home now,' Elena said, 'but you don't have to come along. I know you want to stay.' She was close to a scene, and the thought of that at Dorothea O'Faye's was unbearable.

'No, I'll go with you,' he said quietly.

Lulu was talking. 'Why don't you stay, Charley? Elena gives permission.'

'You don't have to go,' Elena repeated. Her eyes were glittering.

Eitel said the wrong thing. 'Do you want to come home with us for coffee?' he asked Lulu.

'I don't think so,' Lulu smiled.

'Sure, come on over to the pig-sty,' Elena said. 'The pigs are looking for a jump in the hay.'

'Good night, Lulu,' Eitel said.

They left without saying goodbye to anyone. At the door, Dorothea caught them. She was very drunk. 'Did it work out all right with my government friend?' she asked heavily.

'Do you expect thanks?' Eitel said.

'You going to be an arrogant phony son of a bitch all your life?'

Staring into Dorothea's eyes, so angry, so leaden with drink, he remembered that once – for no matter how short a time – they had shared the same bed. It gave Eitel a pang. Where, in what cemetery of the heavens, did the tender words of lovers rest when they loved no longer?

'Let's go, Elena,' he said, not answering Dorothea.

'You don't deserve what any dog does for you,' Dorothea shouted as they escaped down the path.

Neither he nor Elena said a word on the drive to their house. After Eitel had put the car in the garage and followed her into the living room, he mixed himself a drink.

'You're a coward,' Elena said. 'You wanted to stay and you didn't.'

He sighed. 'Oh, baby, not you, too.'

'Oh, sure. Not me too. You wanted to take Lulu somewhere and I ruined it, didn't I?'

How much like a wife she had become, he was thinking. 'You didn't ruin anything,' he said automatically.

'You think I need you so much?' she flared at him. 'Want to know something? When I get drunk I'm a million miles away from you.'

'I love you when I get drunk,' he said.

'Why do you lie to me this way?' Her face was furious with the effort not to cry. 'I can live without you,' she said. 'Tonight at the party I knew I could walk out and never miss you at all.' When he said nothing, she only became more angry. 'I'll tell you something,' she went on, 'that friend of yours, that disgusting man Don Beda, asked me to go home with him and his wife, and he said things to me . . . he thinks I'm dirt. Well, maybe I like high society and the way it thinks I'm dirt. I wanted to go with him,' she shrieked, 'I'm the same thing he is. So don't think you owe me anything. If you want to have your fun, don't think I'm the one who's stopping you. I can have my fun, too.'

It was horrible to smile at such a moment, but he could not avoid it. 'My poor baby,' he said.

'I hate you,' Elena shouted and went into the bedroom.

Oh, he was so drunk. Poor little underdog, he thought about Elena. She would never believe that he would marry her, but he would. He sat by himself looking for the words which would present his offer most attractively. Abruptly, he began to laugh. At the moment he felt as if he knew everything. It seemed so absurd that less than an hour ago he had wanted more than anything to sleep with Lulu. At that moment Elena must have been equally tempted by Don Beda. She would not have called him disgusting otherwise. Like a soft breath on the ash of his desire for Lulu, there came the thought that perhaps he might do worse than to accept Beda's invitation. There was something very disturbing and yet not unpleasant at the thought of giving Elena up to such a party. With the bravery of a man who watches in an operating mirror while surgery is performed on his body, Eitel felt as if he were staring into himself. Once, how long ago? a girl had no more than to scratch him with a word, and out would run the blood of the shy, passionate adolescent he had been. He sighed, evolving drunken systems of philosophy where time was liquid, and liquid dried, and time was gone.

All this while, Elena was undoubtedly suffering. There was something comic about her, he thought; the essence of good comedy was always displaced drama, and she took herself very seriously. He would give her drama then; this was the time for his marriage proposal. So he got up and went into the bedroom and looked at Elena lying on the coverlet. Her face was buried in her arms, the classic pose of grief for the mediocre actress, and it was right that Elena being sincere and comic should lie in such a way. He touched her lightly on the back and she stirred. Probably she wanted to tell him she had not meant what she said about Don Beda.

'Go away,' Elena told him.

'No, darling, I want to talk to you.'

'Please leave me alone.'

He began to smooth her hair. 'Darling,' he said, 'I've ruined a lot of things, but you must know that I care about you. I can't stand the thought of hurting you.' It was true in a way. 'I mean, I want you always to be happy.' Indeed if he could have granted happiness to anyone, he would have granted it to her.

'Just words,' Elena blurted from the pillow.

'I want us to be married,' Eitel said.

She sat up then and turned her face to his.

'You see, what I thought is that we could go on like this, and when you felt that it wasn't good any more, well, then, before we broke up we could get married and then we could get divorced. I mean I know how much you'd like to get married because you feel that no one cares about you that much, and I want to show you that I do.'

Tears came into her eyes, ran down her cheek, and slowly

244

dripped on to her hands. She sat there limply with her hands in her lap.

'What do you think, darling?'

'You have no respect for me,' she said in a wooden voice.

'But I have so much respect. Can't you see?'

'Don't talk about it,' she said.

He felt the kind of mild dismay which comes just before a disaster. 'You don't understand,' he said. 'You see, no matter what happens, we'll get married.'

She shook her head from side to side in a slow bewildered way. 'Oh, Charley,' she said, 'I hate myself. I've been trying to get up the courage to leave you, and I can't. I'm afraid.'

'Then you must marry me the way I said.'

'No. Don't you know I could never do that? Don't you realize the way you asked me?'

'But you have to marry me,' he said with panic. The exit had been prepared, and now she was closing it. If they didn't marry, he would remain wedded to her.

'When you don't want me, I'll go,' Elena said. 'But I don't want to talk about it any more.'

Finally, she had gained his respect, and he could never explain it to her. With numb fingers he touched her foot. The essence of spirit, he thought to himself, was to choose the thing which did not better one's position but made it more perilous. That was why the world he knew was poor, for it insisted morality and caution were identical. He was so completely of that world, and she was not. She would stay with him until he wanted her no longer, and the thought of what would happen afterward ground his flesh with pain as real as a wound. 'I'm rotten,' he said aloud, and with the desire to prove his despair, he began to cry, clutching her body to him, his fists against her back, while his chest shook from the unaccustomed effort to weep.

Elena was tender to him. Like a sad mother, she stroked his hair. And in a wise little voice, she said, 'Let it sneak up on you, darling. Don't force yourself to cry.' As she caressed his face with her fingers, a slow unhappy smile played over her mouth. 'You see, Charley, it's really not so bad. I can always find another man.'

By an unmistakable cruel spill to his stomach, he knew then

245

that he still lived in an exquisitely painful jail of jealousy. For that minute and for another minute he loved her as he had never loved anyone, loved her and knew that the life of such a love was but a minute because all the while he loved her he knew that he dare not love her. Young as she was, he had heard experience in her voice which was beyond his own experience, and so if he stayed with her, he would be obliged to travel in *her* direction, and he had been fleeing that for all of his life.

So he cried again into the pressure of his mind, 'Why is my brain always so alive when I'm too drunk ever to do anything about it?' and then the woe of his life washed up on him at all he had not done, and all that he would never do, and he wept, he wept the harsh tears of a full-grown man, for indeed it was the first time in twenty-five years that he had wept at all. Yet all the while he wept, part of his lament was for Elena because he knew that since she would not marry him, he must find another way to become free.

19

I arrived at the party after Eitel had left, having spent most of the evening debating whether to go. My invitation had come from Dorothea, and I didn't know if she was being kind, or whether Lulu wanted to see me. The more I debated, the more I knew I would go, and I found myself enjoying the fantasy that Lulu was racked because it was after one o'clock, now after two in the morning, and I still had not arrived. I even expected my phone to ring, and was bothered by the thought of Lulu calling everywhere in town, every bar, every club, never thinking to call my house because obviously I would not be there – since I had not appeared at the party, I must have something better to do. And so I paced around the house, close to desperate with my desire to see her again. It had not been easy since she left, but to talk about how I spent my time – the hours I drank, the hours I tried to write, the afternoons I spent with my bankbook as though by studying it long enough I could teach my savings to grow – would be endless for me. For two days I took up my camera and went scouting through the desert, taking infra-red pictures at odd angles of cactus against the sky. Yet that did not work either. I was frightened. For the first time since I had been in Desert D'Or, I had gotten into a fist fight at a bar, and I was beginning to wonder what there was in me. Sometimes I thought I was beginning to be the kind of man who would jump and dig my heels, and these days I had been looking for fights. So I tried with all my strength to keep from going to Dorothea's party, and ended by getting into my car.

It was close to three in the morning when I drove up to The Hangover, and as I passed through the door, the excuses I had made all evening disappeared, and I was left with the hungry angry understanding that I had to see Lulu. But I had come very late and I thought she was gone already. The hour of the party had long been passed; scattered dishes of the buffet supper were hidden here and there, a cigarette stuck like a ski pole into a knoll of potato salad, a bite of ham swimming in a highball glass, an overturned plate underneath a coffee table. The people who were left had concentrated into some small activity whole caricatures of themselves, so that the drunk at the one-armed bandit who dropped quarter after quarter in a solemn, rhythmic way seemed to have become the gambler turned inside out, showing in contrast to his sober passion that he could dominate the machine, the knowledge that now he merely fed it in homage, and seemed never so surprised as when occasionally the box gave back some coins with a clatter. A young call girl had fallen asleep on a couch, her mouth open, her arms trailing in dead weight to the floor, her deep sleep crying the end of that alertness, interest, and attention so necessary to the practice of her trade.

That way, too, did I find Martin Pelley. His chin on his chest, his breathing laboured; he was not asleep but merely stunned. 'I've had it,' he said to me, 'Sergius, do you know what I am?'

'Yes, what are you?' I said.

'I'm a bellboy.' Pelley sighed. 'I'd get a bigger kick out of spending the evening with the boys playing some cards.' Back went his chin on his chest. 'Get it while you're young,' he said drowsily and a first snore whistled from his nose.

In the den the party was still rowdy, in the kitchen people told jokes, in the bathroom private crises occurred, little moments from the hour of truth, forgotten even as they were washed away. I found Lulu in the pantry, her arms around the shoulders of two men, her voice quavering a burlesque of an old-time song. The three sang together, they searched for harmonies in their discord, and even as Lulu, seeing me, slipped apart from them and gave me her hand, the two men continued to sing, closing ranks on the absence like a prize platoon which stands at attention in the sun and ignores those weaklings who faint away.

'I want to talk to you,' I said to her.

'Oh, Sergius, I'm drunk. Do I show it?'

'Where can we talk?' I asked again.

She seemed not nearly so drunk as she claimed. 'We can go upstairs,' she said.

If there was a chance I might have hope, she took care to set up our station in the master bedroom where the women's coats were hung, and we talked through steady small interruptions, coming at last to pay no attention to whoever was fumbling for her wrap in the rosy lighting of the bedroom.

'Sergius, I've been very cruel to you,' Lulu began.

'How's it going with Tony?' I interrupted.

'Sergius, I think you're a darling. But I don't think when people have been intimate, they ought to discuss what's happening with them at the present. You see, I want us to be friends,' she said with just a little emphasis.

'You don't have to worry,' I said, 'I'm indifferent to you.' At that moment I was indifferent to her. If I had spent my days not knowing whether I loved her or was capable of killing her, I had arrived for the moment at that passing calm which teases us that we are cured. I was to feel her loss again; months from now I would catch a quick knife seeing her name on a cinema marquee, reading a word she was supposed to have said in a gossip column, or I would see a girl who by a gesture or a trick of speech would bring back Lulu for me. All this is pointless; what carried the moment was that I was indifferent to Lulu, I thought she could no longer hurt me. So I could be generous. I could say, 'I'm indifferent,' and feel the confidence of a man who has lived through a landslide.

'You'd be a nice girl,' I tried, 'if only you had a good opinion of yourself.'

She laughed. 'You're a boob when you try to be a psychologist. Sergius, be friendly. I think you're honestly more attractive tonight than I've ever seen you.'

From the way she said it, I knew that I was now someone who had never been particularly attractive to her.

'Lulu,' I asked, startled to hear myself, 'is it really all over?'

'Sergius, I think you're sweet and good and I'll never forget you,' she said with her desire to be kind, having forgotten me already.

I looked at her. 'Come on, let's go to bed.'

'No, I'm drunk, and . . . I don't want to hurt you.'

'Try,' I said. But I wasn't sure if I meant it, and who could fool Lulu that way?

'Sergius, sweetie, I don't want to talk about it. You see with us, it wasn't always very perfectly physical, I mean it wasn't a physical-type affair. I think that's due to chemistry, don't you?'

'What about the time . . .?' I asked, and went on, telling her what she had worn, what we had done, hammering at her with every detail of what she had said and how she had said it, and Lulu listened with a cinema smile, the young girl eager and sympathetic, sorry for the nice-featured actor she does not love.

'Oh, Sergius, I'm terrible,' she said. 'I must have been drunk.'

'You weren't drunk.'

'Well, it was always very nice with you.'

That did it. By an effort, admitting I was done, I said, 'Do you expect to see Tony a lot?'

'Maybe I will, Sergius. He's full of laughs.'

A drunk blundered by, searching the upstairs hall for an empty bowl, and she drew against my arm. 'I'm worried, dear,' she said in a voice which showed that we were finally old friends. 'Herman Teppis is going to see me the day after tomorrow. I wanted to get advice from Eitel but he was too difficult.'

'Why are you worried?'

''Cause I know Teppis.' She shivered suddenly. 'Don't tell a soul about Tony,' she whispered. 'Promise!'

Downstairs, guests were still leaving. 'Sergius, drive me to the Yacht Club,' she asked. 'I won't be a minute, just wait for me to powder my nose.'

With her indifference to concealing herself, she did her make-up by the bedroom mirror, studying the shape, the spread, and the colour of the powder and shadow she painted on herself. There was a moment when I thought she studied her features too long and the face in the glass became more alive than the girl who looked in, and I felt how she was bothered, almost as if I could hear a whisper of that wind which says, 'That is you, that is really you. It is you whom you are looking at, and you can never quit your face,' for as we went down the stairs she was silent, she was worried, she was looking for the girl who lived in the mirror.

The party was breaking up as we went out. Dorothea kissed

Lulu. 'You be careful, honey-bun, you hear?' she said, and we pushed through the door. On the street beyond the gate of Dorothea's there were adolescents waiting, a dozen of them, waiting in the false dawn of four o'clock in Desert D'Or.

'That's her, that's her,' several of them cried as we came out.

'My God, I recognize one of them,' Lulu said. 'She's from the city.'

'Miss Meyers, we're on an autograph party,' the leader said formally. 'Will you please sign our books?'

'Lulu, sign mine first,' another begged.

I stood beside Lulu while she decorated her name in album after album. 'Thank you very much,' she wrote, 'my very best . . . hello, again . . . best in the world . . . a million thanks . . .' So it went. When we were free at last and I was driving her on the road to the Yacht Club, driving the car myself for this last time, she lay back against the seat and fluffed her hair. I caught a glimpse of her face and the worry was gone. 'Oh, Sergius,' she said with the glow of adulation still warm, 'isn't this a wonderful life?'

20

Two days later, a half hour before he was to see Lulu, Herman Teppis was waiting for Teddy Pope. From time to time it was Teppis' habit, as Lulu had told me, to have a big chat, or so he called it, with some of his stars. The institution, known to the public through a run of magazine articles written by publicity men, had been advertised as the secret of good family relations at Supreme Pictures. Teppis was always giving little talks at his home, his country club, or the studio commissary, but the big chat took place in his office, the doors closed.

Teppis' office was painted in one of those subsidiaries of a cream colour – rose-cream, chartreuse-cream, or beige-cream – used for all the executive suites at Supreme Pictures. It was an enormous room with an enormous picture window, and the main piece of furniture was the desk, a big old Italian antique which had come down from the Middle Ages, and was said to have been bought from the Vatican..Yet, like an old house, which is made over so completely that only the shell remains, the inside of Teppis' desk was given to a noiseless tape recorder, a private file, a refrigerator, and a small revolving bar. The rest of the room had some deep leather chairs, a coffee-coloured carpet, and three pictures: a famous painting of a mother and child was set in a heavy gold frame, and two hand-worked silver cadres showed photos of Teppis' wife and of his mother, the last hand-coloured so that her silver hair was bright as a corona.

The afternoon Teddy Pope came to see Mr Teppis, he was greeted warmly. Teppis shook his hand and clapped him on the back. 'Teddy, it's a pleasure you could manage to get here,' he said in his hoarse thin voice, and pressed a button under his desk to start the tape recorder.

'Always happy when you want to talk to me, Mr T.,' Teddy said.

Teppis coughed. 'You want a cigar?'

'No, sir, I don't smoke them.'

'It's a vice, cigars. My only vice, I say.' He cleared his throat with a short harsh sound as though he were ordering an animal to come up. 'Now, I know what's going on in your mind,' he said genially. 'You want to know why I want to see you.'

'Well, Mr T., I was wondering.'

'It's simple. I'll give you the answer in a phrase. The answer is I would like to spend the kind of time I ought to with all you young people, all you young stars I've seen growing right on this studio lot. That's a lack in my life, but it don't mean my personal interest is at long distance. I think about you an awful lot, Teddy.'

'Hope you think nice things, Mr T.,' Teddy said.

'Now what are you nervous for? Have I ever hurt you?' Teddy shook his head. 'Of course not, I got a real affection for you, you know that. I'm an old man now.'

'You don't look old, H.T.'

'Don't contradict me, it's true. Sometimes I think of all the years I been sitting in this room, the stars that came, the stars that fell. You know I think of all the stars I made, and then all these up-and-coming starlets. They're going to be heard from in a couple of years, but they'll never push you out, you can depend on that, Teddy, you can say H.T. said to me, "You can depend on that almost as a promise," because what I want to say is that I feel the very real affection which all of my stars and starlets feel for me, I can tell when we have these chats, they think I got a large warm heart, I can never remember a single one leaving this office without their saying, "God bless you, H.T." I'm a warm individual. It's why I've been a success in the industry. What do you need to be successful here?'

'Heart,' said Teddy.

'That's right, a big red heart. The American public has a big heart and you got to meet it, you got to go halfway up to it. I'll give you an example. I'm the father of a grown woman, you know my daugher Lottie, I love her, and I hear from her every single day. At ten o'clock in the morning the call comes through and my secretary, she clears the switchboard for me. If I can't be punctual to my daughter, how can I expect her to be punctual to me? You see, Teddy,' he said, reaching forward to pat Pope's knee, 'it don't matter the love I got for my daughter, there's a lot left over for my other family, the big family right here at Supreme Pictures.'

'The family feels the same way about you, H.T.,' Teddy said.

'I hope so, sincerely I hope so. It would break my heart if all the young people here didn't reciprocate. You don't know how much I think about all of you, about your problems, your heartaches, and your successes. I follow your careers. You know, Teddy, you'd be surprised how much I know about the personal lives of all of you. I even follow to see how religious you are, because I believe in religion, Teddy. I've changed my religion and a man don't change his religion like he takes a drink of water. I can tell you I've found great consolation in my new faith, there's a great man in New York, a great religious man, I'm proud to call him one of my dearest friends, and he made things so you and me can go through the same church door.'

'I guess I haven't been going to church enough lately,' Teddy said.

'I hate to hear that. I'd give you a lecture if there wasn't something else I want to talk about.'

Teppis held up his arms. 'Look, what am I showing you? Two hands. Two hands make a body. You see, I feel as if I come from two faiths, the one I was born with, and the one I changed to and elected. I think I've inherited the wealth of the tradition from two great faiths. Am I confusing you?'

'No, sir.'

'You take my first faith. One of the most heart-warming customs of the people I was born in, it was the concern the parents of the family took in all the doings of their children, the engagements, the weddings, the births of young people. I could tell you stories make you cry. You know the poorest house, dirt-poor people, they would take the same interest in arranging the marriage of their children as for a royal marriage. Now, this is a democratic country, we can thank God for that, we don't approve of royal marriages, I don't approve of it myself, I would never dream of doing such a thing, but there's a lot to be said on both sides. I was talking to the Bey Omi Kin Bek on this very subject, and you know what he said to me, he said, "H.T., we don't arrange marriages the way the American public tends to think, we just encourage them, and then it's up to the kids." That's a first-rate article genuine royalty. I'll say to any man I'm proud to have the Bey for a friend.'

'I think a lot of people like to look down on royalty,' Teddy said.

'Sure. You know why they do it? Envy.' Teppis took out his handkerchief and spit into it. 'People are envious of the people at the top.'

'My idea,' said Teddy, 'is that royalty is like everybody else. Only they express themselves more.'

'You're wrong,' Teppis interrupted. 'Royalty pays a terrible price. Let me tell you a story. What is it about public men that makes them different? It's that they're in the eye of the public. They got to lead a life as clean as a dog's teeth, privately, not only public. You know what a scandal is to a public figure? It's a bomb ten times bigger than the atom. They got to do certain things, it breaks their heart to do them, and why? The public responsibility demands it. That's true for royalty and it's true for movie stars, and fellows like me, people like you and me, that's who it applies for. Those are the laws, try and break them. We're talking like equals now, aren't we, Teddy?'

'Face to face,' Teddy said.

'You look at that picture I have,' said Teppis, pointing to the painting. 'I would hate to tell you how much I had to pay for it, but the moment I looked at that French picture with that beautiful mother and her beautiful child, I said to myself, "H.T., it don't matter if you got to work ten years to pay for it, you got to buy that picture." You know why I said that to myself? Because that picture is life, it's by a great painter. I look at it, and I think, "Motherhood, that's what you're looking at." When I think of you, Teddy, and I know what goes on in your heart, I think that you think about settling down with a beautiful bride and children that come out to greet you when you come home from work. I never had anything like that, Teddy, 'cause when I was your age, I worked long hours, very long hours, hours that would break your heart to tell you about them, and when I'm

255

alone, I sometimes think to myself, and I say then. "You know, H.T., you missed the fruits of life." I would hate for a fellow like you, Teddy, to have to say the same thing. And you don't have to. You know with all that's due respect to my wife, may she rest in peace, she had to work very hard herself, only for those early years, but she never complained once, not a peep.' Tears filled Teppis' eyes, and he wiped them away with a clean handkerchief he kept in his breast pocket, the aroma of his toilet water passing across the room. 'Take any girl you would marry,' Teppis went on, 'you wouldn't have such problems, you could give her all the financial security, you know why, she'd make you settle down. I'd even sit down with you and your business agent and we'd have a talk how to straighten you out financially so you wouldn't have to borrow from us ahead of your salary.' Teppis frowned at him. 'It's a shame, Teddy. People will think we don't pay you nothing the way you got to borrow money.'

'I'd like to talk to you about that, Mr T.,' Teddy said quickly.

'We'll talk about that, we'll go all into it, but now's not the time. You just remember, Teddy, that you're an idol of the American public, and an idol never needs to worry about money so long as he's clean with his public.'

Teppis poured himself a glass of water, and drank it slowly as if he would measure the taste. 'I know a young fellow like you with the world at his feet,' he went on, 'there's a lot of times he don't want to get married. "Why should I get married?" he says to himself, "What's in it for me?" Teddy, I'll tell you, there's a lot in it for you. Just think. The whole world is in a strait jacket so it says, "You, over there, you get in a strait jacket, too." Know why? The world hates a bachelor, he's not popular. People try to drag him down. The stories you hear, ninety-nine per cent of the time unfounded, but I'd be ashamed, I couldn't look you in the eye to tell you the kind of stories I have to listen to. It's enough to revolt your stomach. I hear a story like that, I let them have it. "Don't tell me that kind of filth about Teddy," I say, "I don't want to hear it. If the boy don't want to get married, it got nothing to do with all those dirty rotten stories you tell me, period." That's how definite I am. People know me, they say, "H.T. is on record as being against slander."'

Abruptly, Teppis pounded his desk. 'A rumour about a fellow

like you, it spreads like hot cakes. We get letters from your fan clubs all over the place. Kokoshkosh, towns like that. Small-town America. Two-Bits, Kansas. You see what I mean. What do you want? You know what these letters say, they say that the members of the Teddy Pope fan club are brokenhearted 'cause they heard the most terrible stories about Teddy. Their loyalty is shaken. Listen, Teddy, I go to your defence, you know why? It isn't because of business reasons, or because I know you for a long time, or even because I like you, although I do. It's because I know deep down that you're going to prove I'm right, and I wouldn't go to bat for a person even if they meant a million dollars to me if I didn't think they would prove that H.T. is right in the long run. That's confidence. Should I put that confidence in you?' Teppis held up a finger. 'Don't answer, you don't even have to answer, I know I can put confidence in you.' He got up and wallked to the window.

'You know something, I've had my confidence rewarded already. I took a look in the papers. That picture of you and Lulu where you're holding hands in Desert D'Or. It's one of the most beautiful, impressive, and touching things I've ever seen. Young love, that's what it said. It made me wish that same famous painter on my wall was still alive so I could hire him to paint the photograph of the young love of you and Lulu.'

'Mr Teppis,' Teddy said, 'that was a publicity picture.'

'Publicity! Listen, do you know how many of the most successful marriages in this industry started with just publicity? I'll tell you. The answer is ninety-nine per cent of the most successful marriages began just that way. It's like a dowry in the old country. I know you, Teddy, you're a clean-cut boy. I've seen a lot of photographs. I don't believe that you and Lulu can look at each other like two love-doves and be fakers. Don't try to tell me Lulu isn't crazy about you. That girl is wearing her heart on her sleeve. Teddy, I'll tell you, Lulu is one of the finest girls I know. She's a real fine American-type girl of real American stock. Such a woman is a gift of God. When I look at my mother's picture on this very desk, you know what I get? Inspiration. I carry her picture next to my heart. You should be able to do the same.'

Teddy was perspiring. He leaned forward to say something,

and said no more than, 'Mr Teppis – you have to allow me the right to say . . .'

'Stop!' said Teppis, 'I don't want to hear your ideas. You're a stubborn boy. Why are you so stubborn when you know what's in your heart? You want to agree with me. But you're confused. You need a man like myself to set you straight.'

In a quiet voice, Teddy said, 'Mr Teppis, you know very well I'm a homosexual.'

'I didn't hear it, I didn't hear it,' Teppis screamed.

'That's the way I am,' Teddy muttered. 'There's nothing to be done about it. What is, is.'

'Philosophy?' Teppis shouted. 'You listen to me. If a man sits in . . . *shit*, he don't know enough to get out of it?'

'Mr Teppis, don't you have a big enough heart to understand my feelings?'

'You're the most ungrateful boy I ever knew. You keep me up nights. What do you think, sex it's the whole world? I forget what you said, do you understand? I wouldn't want it on my conscience. You watch. I'll drive you right out of the movie business.'

'Let me try to say . . .'

'Lulu, that's what you got to say. I know what goes on. You're a coward. You got a chip against society. You should love society with all it's done for you. I love society. I respect it. Teddy, you're a sick boy, but you and me can lick this thing together.' Teppis held up a fist. 'I don't want to persecute you, but I never heard of anything so perverted in my whole life.'

The buzzer sounded. 'All right, all right,' Teppis said into the inter-office phone, 'you tell the party in question to wait. I'll be with that individual in a minute.'

'Mr Teppis,' Teddy said, 'I'm sorry. Maybe I'd like to have children, but I've never once had relations with a woman.'

Teppis clicked the switch back to its 'off' position, and stared for many seconds at Teddy Pope. 'Teddy, we've talked a lot,' he said. 'What I want is that you promise me you won't make up your mind ahead of time that you personally aren't able to boff a beautiful sexy girl like Lulu. Do I have to be there to help you? I'm telling you, you can. That's all I ask of you. Teddy, don't make up your mind. Sleep on it. Is that a bargain?'

Pope shrugged wearily.

'That's the boy. That's Teddy Pope talking.' Teppis walked him to the door. 'Now, Teddy, nobody is forcing you into anything. If you said yes this very minute, I would still say, "Teddy, sleep on it." Now, could anybody claim I was trying to push you into a single thing?'

'Who would dare?'

'You're right. I don't force people. Never. I talk things over with them. Someday, Teddy, you're going to say, "God bless you, H.T."'

Once Teddy was out of the door, Teppis flipped the buzzer again. 'All right, send Lulu in,' he said. He waited by the door to greet her and held Lulu at arm's length while he looked at her. 'I wish I could tell you the kind of pleasure it is to have you lightening up this office,' he said to her. 'Sweetie, you take a load off all my worries, and on that desk are sitting one thousand worries.' Now, he held her hands. 'I love a girl like you who brings sunshine into this room.'

Probably Lulu had managed to look no more than seventeen. 'I love you, too, Mr T.,' she said in her husky little voice.

'I know you do. Every one of my stars, they tell me that. But with you, I know it's sincere.' He guided her to the chair in which Teddy had been sitting, and from a drawer in the Italian desk, he took out a bottle of whisky and dropped some ice cubes in a glass.

'Oh, Mr T., I'm not drinking these days,' said Lulu.

'Nonsense. I know you. Sweetie, you got no respect for me. You think you can twist me around your little finger,' he said cordially. 'Well, I got news for you. There's no man in the world you can't twist around your finger. But I understand you, sweetie. I'm crazy about you. I don't want you thinking you got to take a drink behind my back.'

'I think you're the only man who understands me, H.T.,' Lulu said.

'You're wrong. Nobody can understand you. Know why? You're a great woman. You're not only a great actress but there's greatness in you as a person – fire, spirit, charm – those are the sort of things you have. I wouldn't want this to get

259

around but I don't care if you take a drink. You've earned the right to do anything you want.'

'Except when I disagree with you, H.T.,' Lulu said.

'I love you. What a tongue. You got impetuosity. I say to myself, "H.T., what is there about Lulu that's smash box office?" and I don't even have to ask myself the answer. It's in a word. Life,' Teppis said, pointing a finger at her, 'that's what Lulu's got.'

He poured himself a small drink and sipped it politely. 'You're wondering why I asked you up here?' he said after a pause. 'I'll tell you. I've been thinking about you. Know my personal opinion of Lulu Meyers? She's the greatest actress in this country, and this country's got the greatest actors in the whole world.'

'You're the greatest actor in the world, Mr T.,' Lulu said.

'I take it as a compliment. But you're wrong, Lulu, I can't act. I'm too sincere. I feel things too deeply which I can't express. There're nights when I stay awake worrying about you. You know what eats my heart out? It's that I'm not the American public. If I was the American public, I'd make you Number One on the Bimmler Ratings. You know what you are now?'

'Seventeen, isn't it, Mr T.?'

'Seventeen. Can you believe it? There are sixteen actors in this country the American public buys ahead of you. I don't understand it. If I was the public I'd buy Lulu Meyers all the way.'

'Why can't there be ten million people like you, H.T.?' Lulu said. She had finished her drink, and after a little pause, walked up to the desk and poured herself another.

'Lulu, do you know your Bimmler last year? It was twelve. This year you should have gone up, not down. Up to ten, to eight. Three, Number One, that's the way it should have gone.'

'Mr Teppis, maybe I'm a has-been.'

Teppis held up his hand. 'Lulu, for a remark like that, I ought to take you over my knee and spank you.'

'Oh, Mr T., what a construction I could put on that.'

'Ha, ha. Ha, ha. I'm crazy about you. Lulu, listen to me. The trouble is you're weak, publicity-wise.'

'I've got the best press agent in the country,' she said quickly.

'You think you can buy publicity? Good publicity is a gift of God. The time is past, Lulu, when any sort of girl, you'll see I'm speaking frankly, the kind of girl who's so-called friends with this man and friends with that man until she's notorious. The public wants what's respectable today. You know why? Life ain't respectable any more. Think they want to be reminded of that? Let me show you psychology. Ten years ago, a woman she was faithful to her husband, she wanted excitement, she wanted to dream she was having a big affair with a star – Lulu, I wouldn't talk so frankly to any other person on earth. Today, you know what, that same woman she has boy friends all over the place, with the man who fixes the television set, people like that. You think she wants to see somebody just like herself on the screen, somebody just as nuts as she is? She don't. She's ashamed of herself. She wants to see a woman she can respect, a married woman, a royal couple, the Number One married lovers of America. That's true psychology.'

Lulu shifted in her seat. 'H.T., you should have been a marriage broker.'

'You tell me that all the time – I'll tell you something. If you could be married to the right kind of boy, let me give you an example: to a star let's say with a Seven Bimmler, a Nine Bimmler, you know what? You think you'd come out with a Bimmler the average between the two of you, you wouldn't, you'd end up with the two highest Bimmlers in the country. Know why? Two plus two don't make four. It makes five, and five makes ten. That's compound interest. You think about it. The right kind of marriage is better than compound interest. Lulu Meyers and anybody, Joe McGoe, I don't care what the man's name is just so he has a high Bimmler, and then you have the Number One royal couple of America, and America is the world, that's where you'd be.'

Teppis blew a kiss at Lulu. 'You're my darling, do you know that? You're my A-1 darling.'

'I hope so, H.T.'

'You take this young fellow of yours, what's his name, this Shamus Sugar-boy fellow.'

'You mean Sergius.'

'I've looked into him. He's a nice boy. I like him. I'd hire him. Not for acting, you understand, but some sort of work, moving sets around, driving a truck, he's the kind of boy who'd be good for that, sincere, well-meaning maybe, but I think about him with you, and you know what I decide? Lulu, that boy is not for you. He's insignificant. He would drag you down. I don't care how many planes he says he shot, he's a bum, that's the sort of person he is.'

'Oh, you don't have to disparage Sergius, Mr T.,' said Lulu, 'he's very sweet.'

'Sweet boys, a dime a dozen. He's a kid. You're a woman. That's the difference. I think we understand each other. What I want to say is something I got in mind that's going to stun you. Want to know who I think you should marry?'

'I can never know what you think, Mr Teppis.'

'Guess. Go ahead, guess.'

'Tony Tanner,' Lulu said.

'Tony Tanner? Lulu, I'm ashamed of you. I looked up his Bimmler myself. One hundred and eighty-nine, that's what a nobody he is. It's a disgrace for a woman not to value herself. I got somebody better to think about. I don't want you to say a word, I want you to sleep on it. Teddy Pope, what do you say?'

Lulu came to her feet. She made a small demonstration of opening and closing her mouth. 'I'm shocked, Mr T.,' she said at last.

'Sit down. I'll tell you something. Maybe you don't know it. I got no desire to hide it from you. Teddy Pope is a homosexual. It makes you wonder, don't it? Could H.T. be the kind of man who gets down on his hands and knees to beg a beautiful girl like you to marry a faggola?'

'You could never be that kind of man,' Lulu said. 'You're too respectable and upright.'

'Let's not get off the sidetrack. I want you to answer me one question as honest as you can. Do you admit, paying no attention for the moment to your personal life, that to be married to Teddy Pope, wouldn't that be the biggest benefit you could bestow on yourself, publicity-wise? The Number One couple of America. Say I'm right.'

'I can't say you're right, Mr Teppis.' Lulu rattled the ice

262

cubes in her glass, and in a voice which mimicked him, she added, 'I think you're being selfish.'

'Nobody else in the whole world could say that to me.'

'I ought to cry,' Lulu said. 'I've told everybody you're like a father.'

'Don't hurt my feelings, Lulu.'

'H.T., I feel as if things can never be the same between us.'

'To talk like that,' Teppis exclaimed. 'It's disgraceful. After all I've done for you.'

Lulu began to weep. 'I don't like Teddy,' she said in a little voice.

'Like him! You stop crying. I know you, Lulu, and I'll tell you something. Teddy Pope is the only man you could ever be in love with. You think I'm crazy. You're wrong. Just 'cause he's a homo, you think it's an insult to you. But I'm an old man, I know people. You and Teddy can hit it off. He's been hurt, he's got a delicate heart, there's a lot for an actress to learn from him about the subtleties of human nature. Lulu, you're the woman who could straighten him out, and then he'd worship the ground you walk on.'

Lulu put a handkerchief to her eyes. 'I hate you, H.T.,' she sobbed.

'You hate me! You love me, that's why you hate to listen to me. But I'll let you know something. You're a coward. A girl with your looks, your appeal, should rise to a challenge. You're the most attractive girl I ever saw in my life. It don't mean nothing if you get a young healthy nobody excited about the kind of woman you are. That's beneath you. It's like a Hercules award for doing ping-pong. That's the sort of ridiculous thing it is. But think of the respect people would have if you could make a man out of Teddy Pope.'

'And what if I couldn't?' Lulu said.

'You're defeated before you start. I'm disappointed.'

'Mr Teppis, I'll quote you: "Look around before you take a step. There could have been dogs in the grass." That's what you said, H.T., I have witnesses.'

'You make me miserable. I thought you were a gambler like me.'

Tears ran down her cheeks. 'H.T., I want to get married,' she

263

said in a tremulous voice. 'I want to love just one man and have a beautiful mature relationship and have beautiful children and be a credit to the industry.'

'That's the ticket, Lulu.'

'But if I marry Teddy, it won't work, and I'll become promiscuous. You'll see. Will you be sorry when I'm like that?'

'Lulu, you could never be promiscuous. You're too fine. Suppose at the very worst, there should be a fellow or two that you would like and admire and diddle around with, while still being married to Teddy. I don't advise it, but it happens all the time, and you know what? The world don't stop moving.'

'H.T., that's an immoral proposal. I'm ashamed of you.'

'You're ashamed of me?' Teppis whispered. 'You said the wrong thing right then. I sit up nights trying to figure out how to save your career, and this is the thanks you give me. You're wild, that's what you are. Know what a star is? She's like delicious perishable fruit. You got to take her a long distance to market, and when she's there, you got to sell her. If you don't, she rots. She's rotten. Lulu, I'm speaking like a man to a woman. There are a lot of high executives in this studio who are fed up with you. Have you got any idea of the number of times I got to argue in your behalf? "Lulu needs discipline," they tell me, "Lulu's too hard to handle. She gives us more heartaches than she's worth." Believe me, Lulu, as God is looking into this room, you've made enemies, hundreds of enemies on this very studio lot. If you don't start to co-operate, they'll get into the process of tearing your flesh and picking your bones.' His voice had started to rise. 'That's exactly the sort of situation it is,' he now said quietly. 'I don't want to depress you, but Lulu, your Bimmler has got to show improvement this coming year. Otherwise, there's only one way for you.' He pointed to the floor. 'The way is down. You'll go down and down. You'll get older, you won't look so good, you won't get work so easy, you won't have a studio behind you. Know what a studio means? It's like a battleship. Look at Eitel. You'll become so ashamed you'll change your name. And that's how you'll end up, a dance-hall cutey, that's the sort of girl. I could cut my throat I'm so aggravated.'

'I'm amazed you should stoop to intimidate me,' Lulu answered.

'You don't fool me,' Teppis said, 'you're scared stiff. Because you know what I think of people who let me down.' He reached forward and squeezed her shoulder. 'Lulu, be my witness, don't even answer me right away, this is the only favour I ever asked you. Would you turn H.T. down? Consider carefully. Weigh your words.'

Lulu burst into tears again. 'Oh, Mr Teppis, I love you,' she cried.

'Then do something for me.'

'I'll do anything for you.'

'Would you marry Teddy Pope?'

'I'd even marry Teddy Pope. I want to marry Teddy after the way you explained it, Mr Teppis.'

'I don't want to talk you into it.'

'I'd marry Teddy in a minute now,' Lulu sobbed, 'but I can't.'

'Of course you can,' Teppis said. 'Why not?'

''Cause I married Tony Tanner this morning.'

'................'

'Mr Teppis, please don't be angry.'

'You're lying.'

'I'm not lying. We were secretly married.'

'God, how could YOU do this to me?' Teppis bellowed.

'It isn't that terrible, Mr Teppis,' said Lulu from her handkerchief.

'You broke your promise. You're torturing me. You told me you'd tell me if you wanted to get married.'

'That was to Sergius.'

'I could spit. It's not worth it being alive.'

'Do you want a glass of water, Mr Teppis?'

'*No.*' He smashed his fist into his palm. 'I'll annul the marriage.'

'You couldn't. Tony would fight it.'

'Of course he'd fight it. He's got his lawyer already.' Teppis stared down at her. 'Would you fight it, too?'

'Mr T., a wife's duty is to her husband you always say.'

'I could rip my tongue out. Lulu, you got married to spite me.'

'H.T., I'll prove you're wrong by spending the rest of my life making it up to you.'

'I'm sick.'

'Forgive me, H.T.'

'I'm going to persecute you.'

'H.T., punish me, but don't hurt Tony.'

'Don't hurt Tony! You disgust me, Lulu, you ain't capable of thinking of nobody but yourself. You could drop dead, I wouldn't even look at your grave.' His arms raised, he started to advance on her.

Lulu prepared to flee the room. 'Come back here,' Teppis said. 'I don't want you to leave like this.'

'I worship you, H.T.'

'You've shortened my life.'

'H.T., I don't care what you do. I'll always say, "God bless you."'

He pointed to the door, his mouth quivering.

'H.T., please listen to me.'

'Get out of here. You're a common whore.'

When she was gone, Teppis began to shake all over his body. He stood in the centre of the room, shaking visibly. 'It's a wonder I don't pop a blood vessel,' he said aloud. The sound of his voice must have calmed him a little, for he went to the inter-office phone, pressed the buzzer, and said hoarsely, 'You send Collie up here right away.'

A few minutes later Munshin was in the office. 'When are the wedding bells?' he asked as he came in the door.

'Collie, you're a dummy,' Teppis bawled at him. 'You're an A-1 stupid moron.'

'H.T.! What's up?'

'Lulu got married to Tony Tanner this morning.'

'Oh, Jesus,' said Collie.

'That Teddy Pope. A degraded homosexual. I had him twisted into a pretzel.'

'I'll bet you did, H.T.'

'You shut up. This whole thing was your idea. I wash my hands of it.'

'You're right, H.T.'

'Don't you even know what's happening in front of you? A fact accompli is what Lulu gives me. I could cut her up.'

'It's what that twot deserves.'

'I'm nauseous. A dime-a-dozen comedian, a coarse person like Tony Tanner. I hate coarse people. Isn't there any class left in the world?'

'You're the class, H.T.,' said Collie.

'Shut up.' Teppis wandered around the room like an animal with a hole in its flank, and collapsed in a chair. 'I made you, Collie,' he stated, 'and I can break you. I hate to think of what you were when I first knew you, a two-bit agent, a nobody, a miserable nothing.'

'It wasn't as bad as that, I hope.'

'Don't contradict me. I let you marry my only daughter, I made you my executive assistant, I let you produce your own pictures. I know you, Collie, I know your tricks, you'll cut my throat some day. But you won't because I'll break you first. Do you hear me? What's your ideas?'

Collie stood calmly, almost placidly. 'H.T., I'll be frank,' he said, 'it's my fault about Tony, I admit it.'

'You better admit it. I don't know what's the matter with you lately. You can't do nothing right these days. That Air Force boy. I'm sick every time I think of that movie we can't make all because you're such a miserable failure.'

'H.T., I've learned everything from you,' Collie said, 'and I'm not worried. I know you can turn this into something tremendous. I even remember you saying that that's what failures were for, to give ideas.' Collie extended his arms. 'H.T., in my book, and I copy your book, you can do more with Tony than you ever could with Teddy. A lot of work, yes, but one thing I learned from you, H.T., Teddy is through. You'll pick up the paper some day and he'll be in the can for scrounging around a character on the vice squad.'

'You got a disgusting imagination,' Teppis said hoarsely.

'I'm a realist. So are you, H.T. I know there's not another studio in this town that could make a nickel handling Tony. But you can.'

'My digestion is upset,' Teppis said.

'I glimpse the kind of campaign you see for Tony. Tell me if

267

I'm right.' He paused. 'No, it's a bad idea. It won't work. It would be too hard to bring off.'

'You talk and I'll tell you,' Teppis said.

'Well, now, this is off the top of my head, of course, but I was wondering if you were thinking of making Lulu keep this marriage quiet until we're done shooting her film. Then we can make the announcement. Maybe even work out a big wedding. The potential it gives us for building up Tony is tremendous. Tony Tanner,' Munshin announced, 'the kid who stole Lulu Meyers right from under a big lover-type like Teddy Pope. People will say, "You've done it again, H.T." And they'll be right.'

Teppis failed to respond. 'Don't give me compliments,' he said, 'I'm too upset. Do you know how my stomach feels?'

Munshin lit a cigarette and smoked in silence for some seconds. 'The doctor told me you ought to lower your nervous tension,' he said.

'You're my son-in-law, and you're a pimp,' Teppis burst out. Then he reached for the button under his desk and clicked it to the 'off' position. 'Did you hear what Charley Eitel said to me once? He said, "Mr Teppis, we all got our peculiarities." I don't like the sound of it. Carlyle, there's word getting around.'

'H.T., believe me. It isn't what you do or what you don't do, people will still talk about you.'

'There's nothing to talk about.'

'That's right.'

'I haven't slept with a woman in ten years.'

'It's the truth, H.T.'

Teppis looked at the ceiling. 'What kind of girl do you have in mind?'

'A sweet kid, H.T.'

'I suppose you put her on the payroll.'

'To tell the truth, I did. A friend of mine introduced me to her in Desert D'Or. Chief, it's better this way, believe me. The kid'll keep her mouth shut because who knows, she might have a career here. She's a cute little stock girl.'

'That's what you always say, Collie.'

'I had a talk with her. She'll button her lip tight as a virgin's bun.'

'You're a foul-mouthed individual,' Teppis told him.

'She's really safe.'

'If it weren't for Lottie, I'd fire you.'

'A genius like you needs relaxation,' Collie said. 'It's wrong, H.T., to miss the fruits of life.'

Teppis tapped one hand against the other. 'All right, I want you to send her up.'

'I'll have her here in five minutes.'

'You get the hell out, Collie. You think a man can break the laws of society? Those laws are there for a purpose. Every time you send up a girl, I don't even want to see her again. I refuse to sleep with her.'

'Nobody can work the way you do, H.T.,' said Collie, going out the door.

After a short interval, a girl in her early twenties with newly dyed honey-coloured hair came in unannounced through a separate door to Teppis' office. She was wearing a grey tailored suit and very high heels, and her hair was caught in a snood. Her mouth was painted in the form of broad bowed lips to hide the thin mouth beneath the lipstick.

'Sit down, doll, sit down right here,' said Teppis, pointing to a place on the couch beside him.

'Oh, thank you, Mr Teppis,' said the girl.

'You can call me Herman.'

'Oh, I couldn't.'

'I like you, you're a nice-looking girl, you got class. Just tell me your first name because I don't remember last names.'

'It's Bobby, Mr Teppis.'

He put a fatherly hand on her. 'You work here, Collie tells me.'

'I'm an actress, Mr Teppis. I'm a good actress.'

'Sweetie, there's so many good actresses, it's a shame.'

'Gee, I'm really good, Mr Teppis,' Bobby said.

'Then you'll get a chance. In this studio there's opportunity for real talent-types. Talent is in its infancy. There's a future for it.'

'I'm glad you think so, Mr Teppis.'

'You married? You got a husband and kids?'

'I'm divorced. It didn't work out. But I have two little girls.'

'That's nice,' Teppis said. 'You got to plan for their future. I want you to try to send them to college.'

'Mr Teppis, they're still babies.'

'You should always plan. I've given to charity all my life.' Teppis nodded. 'I hope you got a career here, sweetie. You been here how long?'

'Just a couple of weeks.'

'An actress got to have patience. That's my motto. I like you. You got problems. You're a human girl.'

'Thank you, sir.'

'Sweetie, move over, sit on my lap.'

Bobby sat on his lap. Neither spoke for a minute.

'You listen to me,' Teppis said in his hoarse thin voice, 'what did Collie say to you?'

'He said I should do what you wanted, Mr Teppis.'

'You're not a blabbermouth?'

'No, Mr Teppis.'

'You're a good girl. You know, there's nobody you can trust. Everybody tells everybody about everything. I can't trust you. You'll tell somebody. There's no trust left in the world.'

'Mr Teppis, you can trust me.'

'I'm the wrong man to cross.'

'Oh, I wouldn't cross a swell man like you. Am I too heavy on your lap, Mr Teppis?'

'You're just right, sweetie.' Teppis' breathing became more pronounced. 'What did you say,' he asked, 'when Collie said you should do what I wanted?'

'I said I would, Mr Teppis.'

'That's a smart girl.'

Tentatively, she reached out a hand to finger his hair, and at that moment Herman Teppis opened his legs and let Bobby fall to the floor. At the expression of surprise on her face, he began to laugh. 'Don't you worry, sweetie,' he said, and down he looked at the frightened female mouth, facsimile of all those smiling lips he had seen so ready to serve at the thumb of power, and with a cough, he started to talk. 'That's a good girlie, that's a good girlie, that's a good girlie,' he said in a mild little voice, 'you're an angel darling, and I like you, you're my darling darling, oh that's the ticket,' said Teppis.

Not two minutes later, he showed Bobby genially to the door. 'I'll call you when to see me again, sweetheart,' he said.

Alone in his office, he lit a cigar, and pressed the buzzer. 'What time is the conference on *Song Of The Heart*?' he asked.

'In half an hour, sir.'

'Tell Nevins I want to see his rushes before then. I'll be right down.'

'Yessir.'

Teppis ground out the cigar. 'There's a monster in the human heart,' he said aloud to the empty room. And to himself he whispered, like a bitter old woman, close to tears, 'They deserve it, they deserve every last thing that they get.'

Part Five

21

For the rest of the time I stayed in Desert D'Or, I quit the house I had for so many months and took a furnished room at one of the few cheap places in the resort which rented by the week. Then I got a job. As if I wanted to make a prophet of Collie Munshin, the job was washing dishes. It was in an expensive restaurant where I had eaten often enough with Lulu, and it had the merit of paying the wage of fifty-five dollars a week.

I could have had other jobs. I could have been a male car-hop as Munshin had warned, or a parking-lot attendant, or I could have gotten work of some sort in one hotel or another, but I chose to wash dishes as though my eight-hour stint in the steam and the grease and the heat, with my fingers burned by plates which came too hot from the machine and my eyes reddened by sweat, was a sort of poor man's Turkish bath for me. And when I was done for the day, I would grab a meal in a drugstore, an expensive drugstore, but it was the cheapest I could find, for it would have been easier to come on a yacht than a hash-house in that part of the desert, and the restaurant where I worked did not feed the help, except for what help I could get from a friendly waitress – the last of Munshin's predictions – who would slip me a Caesar salad or a peach melba which I would eat with water-puckered fingers, hardly missing a beat on the plates as they erupted from the gargoyle of a machine which threw its shadow over me, while the most simple lesson of class, the dirge of the dishwasher, steamed furiously in my mind: did those hogs out there, those rich hogs, have to eat on so many plates?

At the other end of the machine, feeding me the gravy-rimmed crockery and the egg-crusted forks, was a fifty-year-old dish-washer with grey hair and lean shoulders, who did not say a hundred words in all the weeks we worked together. He worked in order to drink, and drank in order to die, and like all drunks persisted in living, his hangovers strung like morning wash under the pale sunlight of the neon tubes in the kitchen, so that he retched for the first four hours of work and nibbled remnants for the rest of his shift, a choice bit of fillet here, a pure string bean there, the perfect sparrow choosing golden grains from a horse-ball feast, but nervously, waiting for the evening rain puddle when he could stop the thirst for which hunger is only a substitute. Watching his hands claw a prize into his mouth and wipe the rest down the slophole of his work table, I came to envy him more than I had envied anyone in Desert D'Or. His work had such advantages over mine. I did not grudge him the food, but it was blood to know that his end of the machine was ten degrees cooler, and his plates were cold when he scraped and stacked them into the racking boxes while they hissed at my end of the tunnel in boiling water, half-live lobsters making one last gasp to scratch their way out of the pot. I learned again the great anger of working at the bottom where the thought that you do not own a Cadillac is as far away as the infantryman's knowledge that he will never get a General's star, but what bites is that the man on the next cot in the endless barracks at the bottom has the soft job, is on permanent latrine duty let us say, and therefore is given the benefit of missing morning inspection.

I had found the orphanage again and I was home; I might just as well never have left home. After work, after my meal in the expensive drugstore, I would go back to my furnished room and I would bathe – what luxuries have the poor – and lie naked and powdered on my bed, covered with heat rash, reading the newspaper until I fell asleep. That way I passed three or four weeks, my mind sleeping on pointless calculations. I would spend an hour going over my budget, deciding on any particular night that I could reduce my expenses to no less than thirty-four dollars a week, which meant after all the pieces were taken from my pay that I could never bank more than fifty dollars a month. So it would be six hundred dollars saved in a year, and after six years and eight months of dodging lobsters, I would earn back what I had lost in twelve days with Lulu, and this thought gave me a sort of melancholy glee, allowing me to relish, like a saint counting his sores, how hard the work would be tomorrow.

It was all my doing. I still had most of my three thousand dollars and I did not have to work, but with Lulu gone, there was no other choice than to sit down and begin the apprenticeship of learning to be a writer. Feeling the fear this ambition gave to me, I was ready to fly anywhere, to the Equator if necessary, but one can always find the Equator, and I did not have to take a step from Desert D'Or. Waiting for me was the stinkhole and the furnace at the back of my modern restaurant, and I buried myself for a week, and another week, and five weeks after that, mortifying my energy, whipping my spirit, preparing myself for that other work I looked on with religious awe, while all the time, romance being the hardiest of the weeds which grow in a home for orphans, I never could rid myself of the sweet idea that one day Lulu would come to the restaurant, she would blunder back to the kitchen, she would see me in my dishwasher's apron and begin to cry, she would love me as she never had before, and the essence of magic would be tasted: you dropped to the bottom only to gain momentum for the leap to the top.

It could not go on forever. My fairy tales began to dissolve in the gossip columns, and each night I tickled my prickly heat by forcing myself to read the film news from the capital. There were many reports of Lulu's marriage, and columnists were fond of calling it 'The Love Match of the Year.' Those fan magazines which had not been embarrassed by signed articles: 'Why I Dream About Teddy Pope And Me – by – Lulu Meyers,' could afford to give space to the big piggy bank of Tony and Lulu Tanner. The story, gelded by the memorable prose of those magazines to the use of the word 'kiss,' declared that every time Tony 'kissed' Lulu, or Lulu 'kissed' Tony, the winner of the bonanza would drop a coin in the piggy bank. 'It fills up so quickly,' Lulu said or her press agent said, 'that Tony and I are always running short of small change.'

How true it all was, or at least how partially true, I could not know, for once I took the job, I buried myself and never went to see Eitel or Faye or Dorothea or anyone I knew in the resort. The result was that I believed the gossip columns and the surprise was that it cured me of magic; I even began to think of

277

quitting my job and starting to write, and finally one evening I went to see Eitel.

I had supposed that everything would be the same. Nothing had happened to me, and so I could not feel that anything had happened to anyone else. At most, when I thought of Eitel and Elena I saw them eating at a quiet table in my restaurant, or Dorothea and Pelley on a carouse, or Marion making a contact. More than that had happened, however. The night I visited Eitel, he was beginning the job of moving his belongings from Desert D'Or to the capital. He had broken up with Elena, he told me, and she was living now with Marion Faye.

In the hours we sat drinking, I got the story from him and I hated to hear what he told me. There was nothing left of him nor anyone else, and I heard details which were very close. It was all his fault, he began by saying. After Dorothea's party, he knew that he would have to make up his mind about the offer from Crane. He could not postpone a decision much longer and there were only two choices. He could stay in Desert D'Or and continue to be the blackmarket thoroughbred of Munshin's secret stable, or he could go back to the capital. But to go back with Elena did not seem plausible; she was hardly the mate for a commercial man. So his thoughts without any hint of something new chased themselves around the old circle, and after the night Eitel wept in her arms, he lived in constant distrust of the tenderness he felt for her.

That he knew the morning he picked up the phone, heard Beda's voice, and realized how careful he had been to forget the conversation they had had the night of Dorothea's party. But it was hardly possible to forget it now. Into his ear came Beda's voice. 'Look, baby, I'm putting it to you. *Sans façons*, will you and Elena come over tonight?'

'Who will be there?' asked Eitel.

'*Sans façons*, I said. Zenlia is getting to be a bore talking about the lush virtues of Elena.'

Eitel was agitated. 'Look, I'll call you back,' he said. 'I want to talk it over with Elena.'

Her reaction surprised him. He had expected, he realized, that she would refuse the invitation, but instead she acted kittenish.

'What do you think will happen there?' she giggled and added just a trifle seriously, 'What are we supposed to do?'

'You're not signing a contract to do anything.'

'I feel funny, Charley.'

'So do I.' He shrugged casually. 'Let's not go,' he said and felt a certain tension to prepare himself against disappointment if she should agree.

Elena merely looked thoughtful. 'Do you think that wife of his is attractive?'

'Well, she's certainly handsome,' Eitel said, 'but I can't say she's my type.'

'What a liar you are.' Elena's face was cheerful. 'I think Don Beda is very attractive,' she said, thereby startling him. 'But of course not as much as his wife.'

'Of course not.'

'You're angry and I was just warning you,' she teased.

'I'm not angry,' he insisted.

'If you want to go, I'll go,' Elena said. 'But I think we're crazy.'

He made a call to Beda, and for the rest of the day found himself in a curious excitement. From the past came a memory. When he was thirteen or fourteen he had kissed a girl for the first time, and before he said good night he begged a promise from the girl to see her the next evening. All the following day he walked the streets troubled and excited, feeling that life itself was there before him like a banquet of surprises. He had been in a flurry waiting for evening to come.

Now, he could feel the echoes of that emotion, and the day passed with a feeling that he was young again. It was marred only by Elena's silence. What a depressing woman she was, he told himself angrily. Certain enough, just as they were getting into his car, she turned to him, a wifely hand on his arm, and said, 'Charley, maybe this is a mistake.'

'What a time to decide,' he groaned.

'You want to go, don't you?'

'Let's call them up. It doesn't mean all that to me.'

She looked unhappy. 'I'm not being a prude,' she said. 'It's just that it would be better if it didn't feel so planned, I mean if it just happened.'

'You told me you used to do things like this to make your

psychoanalyst think you were more interesting. What's more planned than that?'

'I was immature then,' Elena said. 'Besides I didn't really enjoy it, not really. It's only with you, I can.' She kissed him softly on the cheek. 'Charley, I want you to promise tonight won't make any difference between us.'

'We don't even know that something is going to happen.' With that, he kicked the starter of his car and they were off.

For a while that evening at Beda's, it looked as if nothing would happen. During several hours they merely sat around and drank, and it was not pleasant drinking. Zenlia was sullen. She would smoke a cigarette out of a long holder, she would blow smoke into the air, and smile distantly at something clever that Eitel or Beda might say.

But as Elena got drunk, she turned merry. Beda was giving her compliments, and under the praise she grew more sure of herself, she began to make little remarks which Eitel had to admit were charming. Her green eyes had light in them, her lips were moist and separated, and her skin glowed against her dark dress. Eitel contributed a word from time to time and tried to catch Zenlia's eye. She seemed indifferent to him; for that matter she seemed indifferent to everyone but Elena. One of the few times Zenlia spoke, it was to say in her clear precise voice, 'You act like a dear cousin of mine, Elena.'

'I do?' Elena asked cautiously.

'Yes,' Zenlia said with a bored proud look, 'my cousin has rather an intense grace.'

'Well, I have rather an intense disgrace,' Elena said in a surprisingly comic English accent.

When all four laughed for the first time that night, Eitel could feel her blossom.

After that, the atmosphere changed. Beda began to dance with Zenlia, then with Elena, then he passed around a stick of tea. 'Prime Mexican pot,' he told them with a wave of his hand. Only Eitel refused to smoke. Another round, and Beda said in a tenor voice, 'Everybody's in a balling mood, thank God,' putting a period to the preliminaries.

Eitel wore the horns that night. There was nothing he could do about it – he was in a panic. After a while the party moved away from him, and he gave up and sat in a chair alone, smoking a cigarette, sipping a drink, trying to soothe the beating of his heart. Everything seemed to take hours.

It came to an end. Elena saw him sitting by himself, and she walked over unsteadily and asked, 'Do you want to go home?'

'No, not until you do.'

'Well, I do now.'

They said goodbye at the door as if they had been playing bridge for the evening, but before they drove away Eitel could hear the sound of laughter behind the fence which enclosed the patio of Beda's house.

On the ride he was silent, and when Elena put a shy hand on his leg he remained immobile, neither giving himself to her by so much as the width of a hair, nor drawing away. It was the same when they went to bed. He lay on his back, his eyes watching the ceiling so carefully that he felt at last as if he could see in the dark. Elena stirred restlessly. She sighed once or twice. He could sense how she hesitated to speak, formed words, and then was silent. When her hand touched his, and her fingers tried to squeeze his palm, he stiffened all over his body.

'Don't touch me,' he said to her in the darkness.

'Charley . . .' she began.

'I'm trying to sleep.'

'You wanted to go,' she said mildly, carefully.

'I didn't know what a stinking brutal bitch you are,' he heard himself whispering.

'Charley, I love you,' she said.

'Love me? You love everything,' he said. 'A gorilla, a hyena, a four-eyed horse.' But he had only begun. 'You love me,' he repeated, 'yes, you certainly do when you can give your yelps and yowls to any two-bit dog.' He was trembling.

'Charley, it wasn't the same,' she said in a small voice. 'I don't love them. It's just a cockeyed part of me.' She was beginning to cry. 'Charley, don't turn on me,' she said. 'I love you. I'm the only one who does.'

'Love, Elena?' he said. 'Love is just a big noise.'

What he could not bear was the thought that she did not love him completely, without thought or interest in anything else alive.

'Oh, you're cruel,' she said.

'Cruel?' he exclaimed. 'Why I've been taking lessons from you.'

'All right, Charley,' Elena said, sitting up in bed, her face filling with hard wisdom and hatred of him, until she was beautiful to his eyes, and more than a little frightening. 'Now, you listen to me,' she said. 'You were the one who arranged everything tonight, and yet you call me a pig. If it had turned out better for *you*, you would be loving me all over again, you would be telling me how wonderful I am.'

He was weary, he was exhausted – a defeated man cannot be asked to have the moral bravery of a victor. So Eitel turned on Elena, and in his best accent he said, 'Must you worship stupidity as if it were your patron saint?'

She wept then. He could hear her struggle to keep her grief, and in the darkness each small sound she made, for she never wept loudly, became swollen in his ear. He heard her slip out of bed, grope her way to the bathroom, felt like a whip against his eyes the glare of the bathroom light before she closed the door, and then he was alone, left with nothing but his rage, his cold animosity, and the knowledge that Elena was crying, her chilled feet standing against the stone of the bathroom floor. Eitel tried to shut her from his mind, and all the while his own feet chilled, his body shuddered from cold perspiration. 'I'll never touch her again,' he swore, and even as he was swearing, he knew he could not leave her alone in the bathroom crying into the hard face of the mirror, the tile, and the chromium. 'It really is my fault,' he thought, and he got out of bed and went to her. She trembled in his arms, her body was ice, and for minutes while he soothed her and tried to calm her weeping, his anger buried in the tenderness he felt he had to offer, he could do no more than say, 'It's all right, baby, it's all right.'

She seemed almost not to know that he was there. 'Oh, Charley, you must forgive me,' she wept at last. 'I kept thinking you would never talk to me any more, and you see, there's nothing, there just isn't anything when I begin to think . . . I mean, without you. Oh, Charley, forgive me. I swear I'll make it up to you, I'll spend the rest of my life.' She was babbling now. In another moment she would be hysterical. But as if it were too important to bury herself in hysteria, to leave one thing she must say unsaid, he could feel her clutching him like a broken-hearted child. 'You see,' she hiccuped, her sobbing uncontrollable, 'I got that way because, oh Charley . . . they liked me, and I was the centre of attention.'

Then he hugged her to him, led her back to the bedroom, and exhausted she fell asleep in his arms while he whispered to her, 'It's all right, baby, do you hear, it's all right,' whispering it even after she had fallen asleep, whispering it into the darkness while the chorus of what she had said, 'I was the centre of attention . . . I was the centre . . .' played its long record into his sleep and into his dreams. He almost felt happy. He had learned how he valued her. Yet the stern taskmaster of his conscience knew that he had denied Elena a most valuable opportunity to grow because he had called her stupid at the instant when she had been most perceptive of his character. So, if he hugged her to him now as a naughty but pardoned child, he fell asleep nonetheless with a deep sorrow.

All next day he felt the vulnerability of his body as though he had been flogged with the rung of a chair. It was only after quarrels or crises that he could feel love for Elena the way he desired. Yet at the edge of this emotion he was surprised at himself. Was the memory to be cured so easily?

Eitel learned. Everything was all right until they tried to make love again. Then Elena was far away, and it was no better for him. He hated her. It was impossible not to remember how she had given herself to the others, and whatever expression might cross her face became deformed to him and infected the past until he saw beyond Beda the legion of her numberless lovers to whom she had probably given herself in exactly this way. Thus, losing the pride that it was he who gave her everything, that there was finally something worth while about himself, Eitel was stripped; he had never felt so small.

Elena sensed it of course. She was tense and difficult and her attempts to stir herself offended him. For all the minutes they would try he could hear nothing in his brain but, 'Love, love is a big noise,' and he felt it spreading from him like a poison fog which must turn bone to rubber, and spirit to glue, so that he not only hated her and hated himself but the life of everything.

What seemed most odious to him was that they had been tender to each other, they had forgiven one another, and yet he did not love her, she did not love him, no one ever loved anyone. These things he would think and afterwards would lie beside her, even caress her with a cunning which asked no more than that she not make a scene. And each night, or almost every night for a week, Elena would encourage him to love her and then would lie stiffly, while he knew she was thinking of all he had said in his rage. He would even tell himself that she had developed since he had known her; in their first weeks together she would not have gone a day like this, and now she had managed a week.

During that time, he finished his script. Through all of the new draft, he had been dreading to do the scene where Freddie returned to the seminary and the story was finally wrapped in the chorus of angels' voices. Eitel had no conceit that he was writing his original story; he knew too well how clever was the new script, how effective, how brilliant of its professional sort, but there was the problem: it was so well done in its own way that the end could not be too artificial; as a commercial script it needed its own kind of false sincerity, and he had not been able to imagine how he would do it. But the last scene turned out perfectly: it was a marvel – he admired the way he wrote so well about things he did not believe at all. Eitel felt powerful.

The script, he had decided, was much too good to give to Munshin on the terms they had made, and therefore it was time to alter the contract. Sitting at his desk, working for Collie's profit, his mind would come back to Crane, and like a salesman with his samples at the door, he would tell himself all the arguments; for a man who had been indifferent to politics these ten years it was a waste to be stubborn. The names he hated to give were the names of men who had talked against his own name; in the last months, if he had learned nothing else, he had learned that he was not an artist, and what was a commercial man without his trade? The arguments knocked at the door, they tipped their hat and came inside to leave a sample, departing with the promise they would be back again.

Eitel wrote a cautious letter to Crane, explaining that soon he might be ready, and when one of the regular phone calls came from Munshin, Eitel told him it would be weeks before he could finish the script.

'What's the delay?' Munshin asked.

'Stop worrying. You'll make a fortune on this,' Eitel said easily. He left Elena for a day and flew up to the capital to talk to his lawyer and visit his business agent.

The end came more easily than he had expected. As Elena had been promising for so long, she had her hair cut one morning and it turned out badly. To his flat eye she looked like a clipped rabbit. He would stare at her from time to time, not able to believe that she was any more to him than a drudge he hired by the day. While he sat in a dumb reverie watching her work, he would recognize how hopeless she became the moment his eyes were on her. She was sweeping with a broom, but so absent-mindedly that three times he watched her move the dust from one corner to the other and then back again. Eitel had had a telegram from Crane the night before. There would be committee hearings in two weeks, and Crane was delighted that he would co-operate. When Elena asked him what was in the telegram, he told her.

'I guess it means you'll be making pictures again,' she said.

'I guess it does.'

'Well . . .' She could think of nothing to say because there was only one question she wanted to ask and she hardly dared.

'When are you going?' she said a little later, waiting he thought for the word that she would go with him. That was all it meant to her, he decided bitterly.

'Couple of weeks, I think,' he answered, and they did not talk about it again.

She had finished sweeping and was sitting at the dining table, staring through the picture window at the yucca tree, stoically, like a peasant, much as her parents must once have stared with stony eyes out the dirty window of their candy store. He came up behind her, touched her shoulder, and said, 'You know, I really like your hair this way.'

'You hate it,' she said.

'No, I wouldn't say that.'

Tears forced themselves out of her eyes and she looked furious at how they betrayed her, for she must have sworn she would not weep. He moved across the table from her and watched Elena's fingers tear at her nails. From his sure distance he felt a kind of sweet sorrow that neither he nor she had been able to make the happiness they should have made. He usually felt such sentiments when an affair ended and if he were ashamed afterward of how easy his emotions were it encouraged him now to feel he could finish their affair today.

'Elena,' he said, 'there's something I want to talk about.'

'You want me to go away,' she said. 'All right, I will.'

'It isn't that exactly . . .' he started to say.

'You're done,' she said. 'All right, then, you're done. Maybe I'm done too.'

'No, now wait . . .'

'I knew it would end,' Elena said.

'It's my fault,' Eitel said quickly. 'I'm no good for anybody.'

'Who cares whose fault it is? You're . . . you're terrible,' she said and began to cry.

'Now look, little monkey,' he said, trying to caress her shoulder.

She threw off his hand. 'I hate you.'

'I don't blame you,' said Eitel.

'You're so good with words. I really hate you. You . . . you stink,' Elena said crudely, hopelessly, while he winced for her.

'You're right,' he said, 'I stink.'

Her fingers tapped on the table in a monotonous irritating rhythm. 'I'm getting out of here,' she said, 'I'm going to pack my stuff. Thank you for a lovely time.' How pitiful was her talent for sarcasm, Eitel was thinking.

'Why don't I leave?' he asked. 'You can stay here for a while. It's your place too.'

'It isn't my place. It never was.'

'Elena, don't say that.'

'Oh, shut up,' she said, 'it isn't my place,' and she began to cry again.

'Elena, we can still get married,' he said, and knew the moment he uttered the words that he did not mean them so insincerely as he had thought.

She didn't answer. She merely fled the room. In a moment he could hear her slamming drawers, and it was not hard to picture how she heaped things from one bag to the other, trying not to show her tears, and therefore sobbing uncontrollably. At last he was out of it. He only had to wait until she was gone.

But it became more difficult than he expected. He did not like to hear her weeping in the bedroom; it shivered the calm he had laid on himself and opened a question. What was she going to do? He held on to himself as if it were necessary to support a heavy weight for five minutes, for five minutes more, and then another five. It was vital not to weaken; even love which lasted beyond its time had continued because it took so long to pack a bag. He even thought of going out for a walk, but he could not do that. He would have to call a taxi, see her into it, close the door, wave goodbye with the sad sheepish grin of the man who knows he has not done well and wishes he could do better. Abruptly it occurred to him that he would look to her at that moment as Collie Munshin must have looked when he left her in Desert D'Or. Something turned over in Eitel. Elena should not be treated so badly.

He could hear her phoning for a cab, hear her voice stumble as she gave her address, and the sound of the phone being dropped back on its cradle. Then her bag was snapped shut, then the other bag. All she had accumulated in her life could be crammed into the space of two pieces of luggage.

When she came out of the bedroom, he was ready to give up. She could have done anything; she could have taken a step toward him, or merely looked helpless, and he would have had to do something – possibly he would even have promised to take her with him to the capital.

But she did not do any of these things. In a dry bitter voice, Elena muttered, 'I thought you'd be interested to know where I'm going.'

'Where are you going?' he asked.

'I'm going over to Marion.'

It brought back his hatred. 'Do you think you really ought to?' he said.

'Do you care?'

He resented that she should use this trick to make him unable to let her go. 'I suppose I don't care,' he said. 'I'm just curious.

When did you arrange it?' His throat felt sore as though very soon it would be an effort to speak.

'I called him yesterday. Then I made my appointment for the haircut. This haircut you don't like. Does that surprise you? Did you think you'd have to kick me out? All right.' She cleared her throat. 'Maybe I'll become a prostitute. Don't worry. I'm not trying to make you feel sorry. You think I'm a prostitute anyway, so how could you feel sorry?' Her eyes were dull. This was one time he knew she would not burst into tears. 'In fact you always thought of me as a prostitute,' Elena said, 'but you don't know what I think of you. You think I can't live without you. Maybe I know better.'

There was the sound of the taxi coming up the drive. Eitel started to get out of his chair, but Elena picked up her suitcases. Like an actress she turned around to make a last speech. 'At least for once I'm giving somebody the gate,' she said, and was out the door. Eitel remained standing until the taxi had driven away, and then he sat down and began to wait for her telephone call. It seemed certain to him that she would phone, but an hour went by, and then the afternoon, and much of the night. He sat drinking, too tired even to pry an ice cube from the tray, and as it got dark, he sighed to himself, not knowing if he were relieved that he was free, or if he were more miserable than he had ever been.

22

When Eitel finished telling the story, we continued to sit in the living room with the litter of a dozen half-filled cartons and several pieces of luggage. 'Do you want me to help you pack?' I said at last.

He shook his head. 'No, somehow I enjoy doing it myself. It's the last opportunity I'll have to be alone for some time.'

I guessed what he meant. 'Everything's been set for you to testify?'

Eitel shrugged. 'You may as well know. You'll be reading about it in the newspapers soon enough.'

'What will I read?'

He did not answer the question directly. 'You see, after Elena left,' he said, 'I couldn't stand to stay here. Not for the first few days. I drove into the capital early that morning, and I went to see my lawyer. There's no use giving you all the bits and pieces. I must have talked to a dozen people. The amazing thing is how complicated it is.'

'Then you're going to have your secret session?'

'No.' Eitel looked away while he lit a cigarette. 'They're not letting me off that easy. You see, those people are artists. If you admit that you're ready for a secret session, they know that you'll testify in public session, too. They get down to bed-rock, don't you see?' Eitel smiled pensively. 'Oh, I gave them a bit of trouble. I walked out of a conference when they told me the session would have to be public, and I went to my lawyer's office, and I raved, and I ranted, but all the time I knew I was going to give them what they wanted.' He took a careful swallow of his drink. 'If I had had something to return to in Desert D'Or ... well, in that case, I don't know, I won't look for excuses. The fact is I didn't have anything. All I could do was admit how clever they are. They know you win an empire by asking for an acre at a time. After we'd agreed on a public session, there came the business of the names.' He gave a little laugh. 'Oh, the names. You have no idea how many names there are. Of course I never belonged to *that* political party, and so it was obvious right along that I could never be the sort of witness who qualifies for Stool Of The Year. Still they knew ways to use me. I had several conferences with two detectives Crane uses for his investigations. They looked like All-American guard and tackle posing for a photograph. They knew so much more about me than I knew about them. I never realized how many papers a man could put his name to in ten years. Who asked me, they wanted to know, to sign the petition against the exploitation of child labour in the salt mines of Alabama? That sort of thing. A hundred, two hundred, four hundred signatures. I could just as well have been on a couch coughing up my childhood. A little word at this cocktail party with that dangerous political operator – some fool of a writer, mind you, who liked to think of himself as a liberal with muscles – he had given me a paper to sign.' Eitel felt his bald spot as though to learn how many hairs he had lost in the process. 'I found it confusing for a while. There were certain people they wanted me to accuse, and there were others, particularly a couple of movie stars I know at Supreme and Magnum, whom they were absolutely uninterested in. When I began to understand what sort of arrangement existed between the Committee and the studios we began to make progress. You see they had a list of fifty people prepared for me. Seven of those people I could swear I never met in my life but it seems I'm wrong. There were so many big parties after all, and my two football players knew all about them. "You were both in the same room on such and such a night at so-and-so's party," they would let me know, and eventually I would produce the sort of political conversation that one might have had. Toward the end, they got friendly. One of them took the trouble to tell me he liked a picture I had made, and we even made a bet on a fight. Finally, it seemed to me as if I liked my detectives just as much as some of the people whose names I'm going to give. For that matter, half the names on my list have repulsive personalities.' Eitel smiled wearily. 'The interrogation took two days. Then

Crane was back and I went to see him. He was very pleased, but it seems there were still more things to be asked of me. I hadn't done enough.'

'Not enough?' I said.

'There were still a few acres to be picked. Crane called my lawyer in, and they took the trouble to tell me that I ought to have a statement to release to the newspapers after I testified. Crane had written it for me. Of course I was free to use different wording, but he had thought, he said, to show me the sort of thing which was probably best. Later my lawyer gave another suggestion. Everybody seemed to think it would be practical to take out a paid advertisement in the trade papers to explain how proud I was to have testified, and how I hoped that others in my position would do their duty in the same way. Do you care to see the statement I'm giving to the newspapers next week?'

'I'd like to see it,' I said. I glanced over a few lines:

> It has taken me a year of wasted and misplaced effort to recognize the useful and patriotic function of the Committee, and I testify today without duress, proud to be able to contribute my share to the defence of this country against all infiltration and subversion. With a firm knowledge of the democratic heritage we share, I can only add that it is the duty of every citizen to aid the Committee in its work with whatever knowledge he may possess.

'It goes about par for the course,' I said.

Eitel was off on other subjects. 'You ought to know,' he remarked, 'that Crane keeps his word. While I was in his office he called up people at different studios, and said a word or two for me. It was the one part of the process I found surprising. My mind's too subtle. I didn't expect he would pick up the phone in front of me.'

'What about your script?' I asked. I had a headache.

'That's the funny part, Sergius. You know when I started to feel ashamed? It was at the idea of double-crossing Collie Munshin. I felt I ought to see him first, and I told Collie that I intended to sell the script as my own. He didn't even get angry. I think he was expecting it. Collie just said he was glad I would be back, and he talked me into staying with him. Do you know, I realized that he does care about me, and I was very touched by that. We worked out a new contract. Collie and I will split evenly if he's able to talk Teppis into letting me direct the film. Tomorrow, when I get in, everything will be settled. All I have to do is approve the galley-sheet on my advertisement.'

'Yes, but how do you feel?' I asked suddenly, not able to listen to him any more.

The ironic disciplined expression on his face gave way for an instant to something vulnerable behind it.

'How do I feel?' Eitel asked. 'Oh, nothing so extraordinary, Sergius. You see, after a while, I knew they had me on my knees, and that if I wasn't ready to take an overdose of sleeping pills, I would have to let myself slide through the experience, and not try to resist it. So for the first time in my life I had the sensation of being a complete and total whore in the world, and I accepted every blow, every kick, and every gratuitous kindness with the inner gratitude that it could have been a good deal worse. And now I just feel tired, and if the truth be told, pleased with myself, because believe me, Sergius, it was dirty work.' He lit a cigarette and held it away from his mouth. 'In the end that's the only kind of self-respect you have. To be able to say to yourself that you're disgusting.' He put his cigarette in his mouth and took it out again. 'By the way,' he murmured, and he looked a bit apologetic, 'I've been thinking that it was a trifle presumptuous for me to tell you to turn down that offer from Supreme.'

'I'm not sorry,' I said not altogether truthfully.

'Are you sure?' He rotated his glass in his fingers. 'Sergius, I've been entertaining the idea of inviting you to be my assistant.'

Suddenly I was angry. 'Did they put you up to it?' I asked. 'Are they still thinking of making my movie?'

He was hurt. 'You go too far, Sergius.'

'Maybe I do,' I said. 'But what if I hadn't come over tonight? Would you have thought of making your offer then?'

'No,' Eitel said, 'I have to admit I didn't think of it until this minute. But that shouldn't matter so much. You can't keep polishing knives and forks all your life.'

There was a minute when I was tempted again. But there came into my mind the thought of seeing Lulu at the studio and how she would say hello to me as Eitel's assistant. So I folded his offer into that mental file we carry with us of those jobs we

292

have turned away, and I said, 'Forget it,' to him, and looked at my watch.

As I got up to go, I said abruptly, 'Do you want me to keep an eye on Elena?'

There was something forlorn about Eitel in the middle of his packing cases. 'Elena?' he asked, 'well, I don't know. Suppose you do what you want to do.'

'Have you heard from her?'

He seemed about to say no, and then nodded. 'I got a letter from her. A long letter. It was forwarded to me while I was in the city.'

'Are you going to answer her?'

'No, I just wouldn't know how to do that,' he said.

Eitel came to the door to say goodbye. As I was walking down the drive he called to wait, and came out his door. 'I'll mail you her letter,' he said. 'I don't want to keep it and I don't want to tear it up.'

'Should I write to you after I read it?'

This, too, he considered. 'I don't think so,' he said carefully. 'You see, I get the feeling that if I allowed myself, I would miss her very much.'

'Well, goodbye.'

For a moment he gave his charming smile. 'Please forgive me, Sergius, for that offer as my assistant.'

'I guess you meant it well,' I said.

He nodded. He was about to say something, he changed his mind, and then just as I was ready to turn away, he mentioned it after all. 'You know, I don't want to worry you,' he said, 'but those detectives asked a lot of questions about you.'

Deep in me, I suppose I was not as surprised as I should have been. 'Well,' I said, and my voice was small, 'what did you tell them?'

'I told them nothing. That is, I gave them a few details of your life, I thought it would sound suspicious not to, but I think I succeeded in convincing them that there was no need to bother you.'

'Only you're not sure,' I said.

'No,' Eitel admitted, 'they may come around to pay you a visit.'

'Well, thanks for telling me,' I said coldly.

Then he looked me directly in the eyes for the first time, and in a low voice, he said simply, 'Sergius, why are you so hard on me? I've always been as honest with you as I could.'

I nodded. There was a moment when my voice thickened just a little, and I had to hurry over my words. I could not help it, I still cared about Eitel, and so I lied just a little and said, 'I'm sorry, maybe you were a little too honest for me today.' His eyes brightened for an instant, and then despite myself, not knowing if I were cruel or if it were more important to be honest, I had to try to hurt him again. 'I suppose,' I said, 'that it wasn't fair to build you up into more than you are.'

He was ready for that, however. 'Yes,' he said, 'you're old enough now to do without heroes,' and he touched me on the shoulder and turned back to his house.

I did not receive the letter until the end of the week. In the meantime I had the opportunity to hear enough about Eitel; each night in my furnished room I would read some item about his fortunes. For the week after he testified the gossip columnists wrote about him as if he were the hero of a sermon, and when that had worn itself down I saw only a few more items. There was an announcement by Supreme Pictures that they had bought an original screenplay entitled *Saints and Lovers*, written by Charles Francis Eitel and Carlyle Munshin, to be directed by Eitel and produced by Munshin. If anyone had curiosity to wonder how Munshin could have collaborated with Eitel, it was explained in most of the gossip columns that Munshin and Teppis had convinced Eitel of his duty to testify before the Committee. It was the sort of story which could not be probed too carefully, but for that matter it never was, and Eitel slipped out of the news for a while. He was busy casting his picture I would see by a line in the papers every now and again.

Long before this he sent me Elena's letter, and I read it through, stumbling through page after page of her handwriting. She wrote with blots and smudges, crossing out words, writing uphill and downhill, adding notes and parentheses and arrows in the margin, and her letter seemed a distance from the conversation I had with Eitel in his living room.

23

Dear Charley,

I can just see you smile when you read this. What a stupid girl she is you're going to think, but there's nothing new in that because we both know I'm stupid and I'm crude, and besides I remember what you once said to me, 'Elena, don't use all that psychoanalytical talk, and think that that's going to make you cultured.' Well, don't forget that I'm cultured in a very funny way because there's no such thing as a Catholic who doesn't have some culture. Only in another way you were right, and that's what I was hoping people would think until you punctured that idea. But you couldn't begin to imagine how scared I still am to write a letter to you, you're such a critic, but in high school I got my best marks in English, it's true whether you care to believe it or not, I even got A's, I didn't tell you, but then you wouldn't have believed it no matter what I said. I hate to write this way Charley because I know I sound like a fishwife as you took the trouble to tell me one time, but the important thing for me is that I'm able to write you a letter.

But I'm not saying what I want to say at all. I started to write this to thank you because in your own way you were very good to me, and you're a much kinder man than you think about yourself, and I could cry for you Charley when I think about you, except I can't yet, why should I lie? I still feel bitter to you, but what I hope is that five years from now or I don't know when, some years in the future, I'll really be able to think about you and be grateful because even though you were a snob and what a snob you are Charley, you hated being that way just as I hate being the way I am, and I mean it.

You see I started this letter for one reason only. I wanted to tell you not to feel guilty because it's ridiculous. You don't owe me anything and I owe you a lot. Something very disturbing has happened since I've been with Marion Faye, as a matter of fact it happened before that, the night we were with your friend D. B. and his wife Z., and we ended up getting exactly what we deserved, and I hate the memory of that night – except I don't know because probably we wouldn't have gotten anywhere anyway. But if I'm really going to tell you the truth, it happened much much earlier than that, even before I met you, the night before as a matter of fact, and you know what the truth is? I don't think I ever loved anybody in my whole life. Not even myself. I don't know what love is. I thought I did with you, but I don't. Because you see I know I don't love Marion, and yet, I'm not saying this to hurt you Charley, but sexually, and Marion's very weird, I don't want to give the particulars but there's one way he's like you, he thinks if he's doing something dirty, that's going to change the world or blow up the world or something of the sort. Anyway there is something about him so that in certain ways it's just as good as it was with you. I know what you're going to think. You're going to say of course it's always been like that with her but it isn't true, and the first time I fooled with Marion, that time when you and I were getting started, I didn't want it to be good with him that night and it wasn't because I wanted to believe I was in love with you. I even lied to you afterward and said I knew Marion when I was a kid but it's not true. I met him in a bar right here in town, and I let him pick me up one afternoon and I knew he was a pimp, I knew his reputation, and even if I didn't, he made no bones about it. Now, I know that I can't fool myself any longer, and I'm no good, I'm no good Charley, I'm a prostitute like everybody else which I never thought about myself. My mother always used to say I was no good, and all of a sudden yesterday I thought to myself what if she's right, and that's frightening, Charley. I don't know how to say it but what if all the stupid jealous people are right?

Anyway here is something I never told you about at all. And that is that the day I left you, I had a funny little moment when I wanted to laugh because you know what popped into my head? – 'Well, girls, here we go again.' That's what I thought, and the reason is that I said the same thing to Collie, that for once I was giving a man the gate. And yet, do you know what's funny, there were three or four men who asked me to marry them, two of them on the first night, and yet I always turned them down 'cause I thought they weren't good enough for me. One of them was even a gangster, did you know that? My doctor used to tell me that I had the idea I was a queen and an empress and a man-eating tiger and of course he was right. I'm very conceited at bottom. I want to give you the best example of how stupid I am. When Collie went out the door and he and I were through, do you know what I did? *I tried to commit suicide.* I was always too ashamed to tell you but it's the truth and the funny thing is I told Marion about it the first afternoon I knew him about how after Collie left I just sat in the hotel room Collie had rented for me, a horrible hotel room 'cause Collie was always so cautious, and the terrible thing about it was that I thought I loved him for so many years and then toward the end I thought I hated him but the fact of the matter was I wasn't feeling anything. And then I started to drink by myself which I almost never do and I just felt alone and just a little bit scared, but the trouble was I started to get dizzy and I got so terribly dizzy that the room wouldn't stand still and the weird thing about it was that this seemed worse to me than anything else, I had the feeling I was going to die if the room didn't stop moving, and so I don't know how I got to that point but I had the feeling I had to kill myself or otherwise I was going to die – isn't that fantastic? Anyway I had a package of sleeping tablets in my room and I took all of them, there must have been five or six, and after I took them I was worried I was going to throw them up but it didn't happen that way, I just got dizzier, and then there was a thought kept coming into my mind. I kept thinking of what Collie would always say to me in the old days when we were having a fight. He'd always say, 'Don't talk about it now, honey. We'll work something out, but right now I'm clearing up a problem in my analysis.' He always used to say that and so while I was sitting in that hotel room drunker than a dog I just kept saying to myself as if I were the voice of Collie Munshin or something, 'Don't worry, Elena, we'll work something out,' and I kept answering him, 'Collie, we sure will 'cause I'll haunt you.' And then I kept saying to myself that I couldn't die because if I did I would haunt Collie and this began to bother me so much that I had the feeling I had to call him up and tell him not to worry, that I wouldn't do anything to bother him, and I was going to make it a nice quiet sophisticated little call but the moment I heard his voice on the phone I was terrified, I thought I was talking to my doctor or to St Peter, I don't know what I thought, but I started screaming at him that I was going to die and I'd taken poison, and I remember Charley that I couldn't stop crying after I hung up the phone and I was feeling so sick and dopey and the room still wouldn't stop moving until I was ready to get down on my hands and knees and pray for it to stay still. And when Collie came over he was very business-like at first and slapped me a couple of times because I guess I was in hysterics and then he asked about the poison and I pointed to the tube and I remember him saying, 'Thank God, you idiot,' and then he began to laugh, and I felt worse than I ever did before or since because I knew I couldn't do anything right, I couldn't even kill myself, and I found out later that all I'd taken were sedatives and not even sleeping pills, and he made me throw them up and had the hotel send up coffee and he kept pouring it down me so that it wasn't even necessary to bring a doctor into it. Why do I tell you this? I don't even know, except that a couple of hours later by night-time when I wasn't sick any more, just very nervous, and I didn't care that I was losing Collie. I just felt that I hated him and he even seemed a stranger to me, I began to get excited at the way he had made me throw up and the way he had seen me throwing up, and I don't have to tell you how weird that is for me because you know how I didn't like for you to see me even without make-up and I've always wanted some kind of personal privacy, so much so that even now I feel ashamed writing about this thing of getting excited because Collie had seen me throw up but somehow that seemed very very exciting, and I went to bed with Collie. This is what I wanted to tell you. It was never very exciting with Collie before, but I have an awful confession to make, and this may hurt you, but do you know that Collie was pretty good, very advanced like you only he was fat sort of, he's crude but he's not so crude, and I always used to act that it was great with him, and in a way it was because it was my fault not his, you see I never trusted him, and when a girl doesn't trust a man deep inside her then I guess she's cold although it's a complicated subject and who am I to talk about it because I couldn't have trusted you the first night I met you, I think maybe I even disliked you a little bit, because I remember I was jealous that Sergius liked Lulu, and you seemed so superior and condescending to me, and yet I wasn't acting with you, you're the first man in my life in a way except even that's a lie because on the night before with Collie I'm telling you about, that is the night before I met you and we went to the party and all, I really let go with Collie, I thought I was in ether or something, and suddenly with Collie I had the feeling that I was free. I don't know how to put it but it just seemed as if you could find something like that no matter where you went, and the funny thing was that Collie and I had a long talk afterward and we decided that he would see me just for a night every now and again, and he would pay me, pay me just like a call girl. I think we arranged it should be fifty dollars, and when he left I guess he wanted to make it clear to me that we weren't living together any more, not in any way except for a quick hour once in awhile, and so he told me that for the following day he was sending you over and what you have to realize Charley is that first day we were together, all that evening at the party and then later in your house, I kept thinking that you were going to be a customer I suppose the word would be and I was fantastically excited. I don't mean to say that I was acting because I wasn't, I was fantastically aroused but you see I didn't know then and I don't know now if it was because of you as a person or because of the situation, and the next day when I began to realize that of course you hadn't thought of me as a call girl, and Collie had never said a word that way, I was very depressed and very happy and I didn't know what I felt. You were so good to me and so decent that I began to get very confused, and that's when I made my mistake 'cause I should have had the sense to clear out then, but all I could think of was that little hotel room I had, and I was afraid I would go nuts in there, and I didn't want to go back to the city because who could I go to see? And so of course I just drifted into things with you and before I knew it there I was in a love affair again, and I didn't believe it, I didn't want to believe it, because you see it made me confused again, and that last time I made love to Collie I realized that in a way you could eat up the whole world if you wanted to, if only you didn't fall for all the talk that the middle-class squares give you, and you were making me fall for them. I hate the kind of thing that happens to women where they go out with a man maybe two or three times and immediately they're forced to start thinking about marriage. That's how my mother got married and a lot of my sisters and what a drudgery sort of life they have, everybody's so afraid to live. I am, too, and it's silly. Once I remember I had a girl friend and she had a steady boy friend and I used to fall into a thing with the two of them on a Saturday night when Collie was off at one of his big movie parties, and I know you won't believe it, I don't want to remind you of Don Beda, but it was very different with those friends because I would feel all right the next day and the three of us liked each other like good friends and I almost never felt low-down about it. I mean as an example it used to be almost as much fun eating breakfast on Sunday as it was the night before, but that's because we kept it uncomplicated and the girl liked me very much and nobody was asking anybody else to solve their whole life for them. But that's what you were asking me and what I was asking you and *I resented it just as much as you did.* That was why I slept with Marion Faye the first week I knew you, but I was a coward, I had to keep telling myself that you were wonderful and that I was in love, that life was marvellous and love was marvellous and Charley I've been such a phony 'cause I've been scared and hanging on to you, and the time Collie came to visit us I didn't want to look at him, he seemed repulsive to me, and the reason he seemed so fat and repulsive was because I kept thinking that I had enjoyed myself with him too, at least one night anyway, and I wanted to believe that I was in love with only you.

I'm so neurotic and maybe I ought to write letters more because I never could talk to you and now I can, I suppose probably because we're through, but there're certain things you really ought to know 'cause you never could see them through my eyes like the sort of thing that happens with taxicab drivers. I don't know why they always feel it about me but they know they don't have to talk to me politely, and even the day I left your place and put in my suitcases and gave him Marion's address, we hadn't been driving two minutes and I was trying to think how I felt when the taxi-cab driver said to me, 'Know this Faye character long, baby?' and he said it with a leer, just the same kind of tough guy leer my father always would have when he talked to a woman, and I got so angry I started screaming at him to keep his dirty mouth shut, right in the middle of the drive. And when I got to Marion's and got inside the door I was ready for anything, I was hoping he would send me out as a call girl right away. Did you ever have to put up with those kind of humiliations?

Anyway, Marion didn't send me out. He just got me drunker and drunker, not that I needed much help, I don't know if you know it or not, but I was drunk when I walked out the door on you, early that morning I'd called up Marion and told him I was coming over, and then I got so scared I filled a highball glass with whisky, and every time I went into the kitchen I would take a sip on it, and so I was looped when I got to his house, and he gave me more and then I don't even remember the rest, all I can remember is that I kept thinking, 'How Collie is going to suffer, good for him!!' And that makes me wonder Charley if maybe in a certain kind of way maybe I loved Collie more than you since I remember thinking about him and haven't thought about you much, not until I started writing this letter. And maybe in a certain way I love Marion more than either of you, I don't know, I don't even care, but for example sometimes with him it's very erratic but when it's good it seems to me that it's just as good as it ever was with you, I don't know maybe I'm shallow, maybe I'm nothing, so what? I guess you were right when you used to tell me all I could think about was myself. But this I do know, at least there's something doing with Marion, he's not a coward and a snob like you, I don't even know what he sees in me, but then that's nothing new because I never could understand what any-body saw in me, but do you want to know the kind of stupid argument I have with Marion. I keep asking him to make me a call girl and he says no, he says he wants to marry me and then I can become a call girl. I suppose he wants to be a champion pimp. Like Don Beda or somebody. It's impossible to marry him, he makes it a joke, and I don't want to get married, I'm sick of the whole idea, and Marion does the sort of thing where he begs me to marry him, it's the truth Charley, and when I ask him why, he says he likes the idea of me joining his mother's coffee-clotch (how do you spell that?) or some remark like that, and he insists we stay drunk all the time or on tea although frankly I don't mind that part of it. Although sometimes on tea I get so scared I'm ready to climb a wall or maybe die of a heart attack. And Marion curses you. I think somewhere along the line you must have hurt him somehow. It's all cockeyed. I don't know where we're going and it's weird, I don't want to hurt you if I say that he insisted on seeing Zenlia and Don Beda but you must have heard about that anyway, and I could tell you other things he does but it isn't important, what I think is so rotten is that I'm writing about him as if he's a stranger and I've done something worse, I've talked to him about you the way I used to talk to you about Collie, very critically that is, and I feel ashamed every time, and the truth of the matter is that I'm a bitch and I never have grown up and you were right to call me a bitch, and I want you to believe that because Charley you're such an unhappy and miserable man and it isn't fair, I don't know why I say it isn't fair but I just wish you had some sort of break, some sort of luck, although what would be lucky for you would take a genius to say, but I suppose I have to confess that I'm as sick as you are to discover that I didn't love you the way I wanted to, and I apologize for the things I've said against you. How could I have done that? Charley, you deserve something good. It isn't fair.

There was a blob of ink, the beginning of a new paragraph which she had scratched out, and then apparently having decided to end the letter she had signed her name. Looking at the scratched-out line, the blot, and the signature, I wondered how long she had sat there, thinking to add something else as if the reason for writing the letter had eluded her, and drunk, her mind must have wandered over the grab bag of her life until she had decided to grab no more, had put her name down, sealed the envelope, and sent it off.

24

After I read the letter, I went out to see Elena and Marion, but she was shy with me and Marion was difficult so I gave it up. I had picked the wrong evening for I was in as bad a depression as I have ever been, and I remember as I was leaving them after a half-hour of stumbled attempts and expired conversations, Elena stood next to me for a moment in the hall. 'You don't like me any more,' she said.

'Maybe I don't,' I muttered to her, and closed the door quietly in her face, my depression lifted because I had hurt her, and then it came back again doubly and I lay in my furnished room and I was nowhere. Reading her letter had laid a cloud on me; seeing her with Marion made it worse. I had thought that I knew everything there was to know about the bottom, but I was to learn all over again as one learns each time in his life that there is no such thing as the old bottom, and no matter how bad one feels, one can always feel worse. So I went down and down until the memory of the past day's depression was nostalgia in its contrast to what I felt today, and my energy began to leave me and I woke up in the morning more tired than I had gone to sleep. I whipped myself those days. I started to write, and I would cover pages with all the scrawls and fish-hooks of the handwriting I learned in the orphanage, and in revenge on Lulu, for the worst to be said about a writer is that he can take a coward's revenge, I wrote long incoherent pages where I tried to destroy her, and all the catechism which had been laid into my skull by good Sister Rose came back to scathe the people I had known at Desert D'Or so that I not only hated Lulu, and hated Eitel and Marion and Elena, but I loathed myself. I never knew such self-pity and I never disliked myself so much, and the worst of it was that I was certain I would never write a good word, and I didn't have talent, and I didn't have a girl, and I wondered if I could ever manage to have a girl again, and all in all I was about as brave as an eight-year-old boy at the bottom of an abandoned mine shaft. I thought it would go on forever, but something happened finally, and my sickness came to term, and I climbed from my hole. But I get ahead of myself, and besides I do not really know the reasons.

One night when I got back from my job, there were two men sitting in my room. They were wearing summer suits in some light-grey material, and each of them was holding his hat on his knees, a dark-brown summer straw with a tropical ribbon around the crown. Eitel had not described them too badly – they did look like All-American guard and tackle, but if we are to use the image, I ought to say that there is a difference between guard and tackle. The one who looked like a tackle was very big, he was rangy, he was mean for the pleasure of it: an archetype of the bastard in Dorothea's book. I knew the moment I looked at him that if it ever got out of control, I could not hope for too much. He could use his hands at least as well as I could, and that would be only the beginning. For he was obviously a man who did not like to lose, and he would know other ways to fight. Before we were through I would come to learn all about his elbows and his knees and how good he was at measuring the heel of his hand against my kidneys, and my neck, and of course the other places. He looked like he had changed more than one man's features in his life.

The guard was a little shorter and a little heavier and he had a friendly face. He was a wrestler. He was the kind of man who would give a pained and modest smile before he got into a bar brawl and then he would throw the nearest man across the room. With it all, they looked to have the intelligence of good athletes, practical intelligence.

'Hello,' I said, 'how long have you been here?'

Then I knew it was going to be bad, because I was tired as always and I had tried to make my voice flat, and it did not hold its pitch. I remember thinking what a serious difference it was going to make that they had come to talk to me in a cheap furnished room instead of the modern house I had had with its built-in bar and the long wall mirror to show them their reflection.

The one who looked like a tackle was holding a newspaper clipping in his hand. 'Your name O'Shaugnessy or McShonessy,' he said, looking at me. He had a peculiar stare. He did not look into my eyes, he looked at the bridge of my nose, and that was a trick to practise because it made me feel even worse.

'The first name is right.'

'Marine Corps or Air Force?'

'Air Force.'

The one who looked like a guard continued to smile at me.

'Why did you pass yourself off as a Marine Corps captain?' the tackle said.

'I never did.'

'Are you trying to tell me this newspaper item is a lie?'

'Oh look, Mac,' I said, 'no newspaper ever makes a mistake.'

He grunted and passed the clipping over to the guard. When the guard spoke it was with a Southern accent. 'Boy, why do you spell O'Shaughnessy without an "h"?' he asked.

'You'd have to ask my father.'

'He was a convict, wasn't he?'

'My father was a lot of things,' I said.

'Yes,' the tackle said, 'he was a convict.'

I sat down on the bed, for they were in the two chairs, and I went through a careful set of movements to open a package of cigarettes, and I believe I succeeded in doing it without letting my hands shake. But it would have been beyond me to manage to light a cigarette for them. I had no idea at all if they were just passing through Desert D'Or for the day and had dropped in on me to have an hour of entertainment, or if this were all part of some bigger mistake. 'Before we go any further,' I said, 'would you mind showing me your identification papers ?'

We continued to sit there for a minute, and then the tackle took a wallet from his breast pocket and passed over an important-looking card with the stamp of the Subversive Committee on it, and SPECIAL INVESTIGATOR in raised letters under a passport photo. His name was Greene, Harvey Greene.

'Well, what do you want?' I asked.

'To find out a few things about a few people, including you.'

'What is there to find out?'

'We'll ask the questions. In case you didn't know, you might be in a little trouble.'

'I don't see the trouble,' I said.

'Tell me, boy, is Lulu Meyers a Red?' the guard asked.

I made a point of laughing. 'You know, I never knew anybody who was a Red. I just never travelled in those circles.'

'But you know Charley Eitel, don't you, fellow?'

'Yes, I do.'

'Eitel was going around here with people who were politically questionable.'

I was beginning to feel a little better. 'Well, he probably gave you their names.'

'He certainly did,' Greene said.

'Tell me about Lulu, fellow,' the guard said.

'We never had a single conversation about politics.'

'What *did* you talk about?' said Greene.

'Private things.'

'You had private and intimate relations with her?'

'Don't you know the answer?'

'We're waiting for you to provide it.'

'I was in love with Lulu,' I said.

Greene's mouth showed a considerable distaste. 'You mean you had depraved and illicit relations with her.'

'I don't think like that,' I said.

'You don't think,' Green told me. 'Because if you did, an Irish boy like you wouldn't go around with these perverts.'

I was very scared then. The only thing about Harvey Greene which fit his name were his eyes – they were a boiled green in colour. Into my mind passed the memory of a policeman with boiled green eyes who had come to the orphanage because a few of us had been making penny raids on candy stores. He had questioned me for half an hour, and he had made me cry finally by forcing me to admit that I played with myself. So I had the anguish – it is truly the word – that the same thing was going to happen again.

But there are very few policemen who can work as a team all the time, and the guard saved me for a little while. I suspect that he and Greene were a little tired of each other. At any rate, the guard was interested in other things than the state of my soul. 'You're lucky, fellow, to hook up with a movie star,' he said with superior humour, but the hundred-twenty dollars a week he must have made, and the wife and children in the suburbs were also in his voice. 'You must have thought it was soft picking up those big dollar bills for going down.'

Underneath everything else I felt, I could sense some opportunity preparing itself. And to my surprise I smiled and said, 'You have a good instinct for personal details.'

'I know enough to know you think you're pretty good,' said the guard.

'I'm not the one to brag.'

'Don't brag. We all know movie stars are frigid,' the guard said. He was forward in his seat and he was getting angry. Greene sat by while this was going on, and shook his head sourly. 'Wouldn't you say they're frigid?' the guard repeated.

'Depends on the man,' I said cautiously.

'Yes,' said the guard, 'that would be your theory.' He was getting flushed. 'So tell us, hot-rod, tell us about Lulu.' But before I had to worry about what I could possibly compromise to that, the guard was talking again. 'I hear,' he started, 'that Lulu . . .' and he continued for a full two minutes. He did not really have a great deal of imagination but at least he had a divided mind on the subject, and so he went on and on. 'Why, I bet no respectable call girl would talk to her,' he said at last.

I got up all my courage, which is to say I showed more courage than I had. 'If you're going to question me,' I said, 'I want to use my tape recorder.'

The guard stopped. The smile went off his face and the flushed eager look, and he sat there looking puzzled. It was the last expression I wished to see on his face. For a moment I was certain I had gone too far, and that when it was all over, and I was in a hospital bed with a broken jaw, and a cast over my collarbone, they would pinch my flesh awake long enough for me to mumble to a police stenographer, 'Yes, I admit I was dead-drunk and rolled off a table.'

The guard reached forward from his chair, and poked a finger into my thigh. 'We hear you wear a lavender shirt that Teddy

Pope gave you,' he said. 'You don't look lavender, boy, but I guess you like lavender.'

'When did they promote you from the vice squad?' I asked.

Greene entered into it then. He looked at the space between my eyes. 'Say one more thing like that,' he said.

I was closer to being hysterical than I care to admit, but there is a curious calm this side of hysteria. At least for me. I was that near to breaking down, and yet my voice came out quietly and evenly and slowly. 'Greene,' I said, 'I've got three thousand dollars in the bank, and I'll use those three thousand dollars for a lawyer. So try and think about the publicity your committee is going to get when it comes out that you've pulled a rock with an Air Force flier.' It sounded good to me and I did not mention the medical discharge.

'You're a subversive and a pervert,' Greene said.

'Put that in writing and I'll sue you for slander.'

'Don't you just talk a lot?' Greene said.

I suppose I would have been something of a hero if I had invited him to come downstairs, but instead I smiled again. 'Everybody talks a lot,' I said.

They got up then to go – I remember thinking with a little amazement that maybe they were a little afraid of me, too – and at the door, Greene stopped and turned around and said, 'Don't leave town without notifying us.'

'Yes, you send me a paper to that effect.'

'Just don't leave town,' he said, and he went out the door, and I waited a minute, and went over to lock it so they would not come back on me, and then I lay down on my bed and let myself go.

Because these finally were the kind of men I had grown up with – their shadow had been over the orphanage – and when all was said I knew that I was not so different from them, not nearly so different as I liked to think. All the while they had been in my room and we had talked, I had been nervously and crucially divided, and much of me had been agreeing with everything they said. So I had another inkling of the kind of secret dialogues which had been going on in me through the years, and I lay there for more than one night, exhausted and empty after washing dishes, and I began to think, at least I learned how to try to think, for to do that, one must be ready to live in a hunt for the most elusive game – our real motive or motives and not the ostensible reason – and therefore I would have to look into myself. But that was not the easiest thing to do, for what did I have to discover? I was nothing, a false Irishman from a real orphanage, a boxer without a punch, a flier whose reflexes were gone, a potential stool-pigeon for every policeman who would use his knuckle, and worst of all, a preliminary boy in the bedroom – that was something to stop thought forever. For who can know more, when to know more is to say to oneself, 'It is not going to be very good for me if I keep on thinking.' What was the worst, if I did not watch out, I would be a patsy in the world, that was the worst which could happen to a graduate from the orphanage. Too many men and too much history seemed to add up to no more than the death of the patsies. And then of course I knew no history, that too occurred to me, and if I was going to speak up to the rough world out there, it was time for me to open a book.

So with the grace of a cow kicking flop, and with the old private worry that perhaps I had taken a punch too many on the head and would never be able to think that well after all, I stumbled into the kind of things which everybody has wrestled with, one way and then another; I thought of courage and of cowardice, and how we are all brave and all terrified each in our own way and our private changing proportion, and I thought of honesty and deception, and the dance of life they make, for it is exactly when we come closest to another that we are turned away with a lie, and blunder forward on a misconception, moving to understand ourselves on the platitudes and lies of the past. And, vaguely, thinking of certain words not as words but as the serious divisions of my experience, and every man's experience is serious to himself, I thought of such couples as love and hate, and victory and defeat, and what it was to feel warm and what it was to be cool. I explored with humility and early arrogance, lying on that lumpy bed, reduced to heat rash and to panic, knowing I was weak and wondering if I would ever be strong. For I touched the bottom myself, there was a bottom that time. I returned to it, I wallowed in it, I looked at myself, and the longer I looked the less terrifying it became and the more understandable. I began then to make those first painful efforts to acquire the most elusive habit of all, the mind of the writer, and though I could hardly judge from my early pages whether I were a talent or a fool, I continued, I went on for a little while, until I ended with an idea that many men have had, and many will have again – and indeed I started with that idea – but I knew that finally one must do, simply do, for we act in total ignorance and yet in honest ignorance we must act, or we can never learn for we can hardly believe what we are told, we can only measure what has happened inside ourselves. So I wrote a few poor pages and gave them up and knew I would try again.

In the meantime I did not hear from the detectives, and slowly I came to decide that it was time for me to leave Desert D'Or, and if I was in real trouble with them, which I doubted, well that for that. I would go to Mexico, the idea appealed to me, and I would take a course on a veteran's allotment in some Mexican art school, or I would study archaeology – a good way to spend one's life in the sun. The Government owed me something after all, and a man has to live and there are not fourteen-thousand-dollar poker games every year. I even began to play with a very curious idea. The more I thought of Elena the more I disliked myself for the way I acted toward her the last time at Marion's, and I came to feel my way to the understanding that a part of how I had judged her letter came from whatever it was I had failed to delight in Lulu, and I would leave to the side whose fault it was there, and how much, and from whom. All the while Elena's letter had its slow effect on me, and I read it over many times, as I had once read Eitel's testimony, and after a while I decided I owed Elena a debt; that was the way I felt. So I was going to visit her and Marion again, and if I thought she was not doing so well with him – and in my heart I was certain it was worse than that – well, I was going to make her an offer. She could come to Mexico with me, and we would even make the trip as brother and sister if she wanted it that way, although looking back I know that this last idea was something I could not have meant too seriously. At any rate, the more I thought about it, the better I came to like the prospect, although at other hours I decided I would be mad to take Elena on. Because, looking back, I know that deep in me I had already come to learn that there are not all that many chances in life, and if Elena and I took to each other, it was going to be no casual affair, and so it was a question of whether Elena and I had the characters to begin to bring out the best in each other, and I was doubtful of that, but on the other hand I was probably young enough to take a chance. So, living with the opposites in ourselves, we move to a decision. Only I meandered and debated and enjoyed the idea I was an altruist until a little too much time went by. And then one night as I was coming off my dishwasher's shift I heard from a waitress about what had happened to Marion and Elena that evening, and it was shocking news. For better or for worse, I had probably waited a little too long.

25

What can I say about it? Like his own flesh, Faye knew the loneliness in Elena. It waited for her, the sullen water behind a dike; let a breach be made and she would be carried away over the flooded land of the past. So he knew that she was the material out of which suicides are made.

For months he had been goaded by the thought that his life had lost its purpose, and in those hours before the dawn when he would lie in bed whipped with a terror of his open door, often convinced that the sounds he heard in the street were finally, finally, the killers he was always expecting, there would be another pain larger than the first because it was made of cowardice alone. 'I'm just a pimp. I never made it any further,' he would think to himself and wonder with the frustration of the explorer whose wanderings are from bar to night club and back again, whether all he needed was a point of the compass, any point, and he could follow it on some black heroic safari.

But the trip had never been made. A year had gone by, two years had gone by, and Faye seemed set up in business forever; nobody thought of him any longer as a rich boy with a hobby. Faye was in trade and he knew it. Already, through the logic of commerce he kept two sets of books, he had a lawyer, he gave away percentages, he had even caught himself prancing around one of the executives who ran the syndicate from the capital to the desert. Worse: a week before Elena came to live with him, he had been beaten up by a hoodlum who took a girl and refused to pay. He had not said anything after the beating, he had not complained about the hoodlum to his protection; they would have taken care of it but that was too humiliating. He hated to admit he had become so respectable that hoodlums respected him no longer. 'I'm a storekeeper,' Faye thought after the beating and his rage was ridiculous to him.

There had been a time when he was fifteen and sixteen when he had wondered endlessly about the man who was his real father. He thought he hated Dorothea's boast that the man was European royalty; often enough he liked to believe that his father had been a brilliant and dissolute priest. Today he would flinch when he remembered how he tried to explain the idea to the priest in the confessional box and had only been scolded; week after week he had been scolded. That was the period when he had been religious, had taken fasts, thought of entering a monastery, and to Dorothea's bewilderment and uncertain pride had spent a week on a retreat. That week had almost driven him mad; with a razor he had sliced a tiny piece off the corner of the altar cloth and left in a panic.

What had happened to that, he would wonder now? He had gone through it all, through old documents on the trials of witches and the practice of the Black Mass, through intrigues and poisons and love-cakes baked on the loins of languishing women and the needles of the lady abbess who probed the nuns to learn if they were witches and Satan had entered. He would feel in his adolescence as if he kept the history of a thousand years, but that had passed: he had been eighteen and nineteen and out on the world, his pride that no one could guess how much he read and what he thought.

Since Elena had come to live with him, there were nightmares. He could not get rid of the idea that she was his nun and he would transmute her into a witch. He made up stories in his mind, novels, volumes, drawing on himself the anguish of the priest who begs God to let the devils enter him in order that he alone be burned in Hell so that the others, the nuns, the parish, the castle, the country, indeed the world be spared. Father Marion has been praying for this, he would think, and all the while he prays, what does he do? It is so little and yet he is so damned for he has traduced the choir boys and left pregnant half the rich wives of the village, driven convents to insanity by whipping them with the staff of the Devil in their cloistered beds, giving to suck at such religious breasts the broom of the Witch, and stealing from the most devoted Sister, the purest, the most spiritual, her devotion itself, so that she loves not God but Father Marion, carnally, insanely, and even this is good, he will tell her, for the body and soul are separate, and to be pure one must seek out sin itself, mire the body in offal so the soul may be elevated. Yet it is never enough to make the Sister a Witch; she must be denounced as well, and yet never too soon, for too soon and she is a martyr, too late and she is dead, and therefore ever so carefully, the priest who takes the Devil to save the world must use the Devil to destroy it, and for that the saintly Sister he has made into Witch must first engulf the others, all the others, the nunnery, the church, the castle and the world, denouncing and accusing unto the point where the others burned, she burns herself and looses a scream from the stake, 'Oh, God, have mercy on Father Marion for he is a saint in Hell.' And he is pure when it is done, when they are all burned and he is left only to his prayers and pleads, 'Oh, my God, I have laboured in Your cause, and have found wanting the souls I have tested and they are not worthy of You.' Yet all the while he prays, he prays in the terror of nightmare, for He, He will punish him, will chase him into Hell and to the Devil, and not for something so small as the seductions and the sodomy, the pious minds of the nuns he has whipped, the burnings he has fired, the accusations, the destructions, but instead a sin so much greater, so terrible and enormous that God Himself must blanch before it. 'Oh, My Lord,' prays Father Marion in a cloister of Marion Faye's brain, 'I have sinned and fallen from Grace, for I wish Damnation upon You.'

Jailed in the keep of his bed with Elena beside him, enduring the venial mortification of having his skin itch near her presence, his nostrils repelled by the odour of her body which Eitel had savoured so much, Faye would wander by marijuana through the jungle and out along the cold stone floor of the nunnery to where Sister Elena would burn, her body on fire, her feet of ice, until the moment when Faye was certain his head would burst, that no skull could be immured against the furies and the temptations which came ever closer. He could only open his eyes and grind his teeth and mutter to the foot of the bed, to the spirit dancing on his toes, 'It's bullshit, it's all bullshit. Cut the bullshit. Cut it dead,' as if indeed his thoughts had become

313

needles to probe the Sorcerer in him, and when the dot of his brain was found where the needle entered without pain, then he was damned, he was discovered. Or was he freed? For beyond, in the far beyond, was the heresy that God was the Devil and the One they called the Devil was God-in-banishment like a noble prince deprived of true Heaven, and God who was the Devil had conquered except for the few who saw the cheat that God was not God at all. So he prayed, 'Make me cold, Devil, and I will run the world in your name.' It went on and on, up and down, until in the fever of these thoughts, he would run a hand toward Elena, wake her, and whisper in her ear, 'Come on, let's knock it around.' Elena was a fire to him since she had come, the ashes of the forest seeded new growth only to be burned again. And as he laboured, repelled by what she gave him, he whipped himself, a priest in horror, his mind away with images of the monk beneath his cassock punishing the lewd Sister who betrayed the Faith. When they were done, some fleeting image of damnation riding him over the empty moment, he would turn from her and try to sleep while his mind picked at the centre of his terror: he must coax Elena to kill herself.

After she came to live with him, he found himself riding quickly in directions he could not see, until to his horror and to his pride he came to understand himself at a moment his body was curled next to hers, seeking warmth on the chill of his limbs. A thought came into his brain, a frequent thought, 'She'll kill herself one of these days,' and before he had even done considering this, his mind like an iron monarch inflicting an alien will added cruelly, 'You have to make her do it.' Faye protested as he had protested against his decision to leave the door unlocked – he had pleaded with himself, he had begged, 'No, that's too much,' only to hear the taunt with which he had always been lashed another step, 'If you can't do this, you'll never be able to do the other things,' and he had shuddered in the dark. His command seemed more awful and more valuable than if he had ordered himself to murder Elena. Murder was nothing. Men murdered one another by the million, and found it easier than love. To make Elena kill herself, however, would be truly murder and so he shuddered at his fascination and knew he was bound to it.

314

But how to succeed? He doubted himself, disbelieved that he was serious, while for all this time his mind ticked forward like the clock of a bomb, set beyond his control. Faye had the feeling so deep in himself that this was finally the situation where he could push beyond anything he had ever done, push to the end as he had promised me so many nights ago, and come out – he did not know where, but there was experience beyond experience, there was something. Of that, he was certain.

Therefore, Elena had been in his house not even an hour when he asked her to marry him, not knowing at the moment why he did this. 'We might as well,' he said. 'You want to, and it's all the same to me.'

Even though she was drunk, she laughed carefully. 'Life is screwy,' she said.

'Sure it is.'

'I went with Collie three years and he never took me to a party.'

'And Eitel never asked you to marry him.'

When she did not answer, only swallowing her drink, he continued to stare at her, and murmured, 'What do you say, Elena, marry me.'

'Marion, I feel funny being here.'

He laughed then. 'I'll ask you tomorrow.'

They began the few weeks of their life together in that way. Elena and he passed days when they were never sober, never completely, and yet they were not drunk either, at least not Faye. He would watch Elena with disgust for she had no capacity to drink, and so she passed from gaiety to high excitement to illness to depression and back to the liquor again. Most of the time she talked a lot and laughed with his friends and told Faye how she felt free with him and how with Eitel she always felt ignored.

But occasionally she would be in panic, and several afternoons and evenings when he left her alone and went out to arrange some date, she seemed to have a terror of being alone. 'Do you have to go out?' she would ask.

'That business won't run by itself.'

Elena would sulk. 'I might as well be one of your call girls. I'd see more of you.'

'Maybe you would at that.'

'Marion, I want to be a call girl,' she would say out of her drunkenness.

'Not yet.'

Her eyes would narrow in an effort to give dramatic effect. 'Just what do you mean by that?' she would say. 'Are you calling me a whore?'

'What's in a word?' he would say to her.

Before he would be out the door, Elena would be clinging to him. 'Marion, come back soon,' she would beg. When he would return several hours later, she would announce as if she had thought the thing for the first time, 'You think I love you?' She would laugh a little. 'I want to be a call girl.'

'You're drunk, baby.'

'Get wise to yourself, Marion,' Elena would shout. 'Why do you think I'm living with you? It's 'cause I'm too lazy to live alone. What do you think of that?'

'Everybody's scared,' he would say.

'Except you. You're so high and mighty. Well, I don't think you're anything.'

These spells would pass and she would weep, ask him to forgive her, tell him she had not meant what she said, and perhaps she did love him, she didn't know, and he would say, 'Let's stop knocking ourselves out and get married.'

Elena would shake her head. 'I want to be a call girl,' she would say.

'You're not the kind who could make it,' he would tell her. 'Let's get married first and then we'll see.'

He had no idea of how he felt about her. He thought he hated her, he considered Elena as no more than a test for his nerves, and in their bed he loathed her; indeed if it were not for the pleasure of studying this loathing, of noticing how he was incapable of losing himself for even an instant and how she was determined to lose herself, it would have been difficult for him, cheated of loathing, to go near her at all. He was urged to lead her through a series of parties, at Don Beda's, at his own home, with some of his girls, with strange men, with Jay-Jay, with anyone who was ready to meet him.

She was morose, she was gay, and he led her moods like a

circus master tapping his whip; she was a trained animal and he could wipe his fingers in her hair. There seemed endless energy in the thought, and he would swear to himself that he was serious, sensing how each new trick broke the old limit until he would exhaust her energy, her pleasure itself, and she would be left with nothing. So he would separate the soul from the body by teaching the body that it may never attain the soul, and the greatest sin is to believe the two may live together.

She tried to call a halt. One morning after they had spent a night at Beda's and Marion asked her to marry him, she said, 'I'm getting out of here soon.'

'And where are you going?' he asked.

'You think you hate me,' she said to him. 'If I really believed that, I wouldn't stay with you.'

'I love you,' he said, 'why do you think I ask you to marry me?'

''Cause you think it's a big joke.'

He laughed at that. 'There's a lot of contradictions in me,' he said, his face boyish for the instant he smiled.

Yet one night unable to sleep he got up and walked around the bed, looking at her, mourning her as if she were already dead, and from some unwilling pocket of his mind there came compassion for her; despite himself it had worked free, a pure lump of painful compassion wrenched from him as cruelly as miscarried flesh, alive but not alive, its pain severe.

She had come to live with the idea she could marry him, and he could even grieve for her since she did not realize how much she depended on his promise. He thought it humorous that the only part of their life which was like marriage was the way she spoiled his house. She was always strewing her clothing through his rooms, spilling food in the kitchen, dropping glasses, burning cigarette holes, and then apologizing or breaking into a rage when he would tell her to tidy a room. He had lived in absolute order before she arrived with her two pieces of luggage, but once she was there and spilled the nervous spoil of her belongings over his home, he lived in a state of mortal exasperation. They had a maid, a middle-aged Mexican woman with a stolid face who came in for two hours every morning and put the place together just long enough for Elena to scatter it again. About the maid they had fights. Elena insisted the woman hated her. 'I heard her call me a *puta*,' she told him.

'She was probably praying.'

'Marion, I'm going or she's going.'

'Then get out of here,' he would tell her. More and more often he would say this, confident that Elena could not leave, and he would taunt her with the fact. 'Who are you fooling?' he would say. 'Where do you think you'll go?'

Elena surprised him. She began to make friends with the Mexican servant. In the late morning, he could hear the two women chatting, and occasionally one of them would laugh. Elena began to say she had misjudged the woman. 'She has a good heart,' Elena told him. He watched with amusement, convinced this was only a passing enthusiasm. She could never be friends, he thought, with a Mexican peasant who would remind her that she too was a peasant. Still, it went too far. The day that the servant brought Elena a wooden napkin ring and Elena hugged her, Faye gave the woman a week's salary and told Elena to clean the house herself. After that they lived in disorder and had quarrels about Elena's visits to the Mexican woman. 'Dirt always looks for dirt,' he told her and that was successful. Elena stayed home.

After a time, he would leave her alone for hours. When he would return, she would be helpless with jealousy. He chose one of these occasions to tell Elena that he could not help it, but he found her less exciting. 'This is temporary, of course,' he said. 'I'm getting too much outside.' Two days later he moved into the other bedroom and all the hours he lay awake he could hear her stirring. Once he listened to her crying, his body moist with the effort to ignore her.

They had one last party. Zenlia had left Don Beda and gone back to the East, and one night Marion invited Beda to come alone. Beda was in a bad mood these days.

'You got a hurt for Zenlia?' Marion asked him.

Beda laughed. 'I haven't had a hurt for a woman in fifteen years. But where I live, you get to suffer from the altitude.'

Elena said in a sullen voice, 'I dig Beda. I dig a man who doesn't hurt.'

'Honey, I dig you,' Beda said. 'You're lovelier than you think.'

318

Elena looked at Faye. 'What do you want?' she asked.

'Leave me out of it tonight,' Faye answered.

'Then stay out of it,' she said to him, and Faye sat in the living room while Elena and Beda were in the other end of the house, Faye sipping at his stick of tea while he repeated to himself the thought which he found endlessly humorous, 'I got a young face and an old body.'

Beda came out at last, leaving Elena behind, and combed his hair while he talked to Marion. 'Your girl is on the edge,' Beda said. He looked pale.

'She's just a little high.'

'Marion, don't ride her. She's a brave girl in her way.'

'Yes,' said Faye, 'everybody is brave, they say.'

'You know,' Beda said, 'people like you give a bad name to people like me.'

'Lover, I didn't know you cared,' answered Marion.

'I'll visit you in prison.'

When Beda was gone Marion walked into the bedroom and looked at Elena. She was lying on her back. 'I should have gone home with that man,' she said stonily.

'He would have kept you for a day.'

Elena turned on the bed. 'You don't say anything about marrying me any more,' she said.

'Do you love me?'

'I don't know.' She looked at the wall. 'Who could love you?' she said.

He laughed aloud. 'I don't understand it. So many chicks think I'm the jack.'

Elena let her breath out. 'I feel very rotten. I feel sick.'

He was angry suddenly. 'You're like everybody else. Do what you feel like doing, and then you think because you feel rotten that it wasn't really you who was doing it.'

'So what if you're right?' she said.

Faye had to explain it to her. He had to explain it to everybody. 'Take the bullshit of the whole world,' he said. 'That's love. Bullshit mountain.'

'You're not so happy,' Elena said.

'That's my fault. If an idea won't work for me, that doesn't mean it isn't true.' He lit another stick and blew tea-smoke down on her. 'Elena, you thought you wanted to marry Eitel. You loved him, you say. Do you still love him?'

'I don't know,' she said. 'Let's forget him.'

'The more I think about it, the more I decide that you were in love with him.' Marion laughed. 'That's it. I understand it now. You were really in love with him.'

'Stop, Marion.'

'It's pathetic,' he said. 'There you were, with your hard Wop heart, and yet you loved him. Would you say you loved him passionately?'

He was beginning to reach a very private part of her, that he knew, and so he went on.

'It's a pathetic story,' he said, 'because you and Charley missed the real connection. Let me tell you a secret about Charles Francis. He's a frustrated teacher. Can you begin to understand that type? Deep-down, a John like Eitel is always obsessed with wanting people to trust him.'

'What do you know?' Elena said.

'You couldn't bring yourself to trust him, could you, Elena?'

'Leave me alone, Marion. Maybe too many people let me down.'

'Just didn't they? No wonder you never got around to telling Eitel about some of the men and boys you did to get a two-bit booking in a night club.'

'Not as much as you think,' she said. 'Believe it or not, I had my pride.'

'Yes,' Marion said, 'and maybe you were too proud to see that Eitel was in love with you. He didn't know it, and you were stupid and didn't play him right, but he was in love with you. Elena, you just don't have the brains of a slob to get married and hide under a stone.'

She took every word he said, and then tried to smile back at him.

'Stick with me, Elena,' Marion said. 'I don't care if you trust me. I'm a specialist on stupid girls.'

'I told you to make me a call girl,' she said in a dull voice.

'Well, I don't think you can make it as a call girl,' Marion said.

'Why not? I could be a very good call girl.'

'No,' Marion said dispassionately. 'You're raw meat. You lack class.'

She winced as if he had struck her. 'Then make me a prostitute,' she jeered.

'Let's get married,' said Marion, sipping at his stick.

'I'd never marry you.'

'Proud, aren't you? What would you say, dearest, if I told you I'm the one who won't marry you?'

'I want to be a prostitute,' Elena repeated.

'I don't handle prostitutes,' Marion said. His chest hurt him. 'I could send you to a friend though. He has a job where you could work sort of half in a whorehouse.'

'What does half in a whorehouse mean?'

'It means in a whorehouse,' Marion said. 'Like on the Mexican border.'

Elena looked frightened. Fear showed and then lapsed again. 'I won't do that, Marion,' she said.

'Are you a snob, doctor? Think of all the poor creeps down there and how they're crawling for you.'

'Marion, you can't make me do that.'

'I can't make you do anything,' he said. 'Only, look, Elena, I'm bored with you. I'm just a little bored with you. Maybe you better get out of this house.'

'I'm getting out,' she said, but her voice lacked size.

'Then get out.'

'I'll go,' she said.

'Go ahead.'

Elena lay on her back and stared at the ceiling again. 'I wish I could be dead,' she muttered. 'I'd like to kill myself.'

'You haven't got the guts.'

'Don't taunt me. It doesn't take guts.'

'You couldn't do it,' Marion said.

'Yes, I could. I could do it.'

He left the room for a minute, felt his fingers trembling among tubes of medicine and hair pomades and plastic bandages in the cabinet, and then he came back with a small bottle which held two capsules. 'I've been saving this for myself,' he said. 'They work like sleeping pills.' He set it on the bedside table. 'Do you want some water?'

'You think I won't take them?' Elena asked. She seemed a great distance from him.

'I don't think you'll do anything.'

'Get out of here. Leave me alone.'

He returned to the living room and sat there listening to his heart beat. The sound seemed to fill his body. 'It can't go on like this,' he thought, and his heart gave another jump when he heard Elena get up from her bed and go to the bathroom. He could hear the water running and then there was silence and then she turned the water on again. It was the bathtub this time. With a kind of surprise at himself, he was wondering, 'Can I really go this far?'

The water had stopped running in the tub. He no longer had any idea of what the sounds meant, and he sat immobile, determined not to move, not for an hour at least. He saw this as his duty to Elena for he suffered remaining in his chair. If only he could have walked around the room or even lit a cigarette he might have felt some relief, but he kept repeating to himself that he must know what she was feeling. And convinced she was dead, he mourned her. 'She was better than the others,' he said to himself. 'She was the strongest of the whole lot.'

For all that hour he sat with his eyes on the clock, and when the time was up, he went to the bathroom door. Elena had locked it and he rattled the knob, he called to her, 'Elena? . . . Elena?' There was no answer and he thought if he waited the door would be unlocked. He rattled it again. He drummed against it with the palm of his hand. Then he began to sob a little. A childhood panic had come on him as if *he* were locked inside, and furious at his panic, he was going to force the door, but he remembered there was a utility key among the collection in his pocket. By an effort he managed to keep his fingers steady while he turned the lock, and there before his eyes was Elena sitting beside the water-filled tub with a robe over her body and the bottle of pills squeezed fiercely in her fist so that she sat like a statue with all her force concentrated into the bones of her fingers, that hand projecting forward over her knees in a mute emphasis so nearly permanent she might have been of stone. Down her cheeks ran tears, and her eyes stared at him as if she had to cling to something, no matter what, even him.

Faye reached forward and pried the bottle from her hand. It still contained the two pills, and he made a sound as if he had been scalded, for he knew what he felt at that instant was relief, and hatred for Elena followed his relief, hatred so intense he could have struck her to the floor.

Elena looked up and managed to whisper, 'Oh, Marty, I'm sorry, I'm so sorry, but I didn't want to do it, I don't want to . . . stop, I swear I don't want to stop,' she pleaded, as if he were an Italian gang bully and she was begging him for his one possible drop of mercy. Then she began to weep a little, softly, out of fatigue. 'I'll get out of here in a day or two. I swear I will.'

Faye knew he was defeated. He could not help it – he had his drop of mercy after all. So he put her to bed and lay beside her through the night, not sleeping, not even thinking, his body aching from exhaustion. The next day she was depressed, and the following day she was depressed, but he had lost, and lived instead in a new despair.

When she began to pack her bags he made no objection, and when she told him she was leaving he merely nodded. 'Where are you going?' he asked.

'I'm going to get a job in the city.'

'All right. Let me drive you back.'

'I don't want to ride with you.' She shook her head.

'Then I'll give you a lift to the airport.'

'I don't have money for a plane.'

'I'll buy your ticket.'

'No, you can't do that.'

'You have to let me,' he said, and the sound in his voice made her look at him. 'Please,' he said again.

'I don't understand you,' Elena said.

'I don't either, but let me buy your ticket.'

So she agreed, and he called a travel agency, made the reservation, and put her luggage into the rack of his foreign car.

On the way to the airport, he passed a car around the only curve in all that reach of desert highway, passed it with the knowledge another car was coming for he could see its light. Too late, he discovered it was a truck. As he raced to reach his own lane there was a passing instant when he realized he would never succeed, and then he heard a shriek from Elena, and felt an impact which struck him with surprising force as the front of the truck slapped at his rear fender, and the wheel twisted out of his hand. Then he felt as if parts of his body were being torn in all directions, and through the sensations he knew that they had rolled to a stop and his head was locked against his arm and he was in pain. He tried to clear his mind, he felt there was one thing he had to remember, and listening to Elena sobbing beside him, he wanted to tell it to her. There was the gun in his glove compartment and if he could only collect himself to speak, he would tell her to throw it into the ditch for they would use that against him, and he had always known that the way he would go to prison would be for something ridiculous like keeping a gun without a permit. 'It's all right,' he thought, holding on to consciousness as if it were something to grip with his battered mouth, 'it's all right. To make it, maybe I need a year like that. More education,' he tried to say, but a spasm of pain was carrying him into coma.

The truck stopped, the car behind them stopped; in one minute a crowd of a dozen people collected about Faye's car. They lifted Elena out first and she was conscious. Her nose bled and she moaned when someone touched her arm, for it was broken. Yet she had strength enough to push to her feet when they had taken her clear of the car, and one arm supporting the other, blood spilling from her nose to her mouth, she took a step and then another before they caught her and set her down, and in her mind she believed at that instant that she was running from them into the darkness as a child flees from a night-haunted bed, and through the blood she whispered – although to her own ears it sounded like a scream – 'Oh, Charley, forgive me. Oh, Charley, forgive.'

And yet there was something else she must say, for it was all confused and the puzzle of love was as mysterious as it had ever been. 'Marion, Marion,' she thought, moving into sleep as pain released her, 'Marion, why didn't you like me a little? Why didn't you know you could have loved me?' Then the ambulance was coming up, and she heard the threat of its siren as she lay on the shoulder of the road.

26

At the hospital, Marion was under police guard, and they would not admit anyone to see Elena until morning. After arguing with the floor nurse for an ugly ten minutes over who would pay Elena's bill, I emptied my wallet of my week's wages, gave it to the nurse, and decided to make a phone call to Eitel in the capital. I was thinking that if he did not come, I would have to make Elena my responsibility, and I knew now that I did not want that at all. Which made me feel that it would be more than a little while before I would enjoy thinking about my character.

Eitel's number was not listed and neither was Munshin's but I remembered the name of Eitel's agent, and managed to place a call to him. From the way the agent spoke I had the picture of a nervous man in a bathrobe, with a cigar in the corner of his mouth, but for all I know he could have looked like an account executive.

'Well, who are you?' the agent was saying.

'It doesn't matter who I am. I'm a friend of his from Desert D'Or.'

'I don't even want to hear of that place. Look, you leave my baby Charley alone.'

'Will you give me his number?'

'What do you want it for?'

'I want it,' I said. 'Believe me, it's urgent.'

'Leave Charley Eitel alone. Everybody persecutes Eitel with their troubles.'

'A very dear friend of his may be dying now,' I exaggerated.

'A woman?'

'What's that got to do with it?'

'Look, Charley Eitel don't have to get out of bed for any

325

woman. He's a busy man now, thank God, so stop persecuting him.'

'Listen, if he doesn't get this message tonight,' I shouted into the receiver, 'he'll persecute *you* in the morning.'

So, after half an hour of perspiring in a telephone booth and two dollars in change and a missed connection, I succeeded finally in reaching Eitel. I was so irritated by then and so agitated that I must have babbled. 'What kind of agent do you have anyway?' I asked him with my first words.

'Sergius, are you drunk?' Eitel said into the phone.

I told him then, and I could hear nothing but silence for twenty seconds. Perhaps I was imagining it, but I had the feeling the news put him in a rage. When he answered, however, it was to say, 'Oh, Lord. Is she all right?'

'I think so,' I said, and gave what details I had.

'Do you suppose I ought to come down?' he asked, and when I remained silent, he added, 'tomorrow we're busy casting.'

'Want me to answer for you?' I said.

'All right, I'll arrange something,' he said into my ear. 'Tell Elena I'm taking the plane and I'll see her in the morning.'

'You'll be able to tell her yourself. They won't allow visitors tonight.'

'It must be serious,' he said half-helplessly, and I had a moment of sympathy for him.

In the morning Eitel arrived at the hospital before me, and I met him on the steps as he was coming out from his visit to Elena. 'I'm going to marry her,' was the first thing he said to me.

There had not been much choice. She was sitting in a hospital bed the hour he visited, her arm in a sling, and her nose covered by medical tape which made her look as if she were trying to hide herself. Elena's eyes looked away from him until he touched her shoulder. 'Oh, Charley,' she said simply. He could see she was heavy with sedatives.

They could think of nothing to talk about at first. She had looked at him, and whispered, 'I hear you're working again.'

He nodded.

'It must have been hard for you to get away.'

'Not that hard,' he said with a touch of his charm.

'Do you feel happy working?' she asked politely.

'It's not so bad. Most of the people at the studio have been decent. I even get compliments about my testimony.'

'Oh, that's nice,' she said.

They tried to smile at one another. 'I guess you have your career back?' Elena went on.

'Part of it. There's a lot of mending to do.'

'But you're going to make a good picture.'

'I'll try.'

'I know you'll make a good picture.' This time she nodded. 'It'll be the same for you again, Charley.'

'Not the same,' said Eitel.

There was a tone in his voice which made her turn the least bit toward him, and in a careful whisper, she said, 'Charley, did you miss me?'

'Very much,' he said.

'No, Charley, I mean the truth.'

'I did, Elena.'

She began to weep silently. 'No, Charley, you were glad to be rid of me, and I don't blame you.'

'It's not true,' he said. 'You know the way I am. I haven't let myself think about anything.' He coughed and his voice missed a word or two. 'One night,' he said, 'Elena, I thought of you, and I knew I would go to pieces if I didn't stop.'

'I'm glad you felt a little bit.'

The moment he said the next few words he knew he had made a mistake. 'How are you?' he asked. 'I mean, the accident must have been terrible.'

It was as if he set a mirror to all the time which had gone by since she had left him, and he could feel her carried away from him on the tide of her misery until he was no longer present, but she was alone on a hospital bed, her past scattered, her future unmade, and the bed and the walls and the instruments of her aseptic room surrounding Elena in a cold white sea. 'It wasn't so bad,' she said, and she began to cry again. 'Oh, Charley, you better go now. I know you hate hospitals.'

'No, I want to take care of you,' he said, the words coming despite himself.

327

'Marry me,' Elena blurted suddenly. 'Oh, Charley, please marry me. This time I'll learn. I promise I will.'

And he nodded, his heart numb, his will sick, thinking there must be some escape, and knowing there was nothing. For on the instant she said these words he heard the other words she had said the night he gave his qualified proposal of marriage. 'You have no respect for me,' she had said then, and like a beggar to the beggar of his own pride, he knew that he could not refuse her. All the while he held Elena he felt cold as stone, but he knew that he would marry her, that he could not give her up for there was that law of life so cruel and so just which demanded that one must grow or else pay more for remaining the same. If he did not marry her he could never forget that he had once made her happy and now she had nothing but her hospital bed.

So he continued to caress her shoulder and asked gentle questions and talked about their marriage, certain all the while that no matter what he felt toward her, they were mates, the wound of one's flesh soothed by the wound of the other, and that was better than nothing. Perhaps in a year if she found somebody else, he could get a divorce.

They were married a week later on the day she was discharged from the hospital, and I read about it in the newspapers. He took Elena to a town outside the limits of the capital and they had the ceremony there with Collie Munshin for the best man – which on reflection did not surprise me too greatly.

In the following month a letter was forwarded from Eitel inviting me to the wedding, and I wrote back and sent a present and explained my absence. I had left Desert D'Or and was working on a book about the orphanage in the room of a cheap hotel in Mexico City two thousand miles away. Afterward, what little I heard followed me like the wavelets of a pebble which has already dropped to the bottom. There was a little scandal and a little charity in what I read about their marriage, and if certain newspapers featured photographs of Marion Faye, the gossip columnists were mild. What was said in the capital I never knew, but it was easy to guess. Then, months later, after his trial, I had a postcard forwarded from Marion, and it showed a picture of a clean, well-lit, sanitary cell block in his prison. 'Re: our conversations,' the card read, 'I have the feeling I'm just getting on to it. Your con friend, Marty.' And at the bottom of the card he added, 'P.S. Are you still a cop?'

When it opened a year and a half later, I paid a dollar and eighty cents and went to see *Saints and Lovers* in a first-run movie palace on Broadway. Its reviews were excellent and the theatre was almost filled. On a sour whim, I bought some popcorn and chewed it through the film. It was not a bad picture as pictures go, and it was well made, and it did not have too many scenes which were embarrassing, but it was nothing magnificent either, at least not for me, and the teen-age girl in the next seat petted with her date and laughed at clever dialogue and yawned once or twice. I hate to admit it, but there was a part of the picture I did admire. For although Eitel had claimed that he knew nothing about the Church, he had a very neat sense of the Church in a small way, a neater sense than I did of the kind of picture to make if Catholics were to enjoy it. For years afterward I thought of writing Eitel a letter but I could not decide exactly what to say and the impulse passed. I felt that I had moved my distance, and it would have been self-righteous to tell him so. The years pass into the years and we count our time in lonely private rhythms which have little to do with number or judgment or the uncertain shifting memory of friends.

Part Six

27

So I had taken the trip to Mexico, and after a great deal of delay and some suspicious red-tape which made me remember the guard and tackle from the Subversive Committee, my papers came through, and I lived on a Government allotment, and enrolled in an art school, and went around with some other Americans. There was a tall coloured boy who had played College basketball and now wanted to be a poet and we would have arguments about literature in half the Mexican dives in Mexico City with the song of the *Mariachis* in our ear, and there was a motorcycle racer who had fractured his skull and he was sentimental and ready for a breakdown, and there were others. I drifted through some months, and I suppose I was like most of the Americans down there who pass the days, except that I was usually depressed. I would think too much about Lulu.

Every Sunday I would go to the bullfights in the Plaza Mexico, and when I came to understand them, they had meaning for me. Through friends, I came to know a few bullfighters, and when my Spanish improved, I used to spend hours in the café with them. After a while I got into an affair with a Mexican girl who was the mistress of a young bullfighter, which in itself was unusual, for most young bullfighters were too poor to keep a girl, and in fact generally left women alone on the prizefighter's undemanding theory that one doesn't want to leave one's fight in the bedroom. This bullfighter was considered very good by some, and he was well-managed and ready to become a matador in another season because he had money behind him and some friends. My friends all warned me that it was dangerous, and he might kill me, but it turned out somewhat differently because there is more than one thing to be said about bullfighters, and when he found out about the affair, he invited me to dinner and we had a long touchy Mexican evening where we skirted the edge of some deadly insults, and then went out dead drunk with our arms around each other's shoulders, although that could not have been so easy from him because he was five feet four inches tall and did not weigh one hundred and ten pounds. And to be altogether fair, he was only nineteen, and all but illiterate, and he had the acne scars of a poor Indian adolescence on his face.

Later he tried to take a Mexican revenge. He gave me a few lessons in the mystical private way that only a Mexican *novillero* would give bullfighting lessons, and with me hardly knowing how to hold a *muleta*, and clutching a cape like it was a Hungarian officer's overcoat, he took me with all my Tom Thumb technique to a breeding ranch and allowed me to go in with one of the calves he was given for the day. And part of the point was that his girl was watching. They are not really dangerous, calves, it is almost impossible for them to kill a man, and when one gets hit four or five times in a row, as I was, it is not really much worse, if you are light on your feet, than being knocked down the same number of times by a bicycle, but I must have made a spectacle, and all the Mexicans sat on the stone *barrera* of the ranch, with the dust blowing, and they laughed and they laughed, and by the end of five minutes, I succeeded in passing the calf, and then passing her again, and a third time before she caught me a blow on the leg and started to step on me, and I remember lying there with the calf bellowing in my ear, and the peons giggling as they diverted her with their capes. But I had a passion. I knew what it was to pass a bull, or more precisely a future mother of bulls, and I wanted to be a bullfighter. What else? Isn't one always more desperate than he thinks?

So then began a very odd six months. I travelled around with the *novillero* and his girl, and I took lessons from him, and all the while he knew that his girl would spend her time with me, until finally he merely paid her expenses and usually did nothing else. The more he suffered at her taste for me, the more he would plead with me to stay every time I wanted to quit them. It was costing me too much of the money I had left, and it was unpleasant because the girl had had a bad life, she had started at fourteen in the Organo of Mexico City, and there was no

334

future in it for anybody. And not that much simple taste if the truth be told. Except that she reminded me a little of Elena.

Every time he would convince me to stay, he would hate me a little more, and it was incredible how he would suffer the hours she spent with me, for like most Latins his imagination for such matters was a volcano of creativity. Grim the next day, if he were scheduled to appear he would go out and fight his fight. Relatively, he was a terrible coward, but a third of the good bullfighters in the world have a coward's art, and they can become more exciting than the brave ones, at least to me. For I was always most intrigued by the bullfighters who projected the most intense fear, and then succeeded to put an imaginative fight together. The cowards know every way a man can fear the bull, and so on those rare days when they are able to dominate the movements of their bodies, they know more of the variations, and the movements, and the moments within the moments when something new can be done.

That was the style of this Mexican *novillero*. He was awkward and terrible when he was afraid, and he was hopeless with a bad bull, but once in a while he would go out, pale and black as death, cold to his bones, for he was beyond fright, and death that particular day was probably as attractive as continuing to live, and he would fight if he caught even a half-decent animal, in ways and with innovations that I had never ever seen before, and no matter what had happened between us, I would find myself thinking of him as an artist. He had a rare pathos as a bullfighter; he made half the people in the plaza feel as if they too were fighting the bull. And the other half of the public hated him, for he was very unorthodox. He was the only *torero* I ever saw who could take three turns of the ring holding ears and tail while members of the conservative *afición* were aiming cushions at his head. So I finally realized that he was a radical priest of his art, and in some half-comprehensive way, his mistress and me were the indispensable thorn of his vocation. But how he hated us. I tried for a long time to write that novel, and some day maybe I will.

At any rate, I learned a little, and finally I quit them, which is too long a story to tell, and I went out on my own, and a lot of things happened to me, because to try to become an American bullfighter in the provinces of Mexico is not the most standard career, but for a long time it was more important to fight a bull than to do anything else, and I have to confess that when I had some sort of small good fight I would start to dream again that I was going to be the first great and recognized American matador. But I suppose I was too old to learn to be really good, because there was not only the question of how much courage did you have, but also the question of how much stamina when there were not only bulls to fight, but bad underbred undersold bulls, and crooked managers and impresarios who would have run a chain gang with a smile. I got hurt several times, and the last was a serious wound which left me sick, and then my working papers were renewed illegally as they always are in Mexico if you live there long enough, and something happened, some mix-up, some slip in passing a bribe, and so I was passed across the border, no matador, no *novillero*, no veteran with an allotment, but just a fancy scar on my leg, and a new set of trips to make, and new self-pity.

With a stop or two on the way, I found my hole in New York, a cold-water flat outside the boundary of the Village, and I had a few girls who made for some very complicated romances, and I suppose I learned a little more – life is an education which should be put to use – and I tried to write my novel about bullfighting, but it was not very good. It was inevitably imitative of that excellently exiguous mathematician, Mr Ernest Hemingway, and I was learning that it is not creatively satisfying to repeat the work of a good writer.

All the while I was keeping myself alive by an unusual occupation. I had come down to my last few hundred dollars, and so I took a gamble and rented a loft in the slums of the lower East Side of New York, painted it white, put up a few bullfight posters, and opened a school for bullfighters. After the first few weeks word of the school passed through the Village, and the classes began to grow. I felt two ways about it. I was a little tired of bullfighting, at least I did not want to spend my life talking about it, and I knew I was far from good enough to be a teacher, but the classes were interesting to conduct, and probably interesting to watch, for I built a killing-machine out of an old wheelbarrow and had sets of horns all over the place. It must have looked like a ballet school, with pairs of students alternating at running the horns and practising passes with the cape and the *muleta*. All up and down the loft while the classes were going, I would have the amusement of hearing from ten to twenty embryo voices clucking and chanting and cooing their 'Hey, toro! Chuh-hay, toro! Mire-tu, toro,' while their T-shirts turned grey with sweat, and they were more or less happy, even if some of them had never even seen a cow. The thing which surprised me, until I came to know the Village better, was that half of my students were girls. They included everything from a Jewish college girl from Brooklyn with a Master's degree, to a young burlesque stripper who was born in a mining town and did non-objective painting. It would have been interesting enough if one wanted to make a career of it, but I resented the time I had to spend, because I was anxious for something else.

Then one day I read in the newspapers that Dorothea O'Faye Pelley was in town, and for once a newspaper was telling a fact. On an impulse, I called several hotels and she was staying at the third one, and before I knew it we had a conversation which drew us together, for she had things to tell me about the people we knew in common. To our mutual surprise we spent the night together at her hotel, and for the next ten days Dorothea virtually lived at my cold-water flat, so that I had the chance to see another side of her character. Dorothea's sables – acquired at wholesale from a furrier friend – would lie draped over one of my ten-dollar armchairs, while she would mop the dirty painted linoleum on my floor and give me lectures on how to handle the janitor, because Dorothea understood the first drama of poverty which is that there are no holds barred on getting rid of the garbage, since all the way from the top of the sanitation department down to the drunken hooligan on the ground floor, it is open war, and everybody runs his own garbage patrol.

In less domestic moments, it was an interesting experience with Dorothea, not nice but electric. Dorothea was that many years older, and she was greedy – who can blame her? – so before it was over she offered to keep me while I wrote a book. But that was a little on the serious divide of the gigolo, and while I had nothing against gigolos on principle, having thought in more than one vain, energetic, and penniless mood that it was one of the lives I could have had, it is still very difficult to keep your dignity as a gigolo, and dignity means something when you are trying to move your way up in life, dignity is handy to have around if one wants to do some worth-while work.

Finally, I convinced Dorothea that it was the West Coast for her, and the East for me, and after she was gone, I found that I had come to live with the conundrum of whether it is better to be the lover or the beloved, and I thought of Eitel and his Rumanian, and the bullfighter and his amour, and how Dorothea adored me, or claimed to, and I felt so little, ignoring the electricity of course. So I was back in the circle of old friends, and I could think of Lulu, and to my pleasure the pain was gone, at least most of it, because I could remember Lulu sitting at Dorothea's feet. I had some ideas for my bullfighting novel, and tried to force work on it, and instead found myself beginning pieces of this novel, at last I understood a little, and as I wrote, I found that I was stronger, I had survived, I was finally able to keep in some permanent form those parts of myself which were better than me, and therefore I could have the comfort that I was beginning to belong to that privileged world of orphans where art is found.

The education I had delayed and delayed again was pressing at me with all its attractions, and I was becoming more aware of all the things I did not know. So for most of that year when I was not working or writing, I would spend my days in the public library, often giving as much as twelve hours at a time if I had the opportunity, and I read everything which interested me, all the good novels I could find, and literary criticism too. And I read history, and some of the philosophers, and I read the books of psychoanalysts, those whose styles I could tolerate, for part of a man's style is what he thinks of other people and whether he wants them to be in awe of him or to think of him as an equal. And I read a few anthropologists, and I studied languages, French and Italian, even a little German, because languages were natural for me, and two months I spent reading *Das Kapital* and might have thought of myself as a Socialist if Munshin had not been right and when I cut it all away, I was still an anarchist, and an anarchist I would always be. Or so it seemed. There were bad days when I thought I would go back to the

Church. Anyway, my education went on, and although I do not think I can measure it, I had months where I thought about what I read in books with more excitement than I had ever done anything, and ever since that year, I don't suppose I have met the expert who was altogether impressive to me. Which, after all, may seem a small boast to make, but in the years when I was in the orphanage, the kind of people who went to college were as mysterious as the titles who got together on a yacht to sail the Mediterranean.

I found as I continued to study that there was an order in what I sought, and I read each book as a curve in some unconscious spiral of intellectual pursuit until the most difficult text at the proper moment was open, and yet the more I learned the more confident I became, because no matter the reputation of the author and the dimensions of his mind, I knew as I read that not one of them could begin to be a final authority for me, because finally the crystallization of their experience did not have the texture apposite to my experience, and I had the conceit, I had the intolerable conviction, that I could write about worlds I knew better than anyone alive. So I continued to write, and as I worked, I learned the taste of a failure over and over again, for the longest individual journey may well be the path from the first creative enthusiasm to the concluded artifact. There were nights in the library when I would look at the footnotes in some heroically constructed tome, and know that the spirit of the rigorous scholar who had written it must know its regret, for each footnote is a step on to deeper meaning which terrifies the order of progression of the scholar's logic, until there is no point in experience, nor any word, from which one cannot set out to explore the totality of the All, if indeed there be an All and not an expanding mystery.

It was not often so metaphysical as that, and I lived weeks of desperation when I would wish to fall in love, and would go through one girl after another, my local prestige as a bullfighter helping me no little, and there would be months when I conducted my classes and could do no work at all, but I had changed since I came to Desert D'Or, and so I could always think of Eitel, and I could see his life, and Elena's life, and the life of the capital, until at times my imagination would take me to all the corners I would never visit again, and their life became more real to me than anything of my own, and I would see them on the round of their days . . .

28

. . . Eitel on a particular night, a period of years after he returned to the capital. It was evening and he had been busy since eight in the morning on his latest film. Now, as the cameramen were storing their equipment for the following day, and the electricians were wheeling the floor lamps into position on the set which would be used tomorrow, and the actors were quitting their portable dressing rooms and nodding good night to him, Eitel felt the gentle melancholy which always came over him when work was ended and the giant sound stage began to close down, almost as if he were recapturing a mood from childhood when he was hurrying back from school on a winter afternoon and a grey wind carried him in its path, blowing him home before the approaching night. One of his assistants was holding a scratchboard at his elbow with some mimeographed requisition that he was supposed to sign, and the wardrobe man was beckoning to him from a yard away, expressing an odd frustration in the little dance he made, as though for weeks he had been trying to get a word with Eitel. Actually, they had had a five-minute conference at lunch, but the wardrobe man was changeable, and whatever they had decided was probably to be decided again.

'No, that's all, that's all,' Eitel shouted, 'we'll work everything out in the morning,' and then with a wide wave of his hand which included the scenery and the equipment and the cave of the sound stage as much as any of the film crew who still were left, he pulled away from the ten minor decisions which nipped at his attention, clapped another of his assistants on the back, and pushed through one of the sound-proofed doors out to the studio street. In their Cadillac convertibles, studio executives were moving by at ten miles an hour, and the stenographers and secretaries were coming through the wide marble exit of the administration building, while along one of the alleys, quitting still another sound stage, a covey of lascars and pirates with their make-up vivid in the twilight came brawling toward him, talking with loud voices, their bright rags of costumes soon to be shucked in the studio's storage rooms. A dozen or more said hello to him. Like a politician, Eitel accepted their greetings, nodding to one, smiling to another, catching a confused and tired view of bloodstained handkerchiefs wound about their heads, and crimson shirts, and full bloused pants with cinematic patches.

When he got to his office in one of the private bungalows reserved for directors he told his secretary to get Collie Munshin on the phone, and then Eitel poured himself a drink and began to shave.

Before he was done, the call came through. 'How'd it go today, lover?' said the producer in his high-pitched voice.

'It was all right, I think,' Eitel said. 'We're still on schedule.'

'I'll be down tomorrow on the set. I saw H.T. today, and I told him this picture was going to be good.'

'Everybody's aware of that, Collie.'

'I know, I know, baby. But this has got to be good.'

'They all have to be good,' Eitel said irritably. As he spoke, he continued to shave with his free hand. 'Look, Collie,' he said in a somewhat different tone, 'I called Elena at lunchtime and told her you wanted a story conference with me tonight. I don't believe she'll call you, but if she does, will you run interference?'

He could feel Munshin's hesitation. This was the third time in a month he had asked such a favour. 'Charley, I'll do whatever you want,' Munshin said slowly, 'but don't forget that tomorrow's important too.'

'Stop being a bully,' Eitel said sharply. 'Why do you think I'm going out tonight?'

Munshin sighed. 'Give the lady my regards.'

By the time Eitel reached the executive parking lot and stepped into his car, it was already dark. He manoeuvred through the few streets of heavy traffic which circulated about the studio, and then accelerated his automobile on to one of the wide boulevards which led to the ocean. In her beach house,

Lulu would be waiting, and she would be annoyed that he was late.

He had been having an affair with her for half a year, and they would see each other sometimes as often as once a week. The biggest problem was to find a place to meet. Lulu's home, in one of the suburbs of the capital, had proved impractical, there were always friends coming in for a drink, and they had been obliged to settle for the beach house. Since it was winter, the weather was rainy, and most of the film colony who lived at the beach had moved back to the city. This left the house more or less secluded, yet it was not impossible that someone he knew would see him enter, and Eitel would park his car a distance away and walk up on foot. By another month, spring would come, and they would have to arrange some other meeting place.

On the drive, Eitel tried not to think about the movie he was making. It was the fourth picture he had directed since *Saints and Lovers*, and it was nothing remarkable. A comedy about two people who find themselves married by accident, there was very little which was not cliché, but the film had a large budget, the largest of any picture which had been assigned to him since he had returned to the capital, and two of the biggest stars at Supreme were acting in it. His career depended to an extent on this comedy, for the partial success of *Saints and Lovers* and the middling returns on his other three pictures had not hurt him, but they had not helped him either. Given the situation, there was more than enough pressure. So, as he rode to Lulu's house, Eitel brooded over what he must face in the next few days, worrying about the animosity which was developing between the female star and a young actress who was giving a good supporting performance, too good – it could overshadow the star – thinking that over the weekend he would have to work with the writer on the dialogue of a climactic scene, it was just not comic enough, and all the while Eitel was wondering with a dull fear whether the pace was too fast or too slow. That was the question one could never answer until the cutting was done, but if his instinct was not serving him right, he could only hope it would be possible to patch the picture. Eitel sighed. He had come in sight of the beach house, and still had not rid himself of the day's work.

Lulu was waiting impatiently. 'I thought you'd never get here,' she said.

'It was an awful day,' Eitel said. 'You don't know how much I was looking forward to this.'

Lulu did not react properly. 'Charley,' she said, 'would you be very angry if we let things go for tonight? I'm sort of upset.'

He controlled his resentment. He had gone to considerable trouble to arrange these few hours and she should realize that. However, he merely smiled. 'We'll do whatever you want,' Eitel said.

'Charley, you know I have a tremendous physical feeling for you. My God, you're the only man I have outside of Tony, and I don't have to tell you what that's like.'

Eitel gave his tender smile again. He had heard she was having two other affairs, but then, one never knew.

Lulu began to walk up and down the living room, picking her way through the beach-house furniture. 'I need your advice,' she said abruptly. 'Charley, there's a crisis on.'

'A crisis?' Eitel was on guard. Could Lulu be about to make demands?

'Tony's in trouble.' Quietly, Lulu began to cry. 'I could kill him,' she said.

'What happened?'

'My press agent, Monroney, was on the phone for half an hour just now. He says I've got to release a statement to the papers, but he doesn't know what I should say. Charley, I don't either, and I have to give the statement in the next ten minutes.'

'But what is it?'

'Tony beat up a waitress in a restaurant in Pittsburgh.'

Eitel clicked his tongue. 'That is a mess.'

'It's terrible,' Lulu said. 'I knew Tony would get in trouble on his tour. Why does the studio send him out on personal appearances? They ought to keep him in a cage. He's been drunk for two days, Monroney said.'

'Well, what do you think you ought to do?'

'I don't know. If I make the wrong move, this could finish my career.'

'More probably, it'll finish Tony.'

She shook her head. 'Not with his luck. He's the biggest thing

in town. The studio has to save him. But I can't afford this.'
Lulu cried out in anger, 'Why does Tony have to do these
things?'

'Don't you think you ought to get in touch with Supreme?'

'No,' she said, 'Charley, you're not thinking. Don't you see
it's Tony they're going to protect. They haven't even tried to
call me. That's the proof. They're going to spread the story that
I drove Tony to it because I'm a bad wife.'

'Supreme can't afford to sacrifice you,' Eitel said.

'The hell they can't. Tony's Bimmler is higher than mine.'

'That's only temporary.'

'Charley, stop giving me a sermon,' Lulu shrieked.

'Don't scream at me, Lulu.'

By an effort she calmed herself. 'I'm sorry,' she muttered.

'What does Monroney say?'

Lulu put her drink down. 'He's an idiot. I'm going to fire him
when this is over. He thinks I should make a statement that I
wash my hands of Tony, and that Tony's brutal and that I know
exactly what that waitress went through, and so forth and so
forth.'

'People won't like it,' Eitel said.

'Of course they won't. But Monroney says that's the best I
can do. His theory is that I have to attack before Supreme
attacks me.' She threw her arms out widely. 'Charley, I can't
think straight.'

'Lulu, baby,' Eitel said, 'let me fill your glass. It's not as bad
as you think.'

'I'm so wound up, Charley. Please help me.'

He nodded. 'I'm no expert on public relations but I have
picked up a little bit.' Eitel smiled. 'Offhand, I'd say it's a
mistake to try to fight Supreme's publicity. They're too strong
for you.'

'I know they are,' she shouted in exasperation.

'But you don't have to oppose their strength. You can use it.'
Eitel paused significantly. 'They don't want to lose you unless
they have to. If you make it possible, Supreme will be happy to
save Tony *and* you.'

'Charley, be specific.'

'Well, you know, people love certain kinds of confessions,'

Eitel said. 'What I would suggest is to take the blame on yourself. Only do it in such a way that everybody feels sympathy for you.'

'I think I see what you mean,' Lulu said. 'But will Monroney know how to exploit it?'

'Have you got a typewriter?' Eitel asked. 'I can work it out in five minutes.'

She sat him down at a desk in her den, and he lit a cigarette, took a swallow of his drink, and began to write:

> Reached at her home, Miss Meyers, who was busy entertaining some children from the Bonny-Kare Society for Under-privileged Children, said today, 'It's all my fault. Tony must not be blamed. I feel terrible about that poor waitress, and I know Tony feels even worse. But the emotional and psychological difficulties which led Tony to commit such an act are all of my making. Deep down, Tony has a wonderful character, but I've failed to give him the love and unselfishness he needs, although in my own cockeyed childish way I love him very much. Perhaps, out of this trouble, which is my responsibility more than Tony's, I will achieve the maturity and humility I've been looking for so long. I'm flying to Pittsburgh right away to be with Tony, and I hope that out of all this something good may come for Tony even more than me.'

'Charley, you're a great man,' Lulu said and hugged him again. 'I'll call Monroney right away.' The phone in her hand, however, she hesitated. 'What about this Bonny-Kare thing?' she asked.

'I know Gustafson very well. It's one of the charity drives he manages. Send him a check for five hundred, and you won't have any trouble there. He'll even release his own statement. "One of the most kindhearted actresses in this town."' Eitel grinned. 'Only have Monroney call him right away. While you're at it, tell him to get the airplane reservation too.'

When the phone calls were finished, Lulu came and sat on his lap. 'I don't have to be at the airport for two hours,' she said, 'but I ought to call my maid to pack a bag and meet me there.'

'Let it wait.'

'Oh, Charley, you're really a man,' Lulu said. 'Monroney thinks it's so good that he tried to tell me he was working on the same angle himself. He's going to send a copy to Supreme as soon as the wire services release it.'

'If the newspapers take it on, and I'm sure they will,' Eitel said, 'you'll be publicity for a week at least.'

'I'll never be able to thank you enough. Why did I know it was you who could do it?' she asked fondly.

'Because we're just old thieves,' he smiled.

'Charley, let's make love,' Lulu said. 'Right now you look good enough to eat.'

They spent a pleasant quarter of an hour, and when they were done, Lulu gave him three quick kisses on his bald spot. 'You're the youngest man I know,' she said.

He felt comfortable. It was warm in the room and warm next to her body and the tension of the day's work had passed from him. He held Lulu fondly and smiled when she began to meow like a kitten. Let her have this rest, he thought; she would be busy enough the next ten days.

Lulu stirred in his arms and he sighed for her. Now her mind was active again. 'Charley,' she said slowly, 'there's one trouble.'

'Only one?' he asked gently.

'Well, you know I was planning to divorce Tony, and now I won't be able to. Not for a year at least.'

'Would you really have divorced him so soon?'

'I don't know. I don't know really. Maybe I do love him.'

'Maybe you do.'

'It's just I hate the idea how he used me. I never should have let you go.'

'We were meant to be friends,' Eitel said. 'It's better this way.'

'Sometimes I'm scared, Charley. I never used to be scared.'

'It comes and it goes.'

She propped herself up and lit a cigarette. 'I saw Teddy Pope yesterday,' she said. 'It's funny. I never liked him but now I feel sorry for him.'

'What is he doing?' Eitel asked.

'He's still looking for work. He told me he might have a job in an independent production. I told him to go East and he said he would, but he won't. I think he's afraid of the theatre.'

'I wish I could do something for him,' Eitel said.

'Teddy's really nice in his own way,' Lulu said, and blew cigarette smoke toward her belly. 'Right in the middle of all his trouble with Teppis, it took courage to go see Marion in jail. Only he was a fool to give that crazy statement. He didn't have to throw it in everybody's face that Marion was his friend.' She touched Eitel's arm. 'I'm sorry, Charley.'

'Whatever for?' He resented this, however.

'Well, I'd forgotten about Marion and Elena.'

'It's all right. Everybody has forgotten.' Eitel shrugged.

'Elena's a good girl,' Lulu said.

Lulu looked sad. 'After I left Teddy, I kept thinking that H.T. was right. Maybe I should have married Teddy. We might have worked out, and we'd both be better off today.' Lulu began to cry. 'Oh, Charley, I'm depressed. I wish I hadn't seen Teddy.'

Eitel comforted her. For a while they chatted, and then he looked at his watch. 'You better get dressed if you're going to make that plane.'

'I almost forgot,' she said. 'I wish I didn't have to go.'

She talked to him while she was in the shower. 'Good luck on your picture while I'm gone,' Lulu called out.

'Thank you.'

'When I'm in Pittsburgh can I phone your house if I need advice?'

'I guess so. Under the circumstances I can find some explanation for Elena.'

'She's jealous, isn't she?' Lulu asked.

'Sometimes.'

'Charley, I hope you have luck with this picture. Lord knows you're due. I thought *Saints and Lovers* was one of the greatest pictures I ever saw, and so did everybody else in town. You should have gotten a Hercules for it.'

'Well, I didn't.'

There was silence while she powdered her feet. 'Charles, are you happy with Elena?' Lulu asked.

'I'm not unhappy,' he said.

'Elena's improved a lot.'

'I suppose her analyst helped her.'

'Don't believe it,' Lulu said. 'I've been going to my head-shrinker for five years and he's never done a thing for me. It's you. You've been good for Elena. You're good for everybody.'

'That's a novel role for me,' Eitel said.

'You're always too hard on yourself.'

'Maybe I'm too easy now.'

Lulu opened the bathroom door and stuck her tongue out at him. 'Nonsense. You just remember that.' She made a point of leaving the door open. 'Charley, tell me about Victor. I was going to send him a present the other day but I forgot to.'

'Vickie,' Eitel said, 'ah, I love Vickie.'

'I never could have thought of you as a father.'

'Neither could I, but I love that baby.'

Did he love him? he wondered, feeling a desire to hold the child in his arms. Victor resembled Elena; not Elena as she was now, he thought, but Elena as he had first known her. Yet what was the truth? There were times when he did not think of Victor for a week at a time.

'How do you know you love him?' Lulu asked curiously.

Eitel was about to answer, 'Because I want him to be better than me,' but instead he smiled.

'Maybe I ought to have children,' Lulu said. 'I wonder if that's the answer for me.'

'Better call your maid and tell her to meet you at the airport.'

When Lulu had finished dressing, he drove her car out of the garage and opened the door for her. 'Just keep your head, and everything will be all right,' Eitel said.

'Want to follow me to the airport in your car?'

'Do you think we ought to be seen together?'

'I guess not.' Lulu reached out and hugged him again. 'Oh, Charley, I love you an awful lot. Do you know you have real dignity now?'

It was a decent compliment, Eitel thought, for what was dignity, real dignity, but the knowledge written on one's face of the cost of every human desire.

'It's nice of you to say that, Lulu,' he said, and then he smiled. 'You know, I wouldn't want this to get around, and I don't suppose I've told it to anyone in years, but my mother was a French maid before she married my father. Of course she worked only in the best homes.'

'Oh, Charley, Charley,' Lulu said, and they laughed then

together. 'Why didn't you ever know,' she asked, 'that you were my big love?'

He kissed her softly on the cheek and watched her drive away. In his ear he became aware of the sound of the surf, and he wandered down to the beach and watched the Pacific waters ride gently, steadily, on to the shore. It was early yet, he did not have to hurry home, and shivering a little, he sat down and stirred his fingers in the sand, remembering, from what seemed out of another life, the time he watched the girl with the surf board and tried to make her interested in what he said. It came over him with the force of forgotten pain how he had lusted for her that day, as if she were the entrance to a life he had never quite known.

Eitel was sad, but it was pleasant sadness. He was looking forward to going home; after days of indifference he felt tender toward Elena now, as he invariably felt tender after he had been unfaithful. Before they went to sleep he would hold her and tell her that he loved her. She did not need these words as much as she had needed them once, but still she would be happy, and Eitel, thinking back over the few years they had been married, was thankful they were passed. The first year had been bad; there had been gossip and memories and for months it had not always been easy for them to approach each other. But that too had passed, and if with the loss of his jealousy he had also lost an emotion he once had felt they still had a bedroom and it was better than most.

The last serious trouble had come when Elena discovered herself pregnant. She had been terrified of abortion and he had felt chained for life. But the child had come and now he loved it or at least he did his best to love it, and as Lulu said, Elena had improved. She could keep house, she could run the servants, she could even entertain. In those ways she had grown and there were many people who envied his marriage. Eitel sighed. Was it not possible after all that there was no such thing as Love, but only that everybody loved in their own way and did the best they could? 'Life has made me a determinist,' he thought in passing.

He got into his car and drove home at a tired pace and climbed the drive which led up to the house they had bought in the hills of the capital, and then he parked in his garage, waited a minute to put himself together for Elena, and went to join her in the living room. She looked up from the book she was reading and he saw at a glance that she was moody. But then she often seemed moody on nights when he had been unfaithful, and he wondered if she knew or if it were merely his uneasiness, and he marvelled at how little he understood of what went on in her mind.

'How is Victor?' he asked as he came in.

Elena smiled drowsily. 'He was very cute today,' she said. 'I have a story to tell you about what he did.'

'Fine,' Eitel said, 'I want to hear it. But first I need a drink.' Alcohol would wash his mouth of Lulu and prepare him for Elena. As he kissed her on the cheek, he tried to be a touch remote so she would expect nothing of him when they went to sleep.

'Was the conference all right?' Elena asked.

'It was fair.'

'Why can't Collie make up his mind?' she said crossly. 'He's so changeable.'

'He is,' Eitel agreed, and sat down beside her.

'I missed you tonight,' Elena said. 'I was disappointed when you called at lunchtime.'

'I know.'

'No, you don't.'

'Oh, baby, I'm tired,' he said softly. 'Don't scold me.'

'I wonder when we'll have an evening together,' Elena said in a dispirited voice.

'Over the weekend. I promise you. Maybe Friday night.'

'I have my dance group Friday afternoon. *I'll* be tired then,' she said. In the last year she had begun to take dancing lessons again, probably more to keep her figure than from any deep ambition, but she was good, and once or twice when they had company, she consented to perform for them.

'No, we'll make time over the weekend, sweetheart,' Eitel said. He pushed himself farther back into the sofa, took a comfortable sip on his drink, and rubbed his eyes. 'How did you spend today?' he asked.

'I played bridge this afternoon.'

'Fine.'

'I hate bridge,' Elena said.

She was clearly not in a good mood, and as fatigued as though he had actually undergone a conference with Collie Eitel sat up and stroked her arm. 'What's the matter?' he asked.

'I saw my analyst this morning.'

'Well, you still see him twice a week,' Eitel said.

'Yes, I know, Charley, but I had a fight with him this morning.'

It was worth thirty-five dollars an hour that she should fight with someone else. 'What caused it?' Eitel said tentatively.

'I don't want to talk about my analysis.'

'All right.'

'It's just that we always talk about the same things.'

He made a point of saying, 'Do you mean your analyst or me?'

'Oh, darling, you know I mean the analyst. He's very smart, but I don't know if I need him any more.'

'Then quit.'

'I think I will . . . except . . .'

'Except what?'

'It was a stupid fight,' Elena said, not answering him directly. 'I told him about the new house we were talking of buying if your picture is a success, and we discussed it, and it came out . . . well, Charley, what came out was that I don't want to buy the new house.'

'You don't?' She had seemed so excited the day they looked at it.

'Well, I do and I don't. We uncovered some ambivalences I have.'

'Yes, yes.'

'Now, don't get angry. I won't use those words any more than I have to, but what we discovered is that I feel the house is too big and that we'll just be too rich.'

'All right, I can understand feeling that way.' But he was annoyed at her. For in another few years, whenever she was ready, she would want a bigger house than the one he planned to buy now.

'The analyst didn't like what I said. He told me I was

regressing and being childish, and that it was my attitude toward money and toward you and a sign of weak ego.' As Elena spoke, he listened critically to her voice. She was more articulate these days, and her voice had lost most of its coarseness, but there were ugly tones returning now.

She touched his hand. 'I don't know what happened, Charley, but I started screaming at him, and I told him he was a fine one to talk with his twenty-room house, and that he was a smug fat slob, and I couldn't stand the way he was so satisfied with himself, and if he didn't like the way I talked, well nobody was asking him to take my money and . . .' She lapsed into silence. 'It was just awful.'

'That kind of thing has happened before.'

'Yes, but Charley, this time I meant it. That's what I do think of him, and I don't trust him any more, and next time I won't make a scene when I tell him, I'll just let him know how unattractive he is. Because you see I don't want the same kind of life for me that he thinks I should have.'

'What do you mean?'

'I mean it's true I owe him a lot, but he doesn't understand me. He really doesn't.'

'I don't follow.'

'Charley, I know how you feel about that new house. You want it more than you think you do, and I suppose we'll get it because we always end up doing what you want.'

'Is that fair?'

'Maybe it isn't, but what I'm trying to say is, I mean, we have the baby, and we'll probably have another baby, and I have good relations with the servants and I do love the dancing classes, and Charley, I love you, I can tell because I still get scared at the thought of losing you, but Charley, listen to me, I don't know if you understand how much I love Vickie, I keep worrying that I won't be a good enough mother to him, but is that enough? Is Vickie enough? I mean where do I go? I don't want to complain, but what am I going to do with my life?'

Eitel caressed her. 'Sweetheart,' he said, and his voice throbbed with a little emotion, 'you've grown more than anybody in the time I've known you, and I won't be worried about you, I can't be worried about you, because I just know that whatever you do, you're going to get better and more good all your life.'

There were tears in her eyes. He had spent the evening watching women cry. 'No, Charley,' Elena said, 'you see, that doesn't answer it. I can't talk to you unless you'll understand this. What am I going to do with my life?'.

He held her to him, and fondled her hair, feeling a sense of protection which bade her to stop here and ask no more; for of all the distance she had come, and he had helped her to move, and there were times like this when he felt the substance of his pride to depend upon exactly her improvement as if she were finally the only human creation in which he had taken part, he still knew that he could help her no longer, nor could anyone else, for she had come now into that domain where her problems were everyone's problems and there were no answers and no doctors, but only that high plateau where philosophy lives with despair. He felt a portent in himself that she would grow away from him, and in years to come, many years to be sure, it might be that he would need her, and would she be forced to stay out of kindness and loyalty and boredom too?

'I'm sorry, Charley,' she said. 'You're tired and it's not fair to bother you.'

But he was indeed too tired for enthusiasm, and he had a moment holding her in his arms where he entered into himself, and with a bleak hatred he thought of Elena, and was maniacal with the contempt he felt for what he had said to her. It was nonsense, it was the weak cowardly cheek-blossomed flower of his sentimentality, for the future was unknown, and it was equally possible that Elena would go on with him until in her slow way she had learned a little more of becoming a lady, and then loyalty or no, Victor or no, memories – what they were – or no, she would begin, biologically, imperatively, to look for another mate, some young crude producer whom she could try to train to be a gentleman while the producer was training her to be still more a lady, and he, Eitel, would be left . . . he smiled with his dry sour eighteenth-century smile, he would be free at last to look for a nurse and a servant. And Victor would come to visit. Everyone who stayed alive had at the least a consolation prize. But this was much too far to go, and so he stopped and said goodbye to the unused artist's depths of his intelligence, noticing with what perceptive comfort it provided him that on this night it was Elena who fell asleep first.

Long after he had failed to be lulled by the quiet rhythms of her breathing, Eitel got up and visited Victor's room, and looked at his child sleeping, but there was only a small emotion he could feel, and so putting on an overcoat, he stepped out on the balcony of their house and looked down to the checkerwork of houses and streets which filled the valley of the capital, and beyond, far in the distance was the ocean and the lights of automobiles on the highway which bordered it. He had come along that road tonight on the drive back to his house, and he remembered how at a stoplight, just before the neon signs and the hamburger stands and the tourist camps which threw up their shoddy skirts to the capital, he had stared out across the water and seen a freighter with its hold-lights and its mast-lamps moving away to the horizon. It was off on a voyage and the men who sailed it would look for adventure.

Almost idly, for the first time in many months, Eitel thought of me then, and wondered, 'Is Sergius possibly on that boat?'

Then the lights changed to green and he raced his motor and rode away and forgot the freighter, but now standing on the balcony of his house, Eitel set out on another voyage, and made the nostalgic journey back to Desert D'Or, thinking wistfully of how once he had adored Elena's body in that unhappy time which marked – could he say it so? – the end of his over-extended youth. It was gone now, gone as the miles on the boulevard past that intersection where he had watched the ship go down the horizon, and with a pang for what is lost forever, he remembered the knowledge he wanted to give to me, suffering the sad frustration of his new middle age, since experience when it is not told to another must wither within and be worse than lost.

'One cannot look for a good time, Sergius,' he whispered in his mind to me, thinking of how I first had come to Desert D'Or, 'for pleasure must end as love or cruelty' – and almost as an afterthought, he added – 'or obligation.' In that way, Eitel thought of me, and with a kindly sadness he wondered, 'Sergius, what does one ever do with one's life?' asking in the easy friendship of memory, 'Are you one of those who know?'

And in the passing fire of his imagination, he made up my answer across the miles and had me say goodbye to him. 'For you see,' he confessed in his mind, 'I have lost the final desire of the artist, the desire which tells us that when all else is lost, when love is lost and adventure, pride of self, and pity, there still remains that world we may create, more real to us, more real to others, than the mummery of what happens, passes, and is gone. So, do try, Sergius,' he thought, 'try for that other world, the real world, where orphans burn orphans and nothing is more difficult to discover than a simple fact. And with the pride of the artist, you must blow against the walls of every power that exists, the small trumpet of your defiance.'

It was his speech, and he said it well. But I would have told him that one must invariably look for a good time since a good time is what gives us the strength to try again. For do we not gamble our way to the heart of the mystery against all the power of good manners, good morals, the fear of germs, and the sense of sin? Not to mention the prisons of pain, the wading pools of pleasure, and the public and professional voices of our sentimental land. If there is a God, and sometimes I believe there is one, I'm sure He says, 'Go on, my boy. I don't know that I can help you, but we wouldn't want all *those* people to tell you what to do.'

There are hours when I would have the arrogance to reply to the Lord Himself, and so I ask, 'Would You agree that sex is where philosophy begins?'

But God, who is the oldest of the philosophers, answers in His weary cryptic way, 'Rather think of Sex as Time, and Time as the connection of new circuits.'

Then for a moment in that cold Irish soul of mine, a glimmer of the joy of the flesh came toward me, rare as the eye of the rarest tear of compassion, and we laughed together after all, because to have heard that sex was time and time the connection of new circuits was a part of the poor odd dialogues which give hope to us noble humans for more than one night.

Fourth Advertisement for Myself:
The last draft of *The Deer Park*

In his review of The Deer Park, *Malcolm Cowley said it must have been a more difficult book to write than* The Naked and the Dead. *He was right. Most of the time, I worked on* The Deer Park *in a low mood; my liver, which had gone bad in the Philippines, exacted a hard price for forcing the effort against the tide of a long depression, and matters were not improved when nobody at Rinehart & Co. liked the first draft of the novel. The second draft, which to me was the finished book, also gave little enthusiasm to the editors, and open woe to Stanley Rinehart, the publisher. I was impatient to leave for Mexico, now that I was done, but before I could go, Rinehart asked for a week in which to decide whether he wanted to do the book. Since he had already given me a contract which allowed him no option not to accept the novel (a common arrangement for writers whose sales are more or less large) any decision to reject the manuscript would cost him a sizeable advance. (I learned later he had been hoping his lawyers would find the book obscene, but they did not, at least not then in May 1954.) So he had really no choice but to agree to put the book out in February, and gloomily he consented. To cheer him a bit, I agreed to his request that he delay paying me my advance until publication, although the first half was due on delivery of the manuscript. I thought the favour might improve our relations.*

Now, if a few of you are wondering why I did not take my book back and go to another publishing house, the answer is that I was tired, I was badly tired. Only a few weeks before, a doctor had given me tests for the liver, and it had shown itself to be sick and depleted. I was hoping that a few months in Mexico would give me a chance to fill up again.

But the next months were not cheerful. The Deer Park *had been done as well as I could do it, yet I thought it was probably a minor work, and I did not know if I had any real interest in starting another book. I made efforts of course; I collected notes, began to piece together a few ideas for a novel given to bullfighting, and another about a concentration camp; I* wrote 'David Reismen Reconsidered' during this time and 'The Homosexual Villain'; read most of the work of the other writers of my generation (I think I was looking for a level against which to measure my third novel) went over the galleys when they came, changed a line or two, sent them back. Keeping half busy I mended a bit, but it was a time of dull drifting. When we came back to New York in October, The Deer Park was already in page proof. By November, the first advertisement was given to Publishers' Weekly. Then, with less than ninety days to publication, Stanley Rinehart told me I would have to take out a small piece of the book – six not very explicit lines about the sex of an old producer and a call girl. The moment one was ready to consider losing those six lines they moved into the moral centre of the novel. It would be no tonic for my liver to cut them out. But I also knew Rinehart was serious, and since I was still tired, it seemed a little unreal to try to keep the passage. Like a miser I had been storing energy to start a new book; I wanted nothing to distract me now. I gave in on a word or two, agreed to rewrite a line, and went home from that particular conference not very impressed with myself. The next morning I called up the editor in chief, Ted Amussen, to tell him I had decided the original words had to be put back.

'Well, fine,' he said, 'fine. I don't know why you agreed to anything in the first place.'

A day later, Stanley Rinehart halted publication, stopped all ads (he was too late to catch the first run of Publishers' Weekly which was already on its way to England with a full page for The Deer Park) and broke his contract to do the book. I was started on a trip to find a new publisher, and before I was done, the book had gone to Random House, Knopf, Simon and Schuster, Harper's, Scribners, and unofficially to Harcourt, Brace. Some day it would be fine to give the details, but for now little more than a few lines of dialogue and an editorial report:

Bennet Cerf: This novel will set publishing back twenty years.
Alfred Knopf to an editor: Is this your idea of the kind of book which should bear a Borzoi imprint?

The lawyer for one publishing house complimented me on the six lines, word for word, which had excited Rinehart to break his contract. This lawyer said, 'It's admirable the way you get around the problem here.' Then he brought out more than a hundred objections to other parts of the book. One was the line: 'She was lovely. Her back was adorable in its

358

contours.' I was told that this ought to go because 'The principals are not married, and so your description puts a favourable interpretation upon a meretricious relationship.'

Hiram Hayden had lunch with me some time after Random House saw the book. He told me he was responsible for their decision not to do it, and if I did not agree with his taste, I had to admire his honesty – it is rare for an editor to tell a writer the truth. Hayden went on to say that the book never came alive for him even though he had been ready to welcome it. 'I can tell you that I picked the book up with anticipation. Of course I had heard from Bill, and Bill had told me that he didn't like it, but I never pay attention to what one writer says about the works of another . . .' Bill was William Styron, and Hayden was his editor. I had asked Styron to call Hayden the night I found out Rinehart had broken his contract. One reason for asking the favour of Styron was that he sent me a long letter about the novel after I had shown it to him in manuscript. He had written, 'I don't like The Deer Park, but I admire sheer hell out of it.' So I thought to impose on him.

Other parts of the account are not less dreary. The only generosity I found was from the late Jack Goodman. He sent me a photostat of his editorial report to Simon and Schuster, and because it was sympathetic, his report became the objective estimate of the situation for me. I assumed that the book when it came out would meet the kind of trouble Goodman expected, and so when I went back later to work on the page proofs I was not free of a fear or two. But that can be talked about in its place. Here is the core of his report.

Mailer refuses to make any changes . . . [He] *will* consider suggestions, but reserves the right to make final decisions, so we must make our decision on what the book now is.

That's not easy. It is full of vitality and power, as readable a novel as I've ever encountered. Mailer emerges as a sort of post-Kinsey F. Scott Fitzgerald. His dialogue is uninhibited and the sexuality of the book is completely interwoven with its purpose, which is to describe a segment of society whose morality is nonexistent. Locale is evidently Palm Springs. Chief characters are Charles Eitel, movie director who first defies the House Un-American Committee, then becomes a friendly witness, his mistress, a great movie star who is his ex-wife, her lover who is the narrator, the head of a great movie company, his son-in-law, a strange, tortured panderer who is Eitel's conscience and, assorted demimondaines, homosexuals, actors.

My layman's opinion is that the novel will be banned in certain quarters and that it may very well be up for an obscenity charge, but this should of course be checked by our lawyers. If it were possible to recognize this at the start, to have a united front here and treat the whole issue positively and head-on, I would be for our publishing. But I am afraid such unanimity may be impossible of attainment and if so, we should reject, in spite of the fact that I am certain it will be one of the best-selling novels of the next couple of years. It is the work of a seious artist . . .

The eighth house was G. P. Putnam's. I didn't want to give it to them, I was planning to go next to Viking, but Walter Minton kept saying, 'Give us three days. We'll give you a decision in three days.' So we sent it over to Putnam, and in three days he took it without conditions, and without a request for a single change. I had a victory, I had made my point, but in fact I was not very happy. I had grown so wild on my diet of polite letters from publishing houses who didn't want me, that I had been ready to collect rejections from twenty houses, publish The Deer Park *at my own expense, and try to make a kind of publishing history. Instead I was thrown in with Walter Minton, who has since attracted some fame as the publisher of* Lolita. *He is the only publisher I ever met who would make a good general. Months after I came to Putnam, Minton told me, 'I was ready to take* The Deer Park *without reading it. I knew your name would sell enough copies to pay your advance, and I figured one of these days you're going to write another book like* The Naked and the Dead,' *which is the sort of sure hold of strategy you can have when you're not afraid of censorship.*

Now I've tried to water this account with a minimum of tears, but taking The Deer Park *into the nervous system of eight publishing houses was not so good for my own nervous system, nor was it good for getting to work on my new novel. In the ten weeks it took the book to travel the circuit from Rinehart to Putnam, I squandered the careful energy I had been hoarding for months; there was a hard comedy at how much of myself I would burn up in a few hours of hot telephone calls; I had never had any sense for practical affairs, but in those days, carrying* The Deer Park *from house to house, I stayed as close to it as a stage-struck mother pushing her child forward at every producer's office. I was amateur agent for it, messenger boy, editorial consultant, Machiavelli of the luncheon table, fool of the five o'clock drinks, I was learning the publishing business in a hurry, and I made a hundred mistakes and paid for each one by wasting a new bout of energy.*

In a way there was sense to it. For the first time in years I was having the kind of experience which was likely to return some day as good work, and so I forced many little events past any practical return, even insulting a few publishers en route as if to discover the limits of each situation. I was trying to find a few new proportions to things, and I did learn a bit. But I'll never know what the novel about the concentration camp would have been like if I had gotten quietly to work when I came back to New York and The Deer Park *had been published on time. It is possible I was not serious about the book, it is also possible I lost something good, but one way or the other, that novel disappeared in the excitement, as lost as 'the little object' in* Barbary Shore, *and it has not stirred since.*

The real confession is that I was making a few of my mental connections those days on marijuana. Like more than one or two of my generation, I had smoked it from time to time over the years, but it never had meant anything. In Mexico, however, down in my depression with a bad liver, pot gave me a sense of something new about the time I was convinced I had seen it all, and I liked it enough to take it now and again in New York.

Then The Deer Park *began to go like a beggar from house to house and en route Stanley Rinehart made it clear he was going to try not to pay the advance. Until then I had had sympathy for him. I thought it had taken a kind of displaced courage to be able to drop the book the way he did. An expensive moral stand, and wasteful for me; but a moral stand. When it turned out that he did not like to bear the expense of being that moral, the experience turned ugly for me. It took many months and the service of my lawyer to get the money, but long before that, the situation had become real enough to drive a spike into my cast-iron mind. I realized in some bottom of myself that for years I had been the sort of comic figure I would have cooked to a turn in one of my books, a radical who had the nineteenth-century naïveté to believe that the people with whom he did business were 1) gentlemen, 2) fond of him, and 3) respectful of his ideas even if in disagreement with them. Now, I was in the act of learning that I was not adored so very much; that my ideas were seen as nasty; and that my fine America which I had been at pains to criticize for so many years was in fact a real country which did real things and ugly things to the characters of more people than just the characters of my books. If the years since the war had not been brave or noble in the history of the country, which I certainly thought and do think, why then did it come as surprise that people in publishing were not as good as they used to be, and that the day of Maxwell Perkins was a day which was gone, really gone, gone as*

Greta Garbo and Scott Fitzgerald? Not easy, one could argue, for an advertising man to admit that advertising is a dishonest occupation, and no easier was it for the working novelist to see that now were left only the cliques, fashions, vogues, snobs, snots, and fools, not to mention a dozen bureaucracies of criticism; that there was no room for the old literary idea of oneself as a major writer, a figure in the landscape. One had become a set of relations and equations, most flourishing when most incorporated, for then one's literary stock was ready for merger. The day was gone when people held on to your novels no matter what others might say. Instead one's good young readers waited now for the verdict of professional young men, academics who wolfed down a modern literature with an anxiety to find your classification, your identity, your similarity, your common theme, your corporate literary earnings, each reference to yourself as individual as a carloading of homogenized words. The articles which would be written about you and a dozen others would be done by minds which were expert on the aggregate and so had senses too lumpy for the particular. There was a limit to how much appraisal could be made of a work before the critic exposed his lack of the critical faculty, and so it was naturally wiser for the mind of the expert to masticate the themes of ten writers rather than approach the difficulties of any one.

I had begun to read my good American novels at the end of an era – I could remember people who would talk wistfully about the excitement with which they had gone to bookstores because it was publication day for the second novel of Thomas Wolfe, and in college, at a Faculty tea, I had listened for an hour to a professor's wife who was so blessed as to have known John Dos Passos. My adolescent crush on the profession of the writer had been more lasting than I could have guessed. I had even been so simple as to think that the kind of people who went into publishing were still more concerned with the few writers who made the profession not empty of honour, and I had been taking myself seriously, I had been thinking I was one of those writers.

Instead I caught it in the face and deserved it for not looking at the evidence. I was out of fashion and that was the score; that was all the score; the publishing habits of the past were going to be of no help for my Deer Park. *And so as the language of sentiment would have it, something broke in me, but I do not know if it was so much a loving heart, as a cyst of the weak, the unreal, and the needy, and I was finally open to my anger. I turned within my psyche I can almost believe, for I felt something shift to murder in me. I finally had the simple sense to understand that if I* wanted my work to travel further than others, the life of my talent depended on fighting a little more, and looking for help a little less. But I deny the sequence in putting it this way, for it took me years to come to this fine point. All I felt then was that I was an outlaw, a psychic outlaw, and I liked it, I liked it a good sight better than trying to be a gentleman, and with a set of emotions accelerating one on the other, I mined down deep into the murderous message of marijuana, the smoke of the assassins, and for the first time in my life I knew what it was to make your kicks.

I could write about that here, but it would be a mistake. Let the experience stay where it is, and on a given year it may be found again in a novel. For now it is enough to say that marijuana opens the senses and weakens the mind. In the end, you pay for what you get. If you get something big, the cost will equal it. There is a moral economy in one's vice, but you learn that last of all. I still had the thought it was possible to find something which cost nothing. Thus, The Deer Park resting at Putnam, and new good friends found in Harlem, I was off on that happy ride where you discover a new duchy of jazz every night and the drought of the past is given a rain of new sound. What has been dull and dead in your years is now tart to the taste, and there is sweet in the illusion of how fast you can change. To keep up with it all, I began to log a journal, a wild set of thoughts and outlines for huge projects – I wrote one hundred thousand words in eight weeks, more than once twenty pages a day in a style which came willy-nilly from the cramp of the past, a lockstep jargon of sociology and psychology that sours my teeth when I look at those pages today. Yet this journal has the start of more ideas than I will have again; ideas which came so fast and so rich that sometimes I think my brain was dulled by the heat of their passage. (With all proportions kept, one can say that cocaine may have worked a similar good and ill upon Freud.)

The journal wore down by February, about the time The Deer Park had once been scheduled to appear. Minton argued that some interest in the book would be lost if the text were not identical to Rinehart's page proofs, and Ted Purdy, my editor, told me more than once that they liked the book 'just the way it is.' Besides, there was thought of bringing it out in June as a summer book.

Well, I wanted to take a look. After all, I had been learning new lessons. I began to go over the page proofs, and the book read as if it had been written by someone else. I was changed from the writer who had laboured on that novel, enough to be able to see it without anger or vanity or the itch to justify myself. Now, after three years of living with the book,

I could at last admit the style was wrong, that it had been wrong from the time I started, that I had been strangling the life of my novel in a poetic prose which was too self-consciously attractive and formal, false to the life of my characters, especially false to the life of my narrator who was the voice of my novel and so gave the story its air. He had been a lieutenant in the Air Force, he had been cool enough and hard enough to work his way up from an orphan asylum, and to allow him to write in a style which at its best sounded like Nick Carroway in The Great Gatsby *must of course blur his character and leave the book unreal. Nick was legitimate, out of fair family, the Midwest and Princeton – he would write as he did, his style was himself. But the style of Sergius O'Shaugnessy, no matter how good it became (and the Rinehart* Deer Park *had its moments) was a style which came out of nothing so much as my determination to prove I could muster a fine style.*

If I wanted to improve my novel, yet keep the style, I would have to make my narrator fit the prose, change his past, make him an onlooker, a rich pretty boy brought up let us say by two old-maid aunts, able to have an affair with a movie star only by luck and/or the needs of the plot, which would give me a book less distracting, well written but minor. If, however, I wanted to keep that first narrator, my orphan flier, adventurer, germ – for three years he had been the frozen germ of some new theme – well, to keep him I would need to change the style from the inside of each sentence. I could keep the structure of my book, I thought – it had been put together for such a narrator – but the style could not escape. Probably I did not see it all so clearly as I now suggest. I believe I started with the conscious thought that I would tinker just a little, try to patch a compromise, but the navigator of my unconscious must already have made the choice, because it came as no real surprise that after a few days of changing a few words I moved more and more quickly toward the eye of the problem, and in two or three weeks I was tied to the work of doing a new Deer Park. *The book was edited in a way no editor could ever have time or love to find; it was searched sentence by sentence, word for word, the style of the work lost its polish, became rough, and I can say real, because there was an abrupt and muscular body back of the voice now. It had been there all the time, trapped in the porcelain of a false style, but now as I chipped away, the work for a time became exhilarating in its clarity – I never enjoyed work so much – I felt as if finally I was learning how to write, learning the joints of language and the touch of a word, felt as if I came close to the meanings of sound and could say which of two close words was more female or more forward. I even had a glimpse of what Flaubert must have felt, for as I went on tuning the book, often five or six words would pile above one another in the margin at some small crisis of choice. (Since the Rinehart page proof was the usable copy, I had little space to write between the lines.) As I worked in this fine mood, I kept sending pages to the typist, yet so soon as I had exhausted the old galley pages, I could not keep away from the new typewritten copy – it would be close to say the book had come alive, and was invading my brain.*

Soon the early pleasure of the work turned restless; the consequences of what I was doing were beginning to seep into my stamina. It was as if I were the captive of an illness whose first symptoms had been excitement, prodigies of quick work, and a confidence that one could go on forever, but that I was by now close to a second stage where what had been quick would be more like a fever, a first wind of fatigue upon me, a knowledge that at the end of the drunken night a junkie cold was waiting. I was going to move at a pace deadly to myself, loading and overloading whatever little centres of the mind are forced to make the hard decisions. In ripping up the silk of the original syntax, I was tearing into any number of careful habits as well as whatever subtle fleshing of the nerves and the chemicals had gone to support them.

For six years I had been writing novels in the first person; it was the only way I could begin a book, even though the third person was more to my taste. Worse, I seemed unable to create a narrator in the first person who was not overdelicate, oversensitive, and painfully tender, which was an odd portrait to give, because I was not delicate, not physically; when it was a matter of strength I had as much as the next man. In those days I would spend time reminding myself that I had been a bit of an athlete (house football at Harvard, years of skiing), that I had not quit in combat, and once when a gang broke up a party in my loft, I had taken two cracks on the head with a hammer and had still been able to fight. Yet the first person seemed to paralyse me, as if I had a horror of creating a voice which could be in any way bigger than myself. So I had become mixed in a false style for every narrator I tried. If now I had been in a fight, had found out that no matter how weak I could be in certain ways, I was also steady enough to hang on to six important lines, that may have given me new respect for myself, I don't know, but for the first time I was able to use the first person in a way where I could suggest some of the stubbornness and belligerence I also might have, I was able to colour the empty reality of that first person with some real feeling of how I had always felt, which was to be outside, for Brooklyn where I grew up is not the centre of anything. I was able, then, to create an adventurer whom I believed in, and as he came alive for me, the other parts of the book which had been stagnant for a year and more also came to life, and new things began to happen to Eitel my director and to Elena his mistress and their characters changed. It was a phenomenon. I learned how real a novel is. Before, the story of Eitel had been told by O'Shaugnessy of the weak voice; now by a confident young man: when the new narrator would remark that Eitel was his best friend and so he tried not to find Elena too attractive, the man and woman he was talking about were larger than they had once been. I was no longer telling of two nice people who fail at love because the world is too large and too cruel for them; the new O'Shaugnessy had moved me by degrees to the more painful story of two people who are strong as well as weak, corrupt as much as pure, and fail to grow despite their bravery in a poor world, because they are finally not brave enough, and so do more damage to one another than to the unjust world outside them. Which for me was exciting, for here and there The Deer Park now had the rare tenderness of tragedy. The most powerful leverage in fiction comes from point of view, and giving O'Shaugnessy courage gave passion to the others.

But the punishment was commencing for me. I was now creating a man who was braver and stronger than me, and the more my new style succeeded, the more was I writing an implicit portrait of myself as well. There is a shame about advertising yourself that way, a shame which became so strong that it was a psychological violation to go on. Yet I could not afford the time to digest the self-criticisms backing up in me, I was forced to drive myself, and so more and more I worked by tricks, taking marijuana the night before and then drugging myself into sleep with an overload of seconal. In the morning I would be lithe with new perception, could read new words into the words I had already, and so could go on in the pace of my work, the most scrupulous part of my brain too sluggish to interfere. My powers of logic became weaker each day, but the book had its own logic, and so I did not need close reason. What I wanted and what the drugs gave me was the quick flesh of associations, and there I was often oversensitive, could discover new experience in the lines of my text like a hermit savouring the revelation of Scripture; I saw so much in some sentences that more than once I dropped into the pit of the amateur; since I was receiving such emotion from my words, I assumed everyone else would be stimulated as well, and on many a line I twisted the phrase in such way, the quick reader (who is nearly all your audience) will stumble and *fall against the vocal shifts of your prose. Then you had best have the cartel of a Hemingway, because in such a case it is critical whether the reader thinks it is your fault, or is so in awe of your reputation that he returns on the words, throttles his pace, and tries to discover why he is so stupid as not to swing on the off-bop of your style.*

An example: In the Rinehart Deer Park *I had this:*

'They make Sugar sound so good in the newspapers,' she declared one night to some people in a bar, 'that I'll really try him. I really will, Sugar.' And she gave me a sisterly kiss.

I happened to change that very little, I put in 'said' instead of 'declared' and later added 'older sister,' so that it now read:

And she gave me a sisterly kiss. Older sister.

Just two words, but I felt as if I had revealed some divine law of nature, had laid down an invaluable clue – the kiss of an older sister was a worldly universe away from the kiss of a younger sister – and I thought to give myself the Nobel Prize for having brought such illumination and division to the cliché of the sisterly kiss.

Well, as an addition it wasn't bad fun, and for two words it did a bit to give a sense of what was working back and forth between Sergius and Lulu, it was another small example of Sergius' hard eye for the world, and his cool sense of his place in it, and all this was to the good, or would have been for a reader who went slowly, and stopped and thought. But if anyone was in a hurry, the little sentence 'Older sister' was like a finger in the eye, it jabbed the unconscious, and gave an uncomfortable nip of rhythm to the mind.

I had five hundred changes of this kind. I started with the first paragraph of the book, on the third sentence which pokes the reader with its backed-up rhythm, 'Some time ago,' and I did that with intent, to slow my readers from the start, like a fighter who throws his right two seconds after the bell and so gives the other man no chance to decide on the pace.

There was a real question, however, whether I could slow the reader down, and so as I worked on further, at some point beginning to write paragraphs and pages to add to the new Putnam galleys, the attrition of the drugs and the possibility of failure began to depress me, and Benzedrine entered the balance, and I was on the way to wearing badly. Because, determined or no that they would read me slowly, praying my readers would read me slowly, there was no likelihood they would do anything of the sort if the reviews were bad. As I started to worry this it grew worse, because I knew in advance that three or four of my major reviews had to be bad – Time *magazine* for one, because Max Gissen was the book review editor, and I had insulted him in public once by suggesting that the kind of man who worked for a mind so exquisitely and subtly totalitarian as Henry Luce was not likely to have any ideas of his own. The New York daily Times *would be bad because Orville Prescott was well known for his distaste of books too forthrightly sexual;* and Saturday Review *would be bad. That is, they would probably be bad; the mentality of their reviewers would not be above the level of their dean of reviewers, Mr Maxwell Geismar, and Geismar didn't seem to know that my second novel was titled* Barbary Shore *rather than* Barbary Coast. *I could spin this out, but what is more to the point is that I had begun to think of the reviews before finishing the book, and this doubtful occupation came out of the kind of inner knowledge I had of myself in those days. I knew what was good for my energy and what was poor, and so I knew that for the vitality of my work in the future, and yes even the quantity of my work, I needed a success and I needed it badly if I was to shed the fatigue I had been carrying since* Barbary Shore. *Some writers receive not enough attention for years, and so learn early to accommodate the habits of their work to little recognition. I think I could have done that when I was twenty-five. With* The Naked and the Dead *a new life had begun, however; as I have written earlier in this book, I had gone through the psychic labour of changing a good many modest habits in order to let me live a little more happily as a man with a name which could arouse quick reactions in strangers. If that started as an overlarge work, because I started as a decent but scared boy, well I had come to live with the new life, I had learned to like success – in fact I had probably come to depend on it, or at least my new habits did.*

When Barbary Shore *was ambushed in the alley the damage to my nervous system was slow but thorough. My status dropped immediately – America is a quick country – but my ego did not permit me to understand that, and I went through tiring years of subtle social defeats because I did not know that I was no longer as large to others as I had been. I was always overmatching myself. To put it crudely, I would think I was dropping people when they were dropping me. And of course my unconscious knew better. There was all the waste of ferocious if unheard discussion between the armies of ego and id; I would get up in the morning with less* snap in me than I had taken to sleep. Six or seven years of breathing that literary air taught me a writer stayed alive in the circuits of such hatred only if he were unappreciated enough to be adored by a clique, or was so overbought by the public that he excited some defenceless nerve in the snob. I knew if The Deer Park was a powerful best seller (the magical figure had become one hundred thousand copies for me) that I would then have won. I would be the first serious writer of my generation to have a best seller twice, and so it would not matter what was said about the book. Half of publishing might call it cheap, dirty, sensational, second-rate, and so forth and so forth, but it would be weak rage and could not hurt, for the literary world suffers a spot of the national taint – a serious writer is certain to be considered major if he is also a best seller; in fact, most readers are never convinced of his value until his books do well. Steinbeck is better known than Dos Passos, John O'Hara is taken seriously by people who dismiss Farrell, and indeed it took three decades and a Nobel Prize before Faulkner was placed on a level with Hemingway. For that reason, it would have done no good if someone had told me at the time that the financial success of a writer with major talent was probably due more to what was meretricious in his work than what was central. The argument would have meant nothing to me – all I knew was that seven publishing houses had been willing to dismiss my future, and so if the book did poorly, a good many people were going to congratulate themselves on their foresight and be concerned with me even less. I could see that if I wanted to keep on writing the kind of book I liked to write, I needed the energy of new success, I needed blood. Through every bit of me, I knew The Deer Park had damn well better make it or I was close to some serious illness, a real apathy of the will.

Every now and again I would have the nightmare of wondering what would happen if all the reviews were bad, as bad as Barbary Shore. I would try to tell myself that could not happen, but I was not certain, and I knew that if the book received a unanimously bad press and still showed signs of selling well, it was likely to be brought up for prosecution as obscene. As a delayed convulsion from the McCarthy years, the fear of censorship was strong in publishing, in England it was critically bad, and so I also knew that the book could lose such a suit – there might be no one of reputation to say it was serious. If it were banned, it could sink from sight. With the reserves I was throwing into the work, I no longer knew if I was ready to take another beating – for the first time in my life I had worn down to the edge, I could see through to the other side of my fear, I knew a time could come when I would be no longer my own man, that I might lose what I had liked to think was the incorruptible centre of my strength (which of course I had had money and freedom to cultivate). Already the signs were there – I was beginning to avoid new lines in the Putnam *Deer Park* which were legally doubtful, and once in a while, like a gambler hedging a bet, I toned down individual sentences from the Rinehart *Deer Park*, nothing much, always a matter of the new O'Shaugnessy character, a change from 'at last I was able to penetrate into the mysterious and magical belly of a movie star,' to what was more in character for him; 'I was led to discover the mysterious brain of a movie star.' Which 'brain' in context was fun for it was accurate, and 'discover' was a word of more life than the legality of 'penetrate,' but I could not be sure if I were chasing my new aesthetic or afraid of the cops. The problem was that The Deer Park had become more sexual in the new version, the characters had more force, the air had more heat, and I had gone through the kind of galloping self-analysis which makes one very sensitive to the sexual nuance of every gesture, word and object – the book now seemed overcharged to me, even a terror of a novel, a cold chisel into all the dull mortar of our guilty society. In my mind it became a more dangerous book than it really was, and my drug-hipped paranoia saw long consequences in every easy line of dialogue. I kept the panic in its place, but by an effort of course, and once in a while I would weaken enough to take out a line because I could not see myself able to defend it happily in a court of law. But it was a mistake to nibble at the edges of censoring myself, for it gave no life to my old pride that I was the boldest writer to have come out of my flabby time, and I think it helped to kill the small chance of finding my way into what could have been a novel as important as The Sun Also Rises.

But let me spell it out a bit: originally The Deer Park had been about a movie director and a girl with whom he had a bad affair, and it was told by a sensitive but faceless young man. In changing the young man, I saved the book from being minor, but put a disproportion upon it because my narrator became too interesting, and not enough happened to him in the second half of the book, and so it was to be expected that readers would be disappointed by this part of the novel.

Before I was finished, I saw a way to write another book altogether. In what I had so far done, Sergius O'Shaugnessy was given an opportunity by a movie studio to sell the rights to his life and get a contract as an actor. After more than one complication, he finally refused the offer, lost the love of his movie star Lulu, and went off wandering by himself, off to become a writer. This episode had never been an important part of the book, but I could see that the new Sergius was capable of accepting the offer, and if he went to Hollywood and became a movie star himself, the possibilities were good, for in O'Shaugnessy I had a character who was ambitious, yet in his own way, moral, and with such a character one could travel deep into the paradoxes of the time.

Well, I was not in shape to consider that book. With each week of work, bombed and sapped and charged and stoned with lush, with pot, with benny, saggy, Milltown, coffee, and two packs a day, I was working live, and overalert, and tiring into what felt like death, afraid all the way because I had achieved the worst of vicious circles in myself, I had gotten too tired. I was more tired than I had ever been in combat, and so as the weeks went on, and publication was delayed from June to August and then to October, there was only a worn-out part of me to keep protesting into the pillows of one drug and the pinch of the other that I ought to have the guts to stop the machine, to call back the galleys, to cease – to rest, to give myself another two years and write a book which would go a little further to the end of my particular night.

But I had passed the point where I could stop. My anxiety had become too great. I did not know anything any more, I did not have that clear sense of the way things work which is what you need for the natural proportions of a long novel, and it is likely I would not have been writing a new book so much as arguing with the law. Of course another man might have had the stamina to write the new book and manage to be indifferent to everything else, but it was too much to ask of me. By then I was like a lover in a bad, but uncontrollable affair; my woman was publication, and it would have cost too much to give her up before we were done. My imagination had been committed – to stop would leave half the psyche in limbo.

Knowing, however, what I had failed to do, shame added momentum to the punishment of the drugs. By the last week or two, I had worn down so badly that with a dozen pieces still to be fixed, I was reduced to working hardly more than an hour a day. Like an old man, I would come up out of a seconal stupor with four or five times the normal dose in my veins, and drop into a chair to sit for hours. It was July, the heat was grim in New York, the last of the book had to be in by August 1. Putnam had been more than accommodating, but the vehicle of publication was on its way, and the book could not be postponed beyond the middle of October or it would miss *all chance for a large fall sale. I would sit in a chair and watch the baseball game on television, or get up and go out in the heat to a drugstore for a sandwich and malted – it was my outing for the day: the walk would feel like a patrol in a tropical sun, and it was two blocks, no more. When I came back, I would lie down, my head would lose the outer wrappings of sedation, and with the crumb of benzedrine, the first snake or two of thought would wind through my brain. I would go for some coffee – it was a trip to the kitchen, but when I came back I would have a scratchboard and pencil in hand. Watching some afternoon horror on television, the boredom of the performers coming through their tense hilarities with a bleakness to match my own, I would pick up the board, wait for the first sentence – like all working addicts I had come to an old man's fine sense of inner timing – and then slowly, but picking up speed, the actions of the drugs hovering into collaboration like two ships passing in view of one another, I would work for an hour, not well but not badly either. (Pages 195 to 200 of the Putnam edition were written this way.) Then my mind would wear out, and new work was done for the day: I would sit around, watch more television and try to rest my dulled mind, but by evening a riot of bad nerves was on me again, and at two in the morning I'd be having the manly debate of whether to try sleep with two double capsules, or settle again for my need of three.*

Somehow I got the book done for the last deadline. Not perfectly – doing just the kind of editing and small re-writing I was doing, I could have used another two or three days, but I got it almost the way I wanted, and then I took my car up to the Cape and lay around in Provincetown with my wife, trying to mend, and indeed doing a fair job because I came off sleeping pills and the marijuana and came part of the way back into that world which has the proportions of the ego. I picked up on The Magic Mountain, *took it slowly, and lowered* The Deer Park *down to modest size in my brain. Which events proved was just as well.*

A few weeks later we came back to the city, and I took some mescaline. Maybe one dies a little with the poison of mescaline in the blood. At the end of a long and private trip which no quick remark should try to describe, the book of The Deer Park *floated into mind, and I sat up, reached through a pleasure garden of velveted light to find the tree of a pencil and the bed of a notebook and brought them to union together. Then, out of some flesh in myself I had not yet known, with the words coming one by one, in separate steeps and falls, hip in their turnings, all cool with their flights, like the touch of being coming into other being, so the last six lines of my bloody book came to me, and I was done. And it was the only good writing I ever did directly from a drug, even if I paid for it with a hangover beyond measure.*

That way the novel received its last sentence, and if I had waited one more day it would have been too late, for in the next twenty-four hours, the printers began their cutting and binding. The book was out of my hands.

Six weeks later, when The Deer Park *came out, I was no longer feeling eighty years old, but a vigorous hysterical sixty-three, and I laughed like an old pirate at the indignation I had breezed into being with the equation of sex and time. The important reviews broke about seven good and eleven bad, and the out-of-town reports were almost three-to-one bad to good, but I was not unhappy because the good reviews were lively and the bad reviews were full of factual error, indeed so much so that it would be monotonous to give more than a good couple.*

Hollis Alpert in the Saturday Review *called the book 'garish and gauche.' In reference to Sergius O'Shaugnessy, Alpert wrote: 'He has been offered $50,000 by Teppis to sell the rights to his rather dull life story . . .' As a matter of detail, the sum was $20,000, and it must have been mentioned a half dozen times in the pages of the book. Paul Pickrel in* Harper's *was blistering about how terrible was my style and then quoted the following sentence as an example of how I was often incomprehensible:*

> '(he) could talk opening about his personal life while remaining a dream of espionage in his business operations.'

I happened to see Pickrel's review in Harper's *galleys, and so was able to point out to them that Pickrel had misquoted the sentence. The fourth word was not 'opening' but 'openly.'* Harper's *corrected his incorrect version, but of course left his remark about my style.*

More interesting is the way reviews divided in the New York magazines and newspapers. Time, *for example, was bad,* Newsweek *was good;* Harper's *was terrible but* The Atlantic *was adequate; the New York daily* Times *was very bad, the Sunday* Times *was good; the daily* Herald Tribune *was better than good;* Commentary *was careful but complimentary, the* Reporter *was frantic; the* Saturday Review *was a scold and Brendan Gill writing for the* New Yorker *put together a series of slaps and superlatives which went partially like this:*

> ... a big, vigorous, rowdy, ill-shaped, and repellent book, so strong and so weak, and so adroit and so fumbling, that only a writer of the greatest and most reckless talent could have flung it between covers.

It's one of the three or four lines I've thought perceptive in all the reviews of my books. That Malcolm Cowley used one of the same words in saying The Deer Park *was 'serious and reckless' is also, I think, interesting, for reckless the book was – and two critics, anyway, had the instinct to feel it.*

One note appeared in many reviews. The strongest statement of it was by John Hutchens in the New York daily Herald Tribune:

> ... the original version reputedly was more or less rewritten and certain materials eliminated that were deemed too erotic for public consumption. And, with that, a book that might at least have made a certain reputation as a large shocker wound up as a cipher ...

I was bothered to the point of writing a letter to the twenty-odd newspapers which reflected this idea. What bothered me was that I could never really prove I had not 'eliminated' the book. Over the years all too many readers would have some hazy impression that I had disembowelled large pieces of the best meat, perspiring in a coward's sweat, a publisher's directive in my ear. (For that matter, I still get an occasional letter which asks if it is possible to see the unbowdlerized Deer Park.) *Part of the cost of touching the Rinehart galleys was to start those rumours, and in fact I was not altogether free of the accusation, as I have tried to show. Even the six lines which so displeased Rinehart had been altered a bit; I had shown them once to a friend whose opinion I respected, and he remarked that while it was impossible to accept the sort of order Rinehart had laid down, still a phrase like the 'fount of power' had a Victorian heaviness about it. Well, that was true, it was out of character for O'Shaugnessy's new style and so I altered it to the 'thumb of power' and then other changes became desirable, and the curious are invited to compare the two versions of this particular passage in this collection, but the mistake I made was to take a small aesthetic gain on those six lines and lose a larger clarity about a principle.*

What more is there to say? The book moved fairly well, it climbed to seven and then to six on The New York Times *best-seller list, stayed there for a week or two, and then slipped down. By Christmas, the tone of the Park and the Christmas spirit being not all that congenial, it was just about off the list forever. It did well, however; it would have reached as high as three or two or even to number one if it had come out in June and then been measured against the low sales of summer, for it sold over fifty thousand copies after returns which surprised a good many in publishing, as well as disappointing a few, including myself. I discovered that I had been poised for an enormous sale or a failure – a middling success was cruel to take. Week after week I kept waiting for the book to erupt into some dramatic change of pace which would send it up in sales instead of down, but that never happened. I was left with a draw, not busted, not made, and since I was empty at the time, worn-out with work, waiting for the quick transfusions of a generous success, the steady sales of the book left me deeply depressed. Having reshaped my words with an intensity of feeling I had not known before, I could not understand why others were not overcome with my sense of life, of sex, and of sadness. Like a starved revolutionary in a garret, I had compounded out of need and fever and vision and fear nothing less than a madman's confidence in the identity of my being and the wants of all others, and it was a new dull load to lift and to bear, this knowledge that I had no magic so great as to hasten the time of the apocalypse, but that instead I would be open like all others to the attritions of half-success and small failure. Something God-like in my confidence began to leave, and I was reduced in dimension if now less a boy. I knew I had failed to bid on the biggest hand I ever held.*

Now a few years have gone by, more years than I thought, and I have begun to work up another hand, a new book which will be the proper book of an outlaw, and so not punishable in any easy or legal way. Two excerpts from this novel come later in this collection, and therefore I'll say here only that O'Shaugnessy will be one of the three heroes, and that if I'm to go all the way this time, the odds are that my best senses will have to do the work without the fires and the wastes of the minor drugs.

But that is for later, and the proper end to this account is the advertisement I took in The Village Voice. *It was bought in November 1955, a month after publication, it was put together by me and paid for by me, and it was my way I now suppose of saying goodbye to the pleasure of a quick triumph, of making my apologies for the bad flaws in the bravest* effort I had yet pulled out of myself, and certainly for declaring to the world (in a small way, mean pity) that I no longer gave a sick dog's drop for the wisdom, the reliability, and the authority of the public's literary mind, those creeps and old ladies of vested reviewing.

Besides, I had the tender notion – believe it if you will – that the ad might after all do its work and excite some people to buy the book.

But here it is:

In the cactus wastes of Southern California, a distance of two hundred miles from the capital of cinema, is the town of Desert D'Or. There I went from the Air Force to look for a good time.

Whether or not it is enough of an explanation, I can only say that I arrived at the resort with fourteen thousand dollars, a particular sum I picked up in a poker game while waiting with other fliers in Tokyo for our plane home. The irony is that I was never a gambler. I did not even like the game, and perhaps for such a reason I accepted the luck of my cards. Let me leave it at that. I came out of the Air Force with no place to go, no family to visit, and I wandered down to Desert D'Or.

Built since the Second World War, it is the only place I know which is altogether new. Desert D'Or, one is told, was called originally Desert Door by the prospectors who assembled their shanties at the edge of its oasis, and from there went into the mountains overhanging the desert to look for gold. There is nothing left, however, of such men; when the site of Desert D'Or was chosen, not enough of the abandoned shacks remained to create even one of those many California museums the size of a two-car garage.

No, everything is the present, and in the months I stayed at the resort, I came to know its developed and cultivated real estate in a way given us to know few places. I can still see the straight paved roads and the curved roads, each laid out by the cross hair of the surveyor's transit. The hotels with their pastel colours are visible again in the subtle camouflage which dominated all style in Desert D'Or. It was a place built out of no other need than commercial profit and therefore no sign of commerce was allowed to appear. Desert D'Or was without a main street, and its shops, where nothing but a variety of luxuries could be bought, looked like anything but stores. In those buildings which sold clothing, no clothing was displayed, and one waited in a modern living room while salesmen opened panels in the wall to exhibit summer slacks, or displayed between their hands the lush blooms of a tropical scarf. There was a jewellery store built like a cabin cruiser; on the street one peered through no more than a porthole to see a necklace hung upon

In the cactus wild of Southern California, a distance of two hundred miles from the capital of cinema as I choose to call it, is the town of Desert D'Or. There I went from the Air Force to look for a good time. Some time ago.

Almost everybody I knew in Desert D'Or had had an unusual career, and it was the same for me. I grew up in a home for orphans. Still intact at the age of twenty-three, wearing my flying wings and a first lieutenant's uniform, I arrived at the resort with fourteen thousand dollars, a sum I picked up via a poker game in a Tokyo hotel room while waiting with other fliers for our plane home. The curiosity is that I was never a gambler, I did not even like the game, but I had nothing to lose that night, and maybe for such a reason I accepted the luck of my cards. Let me leave it at that. I came out of the Air Force with no place to go, no family to visit, and I wandered down to Desert D'Or.

Built since the Second World War, it is the only place I know which is all new. A long time ago, Desert D'Or was called Desert Door by the prospectors who put up their shanties at the edge of its oasis and went into the mountains above the desert to look for gold. But there is nothing left of those men; when the site of Desert D'Or was chosen, none of the old shacks remained.

No, everything is in the present tense, and during the months I stayed at the resort, I came to know it in a way we can know few places. It was a town built out of no other obvious motive than commercial profit and so no sign of commerce was allowed to appear. Desert D'Or was without a main street, and its stores looked like anything but stores. In those places which sold clothing, no clothing was laid out, and you waited in a modern living room while salesmen opened panels in the wall to exhibit summer suits, or held between their hands the blooms and sprays of a tropical scarf. There was a jewellery store built like a cabin cruiser; from the street one peeped through a porthole to see a thirty-thousand-dollar necklace hung on the silver antlers of a piece of driftwood. None of the hotels – not the Yacht Club, nor the Debonair, nor the Yucca Plaza, the Sandpiper, the Creedmor, nor the Desert D'Or Arms – could even be seen from the silver antlers of a piece of driftwood transported across the desert from Pacific waters. None of the hotels I remember so well – not the Yacht Club, not the Debonair, not the Yucca Plaza, the Sandpiper, the Creedmor, nor the Desert D'Or Arms – could even be seen from outside. Concealed behind cement-brick fences or wooden palings painted in the prevalent palette of Desert D'Or, one rarely saw a building which was not green, yellow, rose, orange, or pink, and the approach on a twisting sandy road was obscured by a shrubbery of bright flowers. As an instance, one passed through the gate to the Yacht Club, the most important hotel in the resort, and followed its private road, expecting a mansion at the end, but came to no more than a carport, a swimming pool in the shape of a free-form coffee table with curved-wall cabañas and canasta tables, and a set of lawn-tennis courts, unique through all that region of Southern California. From there, along yellow sidewalks which crossed and crossed again a meandering artificial creek by way of trellised footbridges, illumined at night with paper lanterns suspended from the tropical trees, one passed the guest bungalows dispersed through the grounds, their anonymous pastel-coloured doors serving to emphasize the intimacy of the arrangement.

(Pages 134–8)

We soon developed another dispute. I had discovered that to make love to Lulu was to make myself an accessory to the telephone. It was always ringing, and no moment was rare enough to hinder her from answering. Her delight was to ignore the first few rings. 'Don't be so nervous, Sugar,' she would say, but before the phone had pealed five times, she would have picked it up. Invariably, it was business. She would be talking to Herman Teppis, or Munshin who was back in the capital, or a writer, or her director for the next picture, or once even her hairdresser – Lulu was interested in a coiffure she had seen. The conversation could not go on for long before she was fondling me again; to make love and talk business possessed a special attraction to her.

outside. Put behind cement-brick fences of wooden palings, one hardly came across a building which was not green, yellow, rose, orange, or pink, and the approach was hidden by a shrubbery of bright flowers. You passed through the gate to the Yacht Club, the biggest and therefore the most exclusive hotel in the resort, and followed its private road which twisted through the grounds for several hundred yards, expecting a mansion at the end, but came instead to no more than a carport, a swimming pool in the shape of a free-form coffee table with curved-wall cabañas and canasta tables, and a set of lawn-tennis courts, the only lawn in all that part of Southern California. At night, along yellow sidewalks which crossed a winding artificial creek, lit up with Japanese lanterns strung to the tropical trees, you could wander by the guest bungalows scattered along the route, their flush pastel-coloured doors another part of the maze of the arrangement.

(Pages 134–9)

We soon found something new to fight about. I discovered that to make love to Lulu was to make myself a scratch-pad to the telephone. It was always ringing, and no moment was long enough to keep her from answering. Her delight was to pass the first few rings. 'Don't be so nervous, Sugar,' she would say, 'let the switchboard suffer,' but before the phone had screamed five times, she would pick it up. Almost always, it was business. She would be talking to Herman Teppis, or Munshin who was back in the capital, or a writer, or her director for the next picture, or an old boy friend, or once her hairdresser – Lulu was interested in a hair-do she had seen. The conversation could not go on for two minutes before she was teasing me again; to make love and talk business was a double-feature to her.

'Of course I'm being a good girl, Mr Teppis,' she would say, giving me the wink. 'How can you think these things of me?' As the end in virtuosity, she succeeded one time in weeping through a phone call with Teppis while rendering a passage with me.

I would try to get her to visit my place but she had grown an

'Of course I'm being a good girl, Mr Teppis,' she would say, giving me a lewd wink. 'How can you think these things of me?' As the ultimate in virtuosity, she succeeded one time in weeping through a phone call with Teppis while entertaining a passage with me.

I would try to get her to visit my place but she had developed a sudden aversion. 'It depresses me, Sugar, it's in such bland taste. Do you know you're a bland boy?' For a while everything would be bland. Her own place was now spoiled by that word. To my amazement at her prodigality, she insisted one day upon having her room suite redecorated. Between morning and evening its beige walls were transformed to a delicate blue, which Lulu claimed was her most flattering colour. So, too, were the sheets. Now she lay with her gold head on pale-blue linen, ordering from that telephone, as essential as any limb or organ, pink roses and red roses; the florist at the Yacht Club must arrange them himself. She would buy a dress and give it to her maid before she had even worn it, she would complain she had not a thing to wear. Her convertible she traded in one afternoon for another car almost its duplicate, and yet the exchange must have cost her a thousand dollars. When she remembered she must drive the new car slowly until it had accumulated the necessary mileage, she hired a chauffeur to trundle it through the desert and spare her the bother. Her first phone bill was five hundred dollars for the month.

Yet when it came to making money she was not without talent. While I knew her, negotiations were in progress for a three-picture contract. She would phone her lawyers, they would call her agent, the agent would speak to Teppis, Teppis would speak to her. She asked an outrageous price and received more than three-quarters of it. 'I can't stand my father,' she explained to me, 'but he's a gambler at business. He's wonderful that way.' It developed that when she was thirteen and going to a school for professional children in the capital, Magnum Pictures had wanted to sign her to a seven-year contract. 'I'd be making a stinking seven hundred and fifty a week now like all those poor exploited schnooks, but Father wouldn't let me. "Free-lance," he said, he talks that way, "this country was built on aversion. 'It depresses me, Sugar, it's in such bland taste.' For a while everything would be bland. Her own place was now spoiled by that word, and one day she told the management to have her room suite redecorated. Between morning and evening its beige walls were painted to a special blue, which Lulu claimed was her best colour. Now she lay with her gold head on pale-blue linen, ordering pink roses and red roses from the telephone; the florist at the Yacht Club promised to arrange them himself. She would buy a dress and give it to her maid before she had even worn it, she would complain she had not a thing to wear. Her new convertible she traded in one afternoon for the same model in another colour, and yet the exchange cost her close to a thousand dollars. When I reminded her that she had to drive the new car slowly until it accumulated the early mileage, she hired a chauffeur to trundle it through the desert and spare her the bother. Her first phone bill from the Yacht Club was five hundred dollars.

Yet when it came to making money she was also a talent. While I knew her, negotiations were on for a three-picture contract. She would phone her lawyers, they would call her agent, the agent would speak to Teppis, Teppis would speak to her. She asked a big price and got more than three-quarters of it. 'I can't stand my father,' she explained to me, 'but he's a gambler at business. He's wonderful that way.' It came out that when she was thirteen and going to a school for professional children in the capital, Magnum Pictures wanted to sign her a seven-year contract. 'I'd be making a stinking seven hundred and fifty a week now like all those poor exploited schnooks, but Daddy wouldn't let me. "Free-lance," he said, he talks that way, "this country was built on free-lance." He's just a chiropodist with holdings in real estate, but he knew what to do for me.' Her toes nibbled at the telephone cord. 'I've noticed that about men. There's a kind of man who never can make money for himself. Only for others. That's my father.'

Of her father and mother, Lulu's opinion changed by the clock. One round it would be her father who was marvellous. 'What a bitch my mother is. She just squeezed all the manhood out of him. Poor Daddy.' Her mother had ruined her life, Lulu free-lancing." He's just a chiropodist with holdings in real estate, but he knew what to do for me.' Her toes nibbled and twisted at the telephone cord. 'I've noticed that about men. There's a kind of man who never can make money for himself. Only for others. That's my father.'

Of her father and mother, Lulu's opinion changed by the clock. One time it would be her father who was marvellous. 'What a bitch my mother is. She just squeezed all the manhood out of him. Poor Daddy.' Her mother had ruined her life, Lulu explained. 'I never wanted to be an actress. She made me one. It's her ambition. She's just an . . . octopus.' Several phone calls later, Lulu would be chatting with her mother. 'Yes, I think it gives me hives,' she would say of some food, 'glycerine, will that do, Mommie? . . . He's what? . . . He's acting up again . . . Well, you tell him to leave you alone. I wouldn't put up with it if I were you. I would have divorced him long ago. I certainly would.

'I don't know what I'd do without her,' Lulu would say on hanging up the phone, 'men are terrible,' and she would have nothing to do with me for the next half hour.

It took me longer than it need have taken to realize that the heart of her pleasure was to display herself. She abhorred concealing an impulse. If Lulu felt like burping, she would burp; if it came to her mind that she wished to put cold cream on her face, she would do it while entertaining half a dozen people. So it went with her acting. She would say without embarrassment to the most casual acquaintance that she wished to be the greatest actress in the world. Once, talking to a stage director, she was close to tears because the studio never gave her a part in a serious picture. 'They ruin me,' she complained. 'People don't want glamour, they want acting. I'd take the smallest role if it was something I could get my teeth into.' Still she quarrelled for three days running, and how many hours of telephone calls I could not guess, because Munshin who was producing her next picture would not enlarge her part. Publicity, she announced, was idiotic, but with her instinct for what was pleasing to an adolescent, she did more than co-operate with photographers. The best ideas always came from Lulu. One occasion when she explained. 'I never wanted to be an actress. She made me one. It's her ambition. She's just an . . . octopus.' Several phone calls later, Lulu would be chatting with her mother. 'Yes, I think it gives me hives,' she would say of some food, 'glycerine, will that do, Mommie? . . . He's what? . . . He's acting up again . . . Well, you tell him to leave you alone. I wouldn't put up with it if I were you. I would have divorced him long ago. I certainly would . . .

'I don't know what I'd do without her,' Lulu would say on hanging up the phone, 'men are terrible,' and she would have nothing to do with me for the next half hour.

It took me longer than it need have taken to realize that the heart of her pleasure was to show herself. She hated holding something in. If Lulu felt like burping, she would burp; if it came up that she wanted to put cold cream on her face, she would do it while entertaining half a dozen people. So it went with her acting. She could say to a stranger that she was going to be the greatest actress in the world. Once, talking to a stage director, she was close to tears because the studio never gave her a part in a serious picture. 'They ruin me,' she complained. 'People don't want glamour, they want acting, I'd take the smallest role if it was something I could get my teeth into.' Still, she quarrelled for three days running, and how many hours on the telephone I could never guess, because Munshin who was producing her next picture would not enlarge her part. Publicity, she announced, was idiotic, but with her instinct for what was good to an adolescent, she did better than co-operate with photographers. The best ideas always came from Lulu. One sortie when she was photographed sipping a soda she shaped the second straw into a heart, and the picture as it was printed in the newspapers showed Lulu peeping through the heart, coy and cool. On the few times I would be allowed to spend the night with her, I would wake up to see Lulu writing an idea for publicity in the notebook she kept on her bed table, and I had a picture of her marriage to Eitel, each of them with his own notebook and own bed table. With pleasure, she would expound the subtleties of being well photographed. I learned that the core was photographed sipping a soda she shaped the second straw into a heart, and the picture as it was printed in many hundreds of newspapers showed Lulu peeping through the heart, at once coy, chaste, hoydenish and lovable. On those few times I would be allowed to sleep the night with her, I might awaken to see Lulu writing an idea for publicity in the notebook she kept by her bed table, and I had a picture of her marriage to Eitel, each of them with his own notebook and own bed table. With pleasure, she would expound to me the subtleties of being well photographed. I learned that the core of her dislike for Teddy Pope was that each of them was photographed best from the left side of the face, and when they played a scene together Teddy was as determined as Lulu not to expose his bad side to the camera. 'I hate to play with queers,' she complained. 'Teddy pulled seniority and they gave him his way. I thought I had mumps when I saw myself. Boy, I threw a scene.' Lulu acted it out for me. 'You've ruined me, Mr Teppis,' she shrieked to my private ear. 'There's no chivalry left.'

In bed, in those interludes she permitted me at her caprice, matters had altered considerably. To my idea of sport which must have left her exhausted, she directed me by degrees to something quite different. Lulu's taste was for games, and if she lay beneath me like a captive, pallid before the fury she aroused, her spirits improved with a play. In my innocence, there seemed a fabulous lewdness to her imagination, and I thought I had managed at a coup to reach the heart of sexual delights. I was convinced no two people ever had shared such excesses, nor even conceived of them. We were extraordinary lovers I felt in my pride; I had pity for those hordes who could know none of this. Yet, like the Oriental monarch who feels a subtle malaise on seeing the beggars of his kingdom, I was at a pitch of greediness to prove everyone else a beggar. For that, Lulu was the sweetest of mistresses. She would never allow comparisons. This was completely the best. I was superb. She was superb. We were beyond all. Unlike Eitel who now could not bear a word of Elena's former lovers, I was more than charitable to all of Lulu's. Why should I not be? She had sworn they were poor sticks to her Sugar. I was even so charitable that I argued in Eitel's

of her dislike for Teddy Pope was that each of them photographed best from the left side of the face, and when they played
a scene together, Teddy was as quick as Lulu not to expose his
bad side to the camera. 'I hate to play with queers,' she
complained. 'They're too smart. I thought I had mumps when I
saw myself. Boy, I threw a scene.' Lulu acted it for my private
ear. 'You've ruined me, Mr Teppis,' she shrieked. 'There's no
chivalry left.'

For odd hours, during those interludes, she called at her
caprice, things had come around a bit. To my idea of an
interlude which must have left her exhausted, she coached me
by degrees to something different. Which was all right with me.
Lulu's taste was for games, and if she lay like a cinder under the
speed of my sprints, her spirits improved with a play. I was sure
no two people ever had done such things nor even thought of
them. We were great lovers I felt in my pride; I had pity for the
hordes who could know none of this. Yes, Lulu was sweet. She
would never allow comparison. This was the best. I was superb.
She was superb. We were beyond all. Unlike Eitel who now
could not bear to hear a word of Elena's old lovers, I was
charitable to all of Lulu's. Why should I not be? She had sworn
they were poor sticks to her Sugar. I was even so charitable that
I argued in Eitel's defence. Lulu had marked him low as a lover,
and in a twist of friendship my heart beat with spite. I stopped
that quickly enough, I had an occasional idea by now of when
Lulu was lying, and I wanted to set Eitel at my feet, second to
the champion. It pleased me in my big affair that I had such a
feel for the ring.

We played our games. I was the photographer and she was
the model; she was the movie star and I was the bellhop; she did
the queen, I the slave. We even met even to even. The game she
loved was to play the bobby-soxer who sat with a date in the
living room and was finally convinced, always for the first time
naturally enough. She was never so happy as when we acted at
theatre and did the mime on clouds of myth. I was just young
enough to want nothing but to be alone with her. It was not
even possible to be tired. Each time she gave the signal, and I
could never know, not five minutes in advance, when it would

387

defence. She had marked him impossible as a lover, and in breach of friendship my heart had quickened with spite. I overcame that quickly enough, I wished to set Eitel at the place nearest my feet, vizier to the potentate, and it charmed me that in my first big affair I should be so proficient.

We played our games. I was the iceman and she was the housewife; she was the movie star and I was the bellhop; she the queen, I the slave; or in reverse of those situations she adored so well, Lulu mimed the prostitute to my client. We even met in equality. The game she cherished was to play the bobby-soxer who petted with a date in the living room and was finally seduced, always for the first time naturally enough. She was never so happy as when we acted at theatre and fornicated on clouds of myth. I was exactly young enough to wish nothing else ever than to be alone with her. It was not even possible to be sated. Each time she gave herself, and I could never know, not five minutes in advance, when it would happen, my appetite was sharp, dressed by the animus of what I had suffered in public.

To eat a meal with her in a restaurant became a torture. It never mattered with what friends she found herself nor with what strangers, her attention would flee, her eye would wander with impatience. It always seemed to her as if the conversation at another table was more interesting and more provocative than what she heard at her own. She suffered the intolerable anxiety that she was missing a word of gossip, a tip, a role in a picture, a financial transaction, a . . . it did not matter; something was happening somewhere else, something of importance, something she could not afford to miss. Therefore, eating with her was like sleeping with her; if one was interrupted by the telephone, the other was broken by her need to visit from table to table, sometimes dragging me, sometimes parking me, until I often wondered what mathematical possibility there was for Lulu to eat a meal in sequence since she was always having a bit of soup here and a piece of pastry there, joining myself and her friends for breast of squab, and departing to greet new arrivals whose crabmeat cocktail she nibbled. There was no end, no beginning, no certainty that one would even see her during a meal. I remember a dinner when we went out with Dorothea O'Faye

PUTNAM (CONT'D.)

happen, my appetite was sharp, dressed by the sting of what I suffered in public.

To eat a meal with her in a restaurant became the new torture. It didn't matter with what friends she found herself nor with what enemies, her attention would go, her eye would flee. It always seemed to her as if the conversation at another table was more interesting than what she heard at her own. She had the worry that she was missing a word of gossip, a tip, a role in a picture, a financial transaction, a . . . it did not matter; something was happening somewhere else, something of importance, something she could not afford to miss. Therefore, eating with her was like sleeping with her; if one was cut by the telephone, the other was rubbed by her itch to visit from table to table, sometimes dragging me, sometimes parking me, until I had to wonder what mathematical possibility there was for Lulu to eat a meal in sequence since she was always having a bit of soup here and a piece of pastry there, joining me for breast of squab, and taking off to greet new arrivals whose crabmeat cocktail she nibbled on. There was no end, no beginning, no surety that one would even see her during a meal. I remember a dinner when we went out with Dorothea O'Faye and Martin Pelley. They had just been married and Lulu treasured them. Dorothea was an old friend, a dear friend, Lulu promised me, and before ten minutes she was gone. When Lulu finally came back, she perched on my lap and said in a whisper the others could hear, 'Sugar, I tried, and I couldn't make doo-doo. Isn't that awful? What should I eat?'

Five minutes later she outmanoeuvred Pelley to pick up the check.

(PAGE 284)

Tentatively, she reached out a hand to finger his hair, and at that moment Herman Teppis opened his legs and let Bobby fall to the floor. At the expression of surprise on her face, he began to laugh. 'Don't you worry, sweetie,' he said, and down he looked at the frightened female mouth, facsimile of all those

389

and Martin Pelley. They had just been married and Lulu treasured them. Dorothea was an old friend, a dear friend, Lulu assured me, and before ten minutes she disappeared. When at last Lulu returned, she perched on my lap and said in a whisper the others could hear, 'Sugar, I tried, and I couldn't make doo-doo. Isn't that awful? What should I eat?'

Five minutes later she insisted upon picking up the check.

(Page 277)

Tentatively she reached out a hand to caress his hair, and at that moment Herman Teppis opened his legs and let Bobby slip to the floor. At the expression of surprise on her face, he began to laugh. 'Just like this, sweetie,' he said, and down he looked at that frightened female mouth, facsimile of all those smiling lips he had seen so ready to be nourished at the fount of power and with a shudder he started to talk. 'That's a good girlie, that's a good girlie, that's a good girlie,' he said in a mild lost little voice, 'you're just an angel darling, and I like you, and you understand, you're my darling darling, oh, that's the ticket,' said Teppis.

1952–4